I0589407

Cloves for Kolosia

Hanna Rambe
Translated from the Indonesian by
Miagina Amal

Dalang Publishing

Cloves for Kolosia
Originally published as *Aimuna dan Sobori* in 2013 by Yayasan Obor, Jakarta, Indonesia (ISBN 978-979-461-854-7)
Copyright © 2013 Hanna Rambe
Translation copyright © 2015 Miagina Amal

Publication of this book was made possible by a generous gift from PT Marimas, Semarang, Indonesia.

Cover design: Herfitrisna Yulianti Asnar
Book design: Son Do
Editor: Elizabeth Ridley
Indonesian literary advisors: Manneke Budiman and Ratna Asmarani

Dalang Publishing LLC
San Mateo, CA
www.dalangpublishing.com
dalangpublishing@gmail.com

ISBN: 978-0-9836273-8-8
Library of Congress number: 2015943598

CLOVES FOR KOLOSIA

Translator's Note

I was thrilled when Lian Gouw from Dalang Publishing asked me to translate Hanna Rambe's latest work, *Aimuna dan Sobori*, into English. The historical novel is set during the 18th century on the tumultuous and fabled Moluccas, an Indonesian archipelago that holds a very dear place in my heart. Having been born in a North Moluccan family, I am familiar with the region's traditions and cultures and fluent in the colloquial dialect. So without much deliberation, I agreed to translate the novel.

The original novel is a lengthy and complex 480 pages of text in the Indonesian language. Hanna Rambe's heartfelt and compassionate depiction of the Moluccan natives' struggles and miseries caused by the spice trade and colonialism pained me immensely.

On a personal level, reading and translating *Aimuna dan Sobori* served as a timely reminder of my roots. In the translation process I not only made sure the foreign reader would be able to easily get into the story and access the souls of its characters, I also paid extra attention to the accuracy of historical data. With the author's permission, the translation renders the islands referenced in the novel as actual sites rather than fictional places.

While Rambe adeptly used local dialect in some of the dialogue between native characters, I sadly had to refrain from incorporating these colorful passages into the translation. They were all translated into English for clarity's sake. However, I did preserve many significant terms and concepts in their true form and thus captured the local "flavor" of the work. We also omitted some recurring repetitions of information in the narration, all with the utmost care not to alter the story or the author's true voice.

Weaving historical facts, fantasy, ideals, and emotions into a captivating and believable fictional narrative is no easy task. I hope my translation does justice to Hanna Rambe's great efforts to represent the Moluccan voice.

My gratitude goes to the perceptive Lian Gouw and Elizabeth Ridley from Dalang Publishing for the immeasurable insights and work they brought to this translation, which was aimed at maintaining the story's integrity and the author's voice while appealing to the western reader.

Miagina Amal
July 2015

2015 Map of Indonesia

Indian Ocean

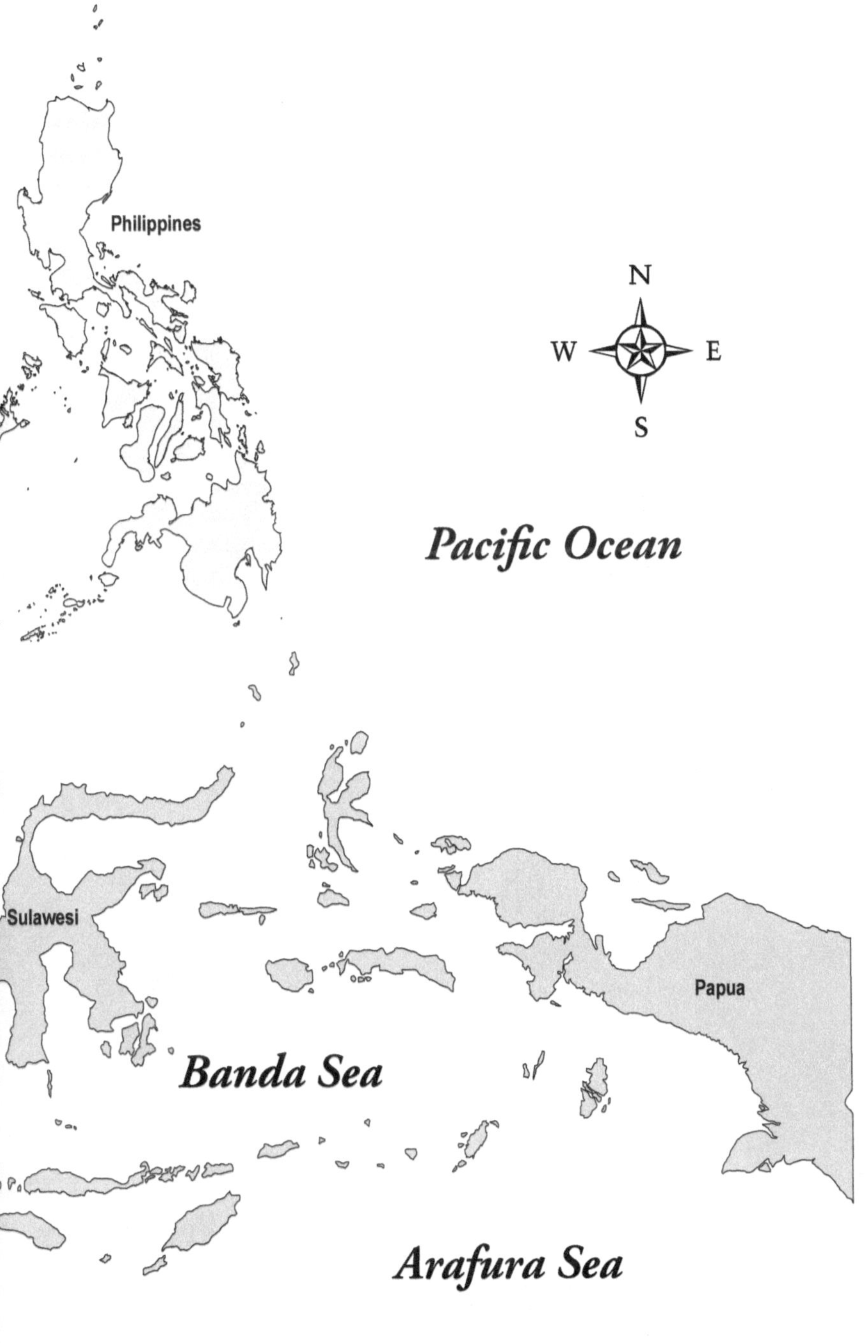

Philippines
N
W
E
S
Pacific Ocean
Sulawesi
Papua
Banda Sea
Arafura Sea

Moluccan Islands
Pacific Ocean
Philippines
Ternate
Tidore
Makian
Halmahera
Bacan
Islands
Sulawesi
Seram Sea
Misool
Papua
Manipa
Seram
Ambon
Saparua
Banda
Islands
Banda Sea
Kei
Islands
Timor
Timor Sea
Arafura Sea

Banda Islands

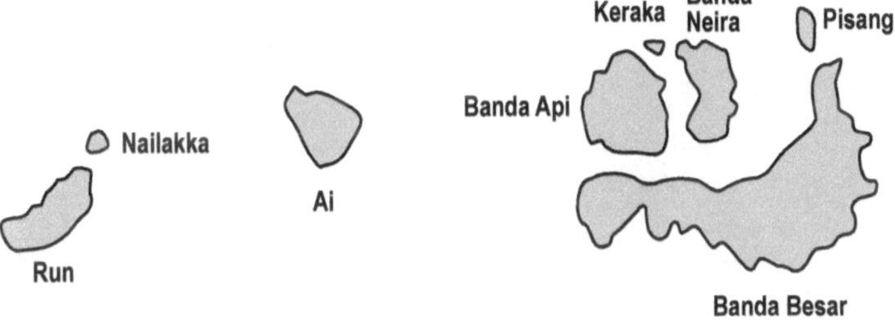

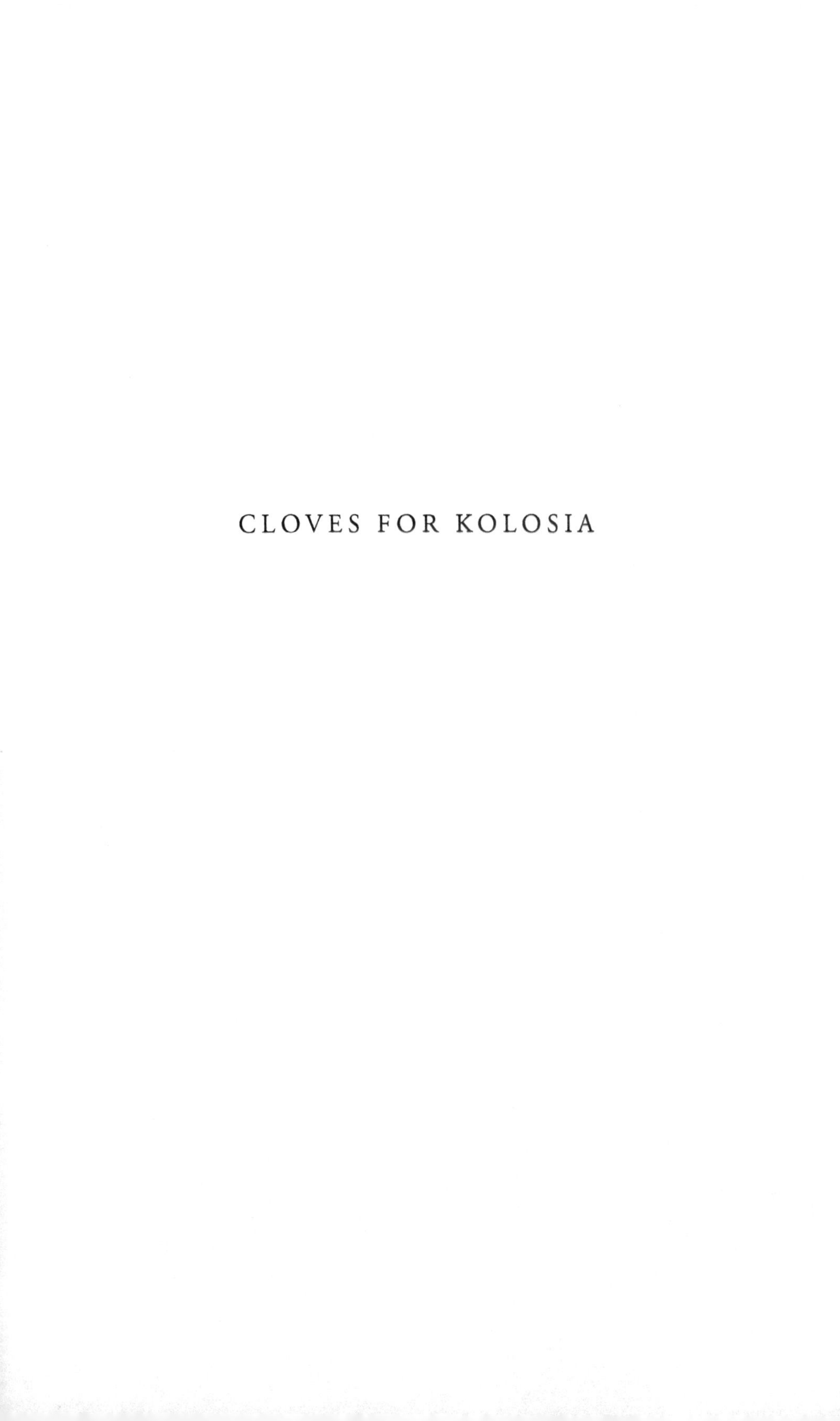

CLOVES FOR KOLOSIA

Chapter 1

The wind blew hard; cold penetrated the woven rattan wall of the hut. Kurubela's only son sat cross-legged on the floor with his hands under his chin. His mother swept dry leaves and bits of straw off the floor while his father lifted baskets of cloves ready for transport.

"Bori, what are you brooding about, Son?"

"I want to wait until you leave. I want to see you out, Father." Bori remained seated on the swept floor. He usually went to bed soon after dark. His behavior tonight surprised his father and mother.

"Why don't you go to bed, Bori? It's late. We'll soon put out the lamp. It will be dark where you're sitting," his father coaxed.

"No, Father. I want to see you out. You'll be gone for a long time. I'll miss you terribly."

Kurubela and his wife exchanged glances. Bori was just a little boy; where had he picked up the notion of missing someone? The baskets filled with clove buds were all lined up, ready to be transported, and Kurubela said, "Bori, I'll blow out the lamp soon; you can wait until it's time for me to leave."

Bori remained seated on the floor with his hands under his chin. He shivered in the total darkness and the cold made his teeth chatter. Yet he did not budge.

The twelve-year-old boy couldn't articulate the strange, deep longing he felt for his parents, who were in their bedroom, only a few

I

feet away. The rooms didn't have any doors; Kurubela thought Bori was still too young to be alone in a room with a door.

Bori knew his parents slept with a machete and a spear ready on the floor. A *salawaku* hung on the wall, and an ax was hidden under the pillow. Once Bori had played with the ax and asked for one under his pillow as well.

"Shush!" his father exclaimed, "You are still a little boy. You can sleep with a weapon when you are older."

Bori was still waiting for that to happen. Outside, the wind blew and leaves rustled. Bats flapped their wings as they swooped down on fruit, crickets chirped in an ongoing dialogue, and an owl hooted, looking for prey. Occasionally, a dog barked on the outskirts of the *kampong*, possibly at a passing reptile.

A rooster crowed. Once. That meant it was past midnight. Bori remained seated. The strange, deep longing for his parents still churned inside him. *It will be a long time before they wake up.* He heard the second crow. His parents were still asleep and he waited patiently. He noticed more noise than usual on the outskirts of the forest.

Suddenly there was a commotion in the distance. He listened intently, frightened. *Who's making such a riot at this time of night?* The sounds were getting louder, closer. A male voice thundered his father's name. He heard the crackling of dry wood burning. His blood ran cold. Everything outside was ablaze, seemingly illuminated by a giant torch. He tried to make sense of what was happening, when someone kicked in the front door.

The small hut wobbled as if shaken by an earthquake. Several angry men brandishing spears and machetes stood in the doorway. Their black silhouettes were in sharp contrast to the glare of the brilliant fire outside.

Shocked, Bori quickly turned to look at his parents' bedroom. They stood wielding spears and machetes. His mother even had an ax in her left hand. "Kurubela! You slave of the Portuguese and English. You dare to rebel against *Pani-pani,* huh? Take this," a heavyset man barked in the darkness.

"You have to die. From now on there will be no more smuggled cloves. You have caused Pani-pani a great deal of loss." The man stabbed Kurubela in the abdomen with his machete, and Kurubela in turn speared the heavyset man. Blood spurted from the wounds of both men.

Bori smelled the unfamiliar stench of blood. He froze. *Cannot move. Cannot scream. Cannot run away. Cannot understand.*

A man, apparently the group leader, shouted something incomprehensible to his friends. Then, they attacked Bori's mother, who wore only a sarong tucked under her armpit. She hadn't had time to arrange her hair in a bun and so her beautiful wavy hair hung loose.

His mother, whom Bori knew had trained in using weapons, especially spears and arrows, threw her ax at the shoulder of one of her attackers. Bori knew she must have aimed for his throat. The man staggered.

Another attacker hit his mother. She fell, but somehow still managed to hack off her assailant's leg and he fell too.

Someone shouted a command and the men hurriedly carried their wounded friends away from the hut. The wooden floor creaked under the weight of the fleeing attackers.

Bori was in shock. He wanted to run to his father and mother, both of whom lay dead on the floor. In the dark, they looked like two huge parcels, glistening in the light from the fire outside. He wanted to hug and kiss them, comfort them, but his mind was unable to control his body. He seemed paralyzed. The heat was unbearable. It was like standing near a giant furnace.

Bori panicked. He rose, knowing he had to leave. Outside the fire grew larger; the fiery flames soared into the sky. Apparently the *VOC* had burned down the whole kampong. The blazing flames nearly licked his hut.

Bori ran outside. He was devastated. He had to leave his dead parents; they could no longer escape with him. He thought of not leaving. He wanted to give them a proper burial and help take care of the other villagers, but the blazing fire made him run.

Outside, people ran around in a panic carrying their infants and their prized possessions. They howled, cried, screamed, cursed, and called out for family members. Bori had only one thought: he had to go to the shack his family had prepared beforehand, deep in the forest.

Bori ran across a jumble of horrors; bodies of children, a hand or a leg, perhaps even a head, miscellaneous baskets. He kept running toward the dark forest, clad only in pajama bottoms. He did not have a sarong, a machete, or ropes, the usual items to bring on a trip to the forest.

The brush he pushed through was engulfed in darkness. The trail his father had cut was almost gone; the vegetation had started to grow back and covered the path, but he had memorized it during earlier treks with his father. He ignored the thistles and thorns that pricked his feet and just kept running.

The screams and howls started to fade in the distance and the giant torch of the burning kampong no longer illuminated the forest. Bori continued to run until at last he came upon a clearance.

He startled. A crudely built shack stood nearby. *Should I enter? What if there are already others inside?* The shack had been kept a secret. Only his immediate family knew its whereabouts: his father, Kurubela's family, the family of Uncle Tarambessi, his mother's younger brother, and several of the crew members of Ngasiran, the captain from Tuban whose ship came ashore once a year to pick up a load of cloves.

Still only a child, Bori was not used to making decisions, so he stood silently by the side of the shack. Darkness prevented him from looking inside. He was afraid that the shack was already occupied.

All the bottled-up emotions wearied him. Finally, he entered. It was quiet and dank, and reeked of mold. He sat on the floor, waiting for a sound, but it remained quiet. Not even a click of a gecko broke the silence.

Exhausted, Bori fell asleep. He still had not had time to reflect on the recent events, and he still had not fully realized that he would never see his father and mother again.

When he woke up he heard someone whimper; another person whispered to hush. This was a secret hideout. Bori wondered who else was in the hut. Perhaps it was the enemy. He rose, ready to flee.

Bori took in his surroundings. A figure moved in the dark. He looked hard and recognized Grandpa Gamati, his mother's father.

"Grandpa," he called, "Father and Mother...." He halted.

"Bori! You survived. Didn't they come with you?" Gamati asked softly.

"They stabbed Father and Mother. They both fell; I couldn't carry them...."

Gamati understood immediately. The villagers from Tupamarangi, Tupawaroka, and Tupawalili, three kampongs scattered on the slope of the mountain, had planned to transport baskets filled with cloves to the seaside that night. Several weeks earlier the three kampongs had harvested the clove buds and by now the buds had dried up and nicely turned fragrant.

The junk belonging to a captain from Tuban on Java should be anchored at the seaside, ready to load the cloves. The junk's crew brought farming tools and several kinds of fabric, such as cotton, and soft fabrics for handkerchiefs, shawls, and head scarves for the men, along with batik cloth for the villagers to trade.

Although the powerful fleet of the VOC always patrolled the seas around Seram and Ambon Island, far into the Banda Islands, the place of origin of nutmeg and mace, the secret trade had been going on safely for several decades.

The agreed-upon seaside meeting routinely took place in the middle of the east wind season when the sea was relatively calm.

Gamati wondered why they were found out this time. *Why was Pani-Pani here? How could they come to a kampong hidden deep in the forest and conduct their* hongi *raids?*

To reach the three kampongs from the seaside, one had to travel up and down the valley and cross the rushing river over a bed of sharp rocks. There was also a sacred banyan tree with snake pits between its roots.

Gamati wondered if perhaps someone had betrayed them. If so, the traitor must have been handsomely rewarded.

Sobori leaned on Gamati's chest, crying over the death of his parents.

Gamati stroked the boy's head and said that they had to start a new life someplace else. He told Bori not to be too sad, lest he get sick. He needed to grow up fast so he could help start a new clove plantation and build a new kampong.

The refugees from Manipa Island built Tupawalili, Tupawaroka, and Tupamarangi after the VOC destroyed the island decades ago. Before the raid Manipa was a beautiful little island not far from Seram's west coast, with a lot of secret clove plantations.

The massacre at Manipa was dreadfully vicious since the natives put up a tenacious resistance, led by the local clergies, and both parties were equal in terms of weaponry. This resistance would be cherished by the people of Manipa for centuries to come.

After the hongi, the survivors fled to Seram. The big island with plenty of open space was capable of housing many refugees.

Suddenly someone moaned softly.

"Who did you bring with you, Grandpa?" Sobori whispered.

"It is Aimuna. She has a leg wound."

"Aimuna is here? Did they attack your kampong too?"

"Yes, they did. I think they attacked us simultaneously," Gamati said sadly.

Now that his eyes had adapted to the darkness of the shack, Sobori saw Aimuna in a corner. He moved toward her. "Muna. You survived. What happened?"

Aimuna started to weep. She lay her head on Bori's shoulder. "Mother...Father...my brother, Limo...the Pani-pani, they are so cruel."

"This means they spared no one." Bori wiped his tears with the back of his hand and yelled, "When I am bigger, I will kill all the people of Pani-pani. If they're dead, they can no longer burn kampongs like they always do."

Aimuna was two years younger than Sobori. Her father, Tarambessi, was Gamati's son. Tarambessi's older sister, Ranila, married Kurubela.

Sobori was their son. Therefore, Sobori and Aimuna were both Gamati's grandchildren. Gamati asked the children to stay quiet. In case the enemy had discovered the place, they had to prevent them from entering the shack.

It was difficult to keep Aimuna quiet. The little girl was used to being spoiled by her father and when the wound on her leg continued to throb, she cried.

Sobori tried to quiet Aimuna and kept stroking her head.

Gamati sat calmly near his two grandchildren. He racked his brain for a solution to the difficult situation at hand.

He had lost everything at once, his wife, children, daughter and son-in-law, his hut, his kampong, and the once-secret clove plantation. Only two of his grandchildren had survived. The youngest grandchild, Aimuna's little brother, Limo, had also been slain. Now they were stranded in a dark place deep in the forest. He did not know how he'd feed the children. One couldn't ask children to suppress their hunger and thirst. He hadn't brought tools in his hurried escape. Without a machete, mattock, crowbar, knife, or ropes, life looked pretty grim.

This was not his first brush with calamity. A long time ago, his kampong in Manipa had been raided by the hongi fleet. They destroyed the clove trees and wiped out the kampong. The surviving villagers fled to the interior of Seram.

The same thing had happened to Kurubela's family, who came from the island of Manipa and also fled to Seram. But the hongi continued to chase them.

Gamati had also learned from his parents that the rest of the people of the Moluccas had always resisted these greedy foreigners, but always lost. The enemy excelled at weaponry. Their vessels were bigger and had more sails. They also had large crews. The main dispute between them was always about the clove trade.

Gamati had agreed with Kurubela, his late son-in-law, that they had to go somewhere far. This time, not just deeper into Seram. Kurubela wanted to go to the islands far up north; he had heard that the VOC didn't have settlements or forts there.

The islands were still sparsely populated. There were a few settlements at the shorelines, and their inhabitants already associated with sailors from faraway lands. The occupants of the deep interiors were not hostile, as long as the new settlers treated them respectfully.

Kurubela, Gamati, and Tarambessi had all agreed. They wanted to have a big ship that could sail far and was able to carry a big load of trading goods. It would take an enormous effort to realize their dream. They'd need a large amount of special woods as well as a lot of workers to first fell the trees and then to build the ship. They might also need other kinds of goods to trade with.

Kurubela, Gamati, and Tarambessi had been saving gold to pay for their dream *arumbae.* They hoped that with the arumbae they'd be able to go far and carry large loads of clove buds. Foreign traders who were adversaries of the VOC, such as the English, the Makassar, and Banten seamen, were known to often visit the northern islands.

Kurubela wanted to move. The intention was kept secret, of course, as they did not want anyone to betray them. It was not a custom among their people to save gold. They had learned this habit from the Chinese traders who came from the north.

The Chinese came from far away. Their land was often beset by massive floods, very long droughts, great famine, and sandstorms that blew from the west. Plagues took many lives as well. The Chinese were also often under attack from enemies who charged at them with thousands of horsemen. When they were at sea, they faced violent storms and their ships were often pirated by Papuan ships that were so fast, they seemed to "fly" on the ocean's surface.

The Chinese said that during bad times the gold they gradually saved came in real handy. Gold was long lasting, even when buried in the ground. In short, it was an excellent commodity.

Kurubela took the Chinese stories to heart. He and his brother in-law, Tarambessi, started to save various pieces of gold jewelry in a porcelain pot they buried in a secret place.

Now, Gamati wanted to realize the dream he had shared with Kurubela and Tarambessi. He wanted to have an arumbae to take his grandchildren up north and settle there.

They would be free there and not forced into treaties with the VOC. Gamati considered this Kurubela and Tarambessi's last request and he wanted to realize their dream. They had to own an arumbae and live free, away from the VOC. Shaken and exhausted, Gamati and his grandchildren fell asleep.

Morning broke with the sounds of small animals. Gamati listened to the awakening of the forest's creatures. Birds chirping loudly and screeching monkeys. Yet it was still dark in the shack, surrounded by lush trees. He listened intently for any suspicious sounds, such as branches cracking under footsteps. He hoped that no one would find this place.

Gamati looked at his two grandchildren. They were still fast asleep. Sobori's hand lay on Aimuna's head as if stroking her hair. Aimuna lay nestled near Sobori's leg. They were both orphans now. His heart sank as he wondered how they would grow up. He realized it was his duty to raise them.

Gamati wiped the tears from his eyes. He had to remain steadfast and strong. The children would rely heavily on him. He was their only caregiver. Gamati waited silently for the sunlight. He was furious with the VOC and wanted to kill them all. But first he had an even more important duty to carry out. He had to raise Sobori and Aimuna. The thought calmed him and repressed his murderous rage.

Several minutes later, a head popped through the door. Gamati's heart skipped a beat. He immediately regretted the absence of a machete at his waist.

"I'm Lawe, *Bapa*. I went to Tupawalili to pick up the cloves, but the village was burned to the ground. So I waited in the forest."

Relieved, Gamati whispered, "Come in, are you alone?"

"No, Ngali is outside."

Lawe let Ngali in. Both men were seasoned seamen. Tall and lean, they exuded physical fitness. Their skin was a lovely dark bronze. Their hair was straight and thick, different from the Moluccans', which was short and tightly curly.

Now there were five people in the tiny shack. Gamati was relieved when he noticed the two men carried big, very sharp machetes. At least now they had weapons. They also needed the machetes to look for food in the forest.

Sobori and Aimuna woke up.

Lawe and Ngali noticed that only Sobori had made it to the shack, and concluded his parents had died in the raid. Assuming the same had happened to Aimuna, they did not question the fact she and Gamati had been alone in the shack.

Gamati told them about the three kampongs that had been simultaneously burned down the night before. Although he did not see it, he was certain that all their hidden clove plantations were also destroyed.

He did not know what had happened to the villagers who survived the massacre. Heaven only knew if they had managed to escape or had been taken hostage.

Next came Lawe and Ngali's turn to share what they saw last night. Lawe spoke while Ngali and the children listened, silently.

The captain from Tuban had anchored his junk in a hidden cove known only to Kurubela and his group. They did not unload any cargo except for some farming tools to be traded for cloves. The crew of over a hundred men were not permitted to leave the ship. They only bathed and cooked. The captain repeatedly reminded them to stay quiet.

"The captain ordered Ngali and me to meet Kurubela. We were going to transport eight to ten *pikuls* of cloves. The two of us can easily carry the cloves on our backs using the baskets. Our plan was to sail north as soon as the cloves were loaded into the junk.

"We brought along the sharpest machetes, so in the event we ran into a snake or a boar, we could kill it with one slash. As we neared Tupawalili, we saw an enormous, raging fire. People wailed and screamed. Someone shouted commands. We decided to change our plan and spent the night in the forest. We could have easily gone back to the junk at the beach, but we wanted to find out what had happened. That is why we came to this shack."

"What about Captain Ngasiran? Is he still waiting? Is he not afraid of getting caught by Pani-pani now present in our area?" Gamati asked.

"I don't know. There is no previous agreement about this type of situation. The captain must have thought that things would proceed as usual. As soon as the cloves are delivered, he releases the trading goods. After that Kurubela goes back to his kampong and we set sail. But it turned out differently this time."

"I am afraid that the Tuban captain will keep on waiting for you and Kurubela's arrival until tomorrow night, when Pani-pani will surely catch them at the cove."

"Let's hope it won't come to that," Ngali answered quietly.

"What's your plan now? Are you going back to the beach with this news of annihilation?"

"It's dangerous to walk in broad daylight. Pani-pani's spies might be in the forest. We don't know whether the ship is gone or still waiting for us. The captain can consider the facts that the two of us didn't return and there's no news from Kurubela or his messenger as a sign that something went wrong. Let's hope the ship has sailed."

After listening to each other's stories, all of them fell silent. Exhausted, worried, defeated, and sad, they wondered what to do now.

Gamati tried to think of someone among his relatives or fellow seamen he could ask for temporary shelter. He had two children with him. If he were alone, he could have easily lived in the forest. Lawe and Ngali were foreigners from the island of Java. They did not have any relatives here on Seram.

Everyone's stomach rumbled. They had to search for food. Gamati suggested looking for fruit in the forest. He and Lawe would go while Ngali stayed in the shack with the children. They had to stay quiet and were forbidden to leave the shack until he returned.

There was plenty of ripe fruit in the forest. The flowers that blossomed by the end of the wet season had grown into sweet fruit.

There was no *saloi* to carry the fruit in and Lawe took off his sarong to use as a makeshift sack. He now wore only knee-length black pants. Gamati and Lawe memorized the location of the fruit trees since they might have to come back for more fruit if they had to stay in the shack.

The fruit cheered the children. The sweet and fragrant mangosteens, santols, and wild mangoes were enough to satisfy their hunger until evening while the sweet fruit juices quenched their thirst.

That evening, they did not have much conversation and went to sleep quickly. Gamati offered to stand guard that night and stayed awake until the next morning. He contemplated whom he could ask for temporary lodging when he remembered the Lando family, who lived in a very remote kampong deep in the interior.

Gamati waited until the morning sun showed in the sky and he could estimate the location of Lando's hut. He asked the two newcomers in which direction their junk was moored. Once he determined the cardinal directions, he decided that they should go south. Lando's kampong was located on the banks of a small river with a swift current. Close to its headwaters was a spring with plenty of fish.

"Let's travel south. A fellow seaman I knew closely back when I was young lives there. If he hasn't moved, we can stay at his place until we find a way out."

"How do we get there?" Ngali asked.

"We head southward. We have to cross the forest, and then cross a river. It's still a very long walk after that. I hope I still remember the route."

"Aren't we going to bring some provisions? Water, especially?" Lawe asked.

"Where do we find drinking water here? We don't even have a jug to carry it with," Gamati answered. "We'll look for it on our way there. Perhaps there are sugar canes or such; we can suck out the juice. We also still have some mangosteen and santols. Surely they'll do," Gamati said, trying to lift their spirits.

They formed a line and started to walk. Gamati held a borrowed machete and headed the procession. Sobori walked right behind him while the third in line was Ngali, who carried Aimuna. There was no way the little girl could walk the entire distance. Lawe closed their ranks and carried a machete and ropes.

Before they started out, Ngali dug a hole to bury their fruit scraps. They did not want to leave any traces of their presence. Gamati said that they needed to reach their destination before nightfall. It was crucial to avoid spending the night in an unknown forest.

Gamati's concern was not without reason. In the deep mountainous interior of the island lived an isolated tribe. The *Halefurus* did not interact with the coastal people. They often required human heads to present to their future wives. According to their tradition, this was some sort of token of their manhood. The unfortunate victims were usually outsiders, not other Halefurus.

"We want to avoid a chance meeting with them," Gamati explained.

"Why does your friend live there? Is he a Halefuru himself?" Ngali asked nervously.

"No, he isn't. He is originally from the island of Halmahera. He is in good standing with the Halefurus," Gamati answered and continued, "His father used to gather massoia bark, and collect wildflower honey. When his father died, Lando took over his father's business. The Halefurus are nice to him, because he's nice to them too."

They walked a long, exhausting walk; luckily the sun was not too hot. They crossed the river with the swift current and climbed steep slopes overgrown with trees until they came upon a cluster of huts. They were stilt huts with rattan walls and roofs made of sago tree leaf stalks. They felt relieved, although they were not sure yet that this was the kampong they were searching for.

Gamati approached a hut in the center of the cluster of huts. It was nearly dark and it was quiet. Curiously enough, there was no one around even though it was the time when people usually came home from their fields. The chirping of birds flying back to their nests served as background music.

"*Tabea!* Tabea! I'm Gamati."

No one answered. Then a teenage boy's head popped out of the door. He looked at the group at the bottom of the ladder, bewildered.

"Son, is this Bapa Lando's house?"

"That's right, but he's not home yet. He'll be home shortly."

"I'm a childhood friend. Please help us. May we come in? It will be dark soon."

The boy did not answer; instead, he went inside the hut. Not long afterward a woman, apparently his mother, climbed down the ladder with a lamp in her hand. She said, "If you are Bapa Lando's friend, please come up. He is on his way home."

They all climbed the creaky ladder and collapsed on the wooden floor of the front porch without being asked. All of them were exhausted and famished, but relieved they had found the right hut.

Less than ten minutes later Lando arrived, bringing along some taro, bananas, and a large bird he had shot with his arrow.

"Lando, do you remember me? I am Gamati from Tupawaroka." Gamati hurriedly climbed down the ladder.

"Oh my dear brother," Lando cried happily.

The two men hugged each other.

"It has been too long since we last met."

"Yes, it has, Lando. Listen, my grandchildren and I are in great danger. My kampong, Tupawaroka; Kurubela's kampong, Tupawalili; and the kampong Tupamarangi all have been destroyed. A hongi expedition came, burned down all the kampongs and killed almost everyone. Kurubela, Ranila, Tarambessi and his wife all died." Gamati wept on Lando's shoulder. His shoulder shook.

Lando was unable to speak and cried too. He remembered that a long time ago, he owed gratitude, if not his life, to Gamati. He waited until Gamati regained his composure, then asked whether they came to his kampong right from their destroyed kampongs or whether they had spent the night somewhere else.

Gamati told him they had spent a night in the forest. He then introduced the two men with him, Lawe and Ngali, crewmen from the Tuban junk. And the children, Sobori, the son of Kurubela with his daughter Ranila; and Aimuna, his son Tarambessi's daughter with Mela, his daughter-in-law.

Riti, Lando's wife, prepared hot water to drink. She was cooking *papeda* and her daughter plucked the bird Lando had brought home so it could be cooked for dinner. *Kolak pisang* would also be ready soon.

When all the dishes were ready, everyone was invited to eat together. This time, three lamps lit the room, two lamps more than they usually put up, and the room was bright.

Lando told his guests to eat as much as they wanted. There was still plenty of food in the kitchen. After dinner, they were invited to wash up, whether by taking a bath or just washing their faces and feet.

Luna and Masna, Lando's teenage daughters, tried to befriend Aimuna. While they were on their way to Lando's hut, Gamati had warned Aimuna to behave nicely and not to be a crybaby. She had to be polite, and friendly with everyone. If she did not behave, she could be asked to leave the house they were staying in.

At first it was a bit hard to make Aimuna take a bath without warm water. Her braid was undone and her beautiful wavy hair let loose, combed, and braided again. Masna gave her a dress she had worn when she was younger. Even though it was still too big for Aimuna, she accepted it since she had no other clothes.

They sat around making small talk, mainly about their trip. Lando purposely did not ask anything more about the hongi raid. He did not want everyone to start crying again. After a while, he suggested they all turn in since everyone was tired.

Gamati and his group were assigned to sleep in the all-purpose room at the center of the hut, where they had dined before.

Lando spread rattan and screw pine mats for bedding, and distributed some sarongs for blankets. The Landos were simple villagers. In accordance with the circumstances of the time, they didn't have many possessions aside from the plantations on communal land co-owned by relatives of the same lineage, or with the rest of the villagers.

Everyone was exhausted after the long and stressful trip. Crossing the river earlier that day had been a challenge since the riverbed was lined with sharp rocks, not to mention the gushing current. It would be nearly impossible to carry a child across if it were flooded. Gamati, Lawe, and Ngali were reluctant to dwell on anything. They fell asleep quickly. Soon, loud snoring filled the room.

The next morning, accompanied by Lando, Gamati reported his group's arrival to the kampong chief. The chief welcomed him with open arms, for he had often heard about how horrific the hongi expedition treated people. He extended his invitation to Gamati to stay for some time in his kampong. They would build a hut for the group and the kampong chief would tell the Halefuru chief not to harm the group of guests since they were refugees, not farmers from Seram.

The kampong chief's welcome put the three men's hearts at ease. They had lodging, they had been cordially welcomed, and they had plenty of food. It was the local tradition of *masohi* at work, and they were thankful for it.

"We call this the spirit of *gotong royong* in Tuban," Lawe said.

Gamati, Ngali, and Lawe worked hard to help Lando on his plantation. They tapped the palm trees and helped cook the sap into palm sugar. No one made *tuak* in the kampong. They planted some yams, cassavas, and taros. Some vegetable seeds, such as purple eggplant, creeping pumpkins, and betel leaves, were obtained from the neighbors.

If the day was bright and sunny, they went to the headwaters of the river to fish. They caught big fish. Riti usually cooked one or two of the biggest fish and smoked the rest of the catch, if any, on the kitchen fire for future consumption. Lando liked to shoot game with his arrows, so they also ate game quite often. Lawe and Ngali thought of the captain from Tuban every time they had papeda with sour fish stew for their meal. It was his favorite dish when he visited Seram.

From everyday conversations with the villagers, they learned that the kampong was very isolated. No outsiders ever came for fear of getting killed by the people from the mountains. The villagers rarely traveled outside their kampong either, because they would have to spend a night in the forest.

News was rarely heard, and nor did it often get out of the kampong. The ten families who lived in the tiny kampong hardly produced anything newsworthy.

It was hard for Gamati, Lawe, and Ngali to figure a way to leave the kampong. They surely did not intend to stay until they were old. The two sailors wanted to get back to Tuban, their hometown. Gamati had to raise Sobori and Aimuna and realize their fathers' dream: to own an arumbae and trade as a free man.

They built a hut in the back of Lando's hut for the three men. The hut had a small porch and a sleeping room separate from the Landos. Aimuna and Sobori slept with the Landos' children.

Aimuna and Sobori adapted quite well to the Landos and their natural surroundings. Together with Luna and Masna, Aimuna started to learn to row a boat in the nearby river. Sometimes Riti came with the girls to the deeper part of the river to catch some fish. Aimuna loved water activities: rowing, swimming, or riding a floating banana tree trunk downstream.

Sobori trailed Bingka, who was a few years older than him. He climbed tall trees, and learned to collect honey by burning damp twigs or leaves right under the beehive. Alarmed by the smoke, the honeybees then fled the hive. Swimming, diving, and rowing became Sobori's favorite pastimes.

Aimuna always wanted to come along with Sobori, but Bingka did not always approve. Aimuna was a girl, and girls should behave and play differently than boys. She should not climb the palm tree, the mangosteen tree, or guava tree. She should not even fly a kite on a hot day.

Gamati made no comment. Muna was just a little girl; it was still all right to play with boys. Only when she grew older did she need to learn how to cook and care for children.

When Bingka did not allow her to join him and Sobori, Muna asked Lawe or Ngali to play by the river or near the forest. She never invited Luna or Masna along. Perhaps their age difference caused the distance.

Lawe and Ngali pitied the little girl. She seemed lonely when Sobori was not around. Sometimes, when Sobori did not take her with him, Lawe saw her hiding behind a tree, crying.

When the two men told Gamati, it saddened him. Once Gamati asked Sobori how he had the heart to leave Aimuna. Sobori answered that actually he had wanted to bring Muna along, but Bingka objected. He gave in, thinking he had to please Bingka. After all, they were guests in his house.

Gamati, who was quite old, began to feel how complex being both a father and a mother was. At times when he did not have any work to do with Lando, he took Aimuna to Lando's plantation and taught her about the plants, their names and properties. The fruit of this tree was bitter, but induced appetite. This here is a squash, and so on.

One time when they came upon a lush betel tree, Aimuna suddenly burst into tears, taking Gamati by surprise. After she calmed down, he asked what had make her cry.

Muna answered sadly that she remembered her mother and grandmother. They loved to chew betel leaf. A betel tree grew right behind their hut and her grandmother used to ask her to fetch some leaves. When she returned with the leaves, her grandmother would smile, kiss both of her cheeks and say, "Muna, smart girl, you can fetch me the betel leaves."

Gamati was deeply stirred; a big lump filled his throat. The grandmother Muna had mentioned was his wife, Arande, a victim of the devilish hongi raid.

"Grandma is gone. I could have picked these betel leaves for her."

Gamati was at a loss about how to console his granddaughter. He nodded and tried to comfort Aimuna. He told her she was even bigger and smarter now and shouldn't cry, knowing her grandmother had gone to a very far place.

Sometimes, Muna amazed Gamati and he exclaimed, "Look at how tall you are now, Muna, and you're so good at rowing the *kolekole*. I bet you already know how to cook delicious papeda with sour fish stew for Bapa Lando."

Riti, Luna, and Masna answered on her behalf, "Of course, Grandpa, she's very good at it."

If Muna was reluctant to take a bath, Gamati coached, "Muna, you're a big girl now. Be good; do as you're told and be my sweet girl."

One day Gamati told Muna to go to Lando's plantation with Ngali while he took Sobori on a boat trip on the river under the pretext of going fishing. In fact, he wanted to have a heart-to-heart conversation with the boy.

On the boat, Gamati told Sobori to take care and protect Muna as long as they lived. Aimuna didn't have anyone left in the world. And neither did Sobori. The cursed night of the hongi raid had brought them together and nothing should be allowed to come between them. He said, "We're lucky to know a lot of people here. The Landos, Ngali and Lawe, they're all caring individuals. However, should you two someday find yourselves alone it's your responsibility to keep Muna safe. Remember that."

Bori was deeply moved. His tongue seemed to fill his throat and all he could do was nod. He wanted to say that in this small world of theirs, the island of Seram, Grandpa Gamati and Aimuna were all he had. He would rather die than lose the two of them.

Gamati was relieved, knowing that Sobori had promised to take care of Aimuna for the rest of their lives. He wanted them to marry so nothing could separate them anymore. But it was against the traditional custom for young children to wed. They had to reach puberty first.

***

Gamati, Ngali, Lawe, and the children stayed with the Landos for more than two years as little changed. During that time it remained extremely difficult to leave the isolated kampong. To go to the coastal areas one would have to spend the night somewhere, but there were no villagers' huts in the forest where one might spend the night.

They also feared they'd run into the Halefurus. Even if the Halefurus usually did not harass travelers crossing the forest, they might need a human head offering during mating season. Thus, it was best to avoid them when crossing the forest.

Gamati remembered how he and Lando had become such close friends. They met several decades ago, when they were both strong and stout young men. Lando was a wildflower honey trader who did business with people in the coastal areas. He obtained most of his honey from the mountain people. Occasionally, he collected honey himself, but since he lacked manpower it was only a small amount, and he simply saved it for his family's use. Good-quality honey from the Halefurus was usually traded for mirrors or big porcelain plates obtained from the Chinese seamen.

One day, Lando came from the forest, limping severely. He could barely walk as he approached Gamati's *lepa-lepa*, which was loaded with salt and sugar. Dried blood covered his left leg, and pain contorted his face. Gamati rushed to help him. He cleaned Lando's wound and dressed it with a piece of clean sarong he had torn. He also applied some nutmeg-scented ointment.

Gamati told Lando to lie down and rest. Lando was not permitted to walk. For three days and nights Lando rested on a mat on the outskirts of the forest while Gamati nursed him.

After Lando's leg wound healed, Gamati and two crewmembers of the lepa-lepa carried him home on a stretcher.

Lando's leg recovered quite nicely, and he soon was able to walk normally. The wound was caused by a snakebite when he was in the forest. He did not know what type of snake it was; he was just glad to still be alive.

Upon thanking Gamati, Lando vowed they would be brothers for life. If one day Gamati should come to visit him in his kampong, he would welcome Gamati with open arms. "I owe you my life, Bapa Gamati. I can never repay you." Tears of gratitude filled his eyes.

It had never crossed Gamati's mind that one day he would actually travel to the far-off kampong to seek help from Lando.

After Lando told this story to Riti, Luna, Masna, and Bingka, they felt a deep respect for Gamati and his family.

One day three guests from the coastal areas unexpectedly came to the kampong. They visited the kampong chief's hut and had long conversations with him.

The chief invited Gamati and his friends to come to his hut so they could ask these trekkers about the route from the tiny kampong to the coastal area.

The trekkers told Gamati that it should be easy to reach the coastal areas if he retraced the trail they had just cleared and followed the river, which was actually the same river that ran not far from their hut. The trekker said, "After a half day's walk, the river will drop into a waterfall.

"You will find several huts nearby. The people are also refugees. They come from other islands, like the Landos. They are not honey collectors, but collectors of massoia bark and wild nutmeg. If you mention Lando's name they will welcome you, since they are related to Riti.

"If you're lucky, you'll meet a young man who owns a kole-kole. The boat is not big, but could carry up to ten passengers. Sometimes, he's willing to take people to the Kolosia village at the coast."

The trekker said it was best to leave as soon as possible, before the bushes on the trail they cleared with machetes started to grow back. Gamati and his group told Lando about their conversation with the trekkers. They had to leave soon. Gamati's group as well as the Landos were saddened by the sudden turn of events. They had grown so close, they felt like a family. But Lawe and Ngali had family in Tuban and they missed their homeland, the island of Java.

Gamati and his men started to prepare their provisions. He and Lawe went to the forest to shoot game. Lando gave them dried smoked fish from his family's stock, and ready-to-eat cakes made from sago flour and rice, so they wouldn't need to build a fire.

Their departure was as unexpected as their arrival two years earlier had been. Soon after their conversation with the trekkers, the hongi survivors left the Landos' hut.

Machetes, ropes, and big knives were very useful when trekking through the dense forest of Seram. Unlike when they first came, they now carried the necessary equipment. Also, the two children had grown and were more mature.

***

The port of Ambon was a niche that divided the land like the wide, gaping mouth of a crocodile. That evening, the harbor bustled with activity. The sun still lingered above the western sea. The golden radiance permeated the entire ocean scene, and created a truly mesmerizing sight.

Several ships were moored in the inner harbor near the fort. The ships were an impressive sight, especially the ones with thick hulls, many windows, and roofed decks with majestic tall masts. Most were warships that had just completed hongi expeditions on Seram, the adjacent island. Men of various size and skin color worked on the decks.

Birds floated in the sky, carried by the rhythm of the wind stroking their wings. The caws of seagulls, kingfishers, shorebirds, and sea eagles interrupted the sound of the breaking waves. A flock of sea eagles glided in formation. Holding their taut legs in a straight line with their bodies, they took advantage of the thermals.

The VOC built the fort on Ambon on an elevated parcel, much like a small hill, with a clear view of the wide ocean. The fort was surrounded by a sturdy fence with an even sturdier gate. There were watchtowers for armed guards at each of the fort's four corners.

In a clearing at a lower area near the fort, several stone structures housed the men and the armory. Beneath was the ocean, barricaded with a specially constructed fence. The warships and boats of the VOC were the only vessels allowed to enter this inner harbor, their private "ocean water pool." The public port and ocean were outside the gate. A sturdy dock separated these two areas and was guarded by armed sentries.

Other smaller vessels were also busy casting their anchors. Some of them had just returned from a hongi expedition, accompanying the bigger ships. Others were just regular fishermen's boats, home from fishing. The local fishermen's boats were forbidden to moor for a long time on the dock. They had to leave as soon as they unloaded their catch.

The dock was crowded with men pulling anchor chains, folding sails, loading and unloading cargo. Some loudly barked commands.

A tall white man stood on the dock. He had stood there for some time and the sun had colored his cheeks red as tomatoes, while his eyes were as blue as the ocean. He had straw-colored hair. His lean body bent in several directions as he scanned the port, apparently looking for someone.

He approached a native crewmember and asked, "Have you seen Tatahini? He works on that large ship over there." He pointed to a warship.

Surprised, the crewman answered, "No, *Tuang*, I haven't seen him."

"You know who I'm talking about, right? He went with the hongi to the islands."

"No, Tuang, I haven't seen him."

The white man headed to the western part of the dock. A group of white men looked like they were going home. Perhaps they had just returned from the hongi.

"I'm looking for Tatahini, a *mardijker* from the Mahardika kampong. Has any of you seen him?"

One of the men said Tatahini had been at the dock earlier. Perhaps he had already gone home.

"No, he can't have gone home. We have an appointment to meet here."

The men said nothing more and left the dock.

A younger white man with brown hair approached him. They shook hands. Apparently the younger man was also waiting for Tatahini. They chatted under the radiant sunlight while waiting.

When the sun touched the horizon, they decided to return to their quarters at the fort. It was quite far from the port. They agreed that perhaps Tatahini would report the next day. Besides, the fort gate would close at exactly nine.

When they reached the fort gate, they instructed the two gate guards that if a man called Tatahini came, he should be allowed to enter the fort. Sergeant Pieter de Stein was expecting him. He should wait in the reception room, since everyone at the fort would be having dinner. Tatahini had to be a man of great importance to the VOC, for although he was a man of color, he was given the privilege of entering the fort.

The dining hall was much livelier than usual that night. All the VOC soldiers who were at the fort came to have dinner. Pieter de Stein, the VOC soldier who was known for his generosity, had donated some wine and special cakes to welcome the soldiers returning from their hongi raid. The mission was said to be very successful. They had torched three kampongs that supplied the clove buds to the VOC's enemies, the traders from China, Malacca, Portugal, and England, who paid the villagers much higher prices than the VOC. They had also killed the kampongs' leaders. They hoped that in the future no one would dare to betray the VOC again. The sultans of Ternate, Halmahera, and the Bacan Islands had all agreed to hand over the entire clove trading to the VOC from Holland. In return, they were to receive a hefty allowance twice a year. Unknowingly, the sultans had become employees of a joint capital venture, the first multinational corporation in the world, the first true conglomerate.

Everyone was in high spirits. They sang and cheered, slapped each other on the shoulders and joked. They profusely thanked Pieter de Stein. The sergeant figured that those who had drunk too much soon would pass out.

Meanwhile, the captains of the warships were being entertained at the residence of the Governor of Ambon, who had thrown a special welcome party, a formal reception.

Not long after, a guard approached Pieter de Stein and notified him that his guest, Tatahini, had arrived and was waiting in the reception room.

Piet rushed to meet his guest. The loud singing and cheering in the dining hall could still be heard from the reception room. Piet knew he shouldn't waste any time. The gate would be closed at precisely nine o'clock and after that no one could enter or exit the fort.

It was a rather small reception room, but tall windows, almost reaching the ceiling, let in a breeze pleasant to both men in the stifling afternoon heat. The flame of the oil lamp flickered wildly in the breeze.

Sergeant Pieter de Stein still wore his uniform. Tatahini, who was extremely dark, wore a long black coat. He looked like a moving big black parcel; only rows of white teeth flashed when he spoke. In the dark, he looked frightening.

Tatahini knew the sergeant very well. So he skipped the small talk and told Pieter right away that the three kampongs in the interior of Seram had been taken care of. They had terminated the leaders of the smugglers, as ordered. They had burned the kampongs and the plantations to the ground, leaving charred bodies sprawled everywhere. They had not spared anyone, not even women and children.

They didn't know the exact location of the secret clove plantations, but they had incinerated all the groves near the three kampongs and the surrounding area, and were confident the fire would have spread and eventually burned the secret plantations.

Sergeant de Stein nodded in delight. He offered Tatahini a glass of wine from the bottle he had taken from the dining hall. Tatahini thanked him but explained that he never drank alcoholic beverages.

"If that's the case, do have some cheese. This is a fine cheese from Holland, you must try it," de Stein said, cajoling him.

Tatahini helped himself to a morsel of cheese, and then another one, as a token of respect, since he did not like cheese. Its peculiar smell and salty taste were too much for him. It was just as salty as *ikang garang* sundried in the yard.

Tatahini continued his story. There was no resistance from the kampongs last night. Perhaps they never expected the VOC to reach them. The kampongs were indeed very far from the coast. They had to cross a valley, climb up a hill, and pass through a forest to reach them.

Judging from the relative ease in penetrating the kampongs and launching the attacks, Tatahini concluded that the villagers had no guards stationed at the kampongs' entrances. They had not even needed to fire the cannon from the moored ships at the beach. They ordered the foot soldiers to advance and attack the kampongs and that was all that was needed.

"It is unusual for these rogue kampongs not to put up a fair fight. Perhaps they assumed that Pani-pani would never get there. Back when we raided Manipa Island, we were met by fierce resistance. The villagers were equipped with sophisticated weapons that matched Pani-pani's. We suffered many casualties."

"What about the bandits' leaders? Were they beheaded? Did you bring their heads with you?" Pieter asked without a hint of horror or unease.

"There was no time, Tuang. We were afraid they'd seek help from other kampongs. We had to act swiftly."

"That's too bad. The heads would have served as solid proof for Tuang Governor," Pieter added.

For a moment the two men fell silent.

"Well, Tatahini, you'll be handsomely rewarded by the governor. Do you remember he promised that whoever would kill the bandits' leaders and destroyed their kampongs would be given a piece of land here in Ambon?"

"Yes, I certainly remember, Sergeant. We should wait for the hongi expedition leader to finish his report and hand it to the governor. Isn't that right, Sergeant?"

"I have deep respect for you, Tatahini. You helped us destroy the enemy. Tell me, how did you know where the kampongs were? How did you find out the leaders' names? And how did you plan a well-timed ambush in the middle of the night?"

Tatahini started to narrate his account. The sergeant was getting drunk. He laughed hard even when there was nothing funny. Tatahini knew he did not need to tell every detail. Anyway, he had to leave before they locked the fort gate at nine.

There was nothing to be proud of in terms of launching a military operation. The kampongs did not fight back; they had no troops. Tatahini told the sergeant how he and his friend found out where the hidden kampongs were. They had befriended the fishermen from various islands who often traded their fish at the Ambon port with the sole purpose to find information about the location of the smugglers' kampongs.

Tatahini was not a native of the Moluccas. His ancestors came from India. Somehow they ended up as slaves of the Portuguese, who brought them to work in Malacca. Then one day the Dutch kingdom conquered Malacca. The Dutch took Tatahini's ancestors to Java and then relocated them to Ambon.

Even though dark in complexion, much like the natives, the mardijkers had different physical characteristics. They had big, round, black eyes. They had wavy hair and sharp noses like Arabs. They also held a higher position than the natives, albeit lower than the whites who worked as VOC officers. Tatahini and his group of mardijkers were given their own settlement in Ambon. They were extremely grateful to be given higher social status than the natives. That was the reason behind their loyalty to the VOC.

Any man would be interested in a parcel of land. He would be able to settle down for good. He could start a life with his family, perhaps start a new business. The mardijkers did not want to return to their native land, for it was unknown to them.

Tatahini did not want to glorify his story and turn himself into a hero to the sergeant. What he did not tell the sergeant was that he and his friend Yacob Schouten had killed Urpati and Reja, their native informers who had guided them to the three hidden kampongs. They had sunk the bodies of Urpati and Reja in the sea after they weighed the bodies down to make sure the bodies would not float.

According to the governor, the VOC would give a reward of free land to anyone who gathered enough information to find the kampongs and destroy them. So the reward should actually have been given to Urpati and Reja.

Since greed got the better of Tatahini and Schouten, they simply reported that the informers were dead, or had fled during the raid. Since their bodies could not be found, the reward would be given to Tatahini and Schouten instead. They were the informers' partners. They did not worry about getting caught. Every VOC officer had done something despicable and foul and broken rules. Conspiracy, embezzlement, and corruption were the trademark of the VOC. They had successfully put shame aside.

Everyone knew Pieter de Stein only earned a meager salary. He was merely a low-ranking officer, but he lived lavishly and he was not hesitant to share with his fellow soldiers. He had a little "game" on the side, bootlegging quality liquors from Makassar and vending smuggled silk from China. His generosity prevented anyone from reporting him to the high officials. A lot of people expected crumbs of his wealth.

Just as Tatahini finished his report, the gate guard came and informed them that he would close the gate soon. Piet walked with Tatahini to the periphery of the residential area. Then, Tatahini hurriedly followed the guard to the gate. The guard locked the gate as soon as he stepped out.

Tatahini's ease at socializing, especially his ability to win the hearts of the right people, had put him in the center of the "right" VOC officials. He had many connections who supplied him with a lot of information. When the VOC needed sensitive information, it was Tatahini they looked for.

Tatahini spoke fluent colloquial Malay and Dutch as well as Portuguese, the language he used with his family. If Portuguese seamen were stranded in VOC territory, Tatahini would act as the interpreter. His wife was fluent in a Chinese dialect because she interacted with several goldsmiths.

And this was how Tatahini and his family, although they were neither born in the East Moluccas nor Ambon, were able to live there. If they were able to put up a good front, they could possibly live there for many generations to come and maintain a better lifestyle than the average native. It was considered normal that an immigrant was more successful than a native. Immigrants worked hard and justified any means that would help them move ahead. Being close to the authorities made it easier to implement questionable tactics.

Chapter 2

Ngasiran, the Tuban captain, had grown weary from scrutinizing the dense bushes at the beach of their mooring spot at the Kastiti Cove. Only the wind blowing from the hills moved the dark green foliage. Neither Lawe and Ngali nor Kurubela and the men from his kampong emerged, even though he was expecting them.

The crew of over a hundred men became restless. The cargo they carried was not easy to manage. There was no storage facility to unload the goods at this illegal port. It was difficult to keep more than a hundred men quiet. They talked and joked while they kept the cargo in place when waves rocked the ship. Even though the east wind was not as wild as the west wind, the tall masts and rolling waves made it difficult to keep the junk steady.

Tonight was their second night at the cove. Ngasiran knew instinctively that his crew members as well as Kurubela and his men could be in great peril despite the fact they carried swords and sharp machetes, and were skillful in defending themselves. As far as he knew, the forest of Seram wasn't home to four-legged predators. The dreaded hongi expedition must have attacked Kurubela's kampong.

Ngasiran had sailed many seas and transited many ports from the west to the east of Indonesia. The waters he cherished and knew best were the seas of the Moluccas.

He loved the rows of beautiful little islands. The stark luxuriance of their deep green forests suddenly appeared on the horizon of a shallow, crystal-clear ocean, packed with colorful fishes and coral reefs. The gentle breeze of the east wind, the friendly and generous natives who loved to sing and dance. Papeda porridge eaten with sour fish stew, his favorite local dish, could never be found in Tuban.

Ngasiran had known Kurubela for a long time. They often traded at the western islands. Ngasiran brought metal farming tools and large porcelain plates said to come from China. The natives considered the plates sacred and mystical and used them in traditional ceremonies. They also liked small urns, flower vases, and finger bowls.

Salt, sugar, rice, and fabrics like batik, cotton cloth, woven fabrics, *selampuri* and silk were favorite items. Captain Ngasiran would get more cloves if his junk brought a full load of these goods from Tuban. They did not buy and sell; they only bartered.

Kurubela often ordered gold jewelry from Ngasiran and had asked to keep this matter a secret. Kurubela owned a large clove plantation and was able to deliver a plentiful harvest, as long as the exchange was made with gold.

When the captain asked why Kurubela and Gamati needed gold while other native clove growers traded with metal tools, Kurubela whispered that gold did not tarnish and was long-lasting.

Unlike the other villagers from his kampong, Kurubela and Gamati wanted to own an arumbae, a large ship just slightly smaller than the captain's junk. They despised the VOC for monopolizing the spice trade in the Moluccas. They also held a grudge against the VOC for murdering many of their family members in hongi raids and for conducting the *extirpation* of clove trees that had bloomed, in order to keep production down.

Kurubela said they could move to another island if they owned an arumbae. There they'd be free to trade with anyone, not only with the VOC. No one in his kampong saved the way Kurubela did. Afraid to become the laughingstock, Kurubela asked Ngasiran to keep his plan a secret.

Ngasiran told him that the women in Tuban wore gold jewelry on their ears, necks, wrists. His wife had asked him for it. The finest pieces came from Malacca and India.

After spending two nights at the cove, Ngasiran knew he had to leave if he wanted to avoid meeting the VOC's patrol vessels. He would have to trade the cargo with anything he could get on the voyage back. He hoped to make some stops at some kampongs on the southeast coasts. Hopefully they'd have cloves to trade. Nutmeg and mace would be even better, or some massoia bark and dried fish.

***

The sun had just emerged shyly from the sea horizon, yet its pale radiance was starting to illuminate the cove's surface. Ngasiran watched in amazement, even though it was not the first time he watched a sunrise. He gazed eastward, silent for a moment. Slowly the pale rays of light turned brighter and the sun became a reddish ball.

The breakfast porridge was served and the crew took turns to eat. The captain and officers ate first. Ngasiran repeatedly ordered his crew to move quietly.

They held a meeting while eating breakfast. The captain had decided they couldn't afford to wait any longer for Lawe and Ngali. If the two of them were safe, he hoped they'd meet next year when the junk returned to Seram.

"But Captain, what about Lodi and Kale, the castaways we found on Bacan Island? We haven't met Kurubela, and we can't just drop them here."

"They are strong, diligent, and nice young men; we all like them. However, they're not Javanese. Could they survive and live on Java like us? And if we were to drop them, where would that be?" Ngasiran asked.

"Perhaps at one of the kampongs that will let us moor at their beach and accept them," the first mate answered.

"I have thought about that too, but these boys are from the northern islands. They are different from the people of Seram. It will be hard for them to adjust here. The hongi destroyed their homes. There is nothing to return to if we drop them on Seram. Those poor boys," Ngasiran said softly.

"Let's call them and ask them if they want to join us. If so, we don't have to drop them. If they don't want to go to Tuban, we'll drop them here. That way, they won't have any regrets later," said the first mate.

Ngasiran agreed. He sent for Kale and Lodi, and invited the two boys to have breakfast. When he posed his question, neither had an answer. Looking devastated, they asked for some time to think.

They asked each other if there would be any chance to return to the Moluccas if they joined the ship and set out for Java. On the other hand, they had no place to go if they did not join the ship. They had no home, no families. All was gone.

Since they had to give the answer soon, Kale and Lodi finally agreed to join the junk wherever it sailed to. They humbly stated they wanted to be crewmembers and, like the others, work hard and become seamen.

All things settled, Ngasiran commanded to raise the anchor, and the junk set sail. They'd sail along the coastline of Seram and make stops at some kampongs that would welcome the Tuban ship. They hoped not to run into a hongi expedition or Papuan ships.

The long and narrow Papuan canoes carried many oarsmen. They were difficult to chase and difficult to avoid in a random encounter. Papuans were excellent marksmen. They speared fish or humans while standing in their extraordinarily fast canoes.

Just like the VOC fleet sailed with a number of warships in convoy, the Papuans sailed in groups too. They pirated whomever they met on their voyage at sea or land. They usually tied up the natives they plundered and loaded them on their boats to sell later as slaves. The VOC needed plantation workers and crew for their warships. They also needed slaves for domestic help at their high officials' residences.

The crewmembers of the Tuban junk carried out their tasks swiftly. They took care to work quietly, fearful of being noticed by a VOC ship should it happen to sail nearby. They left the Kastiti Cove at noon. Fortunately the sky was clear and there was no threat of rainfall. The voyage ran smoothly, even though they sailed against the wind.

The crewmember who was in charge of the ship's food rations reported to the captain. They had to trade for food supplies next time they moored. Due to the failed trade they had been unable to restock rice and sago while moored at the Kastiti Cove. Now they were low on rice.

Lodi carefully stacked the baskets filled with trading items they had unloaded at the cove. He had to make sure they would not topple and scatter when waves hit the junk. Circumstances had forced him to leave the small archipelago he called home and he was heartbroken. He came from Bacan. The island was ruled by a regent they called the *sultan*.

Once a year, the sultan sent an emissary to collect taxes. The islanders had to hand over their harvests of fruit, cloves, or any other spices. Lodi still remembered the arrival of the sultan's hongi, back when he was a child.

They had come in large, decorated boats. At the beach, the kampong chief officially greeted the tax collectors with a ceremony. They were welcomed with dances and music. Betel nut and betel leaves arranged on brass plates were served to them. The harvests, stockpiled in the kampong storage, were to be handed to the emissary after the ceremony was over. It had been a while since the last sultan's fleet came to their beach.

Lodi was all grown up and ready to ask for the hand of a neighbor girl in marriage when strangers attacked his kampong, even though it was located far from the coastline. The enemies came in the still of the night when everyone was fast asleep. They massacred the villagers, taking hostage those who were still alive. They also looted all the baskets of cloves.

He was still alive only because the girl his parents were going to propose to for him shielded him with her body when an enemy soldier attacked him with a machete. He then managed to flee to the dark forest.

Three days after the assault, Lodi returned to his kampong to see about his family and his bride-to-be.

The kampong had burned to the ground. No one had bothered to bury the dead; the stench of corpses was overwhelming.

He fled to the forest again and from that time on, lived there alone. Sometimes, he talked to trees, or the fish in the stream. Sometimes, he wept, feeling wretched and miserable. He did not have any spare clothes, so he never changed, but often bathed in the stream. He ate any fruit the forest offered. His tangled hair was matted into whorls of a reeking, unkempt mass. He looked terrible.

One day, when he wandered in the forest, he heard a sound much like a groan. He figured it had to be the spirits of the forest. Frightened, he tried to get away when the groaning turned into a faint cry for help. After overcoming his fear, he searched for the source of the cries. He found a young man near a small stream. He was part of a group of young men who apparently had tried to drink from the small stream. The rest of the group had died and their bodies had started to reek.

Lodi dragged the young man away from the corpses. He felt bad having to drag him across the rough forest floor. Lodi was weak himself from the hard life and meager diet in the forest. Lodi searched for some rattan filled with water. He slashed it with his machete, the only thing that he had brought from his kampong, and gave the rattan to the young man. Water flowed from the vine-like plant.

The young man gradually recovered. Lodi searched for fruit and was able to get an ample amount of ripe mangosteens. The fruit was their ration for the day.

After several days, the young man was finally able to walk and climb trees. His name was Kale. He came from Ambon, another island. The VOC had taken him as a slave and forced him to work as a crewmember on one of their warships. He looked slightly different from Lodi. His mother came from Makassar, while his father was a native of Ambon. Kale had wavy hair, a medium build, and was not muscular. He had round, glistening black eyes and a common dark brown skin tone.

The two young men talked in the Malay trading language common to the coastal areas, especially the northern islands ruled by sultans. When the hongi raided Bacan Island, Kale and several other young men, all of whom later died at the stream, ran away from the ship. They did not want to attack the natives and no longer wanted to be slaves, so they fled to the forest.

Much to their horror, all the villagers were killed, and that left them with no temporarily shelter. They stayed hidden in the forest until the VOC soldiers left the next day. Kale did not know whether the VOC was looking for them or not. They lived under harsh conditions, but still survived for a few weeks.

One day they came upon a pond where carcasses of animals lay. They were famished, so without a second thought, they drank from the pond. Not long after, an intense stomach pain struck them. The young men died one by one. Kale was the sole survivor and that was how he met Lodi.

Ever since, they wandered together. They planned to leave the island. They never added up how long they had wandered together like brothers, counting on each other. They often sat around on the beach when they finished preparing their meal. Kale knew a tree whose bark could be pounded and made into some sort of stiff fabric to cover their bodies. They shivered in the cold night. The fabric did not warm them. But it was better than being naked; at least they were decent. Apparently there were no mountain people or Halefurus in the interior of Bacan Island. They never found a trace of another human being during their aimless wanderings. Until one day, a great drought dried up a lot of branches and twigs and the heat in the forest was stifling. Lodi and Kale headed to a nearby cove and soaked for a long time in the crystal-clear water. Vibrantly colored fish swam around them, but they made no attempt to catch some. They did not have a fire to cook. Suddenly Kale heard splashing, much like an oar hitting water. They were afraid it was a ship belonging to the

VOC or Papuans. They hid in the nearby groves and watched for an approaching boat.

A large and mighty ship, with a tall mast and a deck with many oarsmen, came nearer. The gong man sat in the middle on the outer deck, and hit his gong to guide the oarsmen.

Lodi and Kale were in awe. They had never seen such a ship. The crewmembers did not have the physical appearance of the average man from the eastern islands: well-built, dark-skinned men with tightly curled hair. Instead their skin had a dark brown or yellowish tone, and they had wavy or straight hair. They certainly were not the VOC. The men did not look hostile, like the Papuans who always carried spears. Neither did they look like the sultan's men or VOC crewmembers, who were pale-skinned and came from a faraway land.

Lodi and Kale decided to approach the strangers and ask to join the ship so they could leave this woeful island. They determined they had to act now or forever be trapped on this wretched island.

Lodi and Kale emerged from the groves and shouted, "Tabea. Tabea." They hoped the men did not just look friendly, but were indeed kind-hearted.

The men on board the junk were alarmed by their appearance and tried to communicate with them, but Lodi and Kale spoke a dialect unknown to the seamen. Finally, they managed to communicate with gestures using their limbs, eyes, and bodies, uttering no sound. The seamen came to understand that the two frail and shabby-looking young men dressed in tree bark were survivors of the hongi expedition. It was heartbreaking, especially to Ngasiran, the captain.

Lodi and Kale were taken on board. The crewmembers gave them clothes and food. After just two nights at sea, Lodi and Kale regained their strength and started to learn to communicate in Javanese, the junk seamen's language. When the junk moored in the Kastiti Cove to pick up Kurubela, they were already at ease with the workings of all matters on board.

Captain Ngasiran and the first mate were fond of the two ill-fated young men and so were the other crewmembers, especially the fishermen. Lodi and Kale were deft fishermen; they could even catch fish with their bare hands when the junk was afloat.

If the disaster at Kastiti Cove had not happened, Ngasiran would have asked Lodi and Kale about their plans for the future. What were they going to do next? Did they want to disembark on Seram and settle there? Or did they want to stay aboard the junk all the way to Tuban? He did not have a chance to ask them before Lawe and Ngali went missing.

The headwind was quite fierce. Every crewmember available was ordered to row to help steady the fully loaded junk. They were also anxious, fearing a chance encounter with the Papuans or the VOC.

Captain Ngasiran and his crew witnessed the misery and devastation that had befallen the victims of the hongi. The man-made catastrophe happened when the regents and sultans of the islands north of Seram were too weary to uphold the resistance and handed the clove trading to the VOC. In return, the sultans received a hefty allowance twice a year.

Ngasiran gazed at the horizon while the morning sun slowly rose. He prayed that no ship would cross their path.

***

The resident of Saparua, a small island right across from Ambon, ascended the ladder of the boat that had transported him from Ambon. The sun was bright in a clear blue sky. Drenched in perspiration, Lucas de Vries took off the coat he wore over a white shirt. The natives were shirtless in this sweltering heat, while he wore a coat.

For a Westerner, Lucas was not tall. He was small-boned, different from most Dutch men in the Moluccas at that time. His eyes were the same color as his thick, wavy brown hair, and his heavy sideburns almost reached his chin. His Hispanic ancestry was obvious. He was in his early twenties.

Lucas breathed a sigh of relief. He had arrived at his new post, with a new appointment. As the resident of Saparua he would direct the governance and regulations on the island as a representative of the VOC.

An older Dutchman greeted him by the ladder. Verhoven was the caretaker of Saparua Island and its fort. They shook hands then walked to the fort.

Saparua's fort was located on a private coastline. The VOC community lived in this fortified area. The resident's quarters consisted of a two-bedroom apartment with a dining room that doubled as an office, and a small veranda in front. The veranda faced a well-kept small garden filled with local flowers. The neighbors were all high-ranking officials of the VOC.

There was a kitchen with a bathroom and a urinal alongside. The housemaid's room and storage were across a roofless path, next to a well. If the resident wished to take a bath, the housemaid would draw water from the well and fill the basin in the bathroom.

Several household helpers led by *Mak* Uti walked to the veranda. They all bowed their heads in respect and greeted him, "Tabea, Tuang Resideng, tabea. Welcome to Saparua."

Lucas de Vries smiled and happily nodded.

"Tabea. Tabea," he replied rather stiffly.

Verhoven explained that these people were his household helpers. Mak Uti used to work for Westerners and could cook European food. She worked previously in a Portuguese household. Kaota, a young man, was the gardener. Roka, a young Papuan bought at the slave market in Ambon, was the errand boy. He would take care of anything Lucas needed done outside the fort, especially at the port.

"Do any of them speak Dutch?" Lucas asked.

"No. They're all natives. You will have to learn the local dialect."

"Very well. I will work on that." Lucas hated the heat that caused him to perspire heavily. He gestured that he needed water to bathe.

All the household staff immediately got busy. Mak Uti, as ordered by Verhoven, prepared mashed potatoes and fried a large fish in butter.

She also prepared a dessert with coconut milk, a substitute for cow's milk.

Verhoven had ordered all the food supplies from the kitchen of the governor's residence in Ambon.

Roka made the trip to and from the port, carrying the baggage of the newly arrived resident. Verhoven cautioned him not to let any of the resident's belongings fall into the sea and waited for Lucas on the veranda.

Resident Lucas de Vries dressed and joined Verhoven on the veranda. He asked if Verhoven had planned anything for him. Currently, the VOC planned another hongi expedition to the southern islands. They were also preparing the pioneering clove plantation there. The plantation was to be identical to those of the natives'. The only distinction was that the VOC would limit the number of clove trees, and the plantation would be closely controlled.

"Yes, Resident. The natives' council of elders will come to the meeting room in the fort. They will report on the preparation of the coming hongi expedition. I will act as an interpreter."

"Hmm. So you have mastered the local dialect? Who taught you?"

"Ha ha ha. There was no teacher, Mr. Resident, I learned from everyday conversations."

"Very well, I shall follow your method. Are there any natives who speak Dutch?"

"There are actually a few, Mr. Resident. They are usually from the church."

"I see. It's lunchtime. Will you be joining me? What's the usual arrangement? Please, tell me."

"Thank you, Mr. Resident. My wife has cooked for me. I am going home to eat now. I will be back later to pick you up in time for the meeting. Do you have any more questions?"

"No, thank you. I'll see you in the afternoon."

The resident of Saparua ate quietly by himself. This was not his first time visiting the East Indies. Lucas de Vries had lived in the Sultanate of Banten for a full year as the treasurer. He was also a good painter, and was given the undercover assignment of archivist. His paintings documented the Sultanate's territory for study in Holland. The VOC did not want their host to know they were spied on and thus Lucas painted under the pretext of engaging in his hobby. Sometimes he made a family sketch of the Banten ruler. The husband, wife, and children. They loved being painted and were unsuspecting.

Lucas de Vries was a good-looking man. His Hispanic looks derived from his mother's side. Yolanda was half Dutch since her father was a Portuguese captain of a trading ship.

After the Portuguese seaman disappeared and her mother died, Yolanda wound up in an orphanage in Amsterdam. When she turned sixteen, the board of caregivers placed her in the home of an aristocrat, with hopes she would have guidance in matters of religion and morality and be wedded, should someone ask for her hand in marriage.

The Hispanic-looking brunette with large beautiful eyes worked without pay and only rested when she slept at night.

Amsterdam was a flourishing trading city. The rich prospered mainly as a result of Holland successfully colonializing new territories in Africa and Asia. Yolanda's beauty enamored Jacob, the eldest son of the aristocrat. Yolanda and Jacob were about the same age, but his parents opposed the union. They were a well-respected family of noble lineage, wealthy and highly educated, while Yolanda came from an orphanage. Moreover, her father had been Portuguese, and Portugal was Holland's rival at sea. She had no education and observed a different religion to boot.

One day after his twenty-first birthday party, Jacob asked Yolanda to bring his freshly pressed garments up to his room on the second floor and then seduced her. He had always wanted to marry the beautiful Yolanda.

She tried to spurn his advances, but he was larger and stronger. His parents were horrified by the idea that their son would marry the maid. Even though Yolanda was a beautiful young woman, they always looked down on her. Jacob had hoped his parents would allow them to marry after the "incident" in his bedroom, but even after Yolanda was far into the last months of her pregnancy, his father refused to settle the issue in that manner. Instead, he wedded Yolanda to their coachman and paid all the expenses, including the childbirth.

This was how Lucas came to bear the surname of de Vries. It was the coachman's surname.

Even though she did not share the coachman's quarters, Yolanda continued to live and work in the aristocrat's mansion.

Then, one day, the aristocrat and his wife quarreled violently about the presence of Yolanda's illegitimate child in the household. They cursed each other and in the end the wife threw Yolanda and her five-year-old son out of the mansion.

Without any provisions, Yolanda and Lucas stepped outside.

Yolanda had refused the aristocrat's offer to have the coachman give them a ride. She also refused what little money the coachman had offered. She was angry and hated everyone.

Lucas remembered very well how his mother had cried during their long walk in the cold autumn wind. They finally arrived at a small house. A fire was lit in a fireplace in the main room and the house was warm. Uncle and Aunt Stam consoled crying Yolanda and told Lucas to play with their children.

The Stams, though not well off, were generous and took in Yolanda and her son.

Lucas remembered being happy there. He had many friends and no one was mean. It was a welcome change after living at the aristocrat's residence.

Alas, the kind-hearted Uncle Stam became ill and died. Aunt Stam was unable to support Yolanda and Lucas.

Yolanda tried to find work as a housemaid. A lot of families were looking for domestic help due to the growing economy, but Jacob's mother had spread the word among the aristocrats that Yolanda was promiscuous and no one would hire her.

The Wijnens, neighbors of the Stams, earned a living as owners of a small circus. They owned a monkey and a dog. Their two children, Eric and Sonya, danced with the animals. Sonya, who had a pretty voice, also sang. They did not make a fortune, but enough to tide them over for several months.

Mr. Wijnen asked Lucas to join them. He taught Lucas to dance and sing, and perform routines with the animals. Mr. Wijnen played the accordion; Mrs. Wijnen played the tambourine.

Since she had failed to find employment, Yolanda allowed Lucas to join the Wijnens' troupe. At least he would be fed and have a place to stay. They had also worked out an arrangement for her.

While the troupe was out performing during the day, she'd cook and clean the Wijnens' house.

Yolanda never spoke about Jacob, but Lucas often found his mother weeping silently when she thought no one else was around. After he found out that his mother often cried secretly, he kept his hurts, ideas, or protests to himself. Lucas grew into an emotionally sensitive and introverted child, different from those around him, who were expressive and open.

His mother taught Lucas to read and draw. Lucas was happy when he learned he could easily and accurately copy objects he saw on paper. People said that he was talented. The Wijnens said that he should be a painter when he grew up. Yolanda knew that Lucas inherited the talent from her father, the Portuguese captain who had abandoned her and her mother.

Thanks to his talent for drawing Lucas now was an archivist in a land oceans away from Holland.

There was a fierce competition between the kingdoms of Holland, Spain, Portugal, and England. All of them were eager to discover new frontiers outside of Europe and invested large amounts of money into overseas expeditions in search of the three most prized spices of all: cloves, nutmeg and its mace, and pepper.

These spices were the staple of every kitchen in the four-seasoned countries. People used the spices to preserve food, add aromas, and enhance the flavor of food and drinks. The spices were also used as natural medicine and in religious rituals. All the religions in the world needed aromatic incense for their places of worship.

People hunted during the summer and by the time snow fell, three months later, the meat would have spoiled. They needed spices like nutmeg and mace to preserve it.

Every country had sacrificed many lives and large amounts of money in their quest to obtain these spices. None lessened their efforts. Now, decades later, these competing kingdoms prospered. Their investment to finance the expeditions yielded profits many times over. With more capital available, they intensified science and research. Their power grew. It became difficult to measure Holland's wealth and glory at sea. And Lucas was in the midst of it.

***

The resident was mildly taken aback when Mak Uti cleared his plate. Lucas had finished eating and his mind had wandered off to his childhood. The new atmosphere of the fort had evoked memories of his tearful mother and the benefactor of his education, the aristocrat who had fathered him. Lucas remembered he had to prepare his drawing tools to bring to the meeting later. He intended to draw sketches of the elders who attended the meeting. He was slightly surprised that the appearance of the Ambonese and Bantenese was very different.

The Ambonese had upright, strong-looking statures. They were dark skinned, and rather quick-tempered. They had tight curly hair, while the Bantenese had thick straight or wavy hair. Some of them wore their hair in a bun at the top of their heads.

The place of the meeting was just a short distance outside of the fort's yard. The ten-member council of elders gave off the air of lordliness; their eyes were intense. The upper parts of their body were only covered with a garment that looked like an unbuttoned shirt. Lucas suspected that was because of the heat.

Lucas and Verhoven were dressed according to the standard of VOC officials; dark, tight-fitting pants, a white inner shirt, and a dark-colored coat made from a thick fabric. Their hair was neatly combed and tucked under their hats. As they entered the meeting room, they took off their hats as a sign of respect to the people inside.

Lucas cast a sidelong glance and noticed the elders' lips were a fiery red. Verhoven said that they chewed a type of leaf with spices. Perhaps as a breath-freshener, he said.

It was customary for the natives to welcome guests by serving betel leaves to honor them. However, the VOC considered it a dirty habit because the betel leaf juices caused them to spit often and so they issued the rule that the natives had to finish their betel leaf chewing before meeting with someone from the VOC. Lucas wondered how he could color the sketches of the elders, since he had only brought a charcoal pencil. The elders came from several kampongs on Saparua and a few neighboring islands that were less populated.

These islands, at the far south of Ternate, Halmahera, and the Bacan Islands had long submitted to the VOC. Previously they paid tributes and taxes to the sultan of Ternate. After he handed over the entire clove trade with foreign seamen to the VOC, the rest of the islands followed suit after unsuccessfully protesting against their new lot. This included Seram, the biggest island in the area.

The foreigners often dealt directly with the high officials from the sultanate. And if a sultan or the king had agreed to something, the people were left with no other choice.

The four sultans of the north area had agreed to receive a periodic allowance so they would not have to concern themselves with the clove trading. They never bothered to ask about the VOC's plans for the clove plantations in their areas.

No one expected that there was a plan to cut down and burn all the existing clove trees. No one knew the intent of the Creator of the universe when out of all the places on earth He chose Bacan, Makian, Moti, Ternate, and Tidore, five small, uncharted islands far on the eastern side of Indonesia, as the only place for the clove tree to grow. No one could explain why only these five little islands were bestowed with the privilege of growing the most sought-after trees in the world.

The clove flower buds had an immense influence. Humans had picked and dried them for thousands of years. The spice was transported to the region now known as the Middle East. Egyptians had preserved their dead through embalming using a mixture of spices of which clove was the most important one. After the body was soaked in the mixture for seventy days, it was ready for the process of mummification. It was believed that those bodies would never decompose.

Those who found the sea or land routes to the origins of the cloves became prosperous and kept the knowledge of the routes secret. They did not want other nations to find the small islands.

For thousands of years the Portuguese were able to keep the secret since other seafaring people were scarce and cartography of faraway lands was primitive. During those times, the people of the small islands, the rightful owners of the clove trees, were safe. The foreign seamen who had traveled far to trade with them were well behaved and respectful. They never used weapons of any type.

Then the idea of monopolizing the trade occurred to the Dutch kingdom. If no other nations could supply the spices, everyone would have to buy the prized spice from Holland and Holland could therefore control the price. Such were the notions that inspired the plan to monopolize the clove trade.

In pursuit of this grand plan, they had to throw aside all feelings of honor and empathy. In competition one had to be shameless, thick-skinned, and ruthless. They could not pity the natives who were made to suffer and even pushed to extinction. They had to abide by the principles that competition was good, that taking profits as high as possible, even up to a thousandfold, was fair in the struggle to prosper. If they formerly lived by the notion that thriftiness was the base of prosperity, they were now driven by greed in their pursuit of wealth.

The routes to the islands had been obtained by stealing. A Dutch sailor applied for work on a Portuguese expedition and sailed with them as far as Malacca. He kept his eyes and ears open and studied everything during the voyage. When the ship returned to Portugal, he resigned and managed to walk off with the land maps and notes for the route to Malacca and Banten. He immediately went back to Holland.

The stolen maps quickly became a big sensation in Holland. The Dutch studied the charted route and elaborated on theories they re-examined before setting sail. The maps helped Holland to find their way to the Indies and all the way to the Spice Islands, the Land of the Thousand Islands in the eastern part of Indonesia.

The Portuguese had come first to the Indies. They had already intended to monopolize the clove and nutmeg trade, long before the Dutch did. When the VOC arrived, the Portuguese were still struggling to sell their idea to the resistant natives. The local sultans soon turned to the VOC for help to force the Portuguese out of the islands. After the VOC ousted the Portuguese, it turned out that the help was not given for free. The VOC asked for a favor in return.

Resident Lucas de Vries had his share of work to reach the VOC's goals. They were going to tour the islands and its kampongs. Anyone who owned clove trees had to report to the VOC and sell the harvest to them at a fixed low price. Trees that had blossomed once had to be cut down and replaced with saplings. If the harvest promised to be abundant, the farmers were ordered to cut down the blossoming trees. This way, the clove price on the European world market would be constantly high.

However, the natives had their own agenda. They secretly planted clove trees in the deep interior, on mountain slopes unreachable from the coast. They even went as far as planting trees on other islands. They traded their harvest with other friendly seamen for everyday goods they needed. Unfortunately the calm, peaceful situation couldn't be maintained for too long. The price of cloves in Europe and the Middle East plummeted. The VOC already controlled the number of clove trees and monopolized the trade. Apparently the supply was abundant. Therefore there must be illegal plantations, secret harvests, and secret traders. There were secret parties who transported the cloves via land routes and caused the prices to drop. The VOC then changed the expeditions of hongi that were initially used to collect taxes by the sultanates to one that delivered disaster.

Lucas observed each of the elders' faces. Later tonight, he'd sketch them and make notes of their heights, the way they dressed, and the names of their kampongs.

The elders told him the number of men drafted to join the hongi mission by the end of the eastern wind season. Almost all of them were married. They expected the single men to marry before the hongi, since there were chances that one would not be able to return home if killed in combat or drown at sea.

"How do you calculate the number of men available? I heard that people usually decline to join the hongi. Their excuse is that they have a family to support," Lucas said.

"That's right, Mister Resident. No one will provide food for their wife and children at home while they're on the hongi."

"In that case they have to stock up food before joining the hongi," Lucas said flatly.

"Yes, but sometimes the season is fierce, Sir. There will be no fish to be dried. Or there could be a long drought and no rice to harvest. Surely, a family can't survive with just papeda to eat."

Lucas busily took notes. He needed to have a meeting with Verhoven later tonight.

"What about boats? I heard that here in Saparua you have *kora-kora*, is that right?"

"Yes, we do, Tuang," the oldest men answered.

"How many of them?"

"Only two kora-koras."

"What about the rowers?"

"Only enough for one kora-kora, Tuang."

"We need more kora-koras."

The elders fell silent. It wasn't their problem. They had provided one kora-kora as well as the rowers. The VOC did not even supply food and drink during the hongi. That was another thing they had to worry about.

The atmosphere of the meeting was a little awkward. Lucas had just been introduced to the elders and he was a bit weary from the heat. He realized the importance of mastering the local dialect if he wanted to have direct conversations. The meeting was abruptly dismissed.

This was Lucas' first appointment as a resident and his first post in the Moluccas. This was also the first time he'd be involved and leading a hongi expedition to extirpate clove trees. However, before his arrival, the fort at Saparua Island had already launched two hongi missions, to Manipa and Seram. After the elders left, Verhoven and de Vries returned to the fort. When they arrived at the resident's home, the alarm sounded.

Verhoven quickly pulled the sword that was always girded at his side and reached for the rifle he always carried. An errand boy who walked with them ran to the fort's gate. He told another boy to carry the resident's belongings to his house. Two other men, some sort of native soldiers, were asked to tag along. Lucas, Verhoven, and the two soldiers sprinted outside the fort.

A riot had broken out at the slave barracks near the new trial plantation site outside the fort. The VOC was going to experiment on a new clove plantation on Saparua, all planted and tended by the VOC. They had brought workers, men and women, to start it. Their barracks were right across from each other and separated by a river. The women over at their barracks were screaming in fright as a number of men were trying to seize a shabby-looking man who brandished a sickle.

The resident lunged to seize the raging man. Infuriated, the man aimed his sickle at the resident's neck. If Verhoven had not instantly shot the man, Resident de Vries would have died with a slashed throat.

For a moment after the rifle went off, everything was still. The resident was in shock. *I've come a long way only to be killed here*, he thought while all the plantation workers gathered around the dead man.

According to the plantation foreman, the man had been bought in Ambon, only last week. He never talked to anybody, and was always wrathful. The sickle never left his hand.

The story broke Lucas' heart. He detested death and wondered, *Why should someone die because of me?* He had seen death too many times during his voyage from Holland to Banten. He thought the punishment for the crew of the ship he boarded was ruthless and most inhumane.

Lucas had no appetite that night. Verhoven, Mak Uti, and the two other helpers ate the dinner prepared for him. The scruffy and unkempt face of the dead man haunted Lucas. He could not forget the man's rage when he wanted to slash his throat. They had never met before in their lives. There was no grudge between them.

The Dutch, people from a faraway foreign land, were the ones who had brought devastation to the natives, the rightful owners of the clove and nutmeg trees. The natives were the ones who planted, tended, and harvested the clove buds that grew in their homeland when, out of the blue, this foreign company, Lucas' employer, came and declared ownership of the trees.

It was not surprising the natives hated whomever represented the VOC. Lucas wondered if this meant that he would always be despised by the natives here. If so, his life in the Indies would be in danger for the rest of his stay as a resident.

Lucas thought of his father, the aristocrat's son who had first paid for his education and then placed him in this job. It seemed highly unlikely that he didn't know of the miserable conditions here. The aristocrat was an educated man, moved in many social circles, and was active in the stock market. *Had he intentionally sent his illegitimate son by the woman he loved to die here?*

Lucas did not have the answer to that question. From now on, he'd be in constant fear of being slashed or speared, of being killed by the natives.

The next day, he asked Verhoven to look for someone who could train him in the use of spears, swords, rifles, and close-range fight. Even though he was not a soldier, he now felt that he needed to learn to use weapons as a means of self-defense. He was propelled to do this, despite the fact he actually hated anything harsh, let alone violence.

***

Gamati led the group. They had walked all night long. Their hearts were heavy since they left the Landos, and it was as if something was missing. They had lived safely with the Landos for two years. Now they had to leave hurriedly without as much as a guide to lead their way.

Bori had grown bigger and was more mature. He was very sensitive to suffering around him, and liked to help people. If he saw Gamati, Ngali, or Lawe carry things he could carry, he offered his help.

Aimuna had gotten taller, and had learned to keep her feelings to herself. She always obeyed her grandfather. All in all, the trip leaving the forest was much easier when compared to their trip entering it two years earlier.

They followed all the instructions from the trekkers at the kampong chief's hut. They walked fast, almost ran, at a steady pace. It was not hard to find the waterfall the men had told them about. It was an amazing sight; Gamati had never been there and he was in awe. The quiet and luxuriant paradise was filled with colorful songbirds and dragonflies with transparent wings. There were swarms of colorful butterflies, fluttering to and fro. The thundering sound of water breaking on the stones below was heard constantly. Gamati thought of his family members who had passed away. They never had a chance to see this beautiful place.

By the waterfall, they met a young man. He was willing to take them to the beach where boats usually moored. There, they could board a boat to the kampong. The boat they were going to use belonged to his uncle, who lived in the interior of the island.

When they asked what he wanted in return for his service, the young man answered that it was up to them. The important thing was to get to their destination first. They could talk about his reward once they reached it. Upon hearing that Ngali and Lawe were from Tuban, and Tuban was the equivalent of Java to all islanders, the young man suddenly said he wanted to come along with them to Tuban.

"Why are you interested in sailing to Tuban?" Gamati asked.

"I heard that everyone there is smart. They can build better boats. They're good at cloth weaving and making batik. They can sail to faraway lands and they are good cooks. I want to learn from them."

"What about your wife and children? And this boat?"

"Wife? I don't have a wife yet. I heard that the girls in Tuban are pretty."

"Aren't the girls here in Seram also pretty? They powder their faces to screen the sunlight, so their faces are smooth. They're good at making sago and weaving mats," Gamati argued.

"That's true, Bapa. But if I could sail to faraway places, there is no harm in doing it, right? I want to escape the hongi; it terrifies me. Now we have to join the hongi every year, Bapa. I do not like it at all," he said softly.

Ah, it is the hongi again, Gamati thought sadly.

They agreed to sail along the river until they reached the beach. Depending on the situation then, they'd decide what to do next. They surely preferred to avoid bumping into the hongi, if possible. They paused twice during their trip to look for food in the bushes along the river. Luckily the river was not rocky at the bottom.

The next morning they arrived in a kampong, a bit far from the coastline, but where the sound of breaking waves still could be heard. People called the kampong Kolosia, which means "waiting." Even though it was not situated right on the beach, people could wait in this kampong to meet up with whomever they wanted to meet according to their arrangements. It was an inter-kampong meeting place for the seamen.

The natives here were also forced to join the hongi. Kolosia still had one year before they would be drafted and this gave them great relief. As soon as Gamati reported to the kampong chief that they were a group of hongi survivors, the chief immediately helped him. Rumors about the destruction of kampongs by the VOC in the interior of their beloved Seram had reached Kolosia.

Apparently Gamati and his group were survivors of the raid. The villagers immediately made a place to sleep available for the group, with food and drinks such as the host could provide. What really touched the hearts of Gamati, Sobori, and the two sailors from Tuban was that even though they had never met the Kolosians before, these kind people treated them like family.

If they had not been welcomed in this kampong, they would have had no other place to ask for shelter. The villagers even allowed Mongonda, the young man they had met at the waterfall, to stay too. They wanted to help him find a solution to his problem.

Gamati could not get over the people's kindness, even though he would definitely do the same thing himself; to help people in great distress was customary throughout the generations. He told Aimuna to be nice to everyone, and she agreed wholeheartedly.

The kampong chief said that they were waiting for a number of boats to moor soon, maybe two or three. All of them were from Ambon, but were not the VOC's boats. Mongonda, Lawe, and Ngali could probably board them when they sailed back to Ambon. There, they could easily find boats that sailed to various places. Perhaps one of them would sail to Tuban.

It was normal for big boats to come to Kolosia at the time of the east wind, when the sea was relatively calm. Some of them traded salt, sugar, or gold with the natives for frying oil made from Java almond, the fragrant massoia bark, or dried fish. If the wild nutmeg trees happened to fruit, they would also take a load of it to Ambon. The crust and rinds of the seeds had many uses.

The VOC usually did not want to trade the wild nutmeg, so the natives could keep them for their own use. The VOC monopolized nutmeg that came from the Banda Islands. These nuts were very fragrant, contained more oil and lasted over long voyages.

Gamati hoped they would not have to stay long in Kolosia. The villagers were nice indeed, but he wanted to live independently. He wanted to have their own clove plantation, and their own ship to sail far. If it was beyond their means they could partner with other good people who were not accomplices of the VOC.

Unlike the secluded kampong of the Landos, Kolosia was a lively kampong. With some thirty families living there, it was quite densely populated. In Seram, it was common for people to inhabit the fertile lands along the rivers or its estuaries. People liked to build kampongs near water. Aside from providing food and drink, the body of water also facilitated transportation. They traveled with boats, through the sea to get to other kampongs. "Our beloved land and seas" was the natives' motto.

Gamati wondered in which direction the Seram Sea lay. Their own kampongs, which were destroyed two years ago, were easier to reach from the south, the sea closer to Ambon. If they ever built another kampong, he would not choose the old site since it could be easily accessed by the hongi expedition. Perhaps it would be better to form an alliance with the people in the north.

Gamati ventured deeper into the forest. He wanted to find out what types of wood were available. He hoped to build a small kole-kole for transport to other kampongs, or a bigger lepa-lepa for fishing. Maybe there were big and sturdy woods to build a *rurehe,* or even an arumbae, the boat Kurubela had always wished for.

The extirpation of clove trees in the northern area that started several years ago, as well as the VOC forcing the natives to move from hills in the interior to the coast, destroyed the long-held indigenous beliefs and customs of kinship.

Gamati remembered how there were systems of alliance of kampongs, namely *uli lima,* the family of five, and *uli siwa,* the family of nine, with specific traditions. Now these customs could no longer be upheld. The VOC had forced everyone regardless of his or her family origin to live in the same kampong. Refusing put one's life at stake.

The old man hoped that someday, when the VOC finally left these islands, peace and serenity would return. Then uli lima and uli siwa would be once again upheld as the rule in kinships, along with the *pelas.*

Gamati felt that their merry traditional parties were never carried out again since the VOC implemented the draft for the hongi. The parties were always filled with *kapata,* the singing and exchanging of rhymes of their ancestors' sagas. They were also losing many epics and oral stories of their relationship to animals through sacred language and satires. The same thing happened with the tradition of boys and girls coming together on the night before a wedding. The cheerful and carefree natives had turned wretched and miserable. Life felt empty now.

Gamati used to love parties. When he was younger, he enjoyed drinking palm wine, just like his son-in-law, Kurubela. However, they took good care not to get drunk. Another thing missing in everyday socializing was humor. The natives were now cautious toward people they just met. Perhaps they were afraid that the strangers were the VOC's accomplices. Fortunately *masohi* among the people of the Moluccas still existed; the spirit of sincerely bearing everything together, for better or worse. Gamati and his grandchildren experienced that during their recent devastation.

Mongonda and Sobori quickly made new friends. Young boys, some of them older than Sobori, invited them to play ball made of rattan twigs called *takarao*. They cut the twigs into thin strips they then wove into a rather large ball. Though closely woven, the ball was very light.

The boys formed two groups and drew lots to decide who would be first. The rule was to kick the ball incessantly, passing it to teammates without letting the ball touch the ground. When that happened, the other group took their turn. The longer a team could keep the ball aloft, the more points they scored. There was no prize for the winner; the applause and cheers were all the boys needed.

After several turns Mongonda and Sobori formed a group. They succeeded in keeping the rattan ball in the air until nearly dark and the second group never had their turn. The two boys received lively applause. The boys from Kolosia were in awe, because neither Mongonda nor Sobori was a native of Kolosia. Gamati was also surprised because he knew his grandson had never played with a rattan ball before.

When they came home, Aimuna showed her grandfather she too could kick the ball. Everyone at the hut stared in admiration while they shook their heads. Gamati told Aimuna that takarao was a boys' game. There were other games for pretty girls like her.

"What kind of games, Grandpa?"

"*Enggo lari,* also hide-and-seek, and *gici-gici.* These are more delicate games."

"But I don't have any friends. I want to learn to play those games, Grandpa. You will have to teach me tomorrow."

"I am a man, Muna. Tomorrow we will find you friends to play with, okay?"

During the following days Mongonda taught Muna to play hide-and-seek and enggo lari. He asked a few little girls to play with them. The young man pitied Aimuna; she was orphaned at such a young age and then had to move from one hut to another.

During the east wind season, people usually flew kites. Getting a kite was very easy in that kampong; almost every grown man could make one. Mongonda made a kite for Sobori. They flew the kite all day. They had so much fun they forgot to have lunch.

Aimuna went with them to the field and asked them to teach her how to fly the kite. When Sobori let her hold the kite, Aimuna maneuvered the kite high and steady. The kite never swooped or fell.

"Wow, Muna, you should've been a boy, you're so good at boys' games," Mongonda teased.

Aimuna smiled proudly. Perhaps, because she was always with Sobori, she thought she should be able to do everything Sobori could do. It made her heart ache for Limo, her little brother who was slain in the raid. They were just one year apart and Limo had been a perfect playmate.

One day Aimuna played hide-and-seek with Lawe, Ngali, Mongonda, and Sobori. It was hard for the men to hide their big bodies when it was Muna's turn to be the seeker. When Muna opened her eyes, she easily spotted Lawe. Mongonda and Sobori couldn't find a hiding spot when Lawe was the seeker. Aimuna laughed out loud; her small body easily fit among the trees.

The arrival of a big ship from Makassar brought an end to this peaceful interlude. The ship brought the long-needed rice and farming tools for the villagers. The VOC never allowed a foreign ship to take farming tools to the interior of the islands. They wanted to offer the tools themselves in exchange for cloves.

By the VOC's standard, the vessel was a "smuggler's ship." The entire crew would meet a fatal end if they were caught. The "smuggled goods" were swiftly unloaded and hidden in a villager's hut.

Soon after loading some drinking water and food supplies such as salt, sugar, sago, and dried fish, the ship set sail. Lawe, Ngali, and Mongonda were aboard. They'd sail for Makassar through Ternate.

If there were no VOC in Ternate the ship would load more nutmeg and mace to be taken to Makassar. There was no hongi in Makassar, so anyone could trade spices freely there, the captain said.

The captain allowed Mongonda, Lawe, and Ngali to board the ship as long as they performed duties like the rest of the crewmembers. In Makassar, they'd find a ship headed for Tuban.

The kampong chief had wanted to serve dinner as a way of saying good-bye and to thank the good captain, but the captain thanked the chief and said they had to leave.

"In this season of calm winds, there are many obstacles at sea. There are Pani-pani ships, the Papuans, and the pirates from the north. All are armed and vicious people. Thank you, Bapa, we're deeply grateful for your good intentions. I hope we'll meet again someday," the captain said before the ship with the three extra passengers on board sailed toward the estuary.

Like the rest of the villagers on the riverbank, Sobori and Aimuna waved as the ship set sail. Gamati noticed Sobori wipe his eyes with the back of his hand as he looked straight ahead. Aimuna's shoulders shook as she tried to suppress her tears among the loud cheering of the crowd.

Gamati himself was deeply saddened. The departure of the three people who had been so good to them left another empty space in his heart. During the last two years he had experienced so many farewells, and so many hellos. He wondered how the young minds of Muna and Bori were to digest such terrible experiences. Gamati was unable to hold back the tears that blurred his eyes.

Aimuna and Bori stayed at the water's edge although many of the villagers had gone home. They stayed behind to hide their tears for the loss of the people who had touched their desolate lives and now had to leave them. First the Landos, and now Mongonda, Lawe, and Ngali.

Lawe, Ngali, and Mongonda waved back as they tried to hide their tears caused by the inevitable good-bye. After he managed to compose himself, Gamati said gently, "Let us go back, dear children. This place is already deserted."

Chapter 3

The commander's shouting broke the morning silence of the forest as the thunder of marching feet shook the earth. A group of men who varied in age trained to attack the enemy. The sizable unit had many squadrons, the commanding officers, the recruits, footmen, and reserves.

The white foreigners and dark-skinned natives trained together. They practiced the technique of running while brandishing their weapons, spears, and machetes. Some carried rifles.

One had to be calm when aiming at a target. Moving targets were hard to aim at accurately. Unsteady heartbeats made one miss the target. The drill sergeants were usually cruel, rude, hot-tempered, and poor instructors. The large crowd of men made so much noise the birds flew away. However, the heavily perspiring men didn't so much as notice. Training in the sweltering heat and humidity exhausted them. They had constructed several bamboo huts they used at night as sleeping quarters.

Ever since the sultans and VOC signed the agreements that granted the VOC monopoly of the clove trade some ten years ago, the VOC hired mercenaries to attack the natives' kampongs that had clove plantations that were "unlisted" in the VOC's registry of trade. The listed plantations were divided into the ones whose trees had just blossomed, those whose trees would blossom soon, and those whose trees had previously blossomed at least once. It was up to the VOC how many times a tree was allowed to bloom. Neither the sultans nor the farmers were included in the making of this decision.

The VOC's intent was to control the supply of cloves on the international market. If the supply exceeded the demand, the price dropped and VOC investors would lose profit.

The native farmers were not happy with their trees being cut down. To top things off, the goods the VOC offered in barter often did not meet their needs. Compared to other seamen-traders, the VOC also asked for far more cloves in the barter.

The natives resisted the VOC. The council of elders, the wealthy noblemen who were leaders of their people, along with other affluent locals, took up arms. A number of fellow Indonesian seamen-traders such as the seamen from Makassar, Tuban, or Gresik, also voluntarily supported the farmers' resistance. Some yellow-skinned, straight-haired folks from far up north sent food supplies or men.

The VOC not only ruled on land, they also flexed their muscle at sea. They patrolled the Moluccan seas and issued high-priced permits to other traders. The price of a permit could be as high as hundreds of kilograms of cloves, which amounted to almost two-thirds of a ship's cargo.

Their fleet also consisted of large, powerful, armed ships, carrying weapons and food supplies and many soldiers. When they caught an "unlicensed" ship sailing the seas once ruled by the sultans, the VOC confiscated all cargo. The captain and his crew were either killed or held as slaves. Thus every seaman avoided the VOC on the eastern seas.

On the larger island of the Bacan islands, the interiors of Seram, which were shielded by rows of hills from the west to east, and Halmahera, home to a number of volcanic mountains, the natives secretly planted cloves. They traded their harvest with foreign seamen at predetermined places that were hard to reach by the VOC's large ships, coastlines with coral reef barriers, coves, or narrow straits.

To control the "rogue" trade, the VOC then engaged the hongi expeditions. The troops now training in the forest were to conduct the hongi expedition by the end of the east wind season. Their first hongi was conducted two years ago.

After a hard day of training, everyone was exhausted. Luckily the lush foliage of the dense forest filtered the harsh sunlight. The soldiers were hungry; their rations were insufficient. The low-ranking soldiers' rations were especially low. Sometimes they mocked each other, saying they were given just enough to keep them from dying.

Several white men started to talk about finding food outside the camp. They hoped to find ripe fruit and figured that if there were plants with juicy stems, there should be edible tree bark as well.

They had heard about a mysterious fruit that was delicious, but also very stinky. Those who loved durian claimed it was a heavenly combination of milk, sugar, and cheese, while those who detested it said it was a foul mix of garlic and rotten fish. Everyone agreed it was very sweet, nothing like any fruit in their country.

That night three white men accompanied by their footmen, two local men, secretly went to the forest after everyone in the camp had fallen asleep. They brought a very sharp machete, an ax, and ropes, but chose not to bring a lamp or a torch because they had heard no one lived in the forest. The natives usually settled at kampongs near rivers or coastlines and a lamp's light would make them visible to others, be it the enemy or their own group leaders.

Their guide was Rebo, a Javanese footman in the troop who was once a prisoner. He had told them he knew the way to a cluster of durian trees he had seen at midday and still would be able to find in the darkness of night. The fruits were ripe, even if they hadn't yet fallen to the ground.

Rebo tied a rope around his waist and told the others to tie their waists to the same rope. That way they could walk safely in a line with Rebo guiding them at the front. After trekking through the forest for about two and a half hours they came to a place scented with the aroma of durian. The group happily inhaled the pungent scent while untying themselves. They couldn't wait to eat the fruit.

Rebo hushed them. "You shouldn't make noise when you're in a forest or a native's plantation in Ambon. There are invisible gentle spirits who guard the forest. Don't ever make them mad." Rebo climbed a durian tree in the darkness. He seemed to know which fruit were ripe to cut. After many durians fell to the ground, Rebo climbed down and taught everyone how to cut open a durian. Caution was needed; durian husks were very tough and thorny.

The lesson in the husking and eating of durian went well. In just a short amount of time, all of the men became devout durian eaters. Everyone truly enjoyed eating durian straight from the tree. They ate voraciously and were reluctant to stop. The amazing thing was that the tree seemed to have endless fruit. When they were full, they started to feel drowsy. Someone whispered that if they went back to the camp now and stank of durian, they would surely be summoned by their leaders and get sanctioned.

"Let us blame it on Rebo. He guided us here. Let him take the blame," someone said in Dutch.

Rebo, who had worked a long time for the VOC, understood the man and answered in broken Dutch, "I was just showing the way. Leksi was the one who had the idea in the first place, so he's the one who has to take responsibility."

"You seem to have magic eyes, Rebo, you can clearly see in the dark. Now let's find some water so we can clean ourselves."

"I don't remember seeing a water source around here. I don't know."

By then, everyone was very sleepy. Only one man thought about getting back to their camp before morning. The others laughed at him and said they'd think about it later. The man himself had forgotten the way back to the camp. Their stomachs filled, they soon dozed off happily. Every so often someone burped loudly.

The chirping of birds woke Rebo. "It's morning already," he whispered to his friend beside him, a native of Ambon. Then everyone awakened and realized they were not in their training camp. Durian husks, still emanating a sweet, strong odor, were strewn all over. Everyone was shocked. It was already morning and they were still in the middle of the forest.

"Rebo. Show us the way back to the camp; let's go now," Leksi said and added, "Shame on you; the sun is already very high up."

They all rose. As they rubbed their eyes, they started to worry. Surely the commandant would punish them when they returned to the camp.

"Rebo, lead the way. Come on, hurry," Leksi said.

Rebo took his machete, fastened it to his waist, and started to walk. The rest of the group followed as he walked around the cluster of durian trees. The five trees must have stood there for decades.

"What about the heap of durian husks?" someone asked.

"What about it? It's garbage; leave it," another man answered.

"It's not just that. Clearly a group of people just ate durian here. We're leaving traces; just what the enemy wants."

"I told you there's no settlement in this forest, so there's no enemy," the man replied.

"If we leave any evidence and our commandant finds it, he'll have proof we weren't in the camp last night," someone else said.

"Who cares?" Rebo argued.

They continued to circle the cluster of durian trees at a fast pace. This went on until well into midday, when the rest of the troops in training were having their lunch break.

There was no lunch for the men in the forest. It seemed everyone in the group had lost their senses. One of them said that he was hungry. They had no food, other than the durian hanging from the trees.

Rebo suggested eating more durians. He climbed a tree, and cut selected ripe durians. The fruit had a high sugar content, and the men immediately felt stronger. Still, they had not eaten anything solid, so their stomachs kept grumbling.

Next, they became thirsty and broke into perspiration. They wanted to dive into a cool stream and drink as much water as they could. Rebo didn't know where to find a water source. Meanwhile they continued to circle the five durian trees.

"Rebo!" someone called. "What are you doing? We have to get back to camp."

Rebo simply stared at him. He had forgotten the way back.

Then someone saw a red ribbon tied around three durian trees laden with ripe fruit. "Hey! Who says that no one lives in this forest?

Look at all these red ribbons! Someone tied ribbons around these trees, perhaps because they've the ripest fruits. The owner must've done this. Why can't we walk away from these trees? We're acting like fools," Leksi said angrily. "It was dark last night, and we're not familiar with this place. Rebo's supposed to know the way back."

"Yes, but look at him, he seems lost and forgot the way back to camp. It seems he can't remember anything. He hasn't spoken a word," another man replied.

They continued to argue over trivial matters, until it was almost dark and two VOC soldiers arrived. They had been assigned to look for the five missing men.

When the soldiers called out, the five durian thieves just looked at them with vacant gazes, not saying anything. The soldiers were natives from Ambon and immediately figured out what was going on. They checked the durian trees and saw the red ribbon.

"No wonder, this tree is marked with a *Sasi* ribbon."

"Why did you steal fruit from a tree protected by Sasi? We have to find a *mauweng* who can undo the Sasi spell." The soldiers hurried back to reach camp before dark.

The news they brought started an argument. The leading commandant was not superstitious. "What are you talking about?" he shouted. "A tree isn't a little girl you dress up to take for a walk." When he was told that the tree could not be disturbed in any way, the commandant almost slapped the Ambon soldier. Someone said they needed to search for a forest shaman to undo the Sasi spell. It was only when the spell was undone that the trapped soldiers would be able to leave the area.

Even though he refused to believe it, the commandant finally allowed the soldiers to look for a mauweng in the nearest kampong, which was quite far from the camp.

The mauweng had no comment when he was told about the incident. He disliked the VOC, but feared showing it. He followed the soldiers to the training camp, which was what the commandant had wanted to avoid. They were supposed to keep the location of the training camp a secret. Next, they headed back to the forest. It was almost dawn when they arrived at the durian tree and the trapped men.

The mauweng took a mouthful of areca nut and betel leaf. Chewing, he started to chant a mantra and stroke the tree that had the red ribbon tied around it. As soon as he finished, the five durian thieves snapped back to reality.

They looked as if they had just woken up from a beautiful dream. They started to ask questions about what happened and why there were so many people. Then they all headed back to camp and now Rebo easily remembered the route they took two nights ago.

The mauweng warned them to always watch for Sasi ribbons when they wanted to pick fruit and never to take fruit from a tree marked by a Sasi ribbon. He cautioned, "If the owner of the tree doesn't show up for one month, you'll remain trapped there for one month and you'll die from hunger long before that." He added, "The Sasi is widely known in these eastern parts of the country."

The mauweng went back to his kampong, leaving the whole camp in an uproar. Everyone talked about the Sasi. The commandant ordered the five insubordinate soldiers to resume their training. He said they'd be punished later, when they were back at the fort.

The story of the Sasi and the confused soldiers who circled the durian trees quickly spread among the VOC officials. Some considered it funny and laughed, while others perceived it as a lesson about fascinating local traditions.

The Governor of Ambon was furious when he received reports about the incident. The natives apparently possessed something that could surpass all the great weaponry of the VOC. People heard him curse.

***

Aimuna held Gamati's hand tightly. Sobori walked in front of them. The three of them had just emerged from the bushes. Bori had a machete in his hand. Gamati held an ax and a hammer. Aimuna carried a coil of ropes around her shoulder. They were all relieved. "Ah...we can already see the ocean," Gamati said.

Sitting on the bare ground, they ate some wild mangos they had picked during their journey. Crossing the forest this time was very different from when they had looked for Lando's hut, right after the hongi raid some two years ago.

Gamati relished the sound of the breaking waves. He recalled a pleasant time in his past when, as a young captain, he sailed freely from island to island. Now he was a displaced man, his kampong obliterated. Still, the sound of surging waves and ripples that caressed the sand was music to his ears.

"Where are we going now, Grandpa?" Aimuna asked sweetly.

"We're now close to kampong Tuna. I have a friend who lives there, a very kind man. Kampong Tuna is on good terms with Pani-pani, so there's no hongi there. If my friend is still alive, I'll ask if we can stay with him, temporarily. I will look for a piece of land and build us a ship. When you two are older, we will make a new kampong."

Aimuna did not dare to ask further questions. It seemed they always searched for a place to stay; they always looked for Grandpa's friends to ask for temporarily shelter. Their hosts were all very nice and loved her and Bori until they had to say good-bye again, crying as they parted, knowing they might never see each other again. Aimuna wondered if there would ever be an end to this. They had traveled by boat for two nights and walked across the forest for a full day. Kampong Tuna was still nowhere in sight. Aimuna wondered, *Will our life only consist of talks about cloves, hongi raids, staying at Grandpa's friends, boarding a boat, crossing forests while being afraid of the Halefurus, only to move all over again to a new kampong?* After she finished eating her mango, Aimuna dozed off.

Bori sat down beside her. When a beetle flew near Aimuna's face, Bori shooed it away protectively.

Gamati was deeply moved by Bori's loving gesture. He thought of his lost family: Arande, his wife; his son, Tarambessi, Aimuna's father; and Ranila, his daughter, Bori's mother. He quietly prayed, "Upulanite, please guard and protect my grandchildren until they're grown and able to take care of each other. Don't allow anyone to take their lives. Have mercy upon them, Upu." Gamati turned away as he did not want Bori to see him cry.

Bori asked Gamati what his plans were for the rest of the day. Were they going to continue to walk in the forest? It would soon be dark.

"No, we won't, dear child. We'll walk along the beach for a short while, until we come to a small estuary. We might find a boat or kole-kole there. Kampong Tuna is near the headwaters." Gamati knew Bori and Muna would be discouraged if they had to walk again. Bori dozed off and Gamati stayed awake, guarding the sleeping children just in case there was danger lurking. He still had a good physique and stamina. Even though he was nearly fifty years old, he was able to stay awake through the night.

When the children woke, Gamati used the available time to give them advice. The two of them had to learn to please other people, especially the people they were staying with. They should always be polite and helpful, lend a hand to carry things, split wood or dry fish. He said, "I am old. If I'm not blessed with a long life, and you do the things I told you, anyone, anywhere, will accept you. Bori, you have to find a vocation to provide for your future wife and children. Never work for Pani-pani, or become its accomplice. They destroyed our family. Take good care of Muna, never let anyone harm her."

"Grandpa, Aimuna is pretty; she looks a lot like my mother. What if a boy wants to marry her?" Bori asked.

Aimuna smiled shyly when Bori complimented her beauty.

Gamati fell silent for a while, then asked, "Do you often think of your mother, Bori?"

"Yes, I do, Grandpa. My poor mother and father, no one has buried them properly in Tupawalili. Every time I think of my mother and want to hug her, I look at Muna."

"And how does Muna react to that? Does she notice you looking at her when you think of your mother? Does she like it or does it bother her?"

"She likes it, Grandpa. She likes it very much. Muna will do anything for me," Bori said softly.

"Then you two should be together from now on. When you're bigger, you can get married and live together in the same house. That way, the Kurubela and Tarambessi families will have heirs and not perish by the evil hand of Pani-pani."

"But Grandpa, you said that Muna and I are family, and family members can't marry each other, right?" Bori seemed surprised.

"That's true, if you're siblings from the same father and mother. It's alright if you've different parents," Gamati explained.

"Oh, I can marry Aimuna, then? Thank you, Grandpa. I'll take care of Muna just as I would take care of my own life." Bori happily hugged Gamati.

Aimuna smiled.

The sugary juice of the mangoes restored their energy, as well as their spirit, and they continued their journey to the estuary. The ocean wind rang in their ears and helped dry their perspiration as well as kept them refreshed.

The rest of the trip was fairly easy. They arrived at kampong Tuna at noon. The kampong, although close to the beach, was invisible from the sea. It was quiet. Many of the villagers were either still working on the field, or out fishing.

Gamati stopped a young man who carried some coconuts on his back. He asked whether someone named Ronasundu, who once was a captain of an arumbae, lived in the kampong.

The young man nodded and added that in fact he worked for Ronasundu as his household servant. He invited them to come along with him to Ronasundu's hut.

Ronasundu's hair as well as his eyebrows had turned white. His eyesight was no longer as sharp as it used to be. While he still could see distant objects, everything near him was blurry. He was still slim and stood tall and straight like a palm tree. His voice was strong and clear, unlike the hoarse, quivering voice typical of old men.

At first Ronasundu did not recognize Gamati, whose hair had also turned white. However, as soon as Gamati called out his name, Ronasundu remembered the captain of an arumbae up north and instantly embraced him. Just as it had happened at the Landos', the two friends cried and cursed the VOC. Muna and Bori tried to fight back their tears.

They were permitted to stay in Ronasundu's hut. Muna and Bori called him Grandpa Rona. He had six children who had all married and moved away. Grandpa Rona and his wife were happy to have visitors, especially children. They hoped the quiet hut would be merrier now that Muna and Bori stayed with them. The two children could play with many children in the kampong.

Ronasundu's oldest son, Lissanei, had inherited the captainship of the kampong's arumbae. Lissanei sailed to many islands, but rarely visited his parents' hut. He only visited for a short time when he happened to be in the northern part of Seram. His wife and children lived on another island. Gamati wanted to meet Lissanei and ask him about arumbaes.

Aimuna and Sobori easily adjusted to their new surroundings. By now, they were accustomed to moving. However, this time, they also had to learn a new language, since everyone in Tuna spoke Malay, which was commonly used by foreign seamen. Except for the verses, chants, and songs performed in traditional ceremonies, their original Manipa dialect was almost forgotten. Their grandfather was the only one who still spoke the Manipa dialect with Muna and Bori, especially when they were having a private conversation.

Ronasundu told Gamati how his kampong came under the patronage of the VOC. This was a terrible thing, Gamati said.

Ronasundu admitted that it was terrible, but the people were tired of war. Almost half of the villagers had died in battles or were lost at sea.

Gamati remembered how they used to live in harmony in their respective kampongs, observing their local traditions. After the raid everything was either destroyed or had perished on Manipa. They had to run and hide in the deep interior, but the VOC had still found them.

Gamati still remembered it vividly. The VOC forced them to live near the coastlines, where it was easier to come with their big, mighty ships. The VOC selected the kampong site for them. They were closely monitored. The inhabitants of the kampong were a mix of many dwellers from many kampongs in the mountains.

All the *henas* and other traditional systems of land ownership had fallen apart. Inhabitants of different henas with different traditions and customs, along with many wise indigenous chiefs, were all mixed up in the new settlements along the coastlines.

"You can see the result. But it's all right, in our hearts and thoughts we're still the people of the Moluccas. We're all still family, together in good and bad times, in the spirit of masohi."

"What about treachery? Does Pani-pani have an accomplice here in this kampong? Do you know who it is?" Gamati asked.

"I don't suspect anyone. There are no spies here. Everyone hates Pani-pani. Every family here is a victim of the first hongi conducted by Pani-pani. Which hongi are you a victim of? It happened repeatedly."

"That's good there are no spies here. They specifically targeted Kurubela and Tarambessi. I'm just worried they'll find out that we're still alive. And then they'll try to kill Sobori and Aimuna, Kurubela's offspring."

"Do not talk about those names here. If they ask, tell them you are a fisherman from Kolosia. And tell Bori and Muna too, so they'll support the story. Tell them never to mention Manipa Island, Tupawalili, Tupawaroka, or Tupamarangi. Just pretend that you're ordinary people."

Gamati told Muna and Bori about their new identities. He repeatedly stressed that they had to be cautious and alert at all times. Thus a new act in their lives began; an act of pretending that they weren't survivors of a hongi raid.

Gamati often went to fish or hunt deer and mouse deer. He contributed a lot of food supplies to eat together. He wanted his grandchildren to grow strong and healthy. He was preparing them for a long, perilous journey ahead.

As sociable as they were, Muna and Bori easily made friends. They often played in the front yard of Grandpa Rona, who was also the chief of the tribal council. Under a full moon the children would merrily play hide-and-seek. Sometimes they sang together or exchanged funny pantoums.

Sometimes the children played snakes. In this game, two players made an arch while the others passed through in single file, lined up like a snake while singing a song. The arch was then lowered at the end of the song to "catch" a player. When the player struggled free, the children laughed and shouted to prevent the player's escape. Grandpa and Grandma Rona liked to sit in the yard and watch the children play. While watching, they ate boiled peanuts, bananas, baked yams, or simply chewed some betel leaves.

One evening when Sobori was not around, Gamati asked Aimuna, what if someday, when he was older, Sobori wanted to marry someone?

Aimuna said she would ask to be treated as his sister. Since she was an orphan, Bori would have to provide for her. She had heard the neighbors say this was the way things were for war victims.

When Gamati asked Muna what type of young man she liked to have as her husband, Muna looked down and suddenly wept. Surprised, Gamati instantly regretted his question. He hugged Muna and patted her head.

Weeping, Muna said that no young man would ever like her. She was ugly, her skin was too dark, and she was an orphan. All the other young brides were always dressed up by their mothers.

Gamati was heartbroken. He adjusted his approach by saying that he was only joking. Had Muna not heard that she and Bori would be together until they grew old? And had Sobori not already said that Muna was as pretty as Aunt Ranila? Why did she feel that she was ugly?

Aimuna stopped weeping and looked at her grandfather. She rested her head on Gamati's chest and asked, "Grandpa, is it true that Sobori wants to marry me?"

"Yes, it is, my sweet little girl. You have to take really good care of him; don't ever hurt him."

"All right, Grandpa," she answered sweetly.

Gamati felt like a heavy burden had just been lifted off his chest. He had conveyed an important message to the children that hopefully laid a solid foundation for their future lives. He considered this an act that could invalidate the VOC's past action: killing his family and the people in his kampong. He only had one duty left; if Lord Upulanite permitted, he would take Muna and Bori to the secluded northern islands the VOC was unable to reach. They would build an arumbae and live as free men.

Time went by quickly in Tuna. Muna was growing up fast. She was tall and slender, like Bori's late mother. The color of her wavy hair was the darkest brown. Grandpa Gamati always told her to put her hair up in a bun. Afterward the bun was secured tightly with a knot so it would not unravel. He did not like it when Aimuna let her hair loose. In his opinion that would capture the attention of men.

He did not want Aimuna to be kampong Tuna's sweetheart, just like his daughter Ranila, Sobori's mother, had been in their old kampong. He wanted to prevent having to disappoint anyone who later would ask for Aimuna's hand in marriage because he would have to turn him down. He asked Muna to learn to row a boat, and to dive. Later, he even asked her to learn to climb and use a machete to cut fruit or tree branches.

When Gamati brought home a mouse deer, he taught Muna and Bori the proper way to skin and cut his kill. It was a task that always made them cry. The sight of a dead, bloody animal never failed to remind Sobori of the wretched night when he witnessed the killing of both of his parents. He remembered them just lying there, not moving, with no one to give them a decent burial. He still wondered if their bodies had burned along with the hut.

Sobori would remember that incident for the rest of his life and had sworn never to spill the blood of a living being, especially that of a human. He figured the offspring of the deceased would suffer the same immense emotional pain he experienced.

Aimuna could not stand to see a beautiful creature that she often watched sprint or play in the forest lie motionless, ready to be cut into pieces. The scent of fresh blood instantly made her nauseous and weak.

Gamati said that once they were used to dressing a killed animal, it would no longer make them nauseous or cry. He said, "We have to endure everything in life bravely, for we don't know what the future holds."

Once Sobori and Aimuna asked Gamati if they could abstain from eating fish, game, deer, chicken, or other animal for the rest of their lives.

"No, definitely not," Gamati said firmly and went on to explain, "You two have to grow up strong, especially since later on you will have to row a boat to the northern islands. You have to make sago, climb coconut trees, and carry out many more tasks. Meat makes you strong."

Aimuna and Sobori did not dare to argue with their grandfather. They ate the meat Gamati brought home.

Gamati taught his grandchildren to hunt using a bow and arrow, but hunting and dressing his kill remained two tasks Bori hated the most.

In Tuna, young men his age were all short-tempered. When they had drunk too much palm wine, they became intimidating and often threatened to kill anyone they argued with. The word *kill* instantly reminded Sobori of his slain parents, covered in blood. His friends enjoyed hunting in the forest. Words such as *kill, smash*, and *crush* came out of their mouths easily.

Among the youths, Sobori was considered a nice, sweet young man. He never fought or threatened to kill his opponent. He never reacted to his friends' unpleasant ridicules or jokes.

Gamati often advised him not to be too timid. "You have to stand up for yourself," he said.

Bori merely smiled.

One day, there was a wedding party in Tuna; a young couple were to start a new household. The whole village was busy with preparations of food and drink to be served at the party. Soon after the traditional ceremony was over, the party was underway. Musicians played drums, gong, bamboo flute, and *arbabu* to accompany the singing and dancing.

People also danced the *lenso*, in which the dancers held a handkerchief, a lenso, in each hand, while others used a long scarf. All the girls wore their best attire and adorned their hair, ears, necks, and fingers. The air was filled with festivity.

Sobori was all but forced to join the other youths in the dancing and singing. But he turned down the invitation politely under the pretext that he had to tend to his sick grandfather.

Aimuna had stayed in hiding at home since the morning, even though a lot of people asked about her.

"Where is the girl from Kolosia who is staying at Ronasundu's hut?"

Gamati, Sobori, and Aimuna did not want to meet a lot of people. They did not want to have to answer questions about their origins. Especially since Aimuna, who was now a pretty teenager, would surely draw attention. Such was their lives on the run. Grandpa and Grandma Ronasundu helped with hiding Aimuna and Sobori.

Long ago, before the hongi raids and clove tree extirpation, right after the clove bud harvest and trade with the seamen, the natives used to have parties for just about every special occasion. First came the season of weddings. Then, there was the season of kampong cleaning, and then the season of sailboat races. All were seasons of merriment.

Now, people only gathered to have a good time at weddings, clove harvest, and clove planting season. They still put on their best attire and amused themselves with dancing to the tune of bamboo flutes, drums, and gongs. *Sopi* or "fiery water" was often served on these occasions, but not every man liked to drink this alcoholic drink. Many avoided it; getting drunk was not considered a commendable act.

Aimuna and Bori grew up in the midst of all this. Bori liked sopi, but never drank enough to make him drunk. He just wanted to please his friends; he was a social drinker. Sometimes Aimuna joined the dance parties. She held a lenso and gracefully swayed her body. People often complimented her dancing; her movements were agile yet elegant. Aimuna smiled quietly. She figured her good rowing skills made her a graceful dancer.

Aimuna and Bori were also good farmers. They already knew how to pick good clove seeds, and knew how deep a hole needed to be to receive a sapling from the seedbed. Soon they were to participate in a harvest and learn which buds were ready to be picked.

The clove plantations in Tuna were not hidden in the interior of the island like the ones in Tupawalili. Here, hundreds of clove trees thrived around the kampong. A VOC officer came regularly to check on the inventory of the trees.

Grandma Rona said that when Muna was a bit older, she would take her to the beach where a lush forest of sago palm trees flourished. She would teach her to make sago flour, the main ingredient of papeda. She said preparing the sago was a woman's job.

On the surface, Aimuna and Sobori's lives were complete. People around them loved them for their diligence, agility, and willingness to please others, especially older people. They were sharp and learned quickly. However, unbeknownst to others, Aimuna and Sobori craved love and affection from family members. Aside from Grandpa Gamati, they had no family. Everyone was nice and friendly, but at any time they could ask Muna, Bori, and Gamati to leave Tuna.

Bori often cried when he and Muna were by themselves in the quiet forest or on the beach. He always remembered his slain parents and their horrible deaths. The fact that no one had buried them continued to haunt him. He never had the chance to hug them one final time. He remembered the inexplicable deep longing, the need to look at them continuously that night before his father sent him to bed and blew out the lamp. That was the last time he looked at them. His longing would never be satisfied.

Aimuna's father had always spoiled her. He loved having a little girl. Limo, her younger brother, liked to tease her. They used to play together on the front porch. Their mother was a great cook who had learned to make simple cakes from a neighbor, a Chinese woman from Ambon.

All of that was now gone and Aimuna worried about what would happen if Grandpa Gamati suddenly died. After all, he was old. Aimuna often cried secretly, in fear of her grandfather's death.

When Sobori and Aimuna were alone and no one watched them, they would hold each other and cry.

Bori would stroke Muna's hair, comforting her, and while Muna wrapped her arms around Bori's neck, they wept together. The support they gave each other provided the strength to carry on.

Although Gamati had told them they could marry since they were not siblings, Muna had not fully understood what that meant. She had always pictured Bori marrying a girl he chose, while she had to accept a marriage proposal from another man. That's when they would be separated.

Aimuna worried. *What if Bori's wife doesn't like me? And what'll happen if my husband doesn't like Bori?* Sometimes she wished they would never grow up and be old. She thought it was better to be children forever, so she did not have to be separated from Bori and Grandpa Gamati.

Many questions filled her child's mind. *Why did people fight so fiercely over cloves? Why did all the foreign seamen not just plant clove trees in their own backyards, like the people here in Tuna did? Why all the brutality over mere clove buds, which were only used for medicine and sweets for dessert after eating a greasy meal?*

Once, Gamati asked Ronasundu why his son Lissanei had never come home. Did he not miss his parents, his home?

For a fleeting moment Rona's face darkened, but he quickly recovered and, smiling, answered that Lissanei's arumbae covered a large area. There were many kampongs to visit and sometimes he had to avoid the pirate ships. Rona said, "Lissanei also avoids Pani-pani's ships, even though he owns their expensive license."

However, months later, someone told Gamati that Lissanei had grown into a man with a questionable character. He liked drinking, pretty young women, parties, and sometimes gambled in Ambon. Ronasundu had been very concerned for a long time.

Then one day, Lissanei left the island, his wife, and his children to run off with the wife of a Chinese man in Tuna. The husband was furious, and held Ronasundu responsible for his son's act. Rona answered that Lissanei was an adult who was responsible for his own acts, and that none of it was his concern. The Chinaman still waited for Lissanei and had pledged to kill him, should he ever return to Tuna.

This incident was a big humiliation for Ronasundu. He was a rich and well-respected man along the coastlines of Seram, and appointed as the chief of the tribal council. He was a charismatic figure, but his son was a gambler and had taken off with another man's wife.

After he heard the story, Gamati never asked Rona about Lissanei again.

***

The room the VOC officials used as a meeting place was small. The tall, open windows let in the sea breeze. The five Dutchmen in the room wore thin shirts. Each of them worked on the reports lying on the large wooden table in front of them.

Martinus de Bruijn, the governor of Ambon, sat at the head of the oval table. He was in his late thirties and once worked as a clerk in an attorney's office. He had golden hair with sideburns extending well below his ears. His eyes were piercing.

On his left was the Hispanic-looking Resident of Saparua, Lucas de Vries, who was barely twenty-five. He was of medium build and had brown hair. His lips seemed always to be curved into a smile. The ladies said that he was a good-looking man, but his formal demeanor made him seem cold and impersonal. Lucas never displayed more than the required friendliness. Two Dutch men who recently arrived in Ambon sat on the governor's right side.

Robert Dumas liked to be called Bertie. The tall, cheerful bachelor had salt-and-pepper hair. He was a botanist who had worked for a short while as a VOC officer in the West Indies, where he conducted research on tropical plants. Since the Dutch kingdom had discovered new regions he had to extend his field of research as his alma mater expanded its breadth of academic knowledge. He was a hard worker but enjoyed drinking.

Karel Timmerman was in his late twenties and had brown hair, an oval face, and attractive brown eyes. He was not a very good-looking man, but he was very athletic and agile, especially when he swam in the ocean and danced. He enjoyed spending his time in bars, particularly when his dance partner was a pretty girl. He was known for his hearty laugh.

All present were adventurers who were willing to face all kinds of dangers with a dream to become prosperous. The news that circulated in Holland was that all the newly discovered regions, be they east or west of Europe, were full of wonders. The areas were shrouded in mystery and filled with the primary spices and treasures of ancient civilizations, all of which needed to be explored, examined, and, if possible, brought back home.

At that time, seamen-traders from China and the Middle East controlled the trade of the primary spices that turned the wheel of life. Prices of pepper, cloves, nutmeg, cinnamon, cardamom, ginger, turmeric, and so on were very high. And these were just the spices used for culinary needs, primarily in the kitchen to enhance taste. And then there were the frankincense and myrrh trees that provided the ingredients needed for the aromatic incense used in religious ceremonies.

The Dutch had wanted to know the location of the spices' origins for a long time. The Middle Eastern seamen were reluctant to tell them and instead made up stories. "Ah, it's at the edge of the world, on the floor of a valley guarded by vicious snakes."

When asked how they then obtained the spices, the Arabs smiled and said, "Well, we used an eagle. We gave the eagle a big piece of fresh, bloody meat and lured it to fly across the valley. We then surprised it with a deafening noise. The eagle would drop the meat on the cloves and nutmeg that lay scattered on the valley floor and the spices stuck to the moist meat. Another eagle, or the earlier eagle that no longer had anything in his beak, was sent to retrieve the fallen meat. A lot of cloves or nutmeg would be stuck to it and all we needed to do was to scrape the spices from the meat before feeding it to the eagles." The Arabian seamen told this story with a serious look on their faces.

The Chinese traders had a different story. They traveled in large caravans and used camels to carry their goods. At times, a caravan would count more than a thousand camels. The journey from

Loyang, at the border of western China, to Baghdad or Damascus took almost two years. If they survived the perilous journey, it would take another two years to get back. The traders' stories were always embellished with amazing and thrilling experiences, but they never revealed that the dried clove buds did not come from China. They had to cross the ocean southeast from their country to obtain them. This was their best-kept secret. As with all fairytales from China, an element of a dragon's "good deed" was also exploited in their stories about the spices.

Since all these stories amounted to nothing more than trickery, the Dutch started to explore the territories to the west and east of Europe on their own. After countless sacrifices and miseries, they finally found their way not only to the seas of Indonesia, but they also even reached the far eastern part of the archipelago, the Moluccas, a small inner archipelago.

The Dutch were not satisfied with only discovering the Spice Islands and trade with the natives. Greed fueled their desire to control the international spice trade and this brought Martinus, Lucas, Karel, and Bertie to an official VOC meeting in Ambon.

The last member, Robert Verhoven, was an officer at Fort Saparua. Prior to the arrival of Resident Lucas de Vries, it was Verhoven who took care of all matters in Saparua. There was no residency post before in Saparua Island, so Lucas was the first official resident there. Verhoven was not that young. He had lived for quite some time in the east. Even his wife was of mixed blood. She had a Dutch father but her mother was a Saparua native. Verhoven was fluent in the local dialect. His job now was to write the minutes of the meeting.

The governor started with a brief abstract of hongi and extirpation. "Gentlemen, I'm sure you all know that our kingdom has become the center of the spice trade. Before, it was Baghdad, Damascus, Alexandria, and Genoa. Slowly, it has moved to our country."

The rest of the men nodded. The governor was the highest-ranking officer; he warranted a formal demeanor.

"The Assembly of the Lords Seventeen, our shareholders who manage the VOC, has just sent us a letter of reprimand. The governor general in Batavia was asked to further reduce the number of clove trees, to ensure the exact amount of clove buds at harvest time to raise the price."

There was a momentary silence.

"Like all of you know, clove trees originally only grew on five small islands up north. But apparently the natives planted many clove trees on other islands. So, unsurprisingly, especially if we had good weather, the harvests boosted the supplies beyond our need. Naturally, the price plummeted. This is the basic principle of trade, am I right?"

No one answered.

"We already extirpated the trees in their places of origins, the five islands up north. We are also closely controlling the number of trees here on Saparua, Ambon, and along the coastlines of Seram. It surprised our trade center in Amsterdam to still have an enormous surplus of cloves. They complained about the low prices. It's the same case with nutmeg; we had to burn several nutmeg warehouses to control the price."

Still no one answered. The three younger men attending the meeting were not particularly interested in what happened in their faraway homeland. They merely cared about the plantations on the islands.

"We've sent many clever men to look for the locations of these illicit trees. The resident of Banda has searched for illicit nutmeg plantations. The strange thing is that despite several hongi and extirpation missions, the supply is not declining. The illicit cloves continue to flood the market. Traders from Portugal, Denmark, Arabia, Makassar, and Java are still able to get their hands on the spices. This is infuriating. We have to work harder, conduct another hongi if we must. Gentlemen, did I make myself clear?"

"Yes, Sir," they answered in unison. It now was the governor's turn to nod happily. He said, "Now let's hear the resident of Saparua. Please, Resident."

"I've not been informed about the exact time of our next hongi expedition. I checked the kampongs in Saparua. There're no illicit clove trees there; only the ones Verhoven had listed. I also met with the kampong chiefs. They have two kora-koras, but only enough men for one. If there's still time, I'll order them to prepare a provision of dried food for the hongi raid. The significant problem we're faced with is to man the second kora-kora."

The governor replied, "Yes, we'll find a solution later. Now let's hear from Verhoven."

"As the resident mentioned, there's no trouble in Saparua other than finding manpower for one kora-kora. On the issue of the coastlines of Seram, were the hidden kampongs on the mountain slopes not raided two years ago? According to the reports, the three kampongs perished, just like Manipa. All the natives are dead.

"In Tuna, all the clove trees that belong to the natives are listed. By and large they just blossomed once or twice. I think we shouldn't destroy these trees. We can't plant more trees without seeds."

"Yes, that's right. Since we extirpated all clove trees on the islands where they originally grew, we must take care not to destroy all sources of seeds," the governor replied. "Please, go on."

"Our officers checked kampongs like Kolosia, Lainuli, Lete-lete, and Batu Putih. They found some clove trees; fifty, sixty, perhaps up to one hundred trees. All are young trees, abundantly blooming around these coastline kampongs. We ordered all the natives to send their next harvest to the VOC in exchange for rice, salt, sugar, clothing, and some metal farming tools."

"How's the natives' preparation for joining the hongi expedition?"

"We told the kampong chiefs every time we checked the trees that it's imperative for them to join the expedition. We still have one kora-kora left without manpower. They said that half of the men did not come home from the previous hongi. Perhaps they died of starvation or drowned. Those kampongs are short of men."

"There are no other kampongs?"

"They're not in my region, Governor. The islands down south are very far from Saparua. They fall under the administrative region of the resident of Banda."

Each of the men around the table consulted the papers in front of him during the brief silence that followed. Then the governor said, "It looks like the most pressing problem we have is the lack of manpower for one kora-kora, right? Where will we find the men for this boat? Most of them are dead."

Another silence ensued.

Then Verhoven said, "If we have to decide quickly, the fastest way out is to buy some slaves. The Papuans used to bring male slaves, but it's been almost a year since a Papua ship came here. The same goes for the pirate ships, which usually came during the west wind season. It's still the east wind season now, so it'll be quite some time before they get here."

"That's a good solution," the governor said. "But unfortunately, the VOC doesn't have enough funds to buy many slaves at one time. Slaves are more needed in Banda to work on the nutmeg plantation. Let's just wait for a letter from the governor-general in Batavia regarding the purchase of slaves," the governor ended.

Verhoven added, "If funding is the main concern, Governor, we could always capture ships that are coming here. We can force the crewmembers to man the kora-kora we're going to use for the hongi, and seize their cargo. This will be far cheaper, I think."

"That's a brilliant idea, Verhoven. But remember, all those ships have licenses from the VOC they paid handsomely for. We can't touch them, for if we do, we're the ones who'll get punished for having violated the VOC's law. The sultans on the northern islands will also be mad at us."

For a moment they were all silent, perhaps to let the information sink in.

A cool breeze eased the terrible heat of the glaring sun that beat on them directly, without a filter of clouds.

The governor added, "I'm sure everyone here has heard that the hongi draft is not popular. The natives hate it. To be honest, we VOC officers don't like it either, having to take so many innocent lives, seize their clove trees, and then destroy their homes. However, we have to execute our employers' orders. I hope you were briefed regarding this matter, prior to being dispatched to this area."

"No, we weren't, Sir. We were only told to research the tropical plants, such as the ones in Brazil. Every plant needs to be studied and catalogued. Someday some of them could be used as trade items, like cloves and nutmeg," Karel said.

"Some time ago, we raided Manipa Island. The natives there didn't approve of the sultan handing over the clove trade to the VOC. They took up arms and fought bravely. They have a stone fort and canons of different sizes. We had to attack them with full power. Now the once-beautiful and productive Manipa Island has been scorched. I don't think anyone lives there anymore," the governor said.

"How long between hongis?" the resident asked, frowning.

"It isn't scheduled regularly. It could be once or twice a year. Sometimes there's no need to conduct a hongi for years. We only conduct a hongi expedition when there are complaints from Holland about the surplus of cloves or nutmeg."

"Do we have to kill the natives and burn their plantations every time we raid them? Why does it have to be that way?" the resident asked.

"Like I said earlier, the natives did not approve of our forcing them to trade cloves with us. They wanted to trade with other seamen who gave them more and better trade items. We therefore had to scare them, deter them. That's why we uprooted them and separated the men from their wives and children. We sold them as slaves here in Ambon, or took them to Java."

The governor's words sent chills up the spines of Lucas and the two young botanists. They thought the killings, burning of kampongs, and separation of families was inhumane.

The governor remained composed. There was no trace of terror or grief, let alone pity, on his face. His tone of voice was flat, as if he were merely greeting someone in the morning.

What kind of man is the governor? Would he treat his subordinates cruelly? Lucas mused. He himself was a gentle, sensitive man with fine artistic sensibilities. He detested crude behavior, loud voices, and cruelty. At school, his teachers taught him to love his fellow man, to forgive the faults of others, excel in self-control, act like a civilized person, and obey the words of God in order to live in harmony as a human being.

Lucas wondered what the governor's voyage from Holland to Ambon had been like. It must have been the same as anyone else's. A perilous journey by day and night with threats of storms, lightning, broken ship's masts, seasickness, illness, and waves as tall as a mountain. Then, when mooring in an unknown place such as the western or eastern coasts of Africa to get some drinking water and to purchase some livestock, one's life could be endangered. The natives hid behind the bushes and threw rocks or spears. Language was always a problem. Disputes often ended in fights and murder with casualties on both sides. Many sailors as well as natives died bloody deaths. It was terrifying.

The ship's captain and his first mate mistreated the ship's crew. While some of the crew were jobless men and war veterans, they were almost never paid. Burdened with hard work, they were deprived of sleep and their food rations were slim. If they complained or protested, they were flogged, or tied to the main mast and left to dry under the sun with no food and drink. The alternate punishment was to be tied and then repeatedly dunked in the ocean.

None of these things ever crossed Lucas de Vries' mind when he accepted the job offer to work in the eastern territory that had been recently "discovered" by the Dutch seamen. The VOC offered him a respectable post. He was to create an archive by recording his surroundings through paintings that accurately depicted his environment. The company needed the archives for further study.

There had been no talks about salary, but his employers promised that on his return from his post, he would live in prosperity, because the place he was to document was an enchanting and magical land, loaded with spices that were very expensive in Europe.

Prior to his appointment as the "Resident of Saparua in the Moluccas," Lucas de Vries served as the archivist in Malacca and Banten. Even here he had witnessed a lot of violent deaths. The main cause was the fight over land and food supplies with the natives. He had imagined that the situation at his new post on Saparua would be more humane than his experiences at his earlier two posts. However, it turned out to be the same.

The governor proceeded to inform the assembly that later in the afternoon, they would conduct a ceremony in the fort yard. Two accomplices who had done the VOC a great service would be presented with rewards. The two men had shown the way to the hidden kampongs they raided on Seram not too long ago.

The governor himself would present the reward. Verhoven, Lucas de Vries, and Karel Timmerman were asked to attend the ceremony to document the men.

"One of them is from Holland, the other is one of the dark-skinned people, called mardijkers. Once, they were slaves of the Portuguese in Malacca. Since we defeated the Portuguese and they lost Malacca, the mardijkers now work for us."

"What did they do for us, Mister Governor?" Karel asked.

"For two years, these two men befriended the native fishermen. Once they won the trust of the unsuspecting natives, they inquired about how to plant cloves, the locations of the secret plantations, and so on. In the end they found out that the natives traded their harvests in the northern islands. It's hard for our big ships to reach those closely crowded islands.

"When we received the letter of reprimand from our superiors regarding the surplus of spices on the market, these two men had discovered the exact location of the secret plantations. They immediately notified us and we attacked and destroyed the kampongs.

"The VOC had promised those who could show the way to the secret plantations a diploma, some gold, and a piece of land on Ambon."

"I heard that non-natives can't own land here. All the land belongs to the *rajas,* sultans, and the descendants of patrilineal kin," Verhoven, the writer of the meeting's minutes, commented casually.

"This land is in the forest. And they will get a property certificate from the VOC. The natives can't do anything. Our accomplice can live here in Ambon with his children for years to come."

At the end of the meeting, the governor invited everyone for lunch together, since they would soon attend the conferral ceremony.

The rather simple ceremony took place in the middle of the fort where the soldiers did their morning drills. On behalf of the VOC, the governor thanked the two men in Dutch with Verhoven as his interpreter.

Again, Tatahini wore a dark-colored garment. He carried himself in a very solemn manner and often nodded respectfully. Tatahini and Schouten were given the certificates, decorated with orange ribbons. Tatahini then thanked the governor for the certificates, and added the promise to bring him any new information that would be of interest to the VOC.

After the ceremony, the resident told the governor that the dark man spoke Dutch and there was no point in having everything interpreted by Verhoven.

"What did you say, Mister Resident? What's his name, it's hard for me to pronounce, can speak Dutch?" The governor thought Tatahini was a bit scary-looking. He continued, "They told me he's neither a native, nor a church member. Where did he learn to speak Dutch? I don't believe it."

"According to Verhoven, he's quite a bootlicker; he often pleased all the high-ranking VOC officials. He speaks Dutch, Portuguese, and Malay. His wife is fluent in Malay and Chinese," the resident answered.

"You fools. Why didn't you tell me? Now Cha...cha...what's-his-name must have made me the laughingstock at his home." The governor felt deceived.

"His name is Tatahini, he lives in Mahardika," Verhoven said.

The governor tried to pronounce the names. "Chachachachini from Mardijker."

The governor then suggested the three bachelors entertain themselves for the remainder of the afternoon at the bars outside the fort. The owners of the establishments were all white women of Dutch or Portuguese descent.

"Resident de Vries can paint beautiful women there. Whether they're of Dutch, Arabic, Chinese, or Javanese descent, they're all young and pretty," the governor said with a smile.

Before they parted, the governor asked Lucas about the incident with the man brandishing a sickle outside the fort. He had just heard the report from someone else. It would be better if the resident reported such incidents directly to him, he said.

Lucas told the governor about the mad face of the victim, and Verhoven's instantaneous decision to shoot the man. It never occurred to Lucas to shoot the man. He did not realize that in just seconds he could have lost his head.

"I didn't expect armed hostages or slaves with sickles or machetes. It's a warning that I'm not popular here. As a white man, I have to be alert twenty-four hours a day. I need to learn to speak Malay as soon as possible. I also need to learn how to defend myself."

"Very well then. Bertie and Karel always have to be alert too, lest they run into people like that as well. Never travel alone when you go to the plantations or drink houses. Bring VOC guards."

The men headed to their respective rooms to change before going to Marianne's bar near the harbor. They also asked to be excused for dinner.

The three bachelors were disgruntled. Their pretty drinking partners did not catch their interests, as none of them spoke Dutch. They needed Verhoven to interpret, but unfortunately he was not with them.

Chapter 4

Ambon was not a large island; it looked like it was almost divided in two between the northern and the southern part. For hundreds of years, perhaps even thousands of years, this island was inhabited. The Ambonese lived in scattered kampongs isolated from each other. Rolling hills stretched across the island. The curved coastline formed many beautiful bays and coves.

Ambon became an important island when a lot of Asian outsiders came and bartered for the inhabitants' spice harvest with farming tools. There were often fights over the cloves and nutmeg.

While there were a lot of clove trees in Ambon, the island actually produced fewer cloves compared to other surrounding islands. The irony was that cloves originated from several small islands north of Ambon.

After Holland discovered the sea route from Europe to Malacca and to Ambon, they built a fort in one of the bays. The fort housed the residence of the VOC representative, its warehouses, soldiers' barracks, an armory, and had many other uses.

The fort grew stronger as time passed, and the VOC's powers tightened its grip on the islands. They soon needed a bigger fort and started to build housings, entertainment venues, markets, and so on, outside the fort. They also began to occupy the hills but left the natives' areas such as the forests and their plantations in the interiors alone.

As the island was devoid of savannas, there were no four-legged grass-eating animals such as horses, cows, goats, or deer. The natives used boats to travel through rivers or the sea, or they walked.

The sultans and their families along with important people traveled on palanquins called *kadeira usung.* The natives were not yet familiar with the concept of getting paid for their services, so the carriers of the palanquins were mostly slaves belonging to the person they carried.

One morning, the governor of Ambon, who was a rather heavy man, traveled using the kadeira usung. He always used one during his formal duties. When the sun was fierce, he needed an extra slave to hold a big umbrella to shade him, even though he already wore a hat.

Behind him was the resident of Saparua, also using a kadeira usung. Next was the governor's wife. All of them wore wide-brimmed hats. The two botanists were on foot and carried their working tools. Behind the palanquins many people followed: mardijkers and Ambonese carried farming tools and baskets filled with clove saplings, along with some food and drink. It was quite a long convoy.

This was an important day for the VOC. They were going to officially distribute clove seeds to the natives with orders to plant and tend the trees until harvest time. This was the first controlled clove plantation of the VOC of which they managed the harvest. It was very different from the centuries-old natural plantation owned by the natives.

The VOC was desperate; they were not successful in controlling the clove supply on the market. The natives had hidden clove plantations and traded their harvest with many other traders who brought the cloves to the international spice market. The supply was abundant, so the price plummeted.

Finally the VOC decided to set up their own plantations. They would control the number of trees, the maintenance, the supervision, and the delivery to Europe. The natives were mere free labor, slaves. The VOC hoped to control the clove supply in the future. If they could achieve that, there would be no need to conduct the costly hongis.

The two botanists were considered experts. They would fertilize the trees and manage the plantation as a commercial commodity. The natives who would be "given" these initial plantations were "selected" individuals. They had submitted to the will of the VOC and were willing to work together. They were the "elites" among the natives of Ambon.

Many natives from other islands had died, and the ones still alive were too weak to put up a resistance. They were tired. It was hard to keep moving from one island to another. Thus, they cooperated.

Some of the older, seasoned clove farmers had prepared the ground for the planting of the VOC's first clove plantation. The planting holes were neatly lined up, wells for irrigation dug, compost made of the forest bed's waste was prepared, and shading plants were available.

While the expertise of the natives in raising clove trees surpassed the knowledge of both botanists, Karel and Bertie, these natives were placed in a lower position at the farm. They were treated as hostages or slaves, even though without them the trees owned by the foreigners would never flourish as it was impossible for young graduates like Karel and Bertie to know anything about clove trees.

The morning trip on board the kadeira usung was not pleasant, especially for the governor and his wife. Morning dew blanketed the lush green forest, while the mist rose from the sea. The resident thought that the scenery was exceptionally beautiful, delicate and emotionally moving. The three passengers of the kadeira usung secretly worried. They knew that the natives were definitely not fond of them.

The two botanists enjoyed the scenery of the lush tropical forest they passed. The various chirping of melodious birds calmed their souls. The slowly rising sun, its golden light, faint at first, tried to permeate the thin veil of mist as far as their eyes could see.

When the golden light gave life to the morning sky as it turned fiery orange, Karel shouted excitedly, "Look, everything's bathed in flaming sunlight. I've never seen something so wondrous. This is the most beautiful morning I've seen in the Indies."

They walked uphill, to the area where the ceremony was to be conducted. The resident and two botanists eagerly looked around admiring the scenery.

For more than a year they had prepared the large plot at the hillside for a "well-organized" clove plantation. It would still belong to the natives, but be supervised by the VOC. They were to distribute one thousand and two hundred saplings. Everything was ready; the VOC was to take care of the food and lodging of the slaves until the trees blossomed for the first time. After that it would be the plantation owner's responsibility.

If the experiment turned out to be successful and the trees blossomed, they had to hand over the harvest to the VOC in return for things needed by the natives like rice from Java, clothing, salt, sugar, and household utensils. Other items the VOC offered were chinaware, lamps, or mirrors. Once in a while they included farming tools.

The VOC was perhaps the first true conglomerate in the world at that time. Many small ships set sail to the east in adventurous search of spices. These were dangerous voyages. The competition was stiff; foul play and deceit were unavoidable. The working conditions were terrible and profit was small. A legal expert proposed forming a business venture with joint capital from hundreds of shareholders. Resident Lucas' father, the Dutch aristocrat, was a shareholder of the VOC, a trading company worth millions, established by the Dutch in 1602.

With the enormous capital, the VOC built ships that were advanced for the time, and equipped the vessels with weaponry and a crew. The Dutch crown granted this private enterprise monopoly over the Asian trade, which included the authority to conclude treaties with local rulers, and even to maintain armies to attack threatening parties.

The shareholders' hopes and fantasies soared. They even aimed to establish their own clove plantations on the islands the prized spice originated from.

Today, the VOC planned to distribute one thousand and two hundred saplings. Several hundred would go to Tanjung Iha, and several hundred more to Tanjung Ketapang. There was a large parcel of land available in Saparua and they would send some four hundred, the largest number of saplings, there. Another two hundred saplings were allotted to the smaller islands around Saparua.

Some of the natives owned "legitimate" clove trees, meaning the VOC knew about their existence and had listed the trees. The "illicit" trees were planted secretly in the interiors of Seram, Halmahera, or Bacan.

For many months, Bertie and Karel worked on opening the plot. They learned a great deal about cloves from natives during the process. It surprised Resident de Vries when he was told that the natives were not experts like the two botanists. The native farmers were far more knowledgeable about cloves than Bertie and Karel. There were tens of them. None of the elderly, solemn-looking, weathered men spoke Dutch. They communicated with the help of an interpreter, an Ambonese with very dark skin who spoke in a booming voice.

"Are they slaves?" the resident asked Ondos, the interpreter.

Ondos nodded.

"Where do they live?" the curious resident continued.

"They live in the huts at the edge of the plantations, Tuang," Ondos replied.

"The natives own the plantations, right? So are these people working for the natives who own the plantation, or for the Dutch?"

"I don't know, Tuang. It could be for the Pani-pani. They give the orders. Tuang Karel and Tuang Bertie can tell you."

"Who feeds them?"

"I don't know, Tuang."

"So what *do* you know? You don't know anything," the resident snapped angrily.

The governor and his wife turned their heads and asked why the resident was yelling.

The resident informed the governor about things that he was inquiring over. The governor answered that the VOC provided lodging and food for the slaves until the trees reached maturity. After they blossomed, the native owner would have to feed the slaves.

"Will the owners be able to afford the slaves' lodging and food?" the resident asked.

The governor merely shrugged and raised his eyebrows.

Lucas was very disappointed. He couldn't help but remember the harsh time when he and his abandoned mother barely had anything to eat. He made a mental note that the company he worked for was cruel. Even though he was a high-ranking official, he was a new employee and did not dare to speak up, let alone protest against the company's policies. Guilt began to gnaw at his conscience.

The ceremony was simple. The governor, vice governor, and resident walked to a row of holes. Three Ambonese approached them with prepared packages of clove tree saplings. The governor was the first to put a sapling in one of the planting holes. Caressing the root and leaves of the plant, he wished out loud for the tree to thrive. Then the vice governor repeated the ritual. The resident of Saparua was last.

After the three saplings were watered, a tall native from the interior of Ambon came forward and chanted a mantra while he tied a red ribbon around each tender sprout.

The governor pulled a face. He had already said that he did not want anything to do with the disastrous red ribbons. However, the native elders insisted that if they did not use the Sasi ribbons, someone would uproot the plants during the night. In the end the governor relented for the saplings' sake.

A man respected among the native plantation owners gave a speech expressing their gratitude for being trusted to tend the trees. The Ambonese who were given saplings all bowed then to the governor and resident; the only one who remained erect was the tall man who had chanted the mantra. He stood calmly and refused to bow.

When the ceremony was over, the governor's convoy returned to his residence in the fort. It was a long trip and, unlike when they had come to the plantation, the sun was high. The convoy ascended the hill that had carved steps leading to the fort. The governor was going to have lunch with the young VOC officials.

The resident did not go straight to the fort. Instead, he headed for a cluster of huts among a grove of coconut trees in the trial plantation.

Lucas de Vries asked a guard to show him the interior of the huts. Even though it was midday, it was dark. The only light came from a cutout in a wall; the dirt floor had no covering. The stench was unbearable. Male and female slaves were housed in different huts. One hut could house ten to fifteen slaves.

Papuan and pirate vessels traded slaves who were mostly innocent natives from the coastal kampongs on the western or eastern islands of Indonesia. The Papuans and pirates, whose weapons were far better than those of the natives, often attacked their kampongs. The natives usually only had machetes or axes for weapons. Families were often separated according to the buyer's purchase. Almost none of the slaves ever returned to their homes. At that time, the VOC purchased many slaves to tend their trial clove plantations.

The resident asked whether the slaves were given mats to sleep on. Not knowing whom he spoke to, the man guarding the huts answered arrogantly, "Mats? For slaves? That's too generous. Slaves sleep on the ground with their hands chained together. If they need to relieve themselves, they'll shout and we'll unlock the chains. We don't want them to run away during the night."

"Why don't you give them mats? It's cold at night because the wind blows from the ocean."

"Perhaps you should ask Pani-pani officials, Sir. I do not have enough mats for all the slaves. I respect your concern for the slaves. Are you from the church?"

"No, I'm not. I work for Pani-pani. I don't think the slaves deserve to sleep on the ground. Like you, me, and many others, they also work for Pani-pani, right?"

"That's true, Sir," the guard answered. "Do you work with the governor here?"

"No, I work in Saparua. I'm the resident of Saparua."

The guard immediately pressed his feet together, corrected his posture, and bowed as a sign of respect.

"Good afternoon, Mister Resident of Saparua. Welcome to the slave huts," he said courteously, with a lowered tone of voice. He appeared to be of mixed Arab or mardijker descent.

The resident did not bow back. He returned the greeting in a low voice and left, quickly. He was upset.

The four people seated at the dining table sighed with relief to see the resident hurriedly come up the stairs of the governor's residence. They had been waiting for the resident for quite some time.

"Finally! Now we can start eating lunch," the governor's wife exclaimed happily.

Lucas apologized for having delayed everyone's lunch. He thought he had told the governor about visiting the slave huts, but apparently he hadn't.

"Oh my, our resident is still a young man, but quite forgetful. Too many things on his mind, I suppose," the governor teased.

They ravenously devoured everything placed before them. Their plates were so clean they looked like they did not need washing. Perhaps their sheer exhaustion and the lunch delay had made everyone hungry. Everyone laughed at their own voraciousness.

Their hostess, the governor's wife, apologized in advance to anyone who couldn't stand intense aromas, for she was about to serve an offensive-smelling dessert, which tasted delicious. Dutch people who had lived for a long time in Ambon said that it was the fruit of paradise.

When the cook brought the fruit to the dining room, the resident, Karel, and Bertie had to suppress the urge to pinch their noses.

"Oh, it's split and husked already, so we don't need a knife?" Karel asked.

"No, we don't need the knives, just take it and eat it. You can suck the flesh, but don't swallow the seed," the governor's wife explained.

"How do I take it from the plate?" the resident asked. It was his first time eating durians.

"Use your hands, the same way you take candy out of a jar. If you haven't washed your hands, go to the kitchen to do so," the governor's wife answered.

The three young Dutch officials marched to the kitchen. Then they returned to the dining room and proceeded to take the fruit from the plate.

"Hmm...it's like a mixture of cream, honey, wine, and garlic." The resident opened and closed his eyes ecstatically while tasting durian.

The plate was soon empty. The governor offered the young officials more durians. There was plenty in the kitchen. All together eight big, perfectly ripe durians vanished from the kitchen. While they enjoyed the dessert, the governor told the story of the durian incident involving soldiers who were training in the forest. They fell under the spell of Sasi and were not able to return to the training camp for two nights.

The five of them roared with laughter, though unsure if the story was true.

Still joking, the governor warned that the story had really happened. He went on to say that he could even summon the five poor soldiers who were the victims of Sasi. The soldiers had been eating durian, the same fruit they just ate. They thought that the tree they had picked the fruit from was a wild tree since it grew in the forest, not on a plantation.

Bertie and Karel asked if they could see the fruit before it was peeled. The governor's wife rang a bell to send for the cook, who returned with two whole durians.

"This would make a good projectile for a catapult," Bertie said.

"Where can we see a durian tree?" Karel asked.

"Try looking for it in the forest when you go with the resident to Saparua. You'll find some there, even if it's not in season. Just remember not to take any durian from a tree with a red ribbon. You'll never find your way home. Wouldn't that be embarrassing? It'll make the natives laugh at us behind our backs." The governor licked his fingers clean.

"I think I want to learn how to put on the red Sasi ribbons. I've a big apple orchard back home in Holland," Karel said.

Everyone laughed.

Later that night, the governor threw an informal dinner party for his three guests. He invited several Dutch officials and families who had daughters. He wanted Bertie, Karel, and Lucas to have decent European lady friends. There weren't too many single Dutch women around.

***

Rosamunda was an eighteen-year-old girl who loved to sing. Her father was of Portuguese descent, and her mother was a mix of Portuguese and Malay. Her father owned a bakery in Ambon.

De Wit, the head of finance for the VOC, came with his wife and his blond daughter, Bertha.

Roosye, a shy fifteen-year-old, was the daughter of a warship captain stationed in the eastern Moluccas. She was born in Holland, and pure Dutch.

The resident had a good singing voice. He used to be a member of the school choir. Karel played the governor's accordion quite nicely. They entertained their guests well into the night.

The modest-looking Rosamunda was the prettiest. Dressed in a white gown with lace around the collar, she looked very feminine. Her shoulder-length brown hair was gathered in a tortoiseshell barrette. Again and again she sang harmoniously with the resident. The governor and his wife, experienced in matters of the heart, quickly noticed that the resident showed more attention to the lovely Rosamunda than to Bertha. They regretted that. Berta was born in Holland and her parents were pure Dutch while Rosamunda, born in Ambon, was of mixed Asian and Portuguese descent. The three young men engrossed themselves in the gaiety of the evening, filled with food, humor, and Dutch music.

If there had not been such merry entertainment that night with the girls, Lucas had wanted to talk about providing the slaves with sleeping mats, but there was no time for it and he decided to broach the subject in the morning when he was alone with the governor.

***

Aimuna and Sobori grew up well and healthy. Grandpa and Grandma Ronasundu as well as the household servants said that they had quickly outgrown their juvenile bodies.

Aimuna was no longer the little girl with cheeks so round that no one could keep from pinching them. The shape of her face was like an upside-down egg, beautifully tapered at the chin. She looked even prettier when she let down her long, wavy hair, but Gamati did not allow her to wear her hair loose.

Her body started to take shape; she began to develop a waistline and little rounds began to appear on her once-flat chest. Changes clearly showed in her gait. She walked quickly, but gracefully.

Grandma Rona owned several sarongs from Java and Makassar. When she told Muna to wear one of the sarongs and a white kebaya, Muna instantly transformed into a young woman, even though she was only twelve years old.

Aimuna's large, beautiful eyes had wide lids. When she lowered her gaze, her half-closed eyes exuded shyness. For some of the young boys in Tuna, this was an attractive gesture.

Her simplicity only added to her overall charm. She never behaved like she was pretty and never flirted with the boys, something the other, older girls often did. Her only makeup was a powder made of crushed *langsat* skin mixed with squid bone. The powder came in small pellets and was used to prevent sunburn. All the girls in Tuna covered their cheeks and brows with it.

One day, Grandma Rona said, "Muna, you're no longer a child. Soon, you'll be a woman. Men will come to ask for your hand in marriage. Girls protect their faces with this powder, to look smooth and fresh. Here, let me show you how to use it." Grandma Rona placed a few pellets and some water on her left palm and made a paste. She then applied the paste to the girl's face. Aimuna did not protest, even though she was not sure about its benefit.

As she grew older, Aimuna's likeness to Sobori's mother, her father's older sister, became more apparent. Bori noticed it and, touched, said to Gamati, "Grandpa, doesn't Muna look like Mother coming back from our burned hut?"

Feeling touched as well, Gamati replied, "Yes, you've a very keen eye, Bori. The most striking resemblances are in her eyes and the way she walks, so agile yet graceful. Exactly like Ranila, before she had children."

Bori grew even faster than Muna. He spent a lot of time on the plantation and at sea. Rowing had shaped his body, and the clean ocean air strengthened his lungs.

Sobori was handsome and tall like his late father. And, even though Aimuna was tall, Bori was still taller. His deep brown skin was darkened by the Moluccan sun. His tightly curly hair was always cropped close to his head, which made him look youthful and energetic. He had a broad chest and his stomach was as flat as a board. He had no excessive fat on his body. Gamati said Bori had inherited the cleft in his chin from his grandpa in Manipa.

The Tuna people often talked about these two young people who were introduced as Grandma Rona's distant relatives from a high mountain slope covered with clouds. People admired them, but they were difficult to approach as their grandfather was extremely protective.

The villagers of Tuna were about to have their *pata cengkei* festival during the next couple of days. The fully matured clove buds that were about to blossom needed to be picked at the same time. If picked too early, the buds would not be fragrant when sun-dried. Just a day later, after the buds blossomed, it would be of no use to sun-dry them, let alone try to use them as a trading item with the foreign seamen. The clove bud would no longer be fragrant and would have lost its preserving qualities.

Grandpa Rona and Gamati suggested Aimuna and Sobori join the rest of the village in the pata cengkei, to gain experience in the clove industry.

On the first day of pata cengkei, Aimuna wore an old sarong. She wrapped the sarong around her, only reaching her knees, and secured the top of it with a rope, so it would not loosen when she moved. Her top was also old and loose. These were understandably work clothes. She was barefoot.

Sobori wore loose black pants and an old shirt. In Tuna, men usually wore black pants and took off their shirts when they worked because of excessive perspiration.

Sobori's task was to pick clove buds. Even though he had no prior experience, he was a fast learner. It was not very hard work, but it was a man's work. He had to climb up a ladder and cut the clusters of clove buds, using a pole equipped with a sharp little knife at its end, called a *gae-gae*. If the tree was very tall and the clusters of clove buds high at the end of the branches, the picker had to climb the tree. This was why women never worked as pickers.

The clove buds were collected in a saloi, a cone-shaped harvest basket. The harvest of one tree did not amount to much. A clove plantation co-owned by all the villagers usually had sixty to one hundred clove trees. The harvest of the plantation after the clove buds were sun-dried would weigh between thirty to forty *catties*.

It was not much, but the combined harvests of all kampongs did amount to a supply capable of impacting the international clove market.

After the reign of the Portuguese and now the Dutch, all the natives of the Spice Islands had taken up a uniform word to call the aromatic spice *cengkeh*, although prior to that each island had its own word for the spice. Those words were now forgotten. People said that the now-popular word *cengkeh* came from the foreigners from the north, the Chinese "ciangkeh" meaning "fragrant nail." The natives of Malacca pronounced it *cengkeh* and the natives of the Spice Islands, including the Tuna villagers, picked up the term.

The women had prepared food and drink for the pickers. The food was usually wrapped in banana or coconut leaves and not served hot like papeda porridge. All the side dishes were already put together with the rice in the banana leaves. For snacks they usually brought seasonal sweet fruit, boiled bananas, cassavas, or yams.

The sun had just risen, but the villagers were already walking in convoy to the clove plantation. Their merry conversations were louder than the chirping of birds in the trees. When they arrived at the plantation at the edge of the kampong, the men quickly propped the ladders against the tall trees.

Two men held the ladder, while the picker climbed up with a saloi basket on his back. Several days earlier, the elders of the kampongs and of the tribal council had checked the trees. They had performed the customary ritual of asking Upulanite, the lord of heavens, permission to pick the clove buds.

Aimuna joined some older women, the mothers, who spread out mats. Later, they would dump onto the mats the clove buds from the salois brought by the men. The faster the clove buds were dried, the better. That day, the sun in the cloudless sky was scorching hot. It rarely rained during the east wind season.

The plantation's site was near the forest home to many species of birds and insects, but the clove buds did not attract pests. Perhaps because clove buds tasted bitter and hot there was no need to fend off the birds. Local natives used to put one or two buds in their chewing wad, to freshen their breath.

The season of pata cengkei was also an opportunity for the youths to socialize. It was their chance to meet for a longer time, to have conversations, joke around, and help each other. They often married after meeting during the harvest. Before the white men restricted the cultivation of clove trees, pata cengkei was far more festive.

The clove trees that held the greatest number of buds would yield the most trade items. The foreign seamen offered many goods for the natives' daily needs for trade with the clove buds. Sometimes they offered items only needed for traditional ceremonies such as large plates, ceramic urns, or glass lights, and also various knives, beautiful silk cloths, and gold jewelry. The last items were usually offered to the kampong's wealthy who owned many clove trees and workers who were close to the sultan's officials. Before the white men came, it was this group who acted as the middlemen in the clove trading. They were also members of the tribal council.

Suddenly, without any prior notification from the kampong's elders, three white men and their native interpreter appeared from the rows of trees at the outskirts of the forest. The pickers were having their lunch break while waiting for the sun to lean west, making it cooler, when all of a sudden they heard shouts of greeting, "Tabea! Tabea samua! Salamat ee!"

They were even more surprised when they saw three white men and a young native carrying tools they had never seen before.

Tior, one of the pickers and a friend of Sobori, stepped forward. He returned their greeting and asked what they were looking for on such a secluded plantation.

Bessy, the interpreter, was a fat young man, fluent in the local dialect. He explained that the resident of Saparua and two botanists wanted to learn about the harvesting of clove buds. The resident also wanted to paint the process of cutting and drying the clove buds.

Tior answered that the pickers could not give them permission. They needed to ask a mauweng instead. However, the mauweng was not at the plantation; he was in the kampong.

The resident said they had to send one man with Bessy to the kampong to see the mauweng and ask for permission to learn about harvesting the cloves and for the resident to paint the process. Sobori was chosen to go with Bessy because he was outgoing, smart, and walked fast.

Aimuna's heart skipped a beat at the thought of Sobori leaving. *Neither Grandpa Gamati nor Grandpa Rona is here to protect me. What if Bori goes missing?* For a while, Muna's thoughts raced. There was not much to do during the lunch break, so she did not make any mistakes.

Bessy walked behind Bori toward the kampong.

As a token of hospitality, the pickers invited the three white men to partake in the provisions they brought. The three Dutch men remembered the governor's warning, "Never socialize with the natives, let alone eat the food they offer as it might be unhygienic or poisoned," and at first were reluctant to take the food.

It was Lucas' first experience of direct contact with the natives, whom the governor and the mardijkers always avoided. Bessy was not around and after all, they were the ones who came uninvited, to seek knowledge. To break the ice, he took one of the food packages wrapped in banana leaves. It contained steamed rice and fish, fragrant with cloves and nutmeg. The packages wrapped in coconut leaves contained fragrant sticky rice mixed with nuts and shredded coconut.

Lucas thought that the natives' food was delicious and fragrant. It suited his taste perfectly. It was a welcome change from the VOC's rations, which consisted of dried, preserved food. They brought everything from Holland; beef, ham, fish, everything was like dry tree bark. Neither the butter nor the cheese used in preparing these foods could improve the flavor.

Walking under the fierce tropical sun had made the three Dutch men hungry. Lucas pointed at his stomach with two fingers.

The pickers, Aimuna, and the other women laughed. They understood what the white man meant.

"Yes, yes, please take more." They pushed the salois filled with provisions toward the resident.

Lucas and the two botanists each ate one more portion of rice in banana leaves and another portion of sticky rice in coconut leaves. They joked about eating Bessy's share and not caring about him starving till dinner.

Bori, Bessy, and the youngest mauweng in Tuna returned long after the pickers had started to work again and the sun was no longer fierce. No one knew the mauweng's real name, because everyone in the kampong simply called him mauweng, although there were the oldest mauweng, a younger one, and the youngest mauweng. Aimuna relaxed when she noticed Bori had come back.

Although Bessy had previously informed the mauweng about the reason for their coming, Lucas repeated the information as he addressed the mauweng directly through Bessy's interpretation.

The mauweng in turn asked, "What is the use of learning about a pata cengkei while the resident had many slaves to do all the work?"

The resident said he had to make a good report. By painting it, the skill and knowledge of the clove harvest could still be learned by others even after they were old or dead.

"With all due respect, Tuang, I can't give you permission to paint the natives. We believe that if you have a painting of a person, you can send bad things to that person by using a shaman's black magic. The villagers will get angry at me."

The resident answered that he and his friends were not shamans with black magic powers. They were from the VOC and just wanted to learn. After he finished his painting, everyone could see it; he would bring it to their kampong. He said, "Pani-pani doesn't have witches or evil shamans."

The natives did not object to the resident painting the trees, the plantation, and the clove buds, but they would not allow him to paint them. Bessy tried very hard to explain the resident's intention in the local dialect, but still they refused to be painted.

Lucas thought that perhaps he would be able to do it some other time, after they knew him better. He knew the natives disliked him, as well as all other VOC officials. VOC trade items were usually of poor quality. Rice, for example, would stink, be wet, and sometimes infested with bugs. Rice from Makassar or Ternate was of much better quality. This was just one of many reasons.

Lucas agreed to paint only the plantation, the size of the trees and the clove buds, in different stages, from being freshly picked to being sun-dried. He also painted the tools: the gae-gae pole with the knife on the end of it, the saloi baskets, and the provisions the natives brought from home.

The two botanists, through Bessy, asked about clove tree pests, how many years it took for a clove tree to blossom for the first time, the difference between a good and bad clove bud, the types of destructive winds, etc.

Lucas asked where the mats used for sun-drying the clove buds came from. The natives answered that they wove the mats themselves. Lucas knew that in a simple society like that of the natives on the Spice Islands, there were no shops. Everything they needed, they made or searched for in the forest. When he asked how he could obtain twenty mats, the mauweng told him to have the slaves at the fort weave the mats for him. Lucas nodded. He would try to follow the mauweng's advice.

After that, Lucas and the two botanists said good-bye. They thanked the natives for the food and the information on clove trees. Bessy wondered why the resident thanked the natives for food. He did not see the resident and the botanists eat anything. After they boarded a boat back to Saparua, Bessy still did not dare to ask about food. He was starving, but did not say anything. None of the natives had offered him anything to eat. Perhaps they forgot, he thought. The natives were never stingy.

As soon as the resident and his group left the plantation, the villagers started to talk about their visit.

How did the resident know that they were having a pata cengkei in Tuna? Why did he come as unexpectedly as a storm, without notifying the kampong chief first? Why did he want to paint people, a taboo in Seram? Why did he need a lot of mats? Do the resident and his friends sit on mats at home?

It was the first time Sobori and Aimuna saw the VOC people their family so despised. The foreigners looked very different from the natives. Not only were their skin, eyes, and hair color different, they were also tall and had pointed noses. Bori and Muna could not understand why the Dutch looked so different from the natives of Tuna.

When the sun was about to set, the pickers gathered their tools and belongings. They put the dried clove buds into the saloi baskets. The buds had dried up nicely; the color was a deep brown. Everyone helped carry the filled saloi baskets as they headed back to Tuna. Too tired to draw bath water from the well near their huts, they stopped at a small stream near the kampong where they took turns bathing.

The women went first, while the men stood guard over the clove buds and the tools. When it was the men's turn to bathe, the women guarded the cloves. The women armed themselves; they feared an attack from Papuan ships or pirates. They were known for kidnapping natives along the coastlines.

When they arrived home, Gamati, Grandpa, and Grandma Rona asked Bori and Muna to tell them about their experiences at the harvest. They all laughed about the awkward and funny mishaps of Muna and Bori. It was, after all, their first time joining a harvest.

After Gamati and his grandchildren had fulfilled the social obligation of chitchat and laughter with the Ronasundus, they returned to their own room at the back of the hut. Gamati said Sobori and Aimuna should go to sleep right away since they were tired. He himself had to wait for an important friend. He asked the youngsters not to tell anyone about this meeting. It concerned their safety.

"Who's the guest, Grandpa?" Aimuna whispered.

"Grandpa Makasuli, he lives not far from Tuna. You've met him, right?"

"Yes, I have. He's also a good friend of Grandpa Rona," Aimuna answered.

"Why don't you meet at Grandpa Rona's front porch?" Bori wondered.

"We just want to finalize the plan of going to the forest for several days. We'll look for honey. I want to teach you and Muna how to survive in the forest. Grandpa Makasuli knows the paths in the forest."

Bori wondered why they had to keep their going to the forest a secret from Grandpa Rona, whom they had trusted like family.

"Bori, listen to me carefully," Gamati explained. "We want to leave this kampong, to escape from the hongi. We and Makasuli's family are not the only ones who want to leave. Dopa, Ages, and Beilang also want to join us. We'll have a lot of friends in our new home. Hopefully there'll be no Pani-pani, no hongi. We can't let anyone in on this secret. I'm afraid everyone'll want to join us, to escape the hongi. I don't want to cause trouble for Grandpa Rona. Pani-pani will be angry at him."

Sobori was exhausted and fast asleep before Makasuli knocked on the door. Aimuna, on the other hand, forced herself to keep her eyes open. She wanted to listen to the conversation about the plan to go into the forest. Gamati allowed her to stay up, as long as she kept quiet.

When Makasuli knocked softly, Gamati opened the door. They were soon engaged in conversation about their plan to go to the forest. There were a few young men who wanted to join them; they were willing to work hard and face danger, if necessary.

Gamati asked about Aimuna. She was a girl, if not still a child. She was not as strong as a man. If the route proved to be challenging, the poor girl needed to be carried on a litter. There was also a chance that she would get kidnapped, as she was a female. However, who would take care of her if they left her? The Ronasundus rarely went out and they weren't sure if they could trust the workers here. Who knew of their real intention?

Makasuli suggested bringing Aimuna along. Teaching Muna and Bori was their pretense for going into the forest, wasn't it? It would look strange if they left Muna here.

"What if she cannot make it? She is just a frail little girl," Gamati said sadly.

"Don't overthink it. If necessary, I'll carry her on my back in the forest. I say we should take her with us," Makasuli urged Gamati.

Aimuna was glad when she heard Makasuli's answer. She would join them in the forest and not lose Bori and Grandpa Gamati. She wouldn't have to wait for the sun to lean to the west before the people she was closest to returned. She was instantly relieved. Suddenly, she was very sleepy and soon fell asleep. They decided that Makasuli's next task was to find a boat that could carry up to ten people.

The next day, a neighboring kampong conducted their *pata cengkei*. Not everyone went there to help. Only some men went, as a token of brotherhood in the spirit of *masohi*. Although at the harvest yesterday there was no help from the other kampong, they brought some baskets filled with provisions that had been donated by the Tuna villagers.

The Tuna villagers never asked for help.

***

The governor was having breakfast with his wife when his butler, a *Borgo*, came in and bowed respectfully. He said, "Good morning, Sir, Madam. There's a man who wants to speak to you. He said it's urgent."

The governor returned the Borgo's greeting, albeit with a sour face. "A guest? This early? Tell him to go to my office at the fort. Where's he from?"

"He didn't say, Sir. He speaks Dutch. Perhaps he just got off the ship from Batavia."

"Batavia? Yes, send him to the fort. I'm not ready to receive guests. Besides, this is my private residence."

"I'm very sorry, Sir. He said this *is* a personal matter; no one can know he came," the butler insisted.

The governor's face turned calm. He indeed had his own clandestine network; he kept it a secret from everyone, even from his wife.

"Ask him to wait in the reception room. Tell him I need to change before seeing him." The governor nodded to his wife and left the dining table. His wife continued to eat her breakfast calmly. When she finished and rang a bell, a household servant came and cleaned the table.

The governor was all dressed up. He had even put on some cologne. His subordinates often laughed at him behind his back. Even though he was a man, he liked to dress up; he loved fragrances and nice clean clothes. He demanded everyone treat him respectfully and always behaved in a formal manner full of pleasantries, especially in church.

As he came through the door, his guest stood and bowed respectfully to greet him. Gonzales had learned to speak Dutch.

"Good morning, Mister Governor of Ambon. Forgive me for coming here unannounced. Thank you for making time to see me. My name is Felipe Gonzales; I'm the captain of the Stella Maris from the Philippines. I'm having some trouble with the ship, so we had to moor temporarily on Bacan Island."

The governor nodded and extended his hand. "Welcome to Ambon. Do you have the password for identification?" he asked coldly.

"Yes, Sir. The sky and the ocean are both blue, but if there are clouds passing, pay attention to the color of sunlight. Is it morning or evening?"

"Hmm. Good. And what is the answer? Is it morning light or evening light?" he pressed further.

"The evening light is livelier, more beautiful, in this hot country, Sir."

"That's true. What's that beauty like?"

"You can check it right away, Sir. It's very satisfying."

The governor's face lit up.

Indeed, he was waiting for a large ship from China. As planned, the ship carried a large cargo of fine porcelain. The snobs in Holland, who had acquired their wealth only recently, had an obsession for collecting fine porcelain from China and Japan. They viewed their collections as a symbol of prosperity reaped from the growing trade.

The Stella Maris also sailed through the Philippines, the center of the gold and silver trade. The governor's accomplice, the ship captain, had loaded many gold and silver pieces for certain people south of the Philippines. First, he would trade with the governor of Ambon, and then with the governor of Batavia, and finally with the other traders in their homeland, Holland.

The ship captain had to look after the trading items he received from bartering the gold he brought. They were catties of nutmeg and mace from the Banda Islands, as well as dried clove buds. Clove buds were heavy and took up a lot of space on his ship. He still had to load catties of white pepper when he reached Batavia.

This was not a trade with the VOC for whom the governor worked, but with the members of his clandestine network of people. No one knew of this little game of private-account trading they used to enrich themselves. When the ship dropped anchor in their homeland and the secret cargo survived, the crew members unloaded them separately from the official and listed VOC's cargo.

The meager salaries they received were the main reason the employees of the VOC were "resourceful" in finding ways to get extra income. They were present at all levels: from governors to couriers, from the ship captains crossing the seas down to the ship's crew members, workers reluctant to return to Holland, all employed their own ingenuity. The tricks were endless.

The ship captain and a select few of his trusted crew who helped with these secret cargos knew they would get quite a large cut of the profit. Gold, silver, and spices were worth a fortune at that time. Many risked their lives in search of these items.

The governor invited Captain Gonzales to have breakfast. He knew that it was impossible for the captain to have already eaten. That early in the morning, the eating house was still closed. After breakfast they walked together to the port, which was nearby. The governor's subordinates wondered why the governor did not use the kadeira usung.

In front of everyone they met, the governor and Gonzales acted very formal. The two men boarded the big ship moored at the port and entered the captain's cabin. The governor checked some papers and nodded his head. Just like in an ordinary transaction, they called a number of carriers to transport the tightly wrapped baskets. However, the carriers were instructed to take the cargo to the governor's residence, instead of to the warehouse inside the fort.

At the governor's residence, the carriers were ordered to carry back to the ship a considerable number of different baskets that were prepared beforehand. Everything looked like the usual trading. Cargo was loaded and unloaded at the Stella Maris.

Then they loaded provisions for their next voyage: some drinking water, dry food supplies such as venison, pork jerky, salted dried fish, rice, fresh fruit, and other food items. The ship was in good condition; nothing was broken. It was just a pretext to moor in order to conduct the secret trade.

The Stella Maris moored for two nights in Ambon before continuing its voyage. The governor said his good-byes to the Stella Maris' captain. "Captain Gonzales, thank you. It turned out that you're a part of our circle. I hope everything will be in your favor, including the wind and the sea. Please take care not to let anyone know about the porcelains. They will fire me if they find out about it, and they will put you in prison. It won't do either of us any good, right? In Batavia, be firm and refuse any extra cargo, even if it's the governor himself who orders you. Just tell him that your ship has reached maximum capacity. We don't want the ship to sink just because you're too afraid to be firm with the governor of Batavia."

Gonzales, who already wore his official captain's uniform, gave a military salute to the governor, and said, "Thank you, Mister Governor. I hope we will meet again next year to trade the same items. Goodbye." He then turned around and ascended the tall ladders of his ship.

Even though Gonzales was a native of Spain, the enemy of the Dutch kingdom, he earned his living working for the enemy's company. His work was dangerous but thanks to the costly "extra cargo" on board his ship, he earned more money. Sailing the fierce seas and smuggling expensive trading items made his life at sea even more exciting. Gonzales dreamt of being a rich and powerful man.

There was a stiff competition among several kingdoms in Europe in discovering new territories at that time. Their main goal was to find the origin of the spices, important commodities in the lands of the four seasons. For centuries, only a few traders could obtain the prized spices from their origin. The others had to buy from them at a very high price. Everyone wanted to purchase the spices directly from the source.

Holland was one of the competing kingdoms. It was hard to live in Holland prior to the discovery of the Spice Islands. There was massive unemployment, and natural disasters happened frequently. Holland's flat and low country was particularly prone to flooding. The stagnant water caused plagues. And of course, there were the wars with the neighboring countries.

The urge to discover the Spice Islands increased. At first, the Dutch only desired to find the origins of the spices. However, after they found the sea route to the islands, they wanted to control the trade.

The Dutch attempted to drive out the seamen from China, Japan, and India who had traded peacefully with the natives prior to their coming. These foreign seamen were not armed. The drive was orchestrated by the VOC, the employer of the governor of Ambon, Martinus de Bruijn; Lucas de Vries, the Resident of Saparua; and the two young botanists.

Another trick VOC employees engaged in to make extra money was to "pinch" well-wrapped packages of cloves ready for shipping. They only pinched one tablespoon of cloves per package, but pinching twenty packages of cloves would glean a substantial amount. This was a true practice of pilfering. The "pincher" would combine and repackage the "pinched" cloves and deliver this load to an address different from the original destination. The profit made would be shared among the crewmembers who pinched the cloves, and the ones who neatly repackaged them.

VOC employees worked hard but their loyalty to the company was merely superficial and their sense of honesty warped. The great difference between the selling price at the spices' sources and the international market fanned their greed.

The Assembly of the Lords Seventeen, the directors of the VOC, were outraged when they discovered there were others who owned supplies of cloves, nutmeg, mace, and pepper outside of their own fleet. They suspected the traders used routes not in the VOC territory. They must have used camels and traveled the caravan route from China through Central Asia to Europe. They could also come via the Philippines through land routes such as Siam or Burma to India, then all the way to Baghdad or Damascus. The officials in Amsterdam were completely unaware of the thieves performing secret operations in their own institution.

After the governor, the harbormaster was the one in charge of the port. When entering or leaving the port, a foreign ship had to report to the harbormaster and pay a fee. If the ship happened to have smuggled cargo or broken a rule, a bribe was paid not only to the harbormaster, but all the way down to the clerk, the cargo weigher, and the area chief. If the ship was large, like a junk or a big traditional ship from Java or Makassar, the harbormaster would ask for the resident's or governor's cut too. But no one knew if he actually gave the bribe to the resident or the governor.

An archivist like the resident of Saparua could earn extra income if he painted family portraits of influential people or sold paintings of landscapes. During his short stay in Banten, while waiting for a ship to go to the Moluccas, Lucas painted a portrait of the sultan's younger brother's family to kill time. He did not ask for anything in return, as he only wanted to have a good relationship with the sultan, so he could turn to him in times of trouble. Unexpectedly, the sultan presented him with a half cattie of pepper. The price of the pepper equaled the price of tens of grams of gold. Lucas turned down the gift, saying that he didn't know how to cook.

As the Resident of Saparua, Lucas de Vries quickly became aware of the treacherous conditions in his working environment, and he did not like it at all. He never dreamt of having to viciously rule over the innocent natives of an island. He had been educated in a school managed by priests who encouraged him to develop his talent in painting and singing. Lucas was fond of things beautiful and subtle.

If it were not for the off-chance meeting with the Dutch aristocrat that one summer, he would have been a singer in the church choir or a painter. On that particular summer day, the young Lucas performed an act with a dog and a monkey in a sidewalk circus. They were performing in front of a seasonal food stall.

The crowd's cheers and laughs drew the attention of a gentleman eating at the food stall. After he paid for his meal, he joined the spectators.

The tall gentleman towered over the children. He enjoyed the show and was drawn to the boy who performed a comical act. The boy's Hispanic looks, especially his brown hair, captured his attention. He felt he knew the boy. After some time, he realized that the boy was none other than Lucas, Yolanda's son; his own flesh and blood.

After the show, he asked Mr. Wijnen, the show's manager, whether the little boy's name was Lucas. Mr. Wijnen nodded, amazed.

The aristocrat then approached Lucas and said, "Lucas. Do you still remember me?"

"Yes, Sir, I do," Lucas, astonished, answered respectfully.

"Where do you live now? I've searched for you everywhere. How's your mother?" he asked anxiously.

Lucas was silent for a moment then said, "She passed away, Sir."

"What? She passed away? How come no one told me? When did she die?" he shrieked.

"You better ask Mr. Wijnen. He knows more than I do."

After the aristocrat found out Yolanda had died from a broken heart, he asked Mr. Wijnen to let Lucas quit the pet show. He wanted the boy to go to school and get a formal education.

Lucas and Sonya, Mr. Wijnen's daughter, studied under the tutelage of some priests from the end of autumn until early spring and Mr. Wijnen refused the nobleman's request. Lucas was like a son to him and the boy helped him to make a living.

The aristocrat said he would pay for Lucas' education. To compensate for the lost revenue caused by Lucas' absence, he would provide the Wijnens with a milk cow. The cow would produce milk and Mrs. Wijnen and Sonya could learn to make cheese. They would have no need to continue with the sidewalk circus, which could only perform for several months of the year anyway.

Mr. Wijnen told the aristocrat he needed three days to think and to talk to Lucas. They agreed to meet in the stall before they parted.

Lucas asked Mr. Wijnen to buy him a sweet pastry from a food stall. Even though he was always very frugal, and they usually had just enough food to keep from being hungry, Mr. Wijnen bought the cake; after all, Lucas had performed very well.

Lucas was not happy with the idea of having to leave the family circus. Even though they had no blood ties, Mr. and Mrs. Wijnen, Sonya, and Erik were his family. He loved them, and he loved the dogs and the monkey from the pet show; they were a part of his life. His heart sank as he pondered, *Why do I have to leave them? There're just too many good-byes in my life.*

Mr. Wijnen felt the same way and Sonya even more so. Mrs. Wijnen said that it would only be temporary. When Lucas finished his schooling, he would return to the Wijnens' house. After all, he had no one else in this world.

Mrs. Wijnen encouraged him to accept the offer. She was always thinking ahead. When he returned, the family would be in a better situation. They would own a milk cow. That was just a start. Perhaps the number would grow with time and then Sonya could take the courses she had always wanted to take.

When the Wijnens asked him who the kind gentleman was and wanted to know why he was so generous, Lucas said that the nobleman was his mother's employer when she worked as a housemaid.

"I see. But he's so generous. We seldom find a kind-hearted and generous aristocrat. Please don't snub us after you're all educated," Erik and Sonya teased.

In the end, the Wijnens gratefully accepted the milk cow and Mr. Wijnen agreed to let Lucas go to school. Lucas concluded that his mother had not told the Wijnens everything. The presence of a nobleman in their lives and her relationship with him was one of the matters she had omitted. Lucas decided to keep the secret forever.

A small coach fetched Lucas. The school he was enrolled in was very far from the Wijnens' house. Mr. Wijnen handed him some pocket money. The money was not his payment as a performer in the pet show, but rather a gift from a father to his son. He said, "Sometimes, things don't turn out to be as good as we imagined. Use this money wisely and, remember, if you're not happy, you can come back to us anytime you want."

Before he left, Mrs. Wijnen said, "Lucas, remember, education is very important."

That was how Lucas ended up studying among the children of aristocrats. He had special courses every afternoon to catch up on all the lessons he had missed. His teachers were happy, for Lucas turned out to be a very smart boy. He also had a wonderful singing voice. They put him in the choir when they held a service.

Lucas also excelled in art lessons and foreign language. Other students asked him to paint their portraits. The aristocrat, as his guardian and sponsor, received reports about his achievements and was very pleased.

Lucas often wondered about the motive behind the aristocrat's generosity. They never interacted. Lucas only saw the aristocrat at his school's anniversary or Christmas party. At these two events, all parents and guardians were invited and given the opportunity to give their charges presents. Lucas always received a complete set of maps and history books of Holland as his yearly gift, while other boys received clothes, shoes, or toys.

The aristocrat would come all dressed up and well groomed, and talked with the teachers and monks who managed the school. When it was time to say good-bye, he shook Lucas' hand and encouraged him to study well. He never once hugged Lucas, or asked if he needed something, let alone ask him about his aspirations.

Lucas pondered, *Mother said he's my real father. Then why is he so cold?*

His mother's stubbornness had prevented their intimacy previously. Now, his mother had passed away. The aristocrat's mother, who had caused all their heartache, was no longer around either. *So what keeps him from being more affectionate?* To Lucas, his father was Mr. Wijnen, while Mrs. Wijnen replaced Yolanda, his mother. His younger siblings were Erik and Sonya.

Lucas had almost graduated from high school when the aristocrat took him out for lunch. Lucas was stunned. The point of their conversation was that the aristocrat invited Lucas to work as a painter-archivist. As such he would paint many things and his paintings would later be studied. His employer would post him to a faraway place, across many oceans.

Lucas said that his teachers often told him that Holland was competing against Spain, Portugal, and England to discover new territories, like in the time of the Romans and Greeks.

His teachers also said that Holland needed tenacious young men like him, who were resilient and willing to struggle, to manage the recently discovered lands. Spain, for instance, had discovered a large bountiful continent in the west. The Portuguese had found routes to the east, while the English had found other routes. Holland did not want to fall behind.

The aristocrat agreed with the teachers. A young man like Lucas needed to work in a company owned by shareholders, he said. The VOC was a large company and growing substantially. He was a shareholder in that company.

"By the time you finish your post there, you'll have ample experience in administration and leadership. You'll also become a better painter and will have enough savings to start a new life in Holland."

Lucas had always wanted to become an independent painter, but he owed a debt of gratitude to the aristocrat and he had been taught to always be grateful. He therefore did not dare to refuse the aristocrat's offer. He did not even ask the questions he needed to ask, such as the name of the newfound land, or what the climate and the natives were like.

He accepted the job offer right away. He knew the Wijnens would be very disappointed. They wanted him to live with them like before. He was disappointed himself for having to abandon his plan to go back to the Wijnens, to feel again the warmth of the people he loved, to be among family.

That was how Lucas de Vries ended up in the east. Working for the VOC, he was able to log many experiences and sights in his memory bank even before his twenty-fifth birthday.

Lucas did not like a lot of things he encountered in his new environment, especially the brutal violence. Ever since he sailed from the Texel port in Holland, misery and death were near. He often thought about the aristocrat, the man who had impregnated his mother on purpose, hoping his parents would force him to marry her. Now, the aristocrat had financed his education and given him a respectable job while many young men were unemployed.

Lucas left Holland on a cold winter day. The gale-force wind whistled in his ears. The aristocrat, bundled up in extra warm winter clothes, waited for him at the dock. He shook hands with the two monks who accompanied Lucas.

His footman took all of Lucas' belongings and carried them on board the ship with a special permit. The two monks left after a short conversation.

Lucas started to feel nervous; he felt awkward being alone with his benefactor, when all of a sudden the aristocrat spread his arms and fondly said, "Lucas, I bet your mother told you who I am? Did she tell you that I loved her and that I wanted the three of us to live in a faraway land?" The aristocrat hugged Lucas tightly. He proceeded to kiss Lucas on both cheeks, his forehead, and the top of his head with an unrestrained affection. It seemed that the aristocrat would never let him go. He cradled Lucas' slight body as if he were a baby. This was everything Lucas had ever wanted from him.

Lucas' heart melted. *He loves me. He hugged me like a real father hugs his son.* A deep yearning and warmth flowed through his veins, from the top of his head down into his feet. Neither father nor son felt the icy December wind. Instead, the warmth of their embrace melted their frozen hearts.

"Lucas, don't ever hate me, Son. Your mother turned down my marriage proposal. I asked her to elope with me to Brazil, but she refused. She hated me so much; I didn't even know she died. Do your best in your new post. I'm staking my good reputation on you."

Lucas only nodded as he tried hard not to cry. An image of his mother as she lay on her sickbed, thin and frail, passed by. He remembered the last time he kissed her forehead, right before the priest closed her coffin.

"Call me Father, Lucas, even if it is only for this one last time," the aristocrat implored.

"Yes, Father," Lucas whispered, then asked, "Would Mother be happy if she could see us together?"

"I don't know, Lucas. Yolanda hated me. I want to heal the wound in your heart and mine. From now on, please accept me as your father even though your surname is de Vries."

The memory of this moment of intimacy and his affectionate father strengthened Lucas during times when he wanted to go back to Holland, fed up and resentful of the vicious thievery he witnessed working for the VOC. He lived frugally, the way he had been taught by his teachers and Mr. Wijnen. He did not want to taint his father's good name.

During the many months Lucas spent on his voyage to the east, death was constantly present on board. There were people who died from grave illness while others fought to death in riots. Crewmembers died from punishment for insubordination. Some people were killed by natives' arrows while forging for fresh water on an African coast.

These were terrible experiences for young Lucas. Yet, because of the aristocrat's plea to call him "Father" and for the sake of his father's good name, Lucas remained resilient. Through it all, Lucas was now content; he had a father, like every other boy.

Chapter 5

The night had just ended. The darkness faded, defeated by the sun that rose as a glorious king from the east. A layer of morning dew covered Seram. The beautiful silver blanket was not too thick and not too thin. The mountains and rows of rolling hills appeared shrouded in mystery. The morning air was cool and fresh.

Seram was an extraordinary island in the eyes of the people of the east. It was a large island. It took days and weeks to circle around it by ship. Stretched from west to east, the island appeared as if divided by a massive row of mountains. The degrees of height varied from high mountains to small hills. This great wall of mountains, home of the reclusive, isolated tribes, was the cause of the climate distinction between the northern and southern side of the island.

When the southern side was having a dry season, the areas north of the mountains experienced a wet season and vice versa. Higher up to the east there was an even bigger island. The people of Seram had never gone there, but the natives of that big island, whom they called the Papuans, often came to the kampongs along the coastline of Seram. They pirated the kampongs, taking the inhabitants as hostages. Papuans always brought a catastrophe, be it on land or at sea. They were excellent warriors; they ran like deer in the savanna and were adept at spearing their target while standing on their ships.

Gamati, Sobori, Aimuna, Makasuli, Dopa, Ages, and Beilang gazed eastward in silent amazement. Although they had spent all their lives living on Seram, the breathtaking sight of that morning still overwhelmed them.

"Grandpa, the sun looks like it's hiding. It's so pretty, just peeking at us. It's usually big and round, high up in the sky and it burns my skin," Bori said.

"Yes, dear child, the sun is our source of light. It looks very small in the morning, and then it gets bigger. At sunset, it's a golden red ball until it's swallowed by the sea. We're fortunate to have been born in such a beautiful place," Gamati answered and continued, "Muna, learn to appreciate the beauty of our homeland. It's such a wondrous place. Our people are warm, kind, and helpful. They enjoy dancing and singing. They have the spirit of masohi. Look to the east."

All of them looked eastward, and immediately fell into silence. The morning panorama amazed them even though it actually was an everyday sight. The morning sun and dew were always mesmerizing during the east wind season, when it rarely rained. However, they were not always paying attention to nature's beauty since they always started their morning with hard work.

Gamati and Makasuli were the adults in the group. Dopa, Ages, and Beilang were in their late teens. Sobori was fourteen and Aimuna was twelve. Aimuna was the only female. She had promised not to be a crybaby, so they allowed her to come along.

It took them two months to prepare for their trip to the forest. The plan was sealed during Makasuli's visit the night after the harvest. Several factors made implementation difficult.

First, that year's harvest had been several catties more than last year's harvest. This raised many issues among the Tuna villagers. They were unsure about the trade with the VOC. What if the VOC ignored the additional cloves and still gave them the same amount of sugar, salt, and rice? There were disputes about who were to speak to the VOC officials. There was also the possibility of hiding the surplus cloves and later secretly trading with other traders who came to Tuna from Ternate, the Bacan Islands, and Makassar. These traders were still interested in good-quality cloves. They offered metal tools, rice, and gold in exchange.

Then there was the question of whether or not to take Aimuna along. Gamati and Sobori were worried that the girl was not strong enough. She could become ill and die in the middle of the forest. On the other hand, Aimuna would rage if she were left, and in reality there would be no one to take care of her once Gamati and Sobori were gone.

The Ronasundus were old and frail and would be unable to protect her if pirates or Papuans suddenly attacked the kampong. Aimuna would most likely be kidnapped. A budding beauty was always in great demand at the slave market.

Gamati could not imagine losing Aimuna or Sobori. He also worried that Lissanei, Rona's oldest son, would visit Tuna while he and Sobori were in the forest. Out of their debt of gratitude, it would be hard for Muna to reject his advances. After all, she was only an innocent girl.

Finally, with the help of Makasuli's reasoning, they decided to bring Aimuna along. Gamati asked her to be resilient and strong during the trip. He wanted Aimuna to be independent and as bold as a man, so she could fend for herself and her family when faced with an enemy. He had raised his daughter Ranila, Sobori's mother, that way.

They brought enough weapons: a machete, ax, a small knife for fruit, a thin, long machete, some ropes, a mattock, and some woven sarongs. Although they knew they had to spend the night in the forest, they did not bring food that needed to be cooked, or sleeping needs, like mats or extra sarongs.

The real reason for their trip was to visit the site of the destroyed Tupawalili kampong. Kurubela and Tarambessi had buried several porcelain pots under the floors of their homes. The porcelain pots were filled with beautiful gold jewelry from China. As long as no one had claimed the land, they could dig up the jars and retrieve the gold. This was to be their starting fund to build a long-distance arumbae ship and finally live a free life.

"Have you asked the *moyang-moyang* for blessings before we enter the forest, Grandpa?" Bori asked solemnly.

"Yes, I have, Bori. A few nights ago I went to the *baileo* and got the blessings from Upulanite. Since we have good intentions, Upulanite will approve."

Sobori looked relieved. Makasuli added that he too had asked for the blessing of moyang-moyang in his kampong's baileo.

Their destination was the Tupawalili kampong. There were no roads that connected the various kampongs on Seram. The kampongs were isolated. Tuna was in the western area of the island, not far from the coastline. Tupawalili was on the north side, deep in the interior, nestled in a hill slope. There was no nearby beach to moor a boat, and the seaside water was dark and deep, surrounded by solid rocks that served as an effective seawall. A boat could smash against those rocks if it attempted to moor at the beach when the sea was restless, especially in west wind season. In short, it was not an ideal beach to moor a boat. The dense forests were home to many varieties of colorful birds. A sharp machete was needed to penetrate the lush growth.

The Halefurus lived in the mountaintops that formed a divide in Seram. They preferred to live with no contact with people outside their tribe. Typically, they were dark-skinned, well built, and muscular. Their kinky hair tended to clump if left to grow. Their noses were wider at the bottom. They were reclusive and known to be headhunters.

The group started to follow a path in the forest. It was very dark and cool. Dense foliage served as the forest roof and blocked the sunlight.

"I hope we won't run into the Halefurus," Gamati said. "I can't remember if this is their mating season. We'll fight them if we have to. They never attack in groups, but their arrows are deadly poisonous."

Gamati instructed the group to form a single file. Bori was right behind him, then came Dopa, Ages, and Aimuna. Beilang followed Aimuna with Makasuli at the end of the line. Everyone held a machete except Aimuna. She carried the ropes, the small knife, and sarongs.

Aimuna was not dressed in her usual girl clothes. Gamati had told her to wear a boy's loose top and knee-length pants, so she could move freely. Her hair was tied into a bun and covered with a man's headband.

Makasuli was actually a descendant of the natives of Banda. Nearly all of his ancestors had perished in a fight against the Dutch over the nutmeg and mace trade. Fortunately, his parents had managed to escape to the southeastern side of Seram.

Makasuli's family who lived near Tuna had always wanted to move. They wanted to get away from the VOC. They wanted to plant nutmeg like their ancestors and trade their harvest with traders other than the VOC. Like Gamati, they wanted freedom.

Several other families from Banda had started a new life someplace else, away from Tuna, which they considered "tamed" by the VOC. Even after more than fifty years had passed, the Bandanese would not forgive the VOC for the slaying of their ancestors. They wanted to get away as far as possible from the VOC. Seram was still too close to Banda and Ambon.

The ground they treaded emanated the particular scent of fertile soil. For hundreds of years decayed foliage had formed a thin layer of humus. Aimuna took a deep breath. "It smells so wonderful. What is this smell, Grandpa?" she asked.

"It's wet soil. The dew never evaporates here because there's no sunlight. So the ground is soft, moist, and fertile."

"Wow, how come there's no soil like this in Tuna?"

"We cleared the land in Tuna. Now there are huts, clove plantations, and large clearances where we dry cloves and salted fish. The trees are far apart, and unlike in a forest like this, sunlight can reach the ground. That's why it doesn't have this lovely smell."

"I love it here, Grandpa. It is shady and cool. Oh, I really love this smell."

"Yes, yes, my little girl. We'll rest later. Now, we have to walk fast. We have to reach our destination before dark."

"Just like when we searched for Bapa Lando's hut?" Aimuna asked sweetly.

"Yes, Muna. That's why you have to stop talking. You have to save your energy."

"So I have to be quiet now, Grandpa?"

"Yes, dear."

The group kept walking. Sometimes they had to duck under the dense growth. At other times they had to climb over large tree roots that had intertwined with the roots of other trees nearby.

They searched for food as they walked. A stand of mangosteen trees bore ripe fruit. They stopped to pick the mangosteens and then continued their walk. Even though the trees' canopies blocked the sunlight, they could still navigate their route.

After some time, Makasuli sensed it was midday. They all sat down on a slope. Gamati told Ages to cut a few stalks of the juicy rattan plant he saw earlier. They needed to drink the water it contained after they ate the mangosteen.

Even though they were not exposed to direct sunlight, they were drenched in perspiration, something that would never happen on the breezy Tuna seashore. There was no more chirping and hooting of birds; they were too deep into the forest where there were fewer small animals. The large animals they were afraid to encounter were big snakes and a big bird with a long, sharp beak and feet so strong it could kick a human. Perhaps there were some wild boars. They were relieved not to have met any of those animals so far.

They continued to walk after the break. After having eaten the sweet fruit and drunk the sugary juice of the rattan, they walked faster. They had to get to a waterfall in a valley before nightfall.

Gamati remembered a cave behind the rocky waterfall. They could spend the night there, sheltered from the dangerous forest and the falling water. The floor of the cave was slightly higher than the rocky floor of the waterfall.

Luckily, the rocky pool of the waterfall was not very deep. Even Aimuna, who was the shortest of the group, could cross it with her shoulders still above the water's surface. Hanging on to a wall of lush vines, they climbed to a flat surface, far from the falling water, and finally reached the mouth of the cave. It was dark inside. Miraculously, they all fit as long as they remained seated.

Gamati said to be quiet lest someone hear them. They consumed the rest of the mangosteen and rattan water in silence.

Gamati looked at his grandchildren admiring their surroundings. They reminded him of Ranila and Tarambessi. His heart ached, and he was silent for a while. It was hard to erase the sweet memories of raising his children with his supportive wife.

They continued their journey to the now-scorched Tupawalili kampong. Mangosteen was in season. Some trees were blossoming, and some were so heavily laden that fruit had dropped and rotted on the ground since no one had picked it.

"Grandpa, is it still far?" Sobori asked.

"We'll get there later today. Hopefully we chose the right path."

"What are you looking for? I thought everything burnt to the ground," Bori said.

"You will see for yourself later, Bori. I hope some things were not consumed by the fire."

"Yes, Grandpa. If we can still find our hut, I want to look for my parents. Perhaps I'll finally be able to bury them."

***

Once again, Gamati wondered who had told the VOC and their accomplices about their kampongs and the secret clove plantations. The plantations were very isolated. *It must have been some native traitors*, he thought.

Gamati never shared his suspicions with anyone. He did not want the burden of having a vengeful grudge. He feared that Bori and Muna would later be tempted to investigate who the traitor was. Perhaps he was one of the Tupawalili villagers. All the villagers refused to trade with the VOC, and before that they all hated the Portuguese. Gamati wondered what the traitor would have received for showing the VOC the way to their secret clove plantations.

It was no use to keep brooding. It was better to work hard to prepare for their leaving Seram. Gamati and Makasuli had planned to move north, to the east coast of Halmahera. A lot of foreign traders went there with their ships. The VOC considered the foreign traders as their adversaries, but their fleet was unable to catch every foreign ship.

Gamati wanted to preserve his lineage. He wanted his family to have an arumbae. If they made it to the new place up north, they could meet ships from other countries and trade with them.

Kurubela, Tarambessi, and Gamati, unlike the rest of the natives in their old kampongs, had listened to the advice of the Chinese traders. They saved their earnings in gold.

The Chinese had taught them that gold was long lasting. It would not tarnish and was easy to sell to rich people. The Chinese taught them also to stash the gold in a special porcelain pot and then bury it in the ground. They said, "Everyone will accept gold. When you've saved enough of it, you can take it to a master shipbuilder and have him build you an arumbae."

The matter was a tightly kept secret between Gamati, Kurubela, and Tarambessi. Other villagers would laugh at them if they knew Gamati and his family saved gold for their future needs. Back then, saving was unknown in the Moluccas. The natives were able to obtain all their daily needs directly from the environment. The sea and rivers provided fish. Sago grew on the beaches. They traded cloves for metal farming tools and for clothes they did not weave themselves.

The natives were easily satisfied with the simple things they had. They had never left their homeland to sell and trade in other lands and had not recognized the necessity to save from their harvests' earnings for graver times.

Their main hardships were caused by long droughts, volcanic eruptions, violent storms, or earthquakes on the bottom of the ocean that resulted in devastating tsunamis sweeping the beaches. They were also plagued by the VOC's hongi raids and their attempt to monopolize the Moluccan seas. Occasionally, pirates and Papuans attacked their kampongs.

Makasuli and his family, as well as the young men of the group, agreed with Gamati. There were actually other families in Tuna who shared the same view as Gamati and Makasuli, but the two men thought that they had enough men to start a kampong on a vacant plot far from the VOC. They undoubtedly would plant cloves and nutmeg. All the foreign traders could come directly to the new kampong.

***

They ate mangosteens and drank the rattan water for breakfast. Then they continued to cut their way through the forest with the machetes. Gamati remembered the directions, the turns and the big trees they needed to pass.

Gamati hoped no one had cleared the ruins of their kampong. He and Kurubela, his son-in-law, had buried several porcelain pots containing beautiful gold jewelry. They had traded their big harvest that happened every four years for gold. The Chinese traders often brought gold to trade with families of the sultan. All the men and women of the sultan's family loved to wear gold jewelry.

Ngasiran, a trader from Tuban, had also traded with gold. Every time Gamati harvested the rare king cloves, the most aromatic and superior of all cloves, he asked Ngasiran to bring gold.

The king clove rarely produced many buds since the trees were difficult to tend. Gamati now wondered how he could get saplings from this variety for his secret clove plantations up north. He did not believe that the VOC had extirpated all the clove trees in the northern islands. He thought it impossible to extirpate all clove trees that had populated the islands for ages. He knew the characteristics of the tree; even if they cut down the trees, the roots would still grow into a new tree. And even if the VOC had destroyed every tree, he knew how to grow clove saplings from seed. He didn't worry much about it. Right now he was more anxious to check on the ruins of Tupawalili.

The group kept walking and, cutting through the brush, they penetrated deeper into the forest. Aimuna did not talk much. She enjoyed the shady and peaceful atmosphere of the forest. She also loved the chirping of the various songbirds in open areas penetrated by sunlight. They had mangosteen again for lunch.

It was after midday when they spotted a grove of young trees ahead. The trees were much shorter than those growing around them.

"There it is, Tupawalili," Gamati exclaimed.

"Tupawalili?" Sobori whispered. A deep melancholy filled him. He relived the moment his father and mother had coaxed him to go to bed that last ill-fated night they were together.

Now he felt he must have had a premonition that day; a feeling of impending doom he had not been able to put into words. Overcome by a strange feeling a very young boy could not explain, he had simply refused to go to sleep that night. Bori remembered wanting to keep looking at his parents' faces and wanting to be there when they carried the baskets of cloves to the beach.

Then the evil men of the hongi raid stormed their hut. Swift as lightning, they murdered both of his parents. Bori remembered lying frozen on the floor until he realized fire threatened his life. There had been no time to approach his slain parents, let alone care for them. He ran until he reached the secret hideout shack.

With nothing more left to say now, he whispered, "Mother, Father, here I come."

Gamati hugged his grandson. He understood. There had been too many deaths in his own life. He said, "Not yet, Bori. This isn't where your parents' hut used to be. We still have to look for it."

Bori was unable to contain himself. Crying on his grandfather's chest, he asked Upulanite to take his life. He missed his parents so much.

"Shush, child, never ask Upulanite for such a thing. We'll all die at the right time. Right now, it's your duty to fulfill your parents' dreams to own an arumbae and sail the seas as a free man," Gamati whispered.

Aimuna leaned her head against Bori's back and cried, hugging him tightly. She had not witnessed her parents' deaths, because Gamati had carried her away while she was fast asleep. Still, Gamati and Bori's pain was hers as well. Ever since that terrible night, her life revolved only around them.

They searched for an open space to sit and eat. Gamati no longer recognized the place. He said they might have to spend the night there. Without rice or sago, they had another meal of only mangosteen.

They ate quickly. Gamati wanted to look for a water source to make them more comfortable. He warned them to walk carefully. There were a few wells in that area.

There were no signs of the kampong roads leading to their baileo or the kampong chief's hut, etc. Gamati remembered his son-in-law's hut faced east, but the fire had destroyed everything. Overgrown bushes and young trees now filled the space where the hut once stood.

Kurubela and Gamati had buried the pots in the yard near the kitchen of the hut. If they could not find the site of the hut, it would surely be hard to determine the location of the buried pots.

Gamati told everyone to rest after they ate the remaining mangosteen while he and Makasuli searched the area.

The rest of the group had no idea what the two men were looking for. Gamati kept looking at the sky. Consulting the location of the sun, he measured the ground with a stick until he finally fixed his gaze on the spot where a patch of tall grass grew. He knew that if there was a well nearby, Sobori's hut should be too. The well had been their source of drinking water and was located a few arm's lengths behind their hut, toward the east.

After he made some calculations, Gamati found the spot he was looking for. Next, he measured the estimated size of the hut, and started to clear the area. The young men helped him.

Gamati was now able to determine the approximate location of the kitchen Kurubela and Ranila had buried three small porcelain pots in the yard nearby it while he and Tarambessi watched. He asked Dopa, Ages, and Beilang to help him dig, but advised them to do it carefully. Sobori came to help.

After a while, Ages spotted something shiny in the hole. Gamati's face lit up. He said to keep digging and fetch the object. It was a porcelain pot. They found another one under it. Only after they dug up the third jar did they stop digging.

Gamati did not want the young men to find out what the pots contained. When they asked, he said they contained ingredients to make medicine.

After their perspiration dried off, Gamati and Makasuli started to trace the location of the backyard where they used to sun-dry the harvested clove buds.

There were three more pots buried in the backyard. They all contained gold that represented savings from several great harvests.

Gamati and Makasuli were satisfied. They had found what they were looking for. They asked Aimuna to hand them the three sarongs she had carried. The bottoms of the sarongs were already stitched into bags. They hurriedly placed the pots inside the sarong bags, along with some dry leaves and twigs. The young men did not see them.

"Are we still going to the ruins of Tupawaroka and Tupamarangi?" Makasuli asked Gamati quietly.

Gamati hesitated for a moment. Considering the dangers of the journey, they had been lucky to be able to bring the young men along to help them. However, if they now continued to look for Tupawaroka and Tupamarangi, they would have to spend a few nights in the wild, needing more provisions and a good place to sleep. The two kampongs were quite far from Tupawalili, and they traveled with two children.

"Perhaps we should come back another time," Gamati said.

"If we wait till later, we have to look for another excuse to tell Ronasundu. I'm afraid he'll become suspicious. Perhaps we should finish now," Makasuli answered.

Gamati had other concerns. He did not want the three young men to know they carried gold and later sneak back by themselves to dig for more gold.

"They didn't see us put the pots in the sarongs, did they?" Makasuli asked.

"I don't think so, but who knows if on our way back to Tuna the sarongs fall and they see the gold. Maybe that'll inspire them to steal it and we'll lose our chance to buy the arumbae."

"You're right. I didn't think that far ahead," Makasuli agreed.

After weighing their options, Gamati and Makasuli decided to only get the gold in Tupawalili this time. Anyway, if they dug up all the gold, Gamati would not have the proper place to keep it in Tuna. He and his grandchildren were only temporary lodgers in Ronasundu's hut.

Gamati and Makasuli agreed to keep some of the gold in Makasuli's hut without even telling his wife or children. Makasuli was afraid they would be tempted. The first thing they would do when they arrived in Tuna would be to count the gold. They then could make an educated guess whether the ship maker in the Kei Islands would accept it for the payment, or demand more.

The Keis were known for their mastery in fine shipbuilding. Makasuli knew a lot of ship builders there. As fellow survivors from the Banda Islands, the Keis often gave him privileges.

"What kind of ship should we order?" Makasuli asked.

"Later, when we get to the northern islands, we need an arumbae to enable us to sail far. Now, we need a boat to sail north. Surely we don't need to ask for an arumbae yet," Gamati argued. "For the short trip north, we only need a small boat. Perhaps a lepa-lepa or a rurehe will do. And we don't have to buy it, we can borrow it from a person who has one, and give him something as a token of our gratitude. We can give him silk fabrics, big plates, or other things he might need."

"Yes, I agree. We have to plan our departure down to the last details. We can't tell anyone, lest they betray us."

Gamati handed the matters of getting a boat and ordering the building of an arumbae to Makasuli. Meanwhile, he would try to collect information regarding the clove tree saplings or seeds.

The journey southeast to the Kei Islands would not be an easy one. They had to wait for the right wind to sail. Then, after receiving an order to build a ship, the shipbuilders had to search for the right type of wood in the forest, fell the tree, and drag it to the workplace.

Gamati and Makasuli knew that in general, the elders and the villagers were against the VOC. Many of their kin had died at the hands of the Dutch. Gamati himself did not want a life filled with conflict. He enjoyed working and sailing in peace for a purpose.

Makasuli was also tired of fighting. He had seen the outcome. His tribe had perished as a result of it.

During the decades ahead, it would be best to start a new, peaceful, and quiet life in a new place. They wanted to avoid another hongi raid. They also did not want to join the hongi draft like the Tuna villagers were forced to do as part of their subordination to the VOC.

Gamati intended to secretly rally several families who were willing to face danger to come with them to Halmahera. When he told Makasuli how surprised he was not to have seen a single clove tree sapling grow between the bushes on the ruins of Tupawalili, Makasuli reminded him that the VOC had burnt the kampong to the ground, and nothing could grow underneath a fire. They did not even find any skeletal remains of humans. Perhaps the skeletons had also burned to ashes.

After they placed the pots of gold inside the sarong bags, they decided to head back to Tuna. Gamati and Makasuli carried the sarongs. Their trip home felt shorter now that they had achieved their goals.

Sobori was slightly disappointed. They had not found any remains of his parents, neither their bones nor any other remains or keepsakes. The great fire had destroyed everything on that ill-fated night. For the rest of their trip, he was mostly silent.

While they were far away from Tuna, Aimuna had been carefree and happy. There was no need for her to be suspicious of the people around her. However, seeing Bori keep to himself and knowing they would soon be back in Tuna, to live in the hut that was their temporary home and where she always had to behave nicely, made her sad. Unlike during their trip to Tupawalili, Muna did not ask many questions. It was Makasuli who talked a lot; he told the youth about the medicinal properties of the trees they found in the forest, how they could be used to cure a wound, fever, etc. The young men were happy to learn new things.

***

The villagers of Tuna were preparing a thanksgiving celebration. The clove harvest in Tuna and a few neighboring kampongs had gone well. Even though the farmers had to hand all the cloves to the VOC in exchange for items of inferior quality, the people of Tuna were still going to throw the party. They invited a mauweng along with some elders, and members of the tribal council. They started the party before the young people arrived.

This party had no particular name nor did it have a particular theme. It was just a means for the young men and women to meet and socialize, and have a good time together. It was a break from their monotonous lives. They needed to dance and sing, eat something different from what they had every day. They needed new opportunities to make new acquaintances and even to find a match. Since it was not an elaborate traditional ceremony, it did not cost a lot. The families donated the food and beverages. The local musicians performed for free. There were conch shell blowers, trumpet players, the soothing tunes of bamboo flutes, drums and gongs. They ensured a merry atmosphere for the party. Anyone could sing, dance, and recite funny pantoums. The young people were allowed, albeit only for that night, to get acquainted and the boys could even make advances toward a younger girl.

The party would be held in the large front yard of Grandpa Ronasundu's hut. He was thought of as a "rich man" in Tuna as he came from a prominent family, and was a middleman in the dried clove trade. People came to him to ask for advice and to establish a business relationship. Those who were dubbed "rich" were generally better off than other inhabitants of the kampong. They had more acreage, more clove trees, and many household servants.

At that time it was common for household servants not to get paid. Most of them were distant or close poor relatives of the family they worked for. It was very rare for a rich man to buy his workers from the slave market. That was why the workers did not look that much different from other natives. The rich men were usually devoted to traditions, so they were well respected.

It was different with the slaves who worked in the households of the Dutch in Ambon or at the VOC fort on Saparua. They usually worked for the white men who were tall, big-boned, and had eyes of many different colors. Some were blue-eyed; others had gray or brown eyes. It was the same thing with their hair color; some were blond, the color of the morning sunlight, while others had gray hair the color of shining silver yarn; and still others had reddish or brown hair. On the other hand, all the natives' hair color was black, and their skin dark brown, with an occasional light brown skin the color of langsat.

Grandpa Rona was delighted that his front yard could be of use to the community. The atmosphere would be lively. His big hut and yard had turned quiet since all of his children married and moved away from Seram. The old couple was frail; they rarely left their hut but loved to watch the merriment of a party at their home.

The youth of the kampong were busy preparing the party. They collected a large amount of bamboo to build a stage for musicians with their instruments and dancers.

In her kitchen, Grandma Rona supervised the cooks who prepared catties of sticky rice, which they had acquired by trading cloves. Sticky rice was only served at festive events, such as weddings, harvest parties, or at the ceremony of appointing a new kampong chief.

The sticky rice was seasoned with Java almonds and wrapped in coconut leaves. The small packets were then boiled in coconut milk, spices, and salt. Savory and fragrant, it tasted so good everyone would eat at least two portions. The rice dish was the guests favorite. Rich coconut milk was not a daily ingredient in the kampong's kitchen, it was also used for every snack at festive events.

And of course, there were various fish dishes. They were, after all, surrounded by the all-giving ocean. There were fishes in various sizes and types cooked in coconut milk, seasoned with cloves and nutmeg, turmeric, and young mangoes; a variety of dishes to indulge every palate.

Grandpa Rona did not like people to get drunk on his property. The sopi, a sugar palm tree wine, was only served very late into the night, when the party was almost over. Grandpa Rona preferred the men to get drunk in their own homes.

"Grandpa, what if they ask for the sopi at the beginning of the party? What should I say?" asked a household servant tasked with keeping an eye on the jugs filled with sopi.

"Hmm, that would be difficult. There can't be a party without liquor, right? Tell them it's not done yet. Tell them to wait for a few moments."

"What if they get angry and won't believe me?"

"Tell them to see me. I'll tell them the sopi is still in the top of the palm tree." Grandpa Rona laughed, and the workers joined him.

Grandma Rona remained quiet.

The day before, the kitchen help had caught a wild goat. The cooks marinated the meat in a mixture of special spices, and then roasted it. Other household servants had prepared pickled clove flower. Clove flowers in full bloom were not as fragrant as the buds. They pickled the flowers in a mixture of water, sugar, salt, and vinegar. This dish was to refresh the mouth after eating rich, spicy food such as roasted fish. It tasted sweet, sour, and aromatic. This dish could not be found in any other part of the world, except for Seram.

Other household servants prepared betel quids, made up of betel leaves, slaked lime, some *gambier*, and betel nut. They would serve this to welcome honored guests. It also refreshed the mouth and breath when chewed after a meal. Sometimes one or two dried clove buds were added to the chewing wad.

A young man came into the kitchen and asked where they should put the extra torches. Grandpa Rona answered they would not need any extra torches since the moon was full.

Grandpa Rona asked his wife whether she had prepared enough sticky rice cakes, roasted goat meat, and other dishes. They had also invited the youth from their neighbor kampongs, including the kampong that had recently received Tuna's help at their harvest.

Grandma Rona did not know for sure, but they had wrapped a lot of sticky rice. It was ready to be steamed and then served to the guests.

"Yes, as long as we do not run out of food. That would be embarrassing. The guests will get angry, and then drink too much. Next, they'd get drunk." Grandpa Rona was also concerned about the supply of betel quids. A shortage would be considered disrespectful to the honored guests.

As per tradition, some elders from the neighboring kampongs were invited as a courtesy. When young people had a party, some honored elders attended the opening and sat around for a while. This was a sign that the elders knew and approved of the party.

The mouthwatering aroma of roasting goat meat and large fish wafted everywhere. The party had not even started yet. Grandpa Rona said to hold the cooking. Once most of the guests were present, they could finish the roasting until the goat meat and fish were fully cooked. That way it would not take long to serve the dishes.

Five middle-aged men came past midday. They introduced themselves as the emissaries from Wael, Rima, and Wane. These kampongs were across the bay from Tuna and they had to come by boat. Tuna and the three villages fell under the jurisdiction of the resident of Saparua.

The men were well built, although some started to have gray hair. They wore all-black outfits and cream-colored headbands made of Chinese silk. They paused a few meters from the hut ladder and called out their greeting, "Tabea! Tabea! We're from the kampongs across the bay."

Grandpa Ronasundu hurriedly left the kitchen and went to the front porch. He nodded and replied, "Tabea. Please come up, *Bapa-bapa.*" He wondered who they were.

The five men ascended the ladder and took a seat on the mats that had just been spread. They made small talk about their boat trip to Tuna and the season of clove harvest, while the household servants served betel quid and drinking water. It turned out that their main mission was to collect some mats.

"If any of you, in this hut or other huts in this kampong, have any extra mats, we'd very much like to collect them," one of the guests said.

"What are you collecting mats for?" Ronasundu was puzzled.

"There was an emissary from Saparua. He said that the head of Pani-pani, a Dutchman, needed a lot of mats. There are a lot of slaves on Pani-pani's new clove plantation, and he said that he needs the mats for the workers to sleep on."

"We do have mats, but only for our own use. It'll take a long time to make them," Rona answered.

"Yes, we said that too. But our kampong chief said to look for mats someplace else. Perhaps others have extra mats."

"No, we don't have extra mats, I'm sorry. We use all of our mats," Rona answered politely.

The guests nodded. They chewed the betel and drank. Since it was still lunchtime, Ronasundu offered them lunch. They thanked him and said they had to hurry to check with the other kampongs before sunset. They asked what the celebration was for. Grandpa Rona said the boys and girls wanted to have a good time after the harvest. The guests nodded and Grandpa Rona saw them out to his front yard.

After the five men left, Ronasundu was silent. He reflected on the visit for a long time. He could not figure out why the Dutch would need mats for the slaves on their new plantation on Saparua. That was very strange. VOC people were usually cruel and far from compassionate to the natives. They would never give their slaves mats to sleep on.

Gamati and his family, Makasuli from Banda, and many more families he knew, were a perfect example. Their families, relatives, and fellow villagers were all separated, each not knowing the whereabouts of the others. It was unclear whether they would ever be reunited. It was said that all the natives of Banda had perished in a fight against the VOC.

Ronasundu pondered, *How strange that Pani-pani now has its own clove plantation on Saparua. Who planted the trees? It must be the natives. It's impossible Pani-pani did it themselves. They wouldn't know how. Now that they have their own clove plantation, will they still need cloves from us, the natives? Hopefully not.*

Ronasundu hoped that he now would be able to trade again with traders from Tuban, Jepara, Malacca, Banten, and Makassar, and also with the Arabs and Chinese. In his simple mind, Ronasundu genuinely believed things still could turn out for the best. He told his wife he regretted that Sobori and Aimuna had not returned from the forest yet. If they were here, they could sing and dance. So far, their lives had been pretty gloomy.

Not long after the departure of the five guests, another group of guests arrived. The three of them were dressed nicely in colorful cotton garments. They covered their heads with silk headbands, a sign that they were not just ordinary people. It seemed that they were officials of the sultanate.

"Tabea! Tabea, Bapa," they called out their greeting respectfully.

Ronasundu bowed to show his respect and invited them to come up.

The servants served a plate of nicely folded betel leaves on the mat as they exchanged small talk. One must always behave with good manners toward the executives of the palace, and he was after all a rich man who took care of all the trades of his kampong. He did not want to be considered disrespectful.

"Looks like you are throwing a party, Bapa," one of the officials said.

"Yes, we are, later in the evening," Rona replied cordially.

"Is it a wedding party?"

"No. The youths of three kampongs in this area just finished the clove harvest. After the hard work, they want to have a good time. Tomorrow they have to go back to the plantations and work again as usual. I let them have fun as long as they don't get drunk."

"So we came at the right time. We heard there is a pretty young woman and a handsome lad in this kampong. The sultan's palace in Ternate is looking for young people to entertain the sultan and his family. They'll sing and dance, and welcome all the visitors to the palace. We'd like to see them; maybe we want to take them to the palace," the leader of the group said.

Ronasundu nodded and answered respectfully, "Forgive me, Tuang. They're not here now. They went to the forest to look for some wild honey. It'll take quite some time for them to return."

Everyone was silent for a moment.

"But they *will* return, right? We'll come back later to take a look at both of them."

"As you please, Tuang, but I really don't know when they will return."

"That's fine. Since we're here, we'll just attend this party and take a look at other girls and boys. Who knows, there might be a few attractive ones we can take to the palace," the group leader said.

"You're all very welcome, Tuang," Rona answered cordially, even though he was a bit concerned. Their presence might disrupt the youths' festive mood.

The three emissaries of the palace never left Tuna that night. They joined the singing and dancing, even though they were not invited.

Although Ronasundu was bothered, he behaved graciously. *If Pani-pani could attack a kampong so small and isolated as Gamati's kampong, there must be a spy, a traitor among the natives. Now who's the spy for these palace emissaries?* Fortunately, he had asked the kampong chief's permission to throw a party.

It was not very dark that night. The full moon was already out before the sun's brilliant ball of fire had disappeared completely. The moonlight was soft. Grandpa Rona was right; they did not need extra torches that evening. The four big torches at each corner of the yard, a sign that a celebration was taking place, were sufficient.

Gradually the young people began drifting in. They took a seat on the mats in the front yard. The younger children who were not invited crowded the stage set up for the musicians. They were curious and excited to take a peek at the festivities. Their parents had given them permission to stay until dark. Their loud chatter and comments made quite a merry racket.

The musicians took their seats on the mats on the front porch. Everyone looked fresh and sharp. The young men wore colorful headbands, which made the handsome ones look even more handsome. The pretty young women looked even prettier wearing special scarves around their shoulders or the napes of their necks. They all had their hair put up in a bun at the top of their heads and decorated it with fragrant frangipani or jasmine. They wore their best sarong with a vibrant color top. All the young women looked beautiful.

Grandpa and Grandma Rona also wore their best attire: dark-colored sarongs and white silk tops. Grandma Rona had put up her wavy hair in a bun on top of her head. She had tucked a frangipani blossom in her bun. Anyone standing near her could smell the lovely scent.

As soon as the sun set, Grandpa Rona welcomed his guests. "Welcome. Please, enjoy this wonderful night," he said then asked everyone to momentarily forget about the impending possibility of war, the hongi raids, clove extirpation, and embargo from the VOC.

He recited a pantoum:

> *When planting bitter melon during the east wind season*
> *Remember to plant on flat lands*
> *Hey, you young men and women*
> *Come and sit to listen to this story.*

Everyone cheered and clapped. "Yes, Grandpa Rona, please tell us a story about the time you were the captain of a ship."

Ronasundu nodded and smiled. His silver hair was completely covered under a headband. "Yes. Later, I'll tell stories. I promise. Now, let's eat first. There's sticky rice, roasted wild goat, and big fish. Enjoy!"

Everyone approached a table constructed of a long board propped up on big rocks that served as the legs. There were several large banana leaves spread on it. Each leaf served a dish: the sticky rice wrapped in coconut leaves, chunks of roasted goat meat, pieces of roasted spiced fish, etc. There were no soupy dishes. Those who liked the pickled clove flower could take some to finish their meal and neutralize the fat.

The young men soon were busy eating, although they sometimes stole a glance at the young women who were serving food. The young women appeared vibrant. Dressed nicely, they looked very attractive. When someone asked about Grandpa Rona's grandchildren, the girl and the boy, he said they went to another kampong and had not returned.

Soon thereafter, someone asked for sopi.

Grandpa Rona said that it was not ready yet. They had started a bit late with the preparation.

Afterwards, Grandpa Rona told a story about a sacred sea eagle from Seram. He was the guardian of several coastline kampongs. When the enemy came from the sea, he would cry loudly. Then a convocation of sea eagles would swoop down to attack the enemy; some would peck at the eyes of the captains of the ships. Meanwhile the alerted villagers prepared a welcome attack. A shower of arrows, sharpened bamboo spears, and stones would meet the enemies if they should moor and attack the kampongs.

When the enemy advanced from the interior, the sacred eagle would perch on the roof of a rich man of the kampong and make noisy calls. Then, when the men were armed and ready, he guided them to the location of the enemies.

Everyone liked the story and applauded. A guest asked why, if the eagle was so sacred and had the powers to protect the kampong, did he not help the natives of Seram to fend off the VOC?

"Pani-pani has more powerful weapons. They have gunpowder, which they can explode from afar. We only have arrows and swords and have to face the enemy up close. That's why," Grandpa Rona explained.

"Ooooh," everyone sighed.

Grandpa Rona asked who else wanted to tell a story. Perhaps someone could share a story about his experiences at sea or in the forest; about cutting the flower of the sugar palm tree to make the sopi. Or maybe someone had encountered the big-horned buck, or a sow that had just delivered her piglets.

A young man rose to the challenge.

He considered his experience special, because just a few days back, he had come in direct contact with a Dutchman. Three Dutchmen had visited the clove plantation where he worked and one of them wanted to paint the clove pickers. Most natives had never seen a Dutchman up close. A lot of them did not even want to meet a Dutchman because they were afraid. The Dutch had a bad reputation.

None of the pickers wanted their face painted. It was taboo to paint a human face. The painting could be used for sorcery.

"What do they look like?" The crowd was curious.

"They're tall, big-boned men. They've very sharp noses. I was afraid to look into their big eyes. Their eyes aren't black. Some have blue eyes. And some have eyes the color of the sky when it's about to rain. I don't think anyone here has eyes with those colors."

"Why did they come to the pata cengkei?" Grandpa Rona asked.

"They wanted to paint the pickers and the clove trees. They also wanted to learn how to plant clove trees and write it down on paper so later our children and theirs can learn to plant clove trees."

Grandpa Rona remembered the guests who came earlier. They were looking for mats, not anything to paint. He told the young storyteller about the guests who said the Dutch were looking for mats.

"Yes, yes, that's true, Grandpa. They were also asking for a lot of mats."

"What do they need a lot of mats for?"

"I didn't ask. Perhaps they wanted to sit around in their homes under the full moon such as tonight," the young man answered.

Everyone laughed.

"Has any of you seen a Dutchman's house? Do they sit on mats or chairs?" a pretty young woman asked.

"That's great, so you've talked with Dutch people," others praised the young man.

"Let's pray to moyang-moyang so the Dutch people won't come to Tuna. I'm afraid that they'll ask for everything we have. They'll ask for our mats, our cloves, our nutmeg, our smoked fish. They might also ask for our pretty girls and then we won't have any pretty girls left."

"Yes, Grandpa, that's scary," the young men and women replied in unison.

After that Ronasundu said that he was tired and sleepy. He and his wife wanted to rest inside. He allowed the party to continue and everyone to have a good time, as long as no one got drunk.

Ronasundu and his wife approached the three emissaries from the sultanate to excuse themselves. The guests did not say they wanted to spend the night. So the couple went to bed. Both of them hoped that Gamati would not return until the party was over. "Poor Muna and Bori," they sighed. "They'll definitely be ordered to join the party."

The musicians began to play. The melodious sound of the solo flute was interposed with the sounds of the arbabu, drums, and gongs. The cool evening breeze caressed the guests, and filled the air with the fragrance of the frangipani flowers in the young women's hair. The youth started to recite more pantoums. They started with an opening piece, then followed with satirical selections and even declared their affection using pantoums.

A handsome young man known as a good fisherman recited:

> *Walking on the beach one evening*
> *My feet were wet and I couldn't run*
> *Hey boys and girls,*
> *Let's sing and dance.*

The crowd cheered and clapped. The fisherman smiled, happy with the response.

The music continued, lively and inviting. People began to dance.

Another young man wearing a Tuban batik headband walked to the stage to answer the pantoum.

> *Your feet were wet, you couldn't run*
> *Leaf of paddy oats can't be picked*
> *The singing and dancing have begun*
> *Bring out the shawls and lensos.*

Everyone cheered while the young men took their lensos, and waved their big handkerchiefs to the flattered girls. A young man who waved a fine silk lenso, perhaps from Tuban or China, responded,

> *If you can't pick the paddy oat leaf*
> *Pick the Marian plums instead*
> *Hey, Miss, here's my handkerchief*
> *Please accept it.*

The pretty girl he approached accepted the handkerchief and they walked to the stage together. Dancing, they swirled and moved agilely to the tune of the dynamic and lively music. Their steps were measured; forward and backward. Sometimes they went around each other or held hands.

Then there was another pantoum response:

What replaces Marian plums?
It's the Java almond season now.
Ah, the flutes, gongs, lensos, and drums
Invite us all to dance.

The dance was called the *lego-lego* dance. It originated from a kingdom up north. Long ago, the kampong chief introduced it to Seram, mainly in Tuna. It had since become a popular folk dance.

The sopi was finally served. The household servant warned the young men not to drink too much. They had only prepared a small amount of the "fiery water."

The music grew louder. Now the low tone of conch shell trumpets coalesced harmoniously with the sounds of the arbabu and singing. Then the musicians played an animated folk song, accompanied by drums and gongs.

A group of girls from a neighboring kampong sung a pantoum:

Wash your bowls by the well
Wrap the clean ones in leaves
My friend, don't yet bid us farewell
If you do, please don't be gone long.

A group of young men from Tuna quickly responded with boisterous voices,

If we don't meet, for a long time,
A deep longing in my heart is all I'll feel
If I leave you for years, it won't be a crime
As long as you wait for me, that's my appeal.

Everyone cheered loudly. The atmosphere was getting merrier. The dancing became livelier; the atmosphere was filled with the vibrant energy of young people. Then a group of girls responded to the previous pantoum:

The moon is big, when it's full.
I'll wait a long time for you
If you bring me a gift of fine Tuban fabric.

There were still more pantoums recited that night. Many were funny or flirtatious. The lively exchange of words accompanied by the beat of the drums and the sound of gongs lightened the atmosphere. This merriment made everyone forget, albeit momentarily, the threat of war on Seram.

The recent harvest of cloves was already wrapped up neatly and ready to be taken to the VOC storage during the next couple of days.

The harvest was stored in Ronasundu's hut. Tuna had harvested a half *bahar* of cloves. Two other kampongs had also deposited their harvests around a half bahar for each kampong. The total of one and a half bahars of cloves was far more than last year's production, which was only one bahar.

It was almost dawn, and all the partygoers were exhausted but happy. There was no unwanted riot that night as no one got drunk. Reluctant to go home, they decided to wait for the sunrise. The girls slept on the mats spread on the front porch; the boys slept on the mats in the front yard.

The sleeping crowd looked serene and peaceful, in contrast to the devastation happening throughout the Moluccas. The emissaries of the sultanate lay sprawled like beggars next to the others. Ronasundu, their host, did not know that his high-ranking guests slept on mats in the front yard.

The sultanate's emissaries had found several attractive boys and girls, but they did not know the youths' families yet. One of the conditions to become a member of the sultan's court was to be offspring from a respectable family, not slaves.

***

The governor had summoned the resident of Saparua. Lucas de Vries had spent two nights in the fort on Ambon. He now sat in the governor's office, along with an assistant who took the minutes of the meeting. Bertie and Karel, the experts on tropical plants who supervised the VOC's pioneering clove plantation on Saparua, were with him.

The governor of Ambon and his staff had been discussing the pilot clove plantation for two nights. Not all of their experiments had worked out. Fifty clove saplings had died of unknown causes. The farmers, a number of middle-aged natives, had not been able to come up with a reason either. The weather was not too hot, and it had rained only rarely.

Resident de Vries voiced his concern about the perishing of the clove trees on the five small islands where they originated before the VOC plantations were established. If that happened, they would have no place from which to acquire new clove tree saplings. He subtly stated they should not have extirpated the God-given clove trees that grew naturally in those islands. It was now proven that the clove trees, cultivated with the utmost care and tended like a human baby, could still perish in a natural way.

Lucas proposed postponing the clove trees extirpation as ordered by the VOC's headquarters in Holland. They should wait until their trial plantations on Ambon, Saparua, and Niwela flourished and their own trees successfully produced new saplings. Lucas pointed out that the VOC executives in Holland did not know the real situation.

Governor Martinus de Bruijn agreed with the resident and the opinions of Karel and Bertie, who worked with the resident on Saparua. However, he was reluctant to recommend the resident's proposal to the main office. They would be furious. Besides, the postal service would take too long to deliver a message quickly enough to make a difference. He said, "The executives in Holland will never agree."

The Assembly of the Lords Seventeen was disgruntled with the surplus on the international clove market. Naturally, the price plummeted. They had invested large capital to acquire the two prized spices. Not to mention the many lives that were lost during the voyage east. The group of aristocrats needed a return on their investment.

The resident did not respond directly to the governor's statements. Lucas de Vries was a sensitive man, even passive in character. He had had a rather sad childhood. His mother had died when he was still a young boy and he grew up with no permanent home. Fortunately, good people like the Wijnens asked him to join their animal show. These bitter experiences had influenced his character. He was used to pleasing other people, especially those he stayed with.

Now, Lucas subtly wondered out loud, "How would The Assembly of the Lords Seventeen react if they were faced with a situation in which all the VOC's clove trees had perished, after all the original trees had been extirpated? No one would be able to obtain any trees anywhere at any price. Is that not too big a risk to take?" Lucas was fully aware that without cloves and nutmeg it would be impossible to preserve all the fish, meats, and liquor that were accumulated during the summer. The process required these spices.

Karel and Bertie, the two botanists who had managed the clove plantations on Saparua for some time, stated their opinions based on their factual observations in the field. They bluntly stated that to destroy the clove trees in their place of origin was dangerous and reckless conduct. They both said that it was an act of foolish, or even worse, mad people. "How can anyone defy God the Great Creator?" Bertie protested.

"We've observed and experienced it ourselves. Without a long drought or storms from the ocean, one-third of the clove saplings died. As for the remaining two-thirds of the clove trees on Saparua, we can't guarantee whether they'd survive and flourish to become mature trees that produce," Karel said.

"If the trees on Saparua don't survive, we still have the plantation on Ambon and Niwela. Let's not be too pessimistic. This is a pioneering project; we're starting a completely new initiative. It's natural to have to learn from errors. It'll take a lot of sacrifice," the governor answered calmly.

Cultivating cloves as a trade item was certainly a new experience for the Dutch. The natives who had known the trees for thousands of years grew and harvested the trees in a natural environment. Cloves were not a main ingredient in the cuisine of either Ambon or Seram. The islanders only pickled the fully opened clove bud.

The natives started to grow clove trees deep in the interiors only after the Dutch arrived with their VOC. The rules the company imposed forced them to do so.

As a human being, the governor understood that the board of directors was motivated by greed, a voracity that bordered on madness. If they exercised some patience they surely would have their return of investment and some share of profit. He wondered how they had decided to demand a three thousand percentage of profit.

Governor de Bruijn figured the notion must have come from the investors. They had no idea of the misery the seamen who sailed to the east or the new continent west from their country had to endure. Many died during the voyage. The underprivileged crew lived in poverty and misery during their voyage and even after arrival at their destination and return to their homeland.

De Bruijn said, "Those who settled on the new islands, such as Ambon and the surrounding islands, rarely became prosperous. I'm like the three of you; I am just a tiny cog in a giant wheel. None of us is empowered to make or change policies. We simply execute the policies handed down by the executives in Holland. It doesn't matter whether we like it or not," he ended and shrugged.

Everyone was quiet for a moment. Bertie and Karel were shocked to hear de Bruijn compare himself to a cog in a wheel. He was the governor, after all. He should be able to adjust policies to local conditions. The two of them had at length discussed the impossibility of meeting the VOC's set profit margin with Resident Lucas de Vries. However, bound by traditional respect for a highly educated superior or someone of noble blood, the three of them did not voice their opinions, which were based on their field observation on Saparua.

Lucas preferred a less hostile approach to the natives. He wanted them to trade their harvest the way they knew. As a newcomer, the VOC should trade according to local rules. He said, "That way we won't need to live in constant fear the natives will ambush us when we're far from our ship. They'll be relieved to know that the foreigners who needed their cloves brought things they needed, such as clothing and metal farming tools."

The three of them wondered why Holland, despite an eighty-year ongoing war with Spain, still had not tired of hostilities.

"The Chinese, Indians, and Arabs have traded here for hundreds of years. They didn't wage war against the natives, nor try to own all plantations and monopolize the spice trade. Why do we, who only recently came here, always have to provoke the natives?" Karel was irritated.

"We have to scare them! Their own kings and sultans agreed to accept a periodic allowance from the VOC in exchange for the clove trade," the governor said, condescendingly.

"Yes, that's right. I still don't think that there is a downside to treating the natives courteously. That way, they'll respect us in return and we could live here peacefully," argued Karel, who had started to learn the local dialect.

"I know that Resident de Vries sympathizes with the natives," the governor turned to Lucas and continued, "Not surprising, given your background and education. The monks must've trained you to value all humankind."

"Yes, Sir. That's why I'm still troubled about the sleeping mats for the plantation workers on Saparua. I'm wondering how I'd feel if I were a Dutch soldier in battle against Spain and was ordered to sleep on the bare floor during the winter. Besides freezing, I'd definitely feel degraded. I feel that I'm becoming a bad person, Sir," Lucas said.

The governor only nodded. He avoided looking Lucas in the eye. The resident was correct, but de Bruijn held a very high position in the VOC and maintained an excellent relationship with the VOC's headquarters for the east in Batavia. The high officials in Batavia worked closely with the main office in Holland, particularly with the Assembly of the Lords Seventeen. The governor would never express his thoughts freely to his superiors like the three men in front of him. He simply executed the orders of the Assembly. Hopefully, the clove saplings would grow as planned. It was the only thing on his mind.

He even fantasized about being far more prosperous upon his return to Holland. His involvement in the secret spice trading in the Far East had fattened his wallet. The deed did not bother his conscience. All was fair in the pursuit of one's dreams. There was no need to be concerned about other people, strangers, to boot, who looked completely different from his own race.

The governor continued the meeting. He returned to the discussion about the hongi and the extirpation expedition to the Banda Islands. They had not finished talking about this big plan.

A map of the southern region of the Moluccas, which they believed to be accurate, was spread on the table. There were many clusters of tiny islands; some were mere volcanoes rising above the water's surface from the ocean floor.

These islands were believed to be the origins of nutmeg. The fruit is very fragrant. Mace, the lacy, brilliant red aril around the seed shell, is even more fragrant than the seed itself.

When the VOC conquered the Banda Islands in 1621, the natives all perished in the war. The nutmeg plantation owners and their workers who occupied the islands now were all settlers. In fact, the VOC had placed them there.

They were the *perkeniers*, big plantation owners who were white men the VOC had lured to Banda with empty promises of high rewards. Later, the perkeniers would learn the hard way that ownership of trees bearing golden fruit only translated into being in debt to the VOC for generations to come. Like the natives, the perkeniers were only allowed to trade with the VOC at a fixed price. Hence, the perkeniers were dissatisfied and found ways to secretly trade with others.

Those who worked on the big plantations under the hot sun were slaves bought on other islands. Most of them came from Java, the islands of Sangihe and Talaud, Seram, Bali, and many others.

The Assembly in Amsterdam was already suspicious of the secret nutmeg trade with other traders. They were mainly suspicious of the traders from Makassar and the Portuguese, who were the first Europeans who came to the Spice Islands.

According to the traders at the international market in Genoa, the Chinese traders brought the spices. They transported their trade items across deserts and snowy fields with large caravans of camels.

The caravans' destination was Holland, the center of the international spice trade at that time. The Assembly of the Lords Seventeen was determined to eliminate this artery.

"That's why we have to conduct the hongi in the southeast region. We'll outfit four large ships with armed soldiers and canons. The provisions have been prepared. We notified the resident of Banda. They are ready to join forces with us," the governor said tersely and continued, "There is, however, a small island that's not ours. There's still an English trade representative there. We have to disarm the fort on Run as well. Who knows if the pilferers might hide there."

The governor's pronouncement was met by silence. The ocean breeze caressed the men's perspiring bodies with cool strokes.

"What other types of vessels do we have to prepare besides the war ships, Mister Governor?" Lucas asked.

"We have to prepare boats to carry our supplies. What has been done to recruit the natives' boats?" the governor said.

"There are several kampongs here on Ambon. I've ordered four of them to join the hongi. They'll bring their own war vessels, which they call kora-kora. The boats will be manned and they'll bring along their own provisions. We'll let their own leaders do the hard work of making all the arrangements."

Everyone nodded while they continued to pore over the map. The governor explained the routes they were going to take. He also laid out the strategy for combat should they come across enemies at sea. He stressed that they had to be combat-ready.

Several kampongs on the southern side of Seram were ordered to prepare kora-koras. They also had to provide their own crew, provisions, and weapons.

"Why do they have to provide their own weapons, Governor?" Lucas asked.

"Here, all male adults always carry weapons when they leave their homes. They usually carry machetes, knives, or axes. When they go to their plantation, they also bring other tools, such as long knives, swords, hoes, and many more. It's mandatory here." The governor shrugged.

"So we don't lend or give them weapons?" Lucas figured that since it was the VOC that had ordered the natives to join the hongi expedition, it was their responsibility to arrange for provisions and weapons.

"Oh, no, no. We already have enough trouble with funding our own soldiers' provisions and weapons. The natives have to take care of their own needs for this hongi to the southeast."

The topic of their conversation soon shifted to the conditions of the season: wind speed, the probability of rain and storm. It was not easy to plan for the hongi expedition even though, at that time, the VOC was a great force in the east. At the end of a dry season, it was sometimes windless. This left the ship becalmed, unable to move as it waited for the wind, and an enemy could easily attack it.

"Mister Governor, do we need to join the hongi expedition? We've no experience in tending nutmeg trees," one of the botanists said.

"Yes, of course. Aren't you two botanists? If you don't know anything about nutmeg trees, it's a perfect opportunity to learn. You two can meet the perkeniers and the slaves of the plantations. Their expertise can be a great asset for us. Who knows, maybe someday we'll be ordered to start a nutmeg plantation on Ambon or Seram. We'll be ready when that happens."

The resident planned to show a selection of his paintings to the governor and the two botanists later that night. As the paintings would be placed in the VOC's archives, he planned to give a detailed explanation of the people he painted, the sceneries and places of importance to the VOC. In the selection, Lucas also included the paintings of places he had visited in Africa, India, Malacca, and Banten.

The governor briefly mentioned that, time permitting, he would invite several families with daughters to join them for dinner and look at the resident's paintings. "The girls would be good company for our two young botanists. Our resident is also a bachelor and might need a lady friend too," the governor joked.

He continued to explain about the mixed marriages on Ambon. "The VOC doesn't bring Dutch girls to the East. Dutch women here are usually the officials' or ministers' wives. If the Dutch men or other white men want to have a wife, they'll choose a local woman. She could be native or half-native. If she's a native, she'll have a different religion, and they can't marry in church. The marriage will be an illegal or unregistered marriage. However, the children will be acknowledged by the law. If the woman is half Dutch but born here, she can't be brought back to Holland."

"So what happens when we have to go back to Holland?" Lucas asked.

"Sadly, she has to be left here."

"Why?" Karel was furious.

"That's how the Assembly of the Lords Seventeen protects the purity of the Dutch race," the governor said.

"Ha ha. Is there any pure race in this world, Mister Governor? All nations that have trading relations will eventually mix racially and influence each other. Some people will fall in love, and some will hate each other. I don't understand the Assembly of the Lords Seventeen's way of thinking. Is it not a rule that once we're married, we're forbidden to divorce?" Lucas shook his head in disbelief.

The governor did not answer. He merely shrugged his shoulders and raised his hands.

The meeting was adjourned. Bertie, Karel, and Lucas left the room and went straight to the beach, far from the fort. The clean ocean air, the beautiful scenery of the fish-eating birds and the crooked-beaked birds flying about with the background of an orange sky eased the minds of the three young men. The waves started to swell as they rolled to the beach. It looked as if it would be high tide soon.

They consoled themselves by listening to the crashing waves and watching the flags of the fishing boats, coming home from fishing on the vast ocean. The information regarding wives who could not be brought home had deeply disturbed them. During church services they were always told that marriage was sacred, a once-in-a-lifetime bond. Now they were told that if they were to marry a non-Dutch girl here they could not take her home. *Wasn't that the same thing as a divorce?*

Lucas gradually discovered that much of his employer's logic was askew and contradictory. His conscience grew more troubled.

Chapter 6

Gamati did not want to be seen by a lot of people when they entered the kampong. He purposely arrived when it was almost dark, and hoped to keep a curious crowd from swarming to the Ronasundus' house. He also did not want anyone to ask what they carried inside the sarong sacks. The gold was very valuable. It was not to be flaunted and only used in an emergency situation. The fewer people who knew they had returned from the forest, the better.

Dopa, Ages, and Beilang walked in the front, followed by Sobori and Aimuna. The two old men brought up the rear. Each of them carried digging tools.

Gamati carried the sack with the gold, which was neatly packed and tied with dry leaves and fibers and hidden under a pile of ripe mangosteens and wild water apples. They brought an ample supply of fruit. If anyone asked what they brought back from the forest, he would show them the fruit.

Makasuli did not stop by Ronasundu's hut; he walked straight home, which was farther than Tuna. He had also hidden the gold he carried beneath some fruit.

At the edge of the kampong, they ran across a couple of Ronasundu's household servants, who offered to help carry the heavy sacks and tools.

Gamati politely said that even though he was an old man, he still had the strength to work. He suggested they help Aimuna who carried the ropes.

Gamati was relieved he at least had the funds to start building the boat they needed to move to the northern islands.

Aimuna and Sobori were also happy. They were filled with impressions of a new place completely different from Tuna. Their eyes had feasted on dark green plants, and rushing streams filled with freshwater fish. They had heard birds with various songs and seen a cockatoo on its nest. They had not only been able to watch agile wild animals, they also had seen several industrious nocturnal creatures. They had inhaled the smell of humus on the forest floor.

Aimuna and Sobori vividly remembered the thrilling trip to the cave behind the waterfall. Too bad it had been such a short adventure.

Aimuna loved the peaceful surroundings amidst millions of leaves and flowers. She asked her grandfather to take her more often to the forest.

Gamati agreed. They were not busy and had a two-month or so supply of dried fish, sago, and firewood. He said, "If you're not lazy and collect the supplies, I can spare several days to go to the forest with you. You also have to learn to use the bow, and find your way in the forest."

Muna was thrilled. Without talks about possible hongi attacks on their village and no need to be anxious about strangers visiting them, the trip to the forest had been relaxing. Life in the forest had felt incredibly peaceful.

Villagers soon congregated in the Ronasundus' hut; such was their tradition. They asked many questions. The household servants prepared meals for the group who had just returned home. Gamati quickly took the fruit he brought from the forest out of his sarong sack. When the visitors were busy peeling the fruit, he sneaked into his room to put away the sack containing gold.

His room was small and did not have a door. As with most homes, there were no cupboards or chests. Even though the sarong was dirty from lying on the forest's floor, Gamati put it near his sleeping mat.

He told Sobori to keep an eye on the room, lest someone enter it. Dopa, Ages, and Beilang feasted on leftovers from the party, fresh fish from the river, and fragrant sticky rice.

People asked about the conditions of the forest. Which fruits were in season, did they run into the Halefurus, what animals did they see in the forest, etc.? They wondered if Aimuna had any troubles in the forest. She was only a young girl, after all.

Grandma Rona jokingly said that Aimuna was going to be a tough Seram woman who was as capable as the men to go into the forest. Grandma looked forward to the day Aimuna would train in using a bow and arrow. In her younger days, Grandma Rona was skilled in using a bow and arrow and dove in the sea. However, she could not stand the sight of blood, so usually someone else skinned and cut her kills.

Muna smiled as she listened to Grandma Rona's story. She would love to take another trip to the forest. Even though they were exhausted, they stayed up late that night telling stories. Dopa, Ages, and Beilang were to spend the night and return home the next morning.

It turned out that the happiness and ease of the evening was short-lived. In the morning, Grandpa Rona delivered bad news. He said to Gamati, "On the evening we had the party while you were away, emissaries from the palace visited. They were elders from the neighboring kampongs."

"Oh, that's a great honor to us and this kampong. Why did they come?" Gamati felt rather proud.

"They heard that there is a good-looking young man and beautiful girl in this kampong. They came to see them."

"What for?" Gamati asked.

"They said that if these youngsters met the palace's requirements, they were going to take them to the palace on Ternate to entertain the sultan and the queen with their dancing and singing."

Gamati asked which family the youngsters the emissaries were interested in belonged to. He was not a native of Tuna, and did not know all of the families there. Grandpa and Grandma Rona answered that both of the youngsters lived in their own hut.

"They were asking for Aimuna and Sobori?" Gamati asked, taken aback.

"That's right, my brother. This is a bad news, I think. They are the only youngsters living in this hut."

Gamati froze.

Many of the villagers would feel happy to hear such news. If their child were to be taken to live in the palace, his or her family would feel very proud. Their child was to be part of the royal family and perhaps bring luck to the rest of the villagers.

A girl chosen for her beauty to be a palace entertainer would be trained in singing and dancing. She would also learn to play several musical instruments such as the flute or the high-pitched arbabu fiddle. She would wear beautiful garments, greet honored guests, and be called a *jojaro ici*, a royal maid.

A boy would be a footman and keeper of the room keys for the sultan's family members. He would hold the royal umbrella when they went outdoors. It was an honorable and esteemed position for the villagers.

However, Gamati had different plans. He was a free islander who wanted to spend the rest of his life at sea. He was a great sailor and trader. After his love for his late wife, the thousands of islands and the vast ocean were the second love of his life.

Gamati felt he had to keep his and Kurubela's lineage going. He could not allow it to perish. Kurubela had to have a sea-loving child, grandchild, great-grandchild, great-great-grandchild, and so on.

Sobori's children needed to own their own secret clove plantation. They had to continue the resistance, or at least refuse to work with the VOC. The same applied to Aimuna. Both of them had to live free, planting and trading their own cloves. They had to uphold their ancestors' traditions. If necessary, they would live deep in the forest. Gamati had plans for a new life in a new place, far away from the VOC.

Gamati was deeply troubled by the story about the palace emissaries' visit. However, his experience in dealing with the VOC, as well as betrayal by other people, had taught him to control his emotions. He never showed a strong reaction to news, not even to Ronasundu.

"Oh, the news about Muna and Bori must have traveled fast. Hopefully, there'll be other boys and girls who'll catch the emissaries' attention. That way, they'll have a choice." Gamati pretended to be humble.

"Yes, let's hope they'll find others in another kampong. The royalties and the sultan lead very comfortable lives in the palace, while we're being oppressed by Pani-pani. Tuna is now a Pani-pani slave. We have been tamed," Ronasundu answered.

"As I said before, Tuna has to wait for its youth to grow up, and learn to sail and trade before we can fight again. It's still a long time to come." Gamati sighed.

"Yes, perhaps I'll die before it happens. We still have a long way to go, Gamati," Rona said.

"So it is. Nevertheless, we have to prepare. We can't just dream about living in the palace and being close to the sultan. We have to work at sea, on the plantations, in the forest." Gamati was passionate whenever he talked about being independent. He hated the VOC and held a grudge against nobility in general for their willingness to work with the Dutch. Yet he never showed it, for fear of a traitor living in Tuna.

The conversation they had that morning was more of a formality. Rona and his wife asked him about the trip. Did they find the site of their scorched kampong? Judging from the length of time they were gone, Ronasundu thought that, even though it was still located on Seram, Gamati's kampong site must be very far. He asked if there had been anything he could salvage from the ruins.

Gamati answered the fire had burned down everything they had; all was gone. Overgrown bushes had taken over the area. Sobori had hoped to find the remains of his parents, but they had not been able to even find any trace of human skeletons.

"Have others started to build new settlements there?"

"Apparently not, Rona. The place is very isolated. We built the kampong so it would be hard for the sultanate and Pani-pani to find us. Unfortunately, they did find and destroy it."

"What happened to the secret plantations of your family in the other two kampongs?"

"We didn't go there; it was too far. I didn't want Aimuna to have to walk that far. After all, she's just a young girl."

"I heard a lot of people own a secret plantation. They planted the cloves far up in the mountains. However, I was getting old at the time they started doing it, so I did not join them."

"Yes, yes, I remember, back when we were still young, we used to look out for each other at the seaside where we traded cloves. You were very kind to the traders from Tuban and Makassar. They spoke highly of you." Gamati chuckled after giving the compliment. It was a time-honored practice among seamen to uphold their brotherly bond. As they sailed the same seas and traded together, they looked after each other in times of need. That was why Gamati had dared to ask first for Lando's and now for Ronasundu's help. Sailors had a strong sense of camaraderie. Later, when he had his own hut and kampong, he would in turn help fellow seamen in need.

Several nights after the conversation, three men visited Rona's hut. They were emissaries from the kampong chief of Tuna and some neighboring kampongs.

Gamati and his grandchildren happened to be in the hut. The men conveyed the message that Tuna had to take part in an upcoming hongi expedition.

"A hongi raid? To what island?" Ronasundu was surprised.

"It has not been decided yet, probably southward. This isn't a sultanate hongi. It's the Pani-pani."

"Why southward?"

"We don't know. We were ordered to convey this message, so you can make the necessary preparations. They need kora-koras and several months of provisions for the expedition. We'll give you more instructions later."

One of the representatives asked, "Are there a lot of young men in this kampong? And how many kora-kora do you have?"

"We've two kora-kora, but we may not have enough men. There aren't many young men here."

"We heard you've a young man living with you. You could send him in addition to others, of course. Once you know the number of men who can join the hongi, you can start to stock up food such as sago, dried fish, salt and sugar, etc."

"What's the age limit for the young men?" Ronasundu asked.

"Fifteen-year-old boys can be enlisted providing they're single. The oldest married man should not be over forty so he still will have the strength to row."

"What if a man just recently married?"

"If he's recently married and has no child, he can't join the hongi. Pani-pani wants to preserve the kampong's population."

"What's our men's duty in the hongi?"

"They will row, man the sails, and handle ropes. Also man the arumbaes, when available."

"Will they also be sent to the kampongs to fight our own people on the islands?"

"We haven't been given such orders yet. We'll tell you more later. For now, just gather the men, then prepare the food supplies. There'll be a training prior to the hongi if we are to fight. That's all for now."

Grandma Rona served a plate of fried banana picked from their plantation. The emissaries ate while chitchatting, then left.

The news struck Gamati like lightning. He was already worried about the sultan's people looking for his grandchildren to take them to the palace. And now the VOC ordered Bori to join the damned hongi, where he would take part in unleashing the same misery their own family had endured.

Gamati had made up his mind to prevent this at all cost. He and Makasuli had planned to move to the far northern islands. However, the time was not yet ripe. They only recently had retrieved the gold and were just about to look for a boat. Since they were going to build a new settlement, they needed more people, especially more young people, beyond just his and Makasuli's families. Several families of Banda refugees wanted to join. However, it was difficult to make concrete plans since they did not even have a boat yet.

Aimuna still needed the training in diving and rowing at least a kole-kole by herself before they executed their plan. Another issue was the safekeeping of the gold.

That night, Gamati tossed and turned as he tried to find a solution for his problems. He used to have help from his wife, his children, his son-in-law; now, despite his old age, he had to face the problems all by himself. He did not remember having this many problems to solve when he was younger.

Gamati mused he needed to visit Makasuli soon. He did not want to be betrayed again. Although he never investigated it, he was sure an insider had guided the men who attacked his kampong. He did not really care to know who the culprit was for fear of being saddled with an unending grudge that could not be avenged. He also did not want Bori and Muna to live burdened by such a grudge.

Kurubela had wanted them to live as free clove traders, sail their own arumbae, and co-own their plantation with the other inhabitants of a new kampong. He had to arrange for Bori and Muna to have offspring. He had to make it happen before he died.

Kurubela used to say that he wanted his children to have a big ship that could sail as far as Tuban or Makassar. He always said that if the foreigners could sail that far, the Manipa natives could too. Gamati felt that it was now his duty to make Kurubela's dream come true.

But he was worried about hiding the gold. Someone might steal it. Gamati used to be a strong, brave man. He never walked away from a fight. During his escape from the VOC, he had turned into a patient man, good at hiding his feelings, and making small talk. As a guest in someone's hut, it would be improper to bring it up if he lost some gold. Finally, he decided to leave the hut as soon as possible. He would take his grandchildren directly to the northern islands. He would visit Makasuli and several other families in two or three days, to finalize their big plan. It pained him to think that Bori and Muna could be ordered to live in the palace or join the hongi.

The next day, an arumbae moored on the beach rather unexpectedly. People soon flocked around it. Lissanei, Rona's oldest son, had come to visit. He usually sailed for months, from island to island. All the villagers of Tuna co-owned the ship. He must have brought imported goods that were hard to get since the embargo by the VOC.

The crewmembers soon unloaded the cargo. Some of them walked inland. Lissanei headed the procession. He was a tall, well-built man who moved gracefully. He had a distinct skin tone, a mixture of copper and bronze, shiny from being constantly under the sun. His curly hair was cropped close to his head.

He apparently was well aware of his good looks and being captain of a trading ship only increased his confidence.

Both of his parents were surprised to see him. He was usually gone longer. It had not been a year since he last visited. His wife and children lived on Ambon. They usually visited Tuna during the dry season, when the weather was clear and the wind favorable.

Lissanei and Gamati both nodded respectfully when Rona introduced them to each other. Gamati hoped Lissanei would not recognize his name. He was well known in the northern islands of Seram. Gamati feared Lissanei would speak about him to the VOC. Luckily, Lissanei did not seem to recognize the name.

Later that day Gamati and Sobori took Aimuna to the beach. Muna had to learn to row a small boat by herself. She needed to learn to control the movements, make turns, slow down by using her oar or speed up by rowing faster.

Gamati was on the kole-kole with Muna, although he did not help her row the boat. Sobori stayed at the beach and watched them from afar. They had chosen a shallow, deserted beach with white sand. It was quite far from the beach where Lissanei's arumbae was moored.

Gamati made a sudden movement, and the boat capsized. Aimuna and Gamati went overboard. Gamati had taught Muna how to save herself when the boat capsized. If the boat sank, she had to swim to safety.

Muna trained every day until her skin burnt. Gamati never told her the purpose of the training. He simply told her she needed to learn how to survive an enemy attack.

On their last day of her training, Lissanei showed up at the beach. He would sail to another island in two days. His arumbae was fully loaded with Tuna produce such as sago, wild honey, dried sea fishes, and long-lasting fruit such as yellow pumpkin and grains.

Lissanei had told his father that his wife in Ambon was gravely ill. His sudden visit to Tuna was to fetch some medicinal herbs. He had heard of an old medicine woman in Tuna who knew some herb leaves and insects for his wife's remedy. He said that as soon as the medication was handed to him, he would set sail for Ambon. He was aware of the death threat from the man whose wife he had taken. After that conversation, Rona and his wife only spoke to Lissanei when in the presence of Gamati and his grandchildren.

To kill time while he waited for the medication, Lissanei looked for Bori on the beach. He actually only wanted to chat about the sea with him. Bori was still young; he must be interested in hearing some stories about the sea and fishing.

When Lissanei saw the boat capsize and Aimuna swim to the beach, his eyes widened. "Hey Bori," he called, "that's a very pretty girl! She's a good rower, a true beach girl. I really like her."

Bori froze. He felt as if lightning had struck him. He never wanted any man to compliment Muna. She was his alone.

"She's only a child, too young to get married, and she's not that attractive." Bori tried to stay calm.

"No, she's not that young. Look at the way her wet clothes cling to her body. Her breasts are formed. She can already marry."

Bori wanted to punch Lissanei right in the mouth even though he was much bigger, but instead, he simply tried to discourage Lissanei. "She still has a long way to go before marriage," Bori said naively.

"That's all right. I can wait. I want to marry that pretty girl. I like her a lot," Lissanei said passionately and added, "Bori, I've sailed to a lot of islands. I know a pretty girl when I see one. I want to have Muna when she's grown up. After all, she has been living in my parents' hut all this time. Are you her relative? I ask you to take good care of her until I'm back." Lissanei slapped Bori on the shoulder as if he were an old friend.

Trained to control his emotions, Bori kept silent. People of the Moluccas never hesitated to express their feelings as they were spontaneous people. When they were happy, they would be very excited. When angry, they would openly and immediately voice their discontent. They were easily involved in quarrels.

As a refugee who moved from village to village, Gamati had trained Bori to be patient, sociable, and full of praise. Bori learned to conceal his real emotions, especially if doing otherwise would spark a conflict.

Gamati also trained both Bori and Muna to speak in a low voice, unlike other people, so others couldn't hear what they said.

He warned them that there could be traitors anywhere. The proof was the attack on Bori's kampong, which had been very isolated. Located far from the seaside, with no river that could be used as an entrance, the attackers from the VOC had still discovered its location. Without help from a traitor they could have never found the kampongs in the dead of the night.

The happiness they felt after the trip to the forest soon evaporated with the problems that started to arise. Aimuna and Bori grew somber as they heard about the conversation with the sultan's emissaries and the hongi draft. Muna thought she would rather die than be separated from Bori. She would not dream of marrying Lissanei. He was a stranger she had just met.

"Grandpa, you have to save us. Let's just go away, far, far away from here." Bori and Muna sobbed when they gathered at the plantation in the evening.

Lissanei was very nice and jolly at dinner. It would be the last time for the three of them to see him before he left Tuna. He told stories about the sea and his many amazing experiences, just like Grandpa Rona. However, Bori and Muna were not impressed. They hated him and hoped it truly was the last time they would ever see him.

The only solution was to leave the hut. Ronasundu was Lissanei's father; he could visit his parents whenever he wished to. On the other hand, they lived there because of Rona's generosity, Gamati thought.

And their gold. He could not imagine what he would do if someone stole it. It represented years and years of their savings.

***

"Tabea! Tabea!" Gamati shouted from the bottom of the wooden stairs to Makasuli's hut. The day had just dawned. The thin silky dew still coated everything. Different bird songs and chirping still filled the air.

Makasuli's head popped out of the front door. He was surprised to see Gamati. "C'mon up, I still need to wash up. Take a seat." Makasuli pointed to a mat on the wooden floor.

The steps creaked when Gamati went up. He immediately took a seat and put his index finger at his lips, signaling Makasuli to be quiet.

Makasuli came closer and asked, "Why are you here this early?"

Gamati sighed that something was weighing on his mind. He could not bring himself to answer straightaway. Makasuli did not push him. He correctly guessed that there was an urgent situation.

After he regained his composure, Gamati asked, "Why's our life so miserable since Pani-pani came here?"

"What happened? Are they going to attack Tuna?" Makasuli asked.

"It is not that. When we came home from the forest, Rona told me emissaries from the sultan's palace had visited him in search of good-looking boys and pretty girls. They knew there was a pair of good-looking youth living in his hut and wanted to take them to the sultan's palace. I hadn't recovered from the shock when several elders of the neighboring kampongs came. Pani-pani plans to conduct a hongi in just a few months. Tuna has to join the hongi expedition to the southern islands. All the young men have to join the hongi to man the kampong's kora-koras. The villagers also need to prepare the food supply for them. I hadn't fully digested this second bad news when Ronasundu's eldest son came to visit his parents. He saw Aimuna, and immediately took a liking to her. He said he wants to marry her in a year or two. What do you think of all that?"

Makasuli scrutinized Gamati's face. He could hardly believe what he just heard. *What an unfortunate series of disasters,* he thought.

"I want to move away quickly. Let's move soon to the northern islands, somewhere far away from Pani-pani. I can't stand living like this. Poor Bori and Muna," Gamati said in despair.

"I understand, but we have to be cautious and carefully plan this. We want to be as safe as possible," Makasuli reasoned.

"I'm an old man. I'll die soon. Who'll take care of Bori and Muna? The two of them have to marry soon and have children. Why does Rona's eldest son have to be such a troublemaker? He already has a wife and children. Why does he want to marry another young girl, and a poor girl at that? Why?" Gamati lamented and held the top of his head.

The two men were at a loss for words and remained silent for a moment. It would not be easy to find a boat. No one sold boats in the vicinity. Boats were usually co-owned by several families or by all inhabitants of a kampong. Making one required teamwork in the spirit of masohi.

Gamati needed a boat to flee from Tuna. People used their boats daily to fish at sea and on the river. He had no idea where to obtain a boat.

Even though they had the gold, they still had to build the boat. The right type of trees had to be found and felled in the forest, then taken to the seaside. The trunks had to be measured, cut, carved, and adjusted. They needed many palm leaves to make the sail. The leaves had to be cleaned, boiled, and dried before they could be woven into a sail. If there were no palm leaves, they could make the sail out of some woven sarongs. They would have to tear the sarongs and sew them into a sail. It was a long and complicated task. Everyone would ask whose boat it was, where they planned to sail to, and so on. Lissanei might hear that they were building a boat.

According to the hongi draft rules, a man who did not have children could not join the expedition. He had to marry and have offspring first, before joining the hongi.

Gamati wanted Bori and Muna to marry as soon as possible. If they were lucky, Muna would become pregnant, but not immediately, so Bori would still have a reason to refuse to join the hongi.

Gamati had started to refer to Lissanei as "the damned man," just like he referred to the VOC and the native traitors.

"Doesn't Lissanei know that Muna and Bori are to be wedded?" Makasuli was surprised.

"I don't know. He never asked Bori or me. I'm pretty sure Rona and his wife told him about us being on the run."

"Perhaps Rona didn't tell him anything. Perhaps he thought there was no point in telling Lissanei since he was going to leave soon. Doesn't he live on another island?"

"Yes, that may be. However, my daughter, Ranila, and my son, Tarambessi, deserve to have their lineage preserved. My family is not going to perish because of Pani-pani. That's why I want to go up north as soon as possible. The traders from China, Malacca, Tuban, and Java often go there. We can trade our cloves with them."

"Where will we get the cloves from?" Makasuli asked.

"We can plant clove trees in a secret plantation, just like before. Pani-pani does not have an office or fort there. The islands are tiny. Pani-pani's big ships will have trouble moving through the shallow water. Fresh water is also hard to find there."

"Where can we build the new kampong and the secret plantation?"

"On Halmahera, which is a large island," Gamati answered.

Makasuli nodded. "In that case, let's walk to the forest. We'll live there temporarily and find our way to the northern seaside. If we happen to find a boat, even if it is only a small lepa-lepa, we'll ask to take us to the southeastern islands. Perhaps to Kei Besar, where there are shipbuilders who make custom ships. The gold will come in handy. I can also help in making the ship."

Gamati shook his head when he heard the word "forest." They had been on the run for safety so many years. Aimuna was still an innocent girl even though she was three years older since their last run, and almost or perhaps already come of age. No man could carry her. It was a taboo, unless she was sick.

Moreover, which forest could they live in? All the rivers, seaside, and small lakes on Seram were like roads that connected kampongs and sultanates. The VOC had easy access to all. Gamati had many experiences sailing islands, straits, bays, and capes, and honestly did not know where they could find a safe forest to hide in. In addition, the damned Lissanei could have his own spies look for Aimuna.

"Gamati, do you know that Lissanei took someone else's wife and ran away? The woman is of Dutch descent, her skin is fair and she has a prominent nose. Her husband is of mixed descent. His ancestors come from Ternate and Makassar. He swore he'll kill Lissanei if he dared to set foot on Tuna again."

"I've heard it. That's what worries me. I'm afraid he'll go crazy and just take Muna whenever he wants to. Even though I saved Muna and Bori from the hongi, they are still in danger." Gamati sighed.

"Did you hear it from Rona himself?" Makasuli asked.

"No, I heard the story from someone else," Gamati answered.

For a moment they both sat in silence, thinking. Until finally Makasuli, as if speaking to himself, said, "My ancestors fled from Banda, without any prior planning. They might have escaped by boat, or on only a log raft or a coconut tree trunk. They went to Kei, and lived there safely for several years before they searched for new places to settle in."

Gamati studied Makasuli's weathered face. Seamen like him and Makasuli usually had dry and wrinkled skin. Their lean, strapping bodies were strong. Observing his friend made him realize they were indeed a family of seamen. They were accustomed to surviving typhoons, rainstorms, and the raging waves of the ocean. Nothing scared them as long as their ship was afloat. *There's no need to be afraid,* he thought.

"Makasuli, I'm only thinking of Aimuna. She's still young, and weak. She sometimes cries secretly. I want to give her a peaceful life. No war, no killing."

"Everyone wants that kind of life, Gamati. Everyone wants to be happy. My children learned to build ships, to face the fierce wind at sea; we had our own hut, our own plantation. Pani-pani destroyed everything. Now, we're all displaced on Seram. Our families are separated; we've no real home, no secret plantation. We can't continue to live like this."

"I agree. Where can we borrow, rent, or seize a boat? On the north shore? I will take my grandchildren there. We have some gold."

"That's good, I like that. I'll never give up. Now, let me ask my wife," Makasuli said quietly and went inside. He returned a moment later. His wife had agreed to face the hardships of living in the forest, together with Gamati's family. She said they should ask the three young men who previously went to the forest with Gamati and Makasuli to come along, since they also originally came from Banda.

"Which forest should we go to?" Gamati asked.

"Let's follow the trail we took to Tupawalili. We can stop there and build a temporary hut from bamboo or rattan. After we rest and regain our strength, we can continue to walk to the northern seaside. During this season, there will be many boats and ships. However, there will also be the Papuans and pirate ships, so we have to be careful."

"Yes, let's do that. Sobori will surely agree and Aimuna always agrees with Sobori. She has learned to row a boat, dive, and swim long-distance. I thought she was weak, but she swam very far when I purposely capsized the boat. We can train her more at the lakes in the forest."

"I agree. Nowadays, everyone, regardless of sex, has to learn how to survive in the forest, row a boat, shoot game for food, weave clothes, and also weave palm leaves to make a sail. Everything," Makasuli said passionately.

"What should I say to Rona? I never want to hurt his feelings," Gamati worried. Ronasundu had been very good to him and his family.

"We'll figure it out later. Let's go fishing now and take Aimuna along. She can practice rowing and diving. Leave Bori to work on the plantation or stay in the hut to chat with Grandpa Rona. He'll like that."

Encouraged by Makasuli's plans, Gamati walked quickly back to Rona's hut. Sobori and Aimuna had been waiting anxiously for him in the front yard. They did not know where Gamati had gone since he had left very early.

"Oh children, are you waiting for me? I'm so sorry; I woke up very early. You were still asleep, so I didn't tell you where I was going. I went looking for a boat to go fishing. Makasuli borrowed a lepa-lepa."

Aimuna and Sobori both wanted to go with him. They both loved being on an open boat at sea. Aimuna loved it when the wind caressed her face and blew through her hair. She especially liked it when the wind filled her ears with long whistles. At sea, she felt as if she was in a different, vast, clean, and salt-scented world.

Once she asked Gamati why there were no women who fished or women who brought cargos of trade items. She wanted to be a trader-seawoman, she said.

Gamati explained that women were not as strong as men. "What if there's a big load of cargo to be loaded or a rainstorm hits the ship?" he asked and joked, "Women will only cry and swallow seawater."

Gamati was only going to take Aimuna with him. She was very excited. Bori wanted to go too, but Gamati said he had sailed many times with other people. He suggested Bori ask many questions about Grandpa Rona's sailing experiences back when he was still young. Bori had to learn more about sailing and the sea. Besides, there would be no one to keep an eye on the hidden precious gold if the three of them went fishing.

Bori and Gamati had placed the package under a very sharp machete. On Seram that meant it was a sacred possession. It was a taboo for anyone other than the owner to touch it, let alone take it. A great misfortune would befall the person who stole it. All the natives of Seram knew about this taboo. The machete acted much like the red Sasi ribbon tied around the trees.

Gamati and Aimuna packed spare clothes and told Grandpa and Grandma Rona they would be gone overnight.

The Ronasundus were surprised and asked why they had to leave so suddenly. Grandma Rona said that there were no provisions ready now at the hut.

Gamati answered that it was fine. He wanted to teach Aimuna how to be a true beach woman. She had to be ready to face dangers and sail the seas without provisions, just like Ranila.

Grandma Rona asked why it was necessary to train a girl that hard.

Gamati grumbled, "Perhaps it wasn't necessary back in the old days, but there's danger everywhere now. Even deep in the forest, far from the seaside, there are enemy attacks. Many of us were killed. If all the men are dead, the women and children have to be able to flee to safety or defend themselves." He didn't mean to be short with Grandma Rona. He was actually mad at Lissanei.

The old couple nodded.

Bori waved at Gamati and Aimuna as they left the hut and asked to bring him some big fish. Aimuna shouted back that they would bring fish if the sea were calm.

On their way to Makasuli's hut, Gamati explained to Muna that she needed to train even harder to control a kole-kole, or even a bigger boat. She also needed to learn to "read" the sea, the wind directions, the seasons and the currents.

Later, he told Muna that they were going to leave Ronasundu's hut as soon as possible. When Muna asked why, Gamati said he did not want Lissanei to marry Muna and it would be hard to turn Lissanei down if they kept living in his parents' hut. Lissanei could easily report to the VOC that there were still living offspring of Kurubela, who was their big enemy.

"We'll first find a boat, Muna, and later we'll have to cross the forest just like we did before. Do you think you can do it, Muna?" Gamati asked gently.

"Yes, I can, Grandpa. Are we leaving Bori in Tuna?" she asked nervously.

"Of course not. He's coming with us, Muna. I want to save both of you, that's why we have to travel so far and head to the northern islands."

Muna nodded. She did not like Lissanei, especially after the way he had looked at her one morning.

"We're lucky he already left, right, Grandpa?" Aimuna looked affectionately at her grandfather.

"Yes, we can't just stay there and wait for him to come back for you, Muna. After this fishing trip, I'm going to marry you and Bori. That way the sultan can't take the two of you as his palace entertainers. Nor can they force Bori to join the hongi."

"I'll do everything you and Bori tell me, Grandpa. I want to go somewhere far away from Pani-pani. They've caused us all these miseries."

They had arrived at Makasuli's front yard and Gamati did not answer.

Makela, Makasuli's wife, emerged from the house to welcome them. She was rather taken aback when she looked at Muna.

"My, you've grown, Muna. You're so pretty and slim." Makela wiped her tears.

"Why are you crying, Grandma?" Muna was surprised.

"I can't help but remember all the people that had to flee from their homes, always running about the islands, moving from kampong to kampong, all because of the war. Also, all the villagers who were killed by Pani-pani. The nutmeg and the cloves put all of us in such misery," Makela lamented while gesturing for them to climb the porch ladder.

They did not wait long. All of the provisions and tools were packed. Ages, Dopa and Beilang, the three young men from the previous trip to their burned-down hut in Tupawalili, were joining them. Aimuna nodded to show her respect.

They walked along the beach until they came to a shady cove. The lepa-lepa was moored there. They all got in and soon left for the open sea.

It was the calm wind season, the best season for sailing. Typhoons were rare; the sky was clear with no threat of rain. On the contrary, right after sunrise, the sun would shine glaringly. At midday, the heat could easily burn human skin.

A deck was positioned on the stern of the lepa-lepa. The three young men rowed the boat quickly. Gamati also told Aimuna to help row the boat, although she might not be that strong. The two older men did not row; they saved their strength to fish, later.

Muna was happy. She loved the vast, clean ocean. It carried her imagination far beyond the seemingly thin horizon. The news of leaving Tuna excited her very much. She actually liked Grandpa and Grandma Rona, who were very kind to her, Bori, and Grandpa Gamati. However, the visit by the demanding Lissanei had left her worried. She had felt like a drowning cat when one morning Lissanei grabbed her hand and flirtatiously said, "Muna, I'll wait for you. In two more years we'll have a nice wedding. Muna, darling, I think of you night and day."

Since she considered it improper, Muna did not dare to tell anyone that Lissanei had groped her chest as he laughed. She had immediately run to her grandfather's room, although Gamati was not home at that time.

Why did he want to marry her? Muna only had eyes for Bori.

They had been at sea less than two hours when they found a spot filled with schools of small fishes. Gamati and Makasuli cast the net. Soon small fishes that made excellent dry, salted fish filled the rattan baskets.

Then the lepa-lepa sailed toward an uninhibited small island. There was a spot near its beach, where schools of bigger fishes were known to gather. Gamati used a pole and hook to fish. The lepa-lepa moved slowly through the water. Muna rowed the boat with vigor and made the men smile. One of the young men told her about how to navigate the water current under the boat and take advantage of the wind direction. She also needed to consider the season they were in, whether it was the dry season, wet season, or the transition season. Currents changed with the season.

Muna nodded and said that if they expected her to master sailing and be able to control a boat, she should train for months, not only once or twice.

"Sure, Muna. Later, we can build a small dugout boat. You can row it with your friends or with Bori, to swim around the beach, to play with the fishes, or when you dive to look for turtles. Maybe later, when we are in the northern islands," Gamati said.

The two old men's hooks kept getting more fish; their bait lured big, meaty fish. Gamati tossed the fish that were too small back into the sea. "Poor little fish," he said and continued, "We must only take the bigger fish. If we catch them all, big and small, there'll soon be no more fish in our ocean, and we'll end up hungry."

The rest of them laughed. They thought that it was highly unlikely that anyone could starve on the flourishing big island surrounded by the sea, with its abundance of fishes in various colors and sizes.

The lepa-lepa returned before dusk with a big catch. Large and small fish filled all the baskets and the boat's floor. *Bori will have a thick meaty roasted fish for dinner, and Grandpa and Grandma Rona will eat all they can of papeda porridge with fresh fish soup*, Aimuna thought happily.

They moored the lepa-lepa in its previous place. This time, slender Aimuna had to carry the last basket of fish, so the men would not have to return to the boat to fetch the remaining basket.

While everyone was transporting the baskets of their catch to Grandpa Rona's hut, Gamati and Makasuli went to the hut of the lepa-lepa owner, near Makasuli's hut. They gave him a half basket of large fish.

The two old men asked if they could buy the lepa-lepa as they needed it to go to another island. After all, he had two lepa-lepas. They were willing to trade it for some gold. If the owner did not want to transfer ownership, perhaps they could borrow it until they finished taking care of their affairs on the other island.

The lepa-lepa owner agreed to trade the boat for some gold. Everyone was tempted when hearing the word "gold," even when it was not much.

***

Martinus de Bruyn, the governor of Ambon, entered his office when the sun was already high in the sky. The meeting of that afternoon was important. Resident de Vries and the botanists Karel and Bertie already waited for him. High-ranking finance officials and sea traffic officers, along with several captains of the VOC's big war ships, were also present. Everyone rose when Martinus entered the room.

As usual, the governor opened the meeting with a statement that he had received a letter from the Assembly of the Lords Seventeen. This time, the topic was not the oversupply of cloves and nutmeg that had made the price plummet. On the contrary, this time it stated that the supply was very low. The shortage was caused by a drought where the spices originated.

A great drought affected the small islands in the north, as well as those in the south. Up north, many plants withered, including the clove trees that grew in the wild. In the south, barren nutmeg trees bore no fruit. The saplings withered and died, including those planted more than two years ago. Many staple crops such as cassavas, sweet potatoes, taros, and many types of pumpkins and eggplants had also withered and died. The same thing also happened to fruit trees. Banana, guava, mango, mangosteen, and sweet orange trees all died due to the lack of rainfall.

The main office in Holland had ordered them to fix the situation. They had to find water and work on an irrigation system while continuing to make the fertilizer. There were many slaves available to do the work. The fact that there were not as many slaves as the Assembly counted and that they all worked under inhumane conditions was not mentioned at all. What it came down to was that the VOC plantations needed to be irrigated one way or another.

Next, all the ships, small and large, had to be ready to sail at any time.

The VOC shareholders and directors in faraway Holland still suspected that smuggling and black market trades in their monopoly areas had caused the decline in the spice supply.

Martinus quoted from the letter, "Keep your eyes open. Patrol the waters! We can't let the natives violate our monopoly. Punish violators severely, even with capital punishment."

No one said anything. The order was directed to the governor. He was the one who was responsible for executing the order.

After a few moments, Martinus said, "We're now confronted by enemies in three different areas. First we have the natives, the owners of the secret plantations and the seamen who trade with traders from Makassar and Tuban, or the English and Portuguese traders up north. Their trade even reaches the Philippines, which is not included in our monopoly. Second is the great drought up north, on Moti, Mare, Makian, and their surrounding islands. And third is the great drought on the Banda Islands in the south, the origin of nutmeg and mace. That area, however, falls under the jurisdiction of another governor. There are perkeniers there with more than enough slaves. However, who, gentlemen, can fight nature's long dry season?"

"That is right, Mister Governor," Lucas, Karel and Bertie answered in unison.

The resident of Saparua was the first called to address the meeting.

Lucas de Vries stated that the pilot clove plantation they built together with the two botanists was actually in good condition. All the clove tree saplings grew as hoped, and they had enough wells of fresh water. They also had enough workers to water the trees, to weed and fend off pests.

The slaves, who came from many areas, had started to learn the local dialect. However, arguments followed by fights frequently occurred between them. Sometimes it led to the death of one of them. They were all temperamental and desperate people, to the point of not fearing death. "I often tried to reconcile them. I even relocate them from the area of the plantation they work on. However, our island is small. It's easy for people to run into each other, even after I moved them. If a slave dies, his tasks fall to the remaining slaves."

After everyone present stated their thoughts and ideas, Martinus mentioned they would conduct a hongi expedition to the northern region. "The situation there needs our immediate attention. I suspect there are still clove trees growing in the wild that belong to the natives. We have to make it a priority to extirpate those trees. We do have the new batch of clove trees on Ambon and Saparua, don't we?"

"Yes, Mister Governor," the resident answered respectfully.

Regarding the condition in the south region, the governor said, "There is a governor there. Let him make the first move. Should he need any help from us, we will send help from Ambon."

Lucas said that Saparua could provide an arumbae and two kora-koras that belonged to the natives. However, there were not enough men to man the two kora-koras as there were only a small number of adults on Saparua.

"What about the arrangement for their provisions?" Martinus asked.

"I ordered them several months ago to start the preparation of dry food for the expedition. They have prepared an ample amount of sago and dried fish; they also dried some venison and fowl. A kampong chief said it was enough for a month's supply of food."

"What if the expedition takes more than a month?" Martinus asked.

"I haven't discussed that with the kampong chiefs yet. Our original plan was only to patrol the tiny islands up north, at the origins of the cloves that have now been struck by the great drought. Those were the trees we were going to extirpate, so I thought that one month's worth of provisions would be enough."

Martinus said, "I think we're facing a natural disaster. There could be many unforeseen conditions. Can you arrange for a larger food supply?"

"The villagers will probably comply if we order them to. Nevertheless, drying and salting meat and fish takes time. We can do it if we don't rush our departure."

Martinus proceeded to ask the leader of the hongi expedition on Ambon if the VOC had enough ships. He needed three large warships with cannons, troops, and food supplies for one month.

The leader confirmed, and also stated that they had made preparations according to the previous order that the expedition would only take approximately two or three weeks.

Several other islands that had become the VOC's underlings also stated that they were ready for one month of voyage.

The leader of the weapons and armory department reported that they were ready. From cannonballs and rifle bullets, down to spears, swords, and bows and arrows, all were ready to use.

"Yes, we plan to sail for a month. What about the wind condition nowadays? Can we rely completely on the sails, or do we need extra oarsmen?" The governor turned to the captains.

One of them answered, "We don't need extra oarsmen if it's a one-month expedition. Now is the perfect season, the north wind season."

The meeting proceeded very smoothly, unlike the usual official meetings. There were only a few questions asked, let alone arguments. Everyone present swiftly agreed upon the governor's ideas and orders. The officer who wrote the minutes of the meeting did his job without any problems.

It looked like one of their main issues was the great drought. It had never happened before, according to the natives and the VOC officials who had lived in the region for a long time. There were dry seasons, of course. Occasionally, the season dragged on for quite some time, but it had never been as long as the one they were having, which already had lasted more than a year.

All of the officials present gave long speeches on various problems they had. At midday, the meeting was still not finished. The heat became unbearable when the sun was right at its highest point. Everyone was drenched in sweat, even though they had opened all the doors and tall windows and the wind blew freely into the room.

The governor suspended the meeting for a lunch break and all of them moved to the terrace of the governor's office to have their lunch outdoors. The governor himself went back to his residence to have lunch with his wife.

One of the VOC captains asked the resident if they could take off their shirts during lunch since the governor was not present.

The resident smiled and answered, "If you feel that it will help, please do so. However, can you bear the shame when the governor suddenly walks in?"

"Oh well, we're used to being bare-chested when we're at sea," the captain complained.

"Let's wait. If the governor himself takes off his shirt when we continue the meeting, we can all follow suit," the storage head officer, who was also used to working bare-chested in his office, answered.

They continued the meeting when the sun leaned toward the horizon and the sea breeze had picked up. With the temperature slightly cooler, the situation was more bearable.

Toward the evening, the governor reminded those present that the next day was Sunday, and requested everyone to attend Mass. They needed to pray for the end of the great drought. The clove and nutmeg trees were their bread and butter. It was important to prevent their destruction. Everyone nodded in agreement.

The governor had heard rumors that the resident of Saparua had taken a liking to Rosamunda, the daughter of a bakery owner in the white men's compound, on the fringes of the harbor. Her father was Portuguese while her mother had Chinese, Javanese, even Ternate blood. Rosamunda was a very pretty girl. Her beauty did not stem merely from a perfect bone structure; she radiated warmth and vigor. She smiled easily and knew all the names of the bakery's clients. She was fluent in the local dialect and Dutch. At home, her family spoke Portuguese.

Dutch men had a choice to marry or not marry. Children born from their couplings with a native woman could be registered and, acknowledged as legal offspring, they could be taken to Holland. However, their mothers could not. The VOC forbade native wives to go to Holland.

The governor did not know whether Lucas was aware of this policy. If he was not, the governor felt sorry for him. He did not know how to start a conversation to bring up the topic. He did not want to be called a meddler who pried into other people's affairs like a nosy woman. In addition, the resident was a rigid and private man.

That was the reason he advised the meeting attendees to go to church tomorrow. He had also received reports that one of the young botanists was enamored with the daughter of a kampong chief whose wife was a Chinese woman. The girl had yellow skin and hair as stiff as palm leave nerves. She had no white blood at all.

Governor de Bruyn and his wife were sympathetic toward Rosamunda. De Freytas, Rosamunda's father, had a good reputation. His cakes were delicious; orders were delivered on time. There were no reports of him swindling his clients. And the most important thing was that tight-fisted or penniless VOC officials were able to purchase the cakes on credit.

According to some high-ranking VOC officials, de Freytas was someone who knew his place. There was only a small number of Portuguese families on Ambon. They refused the offer to relocate to other islands shortly after they fled from Makassar. The governor and his wife were sure that Rosamunda had many good qualities. It would be a shame to leave her here if the resident and Rosamunda married and later Lucas had to return to Holland. It was not clear either if de Freytas would accept a Dutch son-in-law.

Rosamunda's skin tone was not very light. It was of a darker shade, that of the color of ripe sapodilla fruit, a great match to her dark brown eyes. After they struck up a friendship at the governor's dinner party, Lucas de Vries frequently used Rosamunda as his model in a series of paintings portraying mixed-race descendants in faraway lands. Over time, the two of them grew close.

The resident was a very private man. While he had an official and charismatic air about him, no one knew what truly lay in his heart.

The meeting ended just before sunset.

Bertie and Karel did not want to turn in early that night. They asked for permission to visit a bar outside the fort. The good-looking and agile Bertie wanted some entertainment. After the long discussions about warfare, he wanted to relax.

The resident of Saparua declined their invitation. He needed to finish many administrative duties. Thus, the two botanists left after informing the gate guards.

Karel and Bertie walked through the harbor district. It was dark and quiet, although many ships were moored there. The roads wound away from the port to the hills. The wind blew fiercely and both men turned up their shirts collars.

Ambon was a small island. There used to be many native kampongs in the forests and along the shores. The hostile arrival of strangers had caused many of the natives to move to other islands.

However, the VOC fort that was built near the big port had encouraged new settlements that gradually crept toward the interior of the island. The VOC even opened new clove plantations on several hillsides.

Along with residential housing, there were inns, and several bars for the seamen to relax and find entertainment.

People often talked about The Buitenzorg, known for its pretty waitresses. Most of the shapely women were of Chinese, Arabian, Portuguese, Malay, or Dutch descent. None of them had dark skin or tightly curled hair. Their hair was wavy or straight. They were all flirtatious and frivolous.

The manager of the bar knew that the two young men were from the governor's office and ordered Mona, the prettiest among the waitresses, to serve Karel and Bertie drinks. She spoke some Dutch and could down many drinks without getting drunk. Mona was the most popular drinking partner of the house. She always wore a flowery Tuban sarong.

The atmosphere was relaxed. It was already late and there were not too many visitors. Perhaps people wanted to get to bed early since they had to go to church the next day.

Karel and Bertie were unwinding. At least here, they did not have to talk about the hongi expedition.

The conversation around them was about a sailing ship from a foreign land that had approached Ambon without the VOC license plate. The VOC patrol had caught the ship yesterday around midday. Of course, the news had created quite a stir among the VOC people.

Mona had a few stories about the ship. The captain was not Dutch. He was quite an old man and, apparently, enjoyed a good fight. "Yesterday, he was involved in a brawl with several officers and they locked him up inside the fort. He might be punished severely," Mona said.

Karel and Bertie added that they knew how cruel the VOC treated people who were insubordinate. Numerous people were punished during their long voyage east, Karel said. The punishments on board fell to crewmembers who were involved in brawls or mutinies, and also to crewmembers who were caught stealing. The crewmembers also died from depression and grave illnesses. Anyway, the two men said, they just wanted to exchange some light and pleasant chitchat that night, and not talk about death.

Another, older, girl joined them. Leoni spoke Dutch fluently. Before the current governor took office, she worked in the household of a Dutch captain. Her late husband had been a crewmember on a Dutch sailing ship. Their conversation soon picked up and the drinks began to affect them.

A group of white, bawdy men entered the establishment. The barmaids brought out their drinks, along with female drinking partners. They engaged in a rowdy conversation that soon turned into an argument. All the men in the group were drunk; their breath smelled of liquor. A man rose and punched his friend in the face. The man punched him back and turned over the tables, causing the glasses and bottles to drop to the floor.

Soon the rest of the guests were involved in the fight. The room was in turmoil; several items crashed onto the floor. Curses reverberated in the dim room. Fortunately, none of the oil lamps on the wall fell down.

Although they were not a part of the group, Karel and Bertie also received punches and kicks from some of the men. A chair struck lovely Mona. She fell to the floor and her face swelled.

Leoni ran outside to seek help. Some men came in and broke up the fight. They forced the group who had started the fight to leave.

Karel and Bertie sneaked out of the drinking house and walked back to the fort. For a moment, the gate guard did not recognize them and refused to open the gate. Karel and Bertie furiously argued with him. Finally, the guard recognized them. Nonetheless he wondered why they looked so dirty, and their faces were swollen.

Bertie explained that there had been a drunken brawl in the drinking house, and they were dragged into the fight. "The fight destroyed the saloon. We were just bystanders," he said.

They entered the guest quarters they shared with the resident. Lucas de Vries was not yet asleep. He went to meet them outside his room. "Back so soon?" He acted surprised.

"Yes, honorable Mister Resident. There were Mona, Leoni, and a group of drunken sailors from a docked ship."

"Hmm. You two were drunk as well?"

"We were about to get there when the others started a fight and punched each other. The entire place was destroyed. Well, it was better than to have no entertainment, right?" They laughed.

"Ha ha. Yes, tonight there was a Mona, and a Leoni, and tomorrow there will be the Governor of Ambon. With those swollen faces, he might not want you in church after all." Lucas laughed and closed his door.

$$Chapter\ 7$$

Aimuna had gone through an amazing metamorphosis. She had grown into an agile, tall, and slim girl; there was not an ounce of fat on her entire body. Lean and fit, she created an image of an athlete. Her hair had grown longer. A beautiful wave of locks started from the hairline above her forehead. It was a shame her skin was no longer brown. It had turned so dark it looked burned. But all in all she was a dynamic young girl.

Since she was training in rowing, she was exposed to direct sunlight for some time. Usually she rowed a kole-kole. The small and light dugout boat was perfect for her, a young, female beginner.

Gamati, once a captain who sailed the seas of the Moluccas, was her coach. Aimuna's oval face and large brown eyes framed with curled eyelashes created a lovely sight. Gamati feared that if a VOC man ever laid eyes on Aimuna, the man would ask her to be his wife.

Aimuna excelled in rowing, beyond everyone's expectation. She quickly learned to bring the kole-kole to an abrupt stop, to turn, and to maintain her balance on it.

Makasuli was quite puzzled by Aimuna's rowing skills at sea. He shook his head in awe. She was surely a grandchild of an experienced captain. "The apple does not fall far from the tree," he whispered to Gamati when they watched her together. They had borrowed the kole-kole from Makasuli's neighbor who also owned the lepa-lepa.

Next, Aimuna had to perfect her diving skills. She first practiced holding her breath as long as she could underwater. Then she learned to move underwater and surface somewhere other than where she had gone in. This exercise required her to stay underwater for a long time.

Gamati had heard from Grandma Rona that Aimuna had turned into a young woman. Aimuna was ready to marry. On the last day of the rowing and diving training, Gamati took her under a big, shady tree on the beach to rest. It was still early.

Aimuna jumped up when a pod of dophins swam by not far from the shore and called out to them, "Hey, dolphins, sweet dolphins. Hey, you, hey." She shouted at the top of her lungs. The wind carried her voice, but the dolphins swam away.

They took out their provisions. Grandma Rona, growing fonder by the day of the shapely Aimuna, had prepared the lunch. She always complimented Muna who was lively, chatty, and helpful to people.

After they finished their lunch, Gamati said, "Muna, I need to talk to you. It's important, so please listen closely."

"Yes, Grandpa," Aimuna answered respectfully.

Gamati said, "Muna, my girl, my beloved grandchild. I am now old. Grandpa Makasuli is old, and so is Grandpa Rona. It's inevitable we'll soon leave this world. You have to learn to take care of yourself. I'm glad you now know how to row a boat."

"Yes, Grandpa."

"Young people live as a couple. Women have men to keep them company while men have to look out for women. Have you ever thought about a man to take care of you, after I die?"

Muna was speechless. She had never really thought about it. She never had any intimacy with any man. She had never thought about someone who would accompany her in life. Her world revolved around Grandpa Gamati and Sobori.

"No, I haven't, Grandpa."

"Why? Didn't you meet some boys at the pata cengkei?"

"I'm not pretty, Grandpa. Who would like me? I'm dark, skinny, and ignorant. I can't sing or dance."

"Who will you live with when you're old?"

"I don't know. If Bori feels sorry for me, he'll take me in. I'll look after his children if he's married."

"Really?"

Aimuna drew circles in the sand with her foot. A tiny crab bit her toe. She kicked the crab off and started to weep.

Gamati hugged her. He patted her back and said there was no reason to cry. "Have you ever thought of Bori other than as a brother, Muna?"

"Yes, I have, Grandpa. He's very kind and handsome. I'm sure a lot of girls like him."

"What about you, Muna, do you like him in a special way?"

"Me? We're related, Grandpa. Doesn't that mean that I can't marry him? People say that wouldn't be decent."

"Who told you that?"

"Grandma Rona and also Bori himself."

"Bori told me you look so much like his mother that every time he misses her, he secretly looks at you. He said that your hair, your eyes, and the way you walk, make him feel Ranila came back from the hongi fire. Bori wants to be with you for the rest of his life."

Muna fought back her tears. She did not want to be told again that she had no reason to cry. She was very touched that she reminded Bori of his late mother. *But we're family. How can we get married?* she wondered silently.

For a moment Gamati remained silent as well. He wanted Muna to be calm when he told her the good news. "Muna, if you love Bori, you can marry him. You two are not from the same father or mother, so you can marry. Only siblings are not allowed to get married. Since you two are first cousins, you and Bori are allowed to marry."

Muna looked at Gamati with wide open eyes. This was news to her. She loved Bori very much, more than her own life. However, people kept reminding her that they were family.

Now, all of a sudden, her grandfather told her they could marry. She wanted to jump and scream, "Thank you, Grandpa, for the wonderful news," but that would be improper. Her face lit up like a morning sun, and she said, "Grandpa, you're not teasing me, are you?"

"No, I am not, sweetie. It's the truth. If you agree, I'll marry you two here in Tuna, soon. After the wedding, we'll head to the northern islands. That way, the sultan's men can't take you and Bori to the palace, and Lissanei can never marry you. When it's safe, we'll sail to our freedom."

"Have you talked to Bori, Grandpa?"

"Yes, yes I have. He liked the idea very much."

"Oh Grandpa, I'm so happy. If only I had known this earlier."

"You and Bori are actually too young to marry, but too many dangers have cropped up. You are too pretty to live in this kampong as a single girl. It would've been a different story if we lived in our own kampong. No one would give you any trouble. You'd have parents and elders to protect you."

They sat together under the shady tree, and enjoyed the happy moment in the soft breeze.

It would be a small wedding, just to let the public know that Aimuna and Sobori had become man and wife and now were able to go anywhere together without a chaperone. From then on, no one would take offense if they went to the forest or rowed out to sea by themselves.

Toward the end of the day, they walked back to the hut. Gamati had asked someone to keep the kole-kole safe.

Back at the hut, Gamati discussed Bori and Muna's wedding plans with the Ronasundus. Gamati wanted them to be married before the sultan's emissaries or Lissanei came back. He wanted to avoid the possibility of having to challenge Lissanei to a duel to settle the issue of Muna; after all, he and his grandchildren owed their lives to Ronasundu.

He asked Rona whether or not they should have a small wedding reception. And if they were to hold a reception, where should it be?

Without knowing that his own son, Lissanei, wanted to marry Muna, Ronasundu agreed that they had to marry Bori and Muna soon. He understood Gamati's anxiety about having the responsibility of raising them at his age. In addition, the youths were under the threat of being taken to the palace or drafted into the hongi.

"I understand your concerns about these two young people. Let's have a small wedding reception here. We can cook the food, and eat together as a celebration. In the evening we'll invite the youth to come to dance and sing. We'll have a party." Ronasundu was enthusiastic.

"I'm old now, Rona. Once they're married they can stay together until they are old."

They discussed with Grandma Ronasundu which families to invite. A number of fishermen and their families; several rich men whose social positions equaled Ronasundu's and were respected elders. They would invite the kampong chief; there was no need to invite the sultan's emissaries.

The cost was not a problem. Ronasundu would provide all the food. However, they had to look for the couple's wedding attire. Since Gamati was not a native of Tuna, and was a widower at that, he did not have such items.

A relative of Makasuli's wife owned fancy sarongs and tops; also headdresses. She was willing to lend the items, as long as they would be returned in good condition.

Within two weeks the wedding preparations were finished. Gamati was to visit the place where he usually communicated with his ancestors' spirits. He would ask for their protection of the young family. He would ask the spirits to bless the couple's fertility so they would conceive quickly and continue his and Kurubela's linage. Gamati did not consider himself done with life's tasks as long as Sobori and Aimuna did not have a child.

Even though Ronasundu and Gamati had met and made contact with people who introduced new religions to the natives, they still adhered to their ancestors' faith. Perhaps the younger generation would be more curious about new ways of thinking and living. They both preferred to adhere to the traditions that had been passed down for so many generations. Luckily, in their families, there was no conflict about this between the elders and the younger generation. Makasuli was different; he had accepted and observed a new religion.

At the reception, Grandma Rona would serve the betel leaves on her treasured family brass plate that shone reddish-yellow, just like gold. It was perfect to serve the folded betel leaves, betel nut, and slaked lime to the most respected guest, and be placed in front of the bride. Grandma Rona would also provide the brass spittoon.

It was customary for Ronasundu, a rich man in Tuna, to have a set of such brass plates and bowls. Before he moved around as a displaced man with his grandchildren, Gamati used to own a set as well. He was thankful that so many people were willing to help him.

He requested that the Ronasundus never mention the names of the bride and groom's parents, or the name of their old kampongs during the wedding reception. "Who knows," he said, "there might be someone among the guests who has heard of Kurubela and knew our family were clove farmers who had traded illegal cloves with Pani-pani's enemies. Just say that we're from the interiors of Ambon and Grandma Rona's distant relatives."

The old couple agreed. The date was set, and they conveyed the invitations through the elders of the tribal council.

The reception was lively and merry. The musicians played their bamboo instruments and conch shell trumpets, drums, and gongs in the large front yard. Their music filled the night with melodious tones. They purposely had chosen a night close to the full moon, so they would not need many torches as the place was bathed in moonlight.

The high tones of the flute always captivated Aimuna. However, as the night grew longer, the sound of drums and gongs became louder and overpowered the thin whistling of flutes. Since both Ronasundu and Gamati hated to see any drunkards, there was no "fiery water" served. Besides, there was not enough time to make the drink.

The party was getting even livelier after dinner. After the singing, soon the pantoum session started.

Someone started to recite a pantoum,

Do not let the betel trees grow tall

lest its leaves will not grow lush

Do not go, my love, but if you leave at all

I pray you will come back in a rush.

"Who might that be? Who are the two lovers?" voices in the crowd called out.

"Sobori and Aimuna, of course, our bride and groom," others replied.

A group of young people started to sing. Some elders who were dressed in loose black pants and ivory-colored tops made of imported Chinese silk joined the singing. Some guests walked up to the musicians and danced in pairs. The women wore exquisite long silk scarves. They danced the lenso.

A young man who admired Aimuna but was often discouraged by Sobori, who was by her side day and night, rose and recited a pantoum,

Near the porch I plant shrubs of jasmine
soon they wither under the scorching sun
The lovely girl is only to look at
I'd like to have her, but don't have gold.

Aimuna wanted to laugh. She knew the pantoum was meant for her. The boy liked her. However, a bride was supposed to sit demurely and not show any emotion. Aimuna held back her laughter and thought, *Anyway, I only care about Sobori.*

Another guest started a new pantoum,

Seagulls fly in the sky this afternoon
One flies back to a wrong nest at high tide
I would have asked for your hand soon
Alas! Someone is already at your side.

"Oh you poor boy!" the crowd cheered Keira, the young man.

That's how the people of Tuna celebrated Aimuna and Sobori's wedding. The couple was very popular. The villagers thought it was a shame they were unable to get to know them better. Aimuna, Sobori, and their grandfather communicated in the Manipa dialect, which was different from the one in Tuna. Therefore, the lingua franca was the colloquial Malay generally spoken along the shorelines. Gamati and his family used their lack of fluency in the local dialect as an excuse for their reclusion.

The party was over when all the guests returned to their homes just before dawn. Only the ones who were assigned to clean the yard remained. They lay down on the front porch to wait for the sun to come up.

Sobori and Aimuna retired to the small bamboo pavilion made for them and Gamati when they first arrived in Tuna. It stood quite far from the kitchen and well behind Ronasundu's main hut.

The next morning, Bori and Muna decided to give Grandpa Gamati some time to rest. To kill time they went to the edge of the forest. Now they could go anywhere by themselves; there was no need to be chaperoned by Grandpa Gamati again. Muna loved the forest; the flying insects with strange wings and the variety of the butterflies, the knobbed hornbills with reddish casques on top of their bills; amazing songbirds, and of course the smell of the damp forest floor.

Gamati hoped he could rest for a few days to recuperate. His weightiest burden, to wed Bori and Muna, had been accomplished. Now he needed to focus on the plan to move and look for a boat, but first, he needed to return to his old village, Tupawaroka, to retrieve the remaining buried gold jewelry.

Gamati remembered that the gold in Tupawaroka was more than Kurubela's in Tupawalili. The gold in Tupawaroka was his and Tarambessi's gold combined. If it was still safe under the ground, they would have enough to place an order for a boat and grease the palms of the kampong elders, the harbor officials, the sultan's emissaries, and influential men on their destination island.

He clenched his teeth in anger. To think of all those years of hard work to save that gold, often with his life on the line, only to now have to give it away to corrupt officials. Ironically, the people who needed the gold were not poor or in need of help. They were just greedy and insatiable. Still, he would not dare not to pay them off. The consequences would be too grave. He consoled himself with the fact that he fortunately had followed the advice of the Chinese seaman who wore his hair in a braid at the nape of his neck.

He still remembered what the Chinese captain had told him: "Gamati, your cloves are of top quality, and so are your son's and son-in-law's. We call your cloves the king's clove. It's the most aromatic of all. It will not grow mold even though we keep it for a long time. We don't mind to trade it for gold."

The Chinese captain had placed some gold jewelry on the woven sarong Gamati laid on the floor of his small boat. The captain had to disguise himself as a fisherman after the VOC enforced the spice trade monopoly. The gold jewelry consisted of necklaces for men and women, plain gold rings, stud earrings, dangle earrings, bracelets, and brooches for clothes or a man's turban. Once, the foreign seamen gave him a small gold plate and small gold bowls to use in traditional ceremonies to honor ancestors, or to serve drinks to honored guests. If no one had stolen it, the items must still be buried in the soil of the Tupawaroka kampong.

The trade had occurred every four years or so, after the pata cengkei.

"What do we need this much gold for?" Gamati had asked. "We need metal tools such as knives, machetes, hoes, and sickles, and axes to use on the plantation."

The Chinese trader replied, "We traded them with other farmers, whose cloves are not as fragrant as yours. You can trade their tools for fabrics, sago, or dried salted fish later."

"But surely we can't use the gold to farm, can we?"

"Gold can be kept dozens of years, even hundreds. It won't stain or perish. Store it in Chinese porcelain jars and bury it deep. Mark the spot with a pole, a big rock, or a tree with shallow roots. Someday, when you're in deep trouble, you can retrieve the gold and trade it. You can use it to buy a boat, move to another place, or in the event of war, you can trade the gold for weapons. During a great drought and time of famine, it will buy you food."

Gamati, his son, and his son-in-law lived by the long-held tradition to obtain what was needed and use it all. When the goods ran out, they searched for more. After all, they lived on an island with an abundance of clove trees. They never knew that they could save something for future needs such as to buy an escape boat, or to buy food in times of great famine. The three of them had thought that it was a good idea, a noble one, even. Therefore, they followed the advice. Now Gamati was reaping the benefit.

If they succeeded in moving up north and Bori and Muna had children and managed to have their clove plantation, they needed a bigger ship. An arumbae could sail from island to island, far away from the VOC. They had to be free seamen on the seas and live on the lands of their ancestors. Gamati, Kurubela, and Ranila had always wanted that.

It turned out that problems still had not completely left Gamati. It was inexplicable how the emissaries who lived in another kampong came upon the information of the small wedding party that had been only attended by Tuna villagers.

Rona remembered the three middle-aged men. Gamati and his grandchildren were visiting the scorched site of Tupawalili when the emissaries came to the hut the first time.

At first, they made small talk. Among the information they gave was that there was a long drought in the northern islands, mainly where the clove trees originated. Even though the islands' population was sparse now, the sultan of Ternate was trying to send food to help. Many ships had been dispatched.

Grandpa Rona added he also heard rumors that in the south, where nutmeg originated, there were recurring showers of ash from the mountain for several days. This type of ash was not good for trees. Many tall java almond trees and the nutmeg trees in their shade were burnt at the top. They might have to be cut down.

The emissaries said that fortunately there was no great drought or earthquake on Seram.

"Let's hope the next pata cengkei several months from now won't be damaged," Grandpa Rona spoke, as if addressing himself.

After they were served a plate of betel leaves and nuts, along with some cakes, one of the visitors asked about the wedding reception some days ago.

Ronasundu and Gamati were surprised but quickly regained their composure. They smiled cordially, and Ronasundu asked what they needed to know about a party that happened several days earlier.

The visitors said that Ronasundu had told them during their previous visit that there were no youth living in the hut, whereas the sultan at the palace had heard there was a couple of handsome youth worthy to be palace entertainers. Then the next thing they heard was there was a wedding reception.

Rona looked at Gamati to answer the question. Gamati explained that at the time of their previous visit, he and his grandchildren were in the forest looking for wild honey and medicinal herbs. That was how he made a living, other than catching fish at the sea to be dried. Gamati hoped that they would not ask about his origin and home kampong. He did not want any mention of Kurubela and Manipa Island, as they were enemies of the VOC.

The emissaries casually asked why Gamati had taken the youth to the forest with him.

Gamati answered, "They need to learn how to provide for themselves so they can be independent when they grow up."

"Are they not brother and sister?" one of the men asked.

"No, they aren't. Their father and mother were brother and sister. They are cousins."

"Where are their parents now?"

"They passed away. Their boats capsized in a storm. The children survived the accident, and I have taken care of them since they were very young. I'm a widower."

There was a momentary silence. When the emissaries asked about Ronasundu's relation to Gamati, he quickly answered that their wives were kin. He hoped that the fact his wife had passed away would stop further questioning and added, "Perhaps through their great-great-grandparents."

"So, where are the newlyweds? We would like to meet them."

"Unfortunately, they are in the forest looking for some medicinal massoia bark."

"We heard that the young woman is very pretty and the young man is handsome and well-built. He is also supposed to be a good rower."

"I think you're mistaken, my lord. She's not pretty at all. She's as dark as black rock. Her legs are as thin as those of a cassowary bird. And her voice is like the screech of a cockatoo."

One of the emissaries gave Gamati a doubtful look. Then he said sharply, "I don't think people dare to send false news to the palace."

"Tuang, I'm a man. I know pretty women. And, I know for sure that my granddaughter, bless the poor girl, isn't pretty. She's lucky her cousin agreed to marry her."

Gamati purposely used the word "Tuang," a polite word to address an honored man, to flatter the emissaries and tame their anger. It was feasible for the emissaries to separate a man and wife to make the sultan happy and to save their own positions in the palace.

Grandpa Rona smiled knowingly as if in agreement with Gamati.

At last, the emissaries bade farewell. They each only chewed a pinch of betel and did not touch the cake. In the Moluccas this was a sign of disappointment.

As luck would have it, the men did not display their arrogance and send someone to fetch the newlyweds in the forest, or order Bori and Muna to see them when they returned from the forest. They still respected Ronasundu as a member of the tribal council in Tuna, so they were not looking for a quarrel.

After they left, Gamati hugged the kind Ronasundu. Tears of gratitude and happiness rolled down his cheeks.

"My brother Rona, please don't ever tell anyone, including your son Lissanei, that we're related to Kurubela. We've already been betrayed once and lost everything. We can't take any more. Please, Rona, promise me."

Ronasundu was very touched by the devastating life of his friend Gamati. He nodded in silence. If it were possible, he would take on half of his friend's misery.

Gamati went straightaway to a corner of the plantation to pray according to his belief. He conveyed his gratitude. His deity had "inspired" the newlyweds to visit the forest that day, and now they were safe. He did not want anyone to separate Sobori and Aimuna, or take them to the palace, away from him. If that were to happen, Kurubela's family would perish, and no free man of his descendants would sail the seas aboard an arumbae.

After he finished praying, Gamati left the baileo and went to the beach, even though lunch was ready and the sun scorching hot. Perspiration trickled down his body. He found a shady spot under a tropical sea almond tree. He stretched his legs in the water and took off his shirt to dry his perspiration. This stretch of shady beach was not a place to moor a ship. A coral reef garden grew under the crystal-clear water surface.

Gamati used to bring the tearful Muna to this part of the beach. She would stop crying once she saw the colorful fishes swim around the "flowers" of the coral reef. When he let her wade into the water, she would scream in delight and try to catch the fish with her bare hand.

Now, old Gamati himself came to find solace here. He gazed at the mysterious deep blue sea. The waves rolled toward the shore and were about to dash against him. The white sandy beach colored the clear water a greenish blue a few meters away from the white sand.

Some memories of disasters he had encountered at sea surfaced. Times when violent winds suddenly hit the ship despite the calm season. When crests of waves as high as a wrathful mountain flung his ship, and threw baskets filled with cloves and fish into a raging sea.

Gamati's mind wandered to his late family members: his daughter, Ranila, and his son-in-law, Kurubela. He remembered the moment Sobori was born. He thought of Tarambessi, his son, and little Limo who had died alongside his parents. Aimuna was the only one left to remind him of his son Tarambessi and his wife.

He missed them all. They were always on his mind. Sometimes they felt so close he thought he could touch them. *How I long for them...when shall we all see each other again?*

The rising temperature and the lulling sound of the breaking waves lapping the shore made him sleepy. Gamati dozed off with both feet in the water.

He dreamed he took Aimuna on board a large arumbae loaded with a cargo of baskets filled with palm sugar, salted dried fish, venison jerky, cotton cloth from foreign lands, and coconuts. They had traded with the Tuban traders and there was even some rice.

They were headed for some distant shore. Sobori was the captain of the arumbae. He looked taller, his curly hair was cropped close to his head and he was clean-shaven. His cleft chin was his main allure. He appeared authoritative even when Muna and Gamati came on board.

"Muna, Muna," Gamati screamed when Aimuna suddenly fell overboard. The sound of his own scream awoke him. Luckily, there was no one around. The leaves of the tropical sea almond tree were colorful; green, red, orange, brown, and yellow, and the wind blew them away. A number of the leaves briefly caressed his face and Gamati realized he had only been dreaming.

Gamati was terrified to lose Muna and Bori. Gazing at the sea while the waves caressed his feet, he let the ocean water rise to his knees, and relaxed.

The sea was Gamati's joy. He grew up surrounded by it; he earned his living from it; his character and traits had been shaped by it. The sea was truly a remarkable place. It provided paths to other islands where he traded. Unfortunately, the path was also used by the traitors who had raided his kampong and plantation. The blue sea, with its wind whistling in his ears, was a food source for his people. He could not imagine living away from the sea. Gamati suddenly realized how much he loved the sea that surrounded his motherland. His perspiration had dried off and he went home to have his lunch.

Later that night, he told Aimuna and Sobori his dream of Muna slipping from his grip and falling into the sea. The newlyweds laughed and said, "Grandpa is old and needs to rest more."

A while back the Ronasundus had requested Gamati and his family eat with them. They enjoyed the merriment the young people brought. However, that night Gamati went by himself and visited with the old couple till deep into the night. He purposely gave the newlyweds a chance to be romantic without his presence.

***

Domingo de Freytas, the owner of the bakery, was celebrating his 65th birthday. He held a small banquet for the high officials of the VOC. The resident of Saparua, Lucas de Vries, would attend the banquet. He happened to be in Ambon along with a number of VOC officials. They were finalizing the plans for the hongi expedition to the northern

200

islands, to extirpate the unlisted clove trees. It seemed they needed to "re-list" those trees.

Lucas worked from early morning till sunset on taking notes and painting his impressions to document his environment. He felt obligated to paint the tasteful cakes of Portugal and Ambon. The recipes of cakes and vegetable dishes that used cloves and mace were confidential, but he documented them anyway. The VOC claimed exclusivity over the spices and even traders found in illegal possession of the spices were sentenced to death. Before coming to Ambon, the governor's wife had never smelled the aroma of the cloves in food.

If anyone asked the de Freytases about the ingredients they used in their cakes, they always answered that they bought the spices from the natives who lived in kampongs far from the white men settlements.

"What are the names of the kampongs?" the officers' wives often asked him.

"I do not know the names myself." De Freytas played dumb.

In fact, de Freytas did use cloves, although not from the illegal suppliers. He purchased overripe cloves. This clove was late in the picking, and the VOC never confiscated overripe cloves. The natives used it for medicine, or seasonings for fish and vegetables cooked in coconut milk. Even clove leaves were still of use to the natives. The de Freytases simply took advantage of these overripe cloves.

The same thing was true about the nutmeg. The fragrant aroma of fresh nutmeg was indeed extraordinary, especially after it was ground into a fine powder. De Freytas often received deliveries of wild nutmeg and mace from Seram instead of Banda. Therefore, he did not break any of the VOC's rules.

As for the cinnamon, he did not know where it came from. Perhaps from the west, since he purchased it from Tuban and Gresik traders. Sometimes he obtained it from the Makassar traders. It was very costly in large quantities. The traders sometimes asked to trade the cinnamon with gold. Nevertheless, de Freytas needed the cinnamon to season his cakes, or fish dishes.

De Freytas had also invited the governor and his wife. However, they would not attend the banquet since they thought that the baker's low social rank was unworthy of their attendance. Also, the Dutch were not too keen on socializing with the Portuguese. The two countries had been at war for decades in Europe, not to mention the growing competition between them to control the seas of the world.

De Freytas was an excellent accordion player. His oldest son played the guitar and a fellow churchgoer was a great violin player. They had enough instruments for a simple dance band.

An affluent spice trader who was a trade agent for the VOC provided the wine. Many guests came. They were mostly members of the local upper class who could afford to patronize the bakery.

Lucas de Vries was immaculately dressed according to his rank. He wore a delicate white shirt, trimmed with lace at the collar and front side, pitch-black pants, and jacket. He wore light brown dress shoes, the same color as his hair.

He looked like a handsome Latino.

Karel and Bertie were also dressed formally. They were much darker than the other newly arrived white men. Other dignitaries who attended the banquet were the secretary, the storage head, the administrative head, the liaison officer, the VOC's purchaser and some church members.

Rosamunda wore a long red dress. A rather large brooch decorated her dress near the neck area. A pair of dangling earrings completed the picture.

Lucas had painted Rosamunda many times, as an example of mixed descendants of the Indonesian natives. Unlike Lucas, Rosa did not look like a Latina. She possessed a unique charm; she was neither European nor Asian. Her warm smile, her bright shining eyes and long, curly eyelashes gave her a truly exquisite look. Her hair color was a distinctive shade of auburn.

The banquet began after the host gave a short speech and then cut the cake. Every guest could smell the fragrant cinnamon in the cake. Almost everyone had come with an empty stomach. They knew a scrumptious buffet awaited them. The table would be decked with many dishes such as rice cooked with shrimp, various soups of fresh fish, and fresh tropical fruit such as ripe, sweet mangosteen and rose apples. They waited for the host's signal to start the feast.

Everyone present seemed happily satisfied with the food and the amount of wine served.

Finally the music was played, and the dancing began. There were not too many young women among the guests. The majority of white people came to the Moluccas to work hard and save money. They seldom brought their wives and family along. Only a few of the couples had children. If the man married a native woman or had a native mistress, their children as a rule would not be accepted in the high-society circles.

The male guests repeatedly asked Rosamunda, her mother, and her younger sister to dance. It had been quite a while since Karel and Bertie were at a party such as this. They ate, drank, and danced with high-spirited gaiety; however, they were not drunk.

The governor always reminded Lucas, Karel, and Bertie that they were representatives of the VOC, and, even though they were all bachelors, they should not behave like wild studs. It would tarnish their reputation and diminish their authority as high officials, he said. Despite the strict rules, the natives opposed them. They could be attacked at any time with a machete or shot at from a hidden spot with an arrow. There were several bars outside the fort if they needed entertainment. There were women to have fun with, and it wouldn't be a scandal to get drunk there.

The governor explained further that the Dutch in the Moluccas were not morally righteous people. Some of the men sent as soldiers were also sidelining as VOC workers. They were not of respectable character or selected men. Many of them were foreign mercenaries, who were jobless in their own native lands. It was inevitable that they liked to drown their sorrows in liquor. They were shameless and immoral, the governor pointed out repeatedly.

The governor realized the VOC's mission was to reap profit, profit, and profit. The high officials were educated men and came from decent families. Therefore, they had to show some degree of sophistication, since they dealt with important people such as the sultans from the northern islands, the warlords of Makassar, the rulers of Tuban and Gresik, the Banten sultan, and many more.

"If we act like wild studs, they will scorn us," the governor said.

Bertie Dumas was particularly happy that night. Paulina de Waal was among the other guests. She was the widow of a VOC officer and dressed very pretty. Her beautiful, light brown, waist-length hair matched her eyes, and she often wore it loose. When she laughed, dimples marked her cheeks. Albeit a little plump, she was a good dancer. Bertie and Paulina danced almost without changing partners.

Bertie did not hide his attraction to Paulina. However, Paulina had yet to respond to his advances. Bertie had only recently arrived on the island and one day would return to his country. She was not quite sure about his plans. She could not tell if he would make a good trader. The only way to survive here was to be a savvy trader of spices and Chinese porcelain.

It was no secret that Karel was attracted to Hermina Meyer. Hermina's father was a Dutch-born German, and her mother was a free-spirited Italian beauty who was quite a libertine and who often modeled for the painters in Rome. Meyer had brought her to Batavia and then to Ambon. After Hermina was born, her mother eloped to Europe with another man, a painter.

Her stepmother, a Dutch woman whose mother was Javanese, raised Hermina in an all-European tradition. Hermina sang and danced very well.

Karel and Hermina danced almost without changing partners. They never left the dance floor and were absorbed in each other. It seemed Karel had made up his mind to marry Hermina.

He figured that besides gaining experience as a botanist with the VOC, he could join the ranks of would-be traders who were present throughout the company's ranks. Besides, he could "trade" like many of his fellow employees of the VOC, from the highest official down to the workers.

Karel had learned the secret of clove pinching during his stay on Ambon. He knew he had to maintain a good relationship with the clerk, cashier, storekeeper, kampong chiefs and the like, and along with anyone else plead ignorance regarding the company's great losses.

Karel was getting to know some foreign traders from Makassar, Denmark, Spain, and also from Siam and China. They frequently sailed from the Malacca port. These traders more often than not did not mind taking part in the plot to smuggle the cloves.

Karel figured that once he became rich, he could take Hermina to Rome instead of Holland. They could live in Italy. Unlike Lucas, Karel did not pay attention to details. He always acted first, and thought of the consequences later.

Engulfed in the band's lilting music, Karel and Hermina danced in a tight embrace. Karel whispered, "Hermina, I want to always be this happy with you. I won't be able to enjoy life without you. Will you be with me until the day I die?"

At first, Hermina thought that Karel was joking and only being witty. The chances of finding a husband on this isolated island were very slim. She hardly had any options.

The white or half-white men were mostly old. Many of them were crippled, having lost an arm, leg, or eyesight because of the war. Some of them were drunks or simply broke. Their wives were native women who went barefoot.

If Karel was serious about his proposition, she would accept it. He liked living in the tropical country, where life was slower. One did not need to rush; there was no fear of getting caught in falling snow. In addition, there was the chance he'd become a rich man in the spice trade.

Lucas could never be as demonstrative and open as Karel about his feelings, although he was delighted to see Rosamunda that night. He was often awestruck when he painted her. Just so he could look longer at Rosamunda, he often pretended it took a long time to finish the painting. Her kind nature had warmed his heart. Moreover, Rosa could keep up a good conversation since she often discussed many topics with her father. De Freytas had traveled a lot and had a wide circle of friends.

Rosamunda also reminded Lucas of his late mother. She was friendly, and she liked to ask small questions that showed her genuine interest in the people she talked with. She also had this little dainty laugh. She never acted formal with the resident of Saparua.

Sadly, there was the VOC policy that prohibited an officer who married a woman of mixed race in the Moluccas from bringing her back to Holland. Lucas had always wanted to return to Holland to become a famous painter. However, he would never leave his wife once he married. He hated the thought of a broken home as he himself had been one of its victims.

He would never abandon Rosamunda just because of the foolish VOC policy. She was far too kind, good, and refined.

Lucas had been thinking about his feelings for Rosamunda for quite a while. However, he never told anyone about it. He did not want people to give him ill advice; tell him to get married illegally and just live together like hundreds of other couples.

Lucas knew that Domingo de Freytas and his wife liked him. They did not know yet that he had Portuguese blood. He wondered whether if they knew, they would accept him as their son-in-law. He also knew that Rosa was still single.

There were not many Portuguese families in Ambon after they were ousted from the Moluccas. Finding partners for young people had become a problem because there were not many options available.

When they danced, Lucas and Rosa talked about the beauty of the sea, the dangers in the forest, and the freezing winter in Holland at year-end. They talked about many things, except their feelings for each other.

Lucas told Rosa about the great drought in the northern islands. He had been commissioned to cut down the clove trees that had bloomed. They needed to destroy the illegal trees and find saplings to plant in the plantations on Saparua. He feared that the existing VOC trees that had not bloomed would not survive while they still searched for the saplings.

"Your assignment, will it involve death?" Rosa asked, frightened.

"Sadly yes, it will, Rosa. Any expedition of clove trees extirpation will result in deaths. The natives hate us. Their retaliation should not come as a big surprise."

Rosa was silent. Her body swayed to the melody of her father and brother's music. She regretted that no one was able to relieve her father and brother from playing the instruments. They had to keep playing while the singers could take turns. Most everyone was a fairly good singer and was used to singing in the church's choir.

Lucas mentioned in passing that when it was time for him to go home, he would try to live in Lisbon.

"Lisbon? Why not Amsterdam, or Paris, where famous painters live? Or, why not Rome, the city of Leonardo da Vinci?" Rosamunda wondered.

"Those cities are too old-fashioned. I'd like to try a new place. Lisbon is an artery of trade between Europe and Asia. I'm convinced that there are new objects there that will become new sensations in Europe."

Rosa believed him. She had heard many things about her ancestors' country from her relatives in Makassar.

"How wonderful it is to be a man," she said softly, "you can go and live anywhere you want. I would love to see Lisbon. However, my father lives here. He might never go there. We're a big family. It'll surely cost a lot for us to sail there," she said.

"Have you ever talked about it with your father?" Lucas asked.

"Yes, I have. He said that it'll cost a fortune. In addition, it's a long and dangerous voyage. It's only a dream to me."

"But who knows, one day your dream may come true, Rosa. A beautiful life always begins with impossible childhood dreams, doesn't it? Keep praying for it," Lucas consoled her.

After he completed his commission with the VOC, Lucas planned to return first to Holland. He had small savings. He would move to Lisbon and since his grandfather was Portuguese, he would get permissions easily. After all of that was taken care of, he would ask Rosa to come along. Unfortunately, it wasn't going to happen soon. Moreover, it would only happen if the VOC granted his return to

Holland. It would take even longer if his father asked him to extend his stay in the east. He had no right to ask Rosa to wait that long. Therefore, he kept his feelings for Rosa to himself. He knew that Rosa was interested in visiting her ancestors' country. He prayed that her dream would come true.

De Freytas' birthday banquet was the talk among high society for quite some time. He had many friends; all the VOC's high officials were his bakery's best customers.

The resident of Saparua, the eligible bachelor, was dancing intimately with Rosamunda. It was factual news, not just groundless rumor. The resident was considered an honorable man of high position. Everyone wondered why he had chosen Rosa, the half-Portuguese girl. There were other Dutch girls. Now that everything was said and done, what else was there left to do?

After the banquet, the resident spent another few weeks on Ambon. The hongi expedition the VOC officials were planning was a large operation, and involved many ships. They needed many crewmembers, extensive weaponry, a lot of provisions and training for the troops.

The clove tree harvest was a few weeks away, hopefully within two months' time. Since the VOC's clove trees had not yet bloomed, they needed to fill the warehouse with cloves from other sources, such as from the conquered islands around Ambon, or, alternatively, from the southern seaside of Seram and from Ternate and Tidore.

The governor had ordered the kampong chiefs to estimate their harvest. After adding the reported figures, the clerk and storekeeper estimated the total harvest of the kampongs to be approximately eight bahars. One bahar was roughly one hundred kilograms of dried clove buds. This was far less than last year's harvest. The situation was undoubtedly caused by the long drought during that year.

However, it would be the same if the supply was excessive. In either case the Assembly of the Lords Seventeen would send a letter of reprimand and demand the illegal traders be eliminated. He wondered out loud, "When will they ever compliment us for our hard work?"

"Their greed is insatiable," the resident of Saparua grumbled.

"Yes, it is, Mister Resident," the governor added quietly, "Greed was the main motive to explore the east. Greed inspired them to order the hongi expeditions, the clove trees' extirpation, the expensive license badge, the spice trade monopoly, the allowance to bribe the sultans, etc. I often wonder where this insatiable greed comes from."

"You're right," Lucas answered.

After the meeting, Lucas, Karel, and Bertie headed for the de Freytas' bakery. There was a possibility that the three ladies they fancied would be there. They wanted to make good use of the little time they still had in Ambon and they all enjoyed eating tasty cakes in the evening.

After three weeks of planning, the governor decided the resident of Saparua was going to lead a hongi expedition to the Banda Islands, southeast of Ambon. Two large war ships outfitted with cannons, soldiers, and extra oarsmen who were native slaves were dispatched to escort his ship.

"There was a volcanic eruption on Banda last year. It burned the nutmeg and Java almond trees, so we need to clean up the area. We have to remove the dead trees and find new tree saplings. Perhaps Karel and Bertie can apply their knowledge there," the governor said.

The three men were astonished.

The resident had already ordered the kampong chiefs in Saparua and the neighboring islands to prepare for their hongi to the north, to the islands where the cloves originated. He wondered why he now had to go south.

Lucas felt that all the time he had spent on studying the maps, climate, winds, and currents of the northern islands for the past several weeks was wasted. Karel and Bertie, who had checked the types of trees, weeds, and pests of clove trees, were now suddenly expected to tend nutmeg trees.

"Gentlemen! The expedition to the southeast doesn't involve any battle. We'll only send two warships to escort the expedition. All you have to do there is to make notes of how many trees were extirpated and how many were left to cultivate. You need to list the names of the plantation owners and the number of slaves per family. The botanists can figure out a plan to find new nutmeg saplings."

The governor planned to lead the hongi expedition to the little islands up north. Two of the islands had a volcanic mountain. One of the mountains rose straight from the dark blue ocean. The clove trees grew on the slope of that mountain.

Four warships were assigned to escort the governor's ship. The ships would sail from Ternate. The kora-koras would be manned by natives and sent by the sultan.

Despite the fact that the VOC had relocated the inhabitants and laid waste to the land, there were still some settlements found. Every so often pirate ships would moor and hide there. Instead of paying for the VOC's license, they robbed any ship sailing nearby.

As a profit-driven establishment, the VOC regarded the pirates as the cause of their loss in revenue. Their previous plan was that the resident of Saparua would lead the expedition to eliminate the last inhabitants of the islands. They were still going through with the plan, only with a different leader.

Unlike the hongi to the northern islands, the expedition to the nutmeg and mace islands in the southeast was planned hastily. Hence, the resident of Saparua and his group needed to return to Saparua to give orders to the natives drafted into the hongi expedition. Before he sailed for his hongi mission, Lucas de Vries had to check on the provisions and weaponry such as swords, spears, and rifles.

Rosa, Paulina, and Hermina purposely came to the port on the day of Lucas' departure to bid him and the botanists farewell. Lucas looked dashing and stout. He was in fact secretly touched. As an orphan, he never had this many women care about him leaving.

***

Bori and Muna's wedding lingered long in the memories of the Tuna inhabitants. The happy couple became the center of attention whenever they crossed the streets. They looked so vibrant and exuberant. It was understandable since they were still in their teens.

Then came the news that the pata cengkei would be held in a few days. All the adults of Tuna made preparations. They prepared the saloi baskets, gae-gae and the knives to tie at its end, numerous mats, and the shabby workshirts. They had to pick clove buds in many plantations.

Bori and Muna joined the others to pick clove buds on the plantations. The Ronasundus and the kampong chief owned many plantations. Someone said that last night the kampong chief had visited Ronasundu's house. The VOC's warehouse on Saparua was empty and the resident had ordered to fill it with cloves from the harvest.

The women had previously prepared ready-to-eat meals, usually of rice wrapped in banana or coconut leaves. Aimuna had also joined the cooking process the day before.

"What if there's only a small amount of clove buds?" someone asked.

"The Pani-pani people can go to the plantations and see for themselves that there are not many buds on the trees," someone else answered.

Now that they were husband and wife, Bori and Muna worked together. Bori climbed the tree with a saloi on his back, while Muna gathered the buds that fell on a large mat she placed under the tree.

The women sorted and sundried the buds right away. As it was the peak of the dry season, the sun was very bright and hot, especially since it was a long dry season.

Although they did not live in Tuna, Makasuli and his wife helped with the harvest. It was the spirit of masohi, of helping each other. Grandpa Rona and Grandpa Gamati did not participate. It was considered appropriate to have them rest.

A number of people who knew Bori and Muna greeted them. Everyone worked fast. The next day, they had to harvest the plantations in other kampongs. Tuna had to hand over around a half pikul and two katis, approximately sixteen kilograms, of clove buds to the VOC.

No one dared to tease Muna during the harvest. They did not want a fight with Sobori. He had grown into a seasoned sailor and was quite strong.

After they finished picking and sun-drying the cloves, they packed the cloves inside the folded mats to bring home. The plantation was quite a distance from the kampong. On their way home, they stopped by a small stream to bathe and to wash their equipment.

The sun radiated its final rays of golden light as it set on the west horizon. Bori and Muna were always entranced by the light. Many of the harvesters sat on a dead tree trunk by the stream, and, for a moment, they were silent as they gazed to the west in awe. It was as if they were in another world. Everything was bathed in an exquisite amber glow, more radiant than gold. Even their skin and faces looked as if they were made out of gold too. The giant amber ball, more radiant than a blazing fire in the stove, slowly faded. Then a part of the sun disappeared. Perhaps it sunk into the ocean.

Sobori looked up. The exquisite amber glow also radiated through the layers of fluffy clouds and colored them.

Muna was silent, her eyes open wide. She had watched many sunrises and sunsets, but this time, she could share her feelings with Bori. For a fleeting moment, she felt as if she were underwater in the warm sea. Her whole body warmed with the exhilaration of knowing she was never going to be alone again as an orphan. She finally had someone to share the sunset, the clouds, and the whispering wind with. Aimuna was content.

When they came home, they had dinner with the Ronasundus in their hut. The young couple knew that Grandpa Rona loved to hear stories from people who had spent their entire day away from the hut. Aimuna told them about the beautiful sunset, its vibrant, amber glow. Grandpa Rona liked the way Muna told the story: simple and lively, such a contrast with the way he was, a frail old man.

Suddenly, Aimuna had trouble eating her dinner. The different aromas nauseated her. She struggled to swallow the food, but could no longer hold it. She jumped up and ran to the well in the back of the hut. They could hear her vomit. She looked pale when she returned.

Grandma Rona immediately understood what it indicated. "Muna might be pregnant," she whispered to Gamati.

"This soon?" Gamati asked.

"It depends on one's health. Some women get pregnant fast, while it's harder for others. Some can't even get pregnant. It's fine if Muna is not ill but pregnant. We'll help her. We'd be happy to have children again in this hut," she said tenderly.

Although Gamati was not convinced that Aimuna was pregnant and thought she might just be ill, he nodded. After Gamati, Sobori, and Muna thanked the Ronasundus, they returned to their smaller hut. As soon as they closed the door behind them, Gamati whispered, "Aimuna, are you really pregnant? I mean, have you ever asked a more experienced woman how it is with pregnant woman?"

"Yes, I have, Grandpa," she answered in a hushed voice.

They were afraid someone would hear them.

"So what Grandma Rona said just now is true?"

"I believe so, Grandpa. Aren't you happy with the news?"

"I certainly am, sweetheart. However, I didn't expect it to happen this soon. You have to be strong, Muna. We're planning to relocate soon. We won't have a home or a kampong. We'll live in the forest while we wait for our big ship. Then we'll sail north. I hope you can eat well soon, and won't be vomiting. There's a lepa-lepa for our voyage north."

"Yes, I hope I'll be strong enough, Grandpa. I'm afraid Lissanei will suddenly show up. This is after all his father's hut and he can pretend to miss his parents. If he ever hurts Sobori, I'll kill myself. I don't want him to touch me."

"Very well. We'll leave soon, regardless of whether you're pregnant or ill. I'll go to Makasuli's to prepare everything."

"Grandpa, please tell us more about what you and Grandpa Makasuli are planning, about our plan to move. Where will we sail to, what kampong, and how will we find food?" Sobori asked.

"We're going to use a lepa-lepa that cost us six gold necklaces. We'll sail eastward, following the shoreline, and pretend to be fishermen. At dark, we will stop by an estuary. We will rest and hide the boat there and Muna can sleep in the cabin. We'll leave again the next morning. We'll continue to sail this way until we reach the kampong of the refugees from Banda where Makasuli's relatives live. There'll be no time to wait for a custom-made ship. We'll just trade for whatever boat is available there, anything larger than a lepa-lepa. Then we'll sail north."

Sobori was silent. He had never sailed far before, except while on the run as a hongi refugee. He couldn't imagine how large the area and forest that they would travel through would be or how vast the ocean they'd sail.

Sobori wondered if there was a chance they would run into Lissanei. The man had said that he was the captain of a large arumbae that belonged to the Tuna kampong. He carried cargo of many trading items. He knew almost every seaman-trader on the seas of the Moluccas.

Bori thought it was strange that except for that one time, Lissanei had never visited his parents during the entire time they had lived in Grandpa Rona's hut, and the old man had never mentioned his son's name. He asked, "Why do you think Lissanei suddenly showed up? Did he long for his parents? Or did he have to deliver cargo?"

Gamati smiled wisely and said, "Bori, the sea is a main road for us islanders. We sail across the seas to get to other islands. It's the source of salt and the fish we eat with papeda. We contemplate on the beach as we gaze at the beauty of a dew-covered Ambon early morning. It's an open road. Everyone can use it. Pani-pani, the ships from Makassar, and the ship of our honorable Sultan of Tidore sail across its waters. It even carries the pirate ships from Papua, and evil Lissanei's ship. Grandpa Makasuli is finding out about the places Lissanei often visits, and when he usually moors there to trade so we can avoid those places."

"Why is it so important for us to leave Seram, Grandpa?"

"Did you forget that aside from Lissanei wanting to take Muna from you, the palace people want to use the two of you as entertainers, and you can get drafted for the hongi?"

"How do we find food in the new place?"

"We'll plant a secret plantation, just like the one we had in Tupawalili. We'll fish, and make salted fish. We'll make venison jerky. We'll trade with the foreigners who come to the island."

"Will there be foreigners who come to trade? I don't want us to be raided again."

"Son, when you're a married man, you can no longer be afraid to face danger. Should there be a traitor and they raid us again, there's nothing left to say. We tried to better our lives. We fought, just like your father and mother, and other brave members of our people. I heard that Pani-pani doesn't have a fort there. The foreign ships that come to the islands are small, but fast. I hope we'll make it. You'll have many children and grandchildren, and one day we'll have our own arumbae."

"I'm not afraid to fight, Grandpa. I just don't want to fight before I have children. I can't forget the way Father and Mother died, bathed in blood. I never want to do something that horrible to a father of any child. When I really think of it, the thought of killing Lissanei disturbs me."

"I understand, Bori. That's why we've to leave Tuna as soon as possible. Now, go to sleep." Gamati put out the lamp and soon they were fast asleep.

In the morning, Gamati went to see Makasuli. The lepa-lepa was ready. They only had to build a small cabin with a roof to protect them from the rain or hot sun.

Aside from Makasuli and his family, six young men from a kampong north of Tuna were to join them. They would take turns rowing the boat.

They expected that the long sail to the Banda Islands southeast of Seram would be safe. Makasuli had heard that the VOC ships patrolled the seas and islands up north. Sailing south, they would not run into the VOC. The whereabouts of the Papuans was the only unknown factor.

Gamati and Makasuli decided to sail as soon as possible. They would bring farming tools such as hoes, long and short machetes, some sickles, kitchen knives and meat cleavers to use when making meat jerky. They did not bring any arrows or spears. If they ran into the VOC and had their boat searched, they would be mistaken for fishermen and farmers.

Besides the six young men, another eight from two different kampongs were to join them. They were between seventeen and thirty years old, young and spirited. Four of them were relatives of Makela, Makasuli's wife. Just like Gamati and Makasuli, they did not want to join the hongi. They considered the hongi evil. Their bonds of kinship forbade them from causing misery to fellow Moluccan people. They leaped at the opportunity to escape the hongi draft.

Gamati checked on the things and provisions they brought along. Besides the iron farming tools, they had brought food: dried salted fish, sugar, and a large quantity of dried sago. If they had to live for a short while in the forest, it would be hard to find a sago palm grove nearby. They had also brought some earthen cookware to cook, some medication, like ointments, and some sarongs they could tear should one of them need a wound dressing.

As for the gold jewelry, only Gamati and Makasuli knew its hiding place. Aside from them, Bori was the only one who knew they had gold.

One afternoon, when their preparation was almost finished, Gamati asked Ronasundu to sit together under the guava trees by the porch. He did not want anyone to overhear his conversation with Rona.

Gamati thanked Ronasundu and his wife for their kindness during his stay with them. He also asked Ronasundu to convey his gratitude to the domestic help. Aimuna had come as a crybaby and lived there until she married. Sobori grew from a boy into a good seaman and a husband while living there.

"We'll remember your kindness for the rest of our lives, my brother." Gamati's voice shook with emotion. "We are poor people, we've lost everything. So sadly, I can't give you any souvenirs. I'll pray that you and your wife will be fine; you can live in peace although you have to bow down to Pani-pani. Perhaps some day, when Bori's more mature and his baby is born, he will continue my fight against Pani-pani. Let's hope that one day, we'll be free traders like our ancestors."

Ronasundu was deeply touched. He had mentally prepared himself for this farewell for a while. "Gamati, my brother, I don't want to stand in the way of your plan. I hope everything works well for you, Muna, and Bori. I'm now very old; it's difficult for me to leave the house. What should I tell anyone who asks about your whereabouts?" Ronasundu fought back his tears.

"Just tell them that we went back to Ambon, to my late wife's kampong. We'll be fishermen there, just like we used to be."

"It's better for me to not know where you're heading, so I can never betray you, even if they tortured me. Good-bye for now, my dear brother, I hope you will have what you wish for. Now, my hut will be quiet again. My wife and I will miss the three of you."

"Thank you, Rona. Send my regards to Grandma Rona. I can't bring myself to see her and say good-bye. We'll definitely start crying and the servants will get curious."

"Yes, very well, my brother. Go in peace," Ronasundu whispered.

They held each other for a while in a tight embrace then Gamati went back to the small hut to get Muna and Bori. They did not bring anything since they had moved their belongings little by little. Aimuna noticed Gamati had been crying.

The sun was not yet fully overhead when they arrived at Makasuli's. They walked separately to a shady cove where the man who had traded the lepa-lepa for six gold necklaces had moored the boat. No one was at the cove.

Makasuli estimated that toward the evening they would reach a place where they could spend the night. It was still on Seram. The place was uninhabited and far from the Halefurus. They had brought ready-to-eat food for their supper.

Aimuna and Makela dressed as men for the long voyage. They had tied their hair back and wore headscarves just like the others. This was necessary to make someone who spotted their boat from land think that it was a fishing boat.

They sailed smoothly. The sky was clear and there were no big waves. Makela accompanied Aimuna in the roofed cabin. Muna was pregnant and Makela had to prepare their supper for later when they moored for the night.

They hoped they wouldn't run into any boats or ships until the sun set. They wanted to avoid questions. There weren't too many vessels sailing to the south or southeast. Perhaps the native fishermen knew about the VOC's upcoming hongi and decided to stay away from the seas. Perhaps the long drought had caused a shortage in produce to trade. Gamati and Makasuli could only guess.

On the other hand, there were usually many boats and ships at sea during the sailing season, which was at the beginning of the dry season. The fishermen worked hard to catch enough fish to dry and store. The Makassar and Tuban traders sailed to Seram. Sometimes there were even parades to show off the beautiful ships of the sultan's fleet.

Gamati still remembered when, back in his childhood, once a year, the fleet of the sultan's *juangas* would sail by the shores of kampongs under the sultanate of Tidore's rule. The royal ship sailed majestically in its grandeur; it seemed to glide on the waves. It was beautifully decorated with colorful silk fabrics tied to the masts. Ornaments made out of woven young coconut leaves, light green in color and pleasing to the eye, hung gracefully on the deck. The sultan's gilded throne, although it was usually empty, was flashy and could easily be spotted from afar.

The juanga's crewmembers wore a festive yellow-and-black uniform. The sultan's deputy was dressed in an all-yellow garment; yellow pants, a yellow top that was heavily decorated with jewels, and a yellow turban.

The villagers loved to stand along the beach, to hail and wave at the fleet as it sailed by. Gamati used to sit on his father's shoulders so he could see clearly. His mother and other family members would also be waving branches of young coconut leaves at the fleet.

There were battles with the white men even then. They were not from the VOC. Gamati had forgotten their name. All he could remember was that despite wars, things were never as miserable as they were now. He had never heard of the destruction of entire kampongs and clove plantations, the killings of natives or their relocation from the mountains to the seaside, the separations of families.

Human nature was as unpredictable as the restless waves of the ocean. The white men attacked their neighboring kingdom. They traded at faraway shores, and imposed their will on others. Changes were inevitable in a society.

Gamati asked himself if he missed the old times, and concluded he did not miss the people who later became his family's enemy. Particularly the second group of white men, who were not only hostile, but had even killed his family. Displaced, he and his grandchildren had been forced to move from one friend's hut to another, from one kampong to another, borrowing boats. He had to raise his orphaned grandchildren without relatives. They had to grow up without their customs and traditions. His old heart ached. Nevertheless, he had to keep going for Aimuna, Sobori, and his future great-grandchild.

Chapter 8

The thin morning mist over the ocean had evaporated in the heat of the long drought. That morning, the fort on the shore of Saparua stood brightly lit by early sunlight. The skies were clear and although the morning had just broken, sea birds were already busy hunting.

People and vessels filled the harbor by the fort. There was quite a racket. Three large ships were ready to sail, their masts rising high in the air. There was only one kora-kora that would join the expedition. The rest were the smaller natives' vessels such as rurehes and lepa-lepas. Another kora-kora could not sail since it did not have enough crewmembers.

The resident of Saparua looked tired, as he had not slept for the last few days. He wore the complete dress uniform for a fleet captain; beige cotton pants, a thin shirt with a beige jacket, and a tri-corner hat. A long, sheathed sword was girded to his waist.

Lucas de Vries had put all his painting tools aboard his ship. There were three large, fully armed VOC warships. They did not bring too many provisions. The island of their destination was quite close. There was a settlement on the island; the host would provide food for them.

Lucas looked around him, and walked along the small port, checking and counting the natives' boats that were ready to join the hongi expedition to the nutmeg plantations southward.

There had been a change in plans. They were not sailing north to the cloves' origins as planned previously, but to the Banda Islands, southeast of Seram. It was the governor's decision at their last meeting, after he had received reports that lately, the supply of nutmeg and mace had dwindled. Supposedly, the nutmeg saplings of the perkeniers on Banda had died because of the long drought. Martinus de Bruijn wanted to verify the report and rather than sending the resident of Saparua on a routine extirpation expedition, he chose to send Lucas to the Banda Islands to find a way out if the harvest of nutmeg had indeed greatly decreased.

The governor of Ambon did not want to be blamed for the VOC's loss in revenue. That would surely threaten his position. The VOC might dismiss him if he could not meet the demand of the international spice market in Holland.

Martinus de Bruijn had also been told that another European country's armada was able to obtain nutmeg and supply the European market.

The Assembly of the Lords Seventeen in Holland claimed that the perkeniers, Dutch plantation owners who were drowning in debts to the VOC, were powerless against these foreign buccaneers. They easily overpowered the natives with their heavy artillery. Their vessels were small and lean and only had one or two masts. They were fast as lightning. According to the slaves on the nutmeg plantations, these pirates came at night. They had become a terror to the natives at the seaside. Holland demanded the governor of Ambon rectify the situation.

In turn, Martinus de Bruijn then ordered the resident of Saparua and his fleet to pursue and capture the pirates, annihilate them, if necessary. Only one of the botanists, Bertie, was assigned to join Lucas on his expedition.

Lucas, who had started to become fluent in the local dialect, asked the leader of the natives whether they were ready to sail. The leader, a middle-aged man with graying curly hair that elegantly contrasted with his dark skin, answered yes. Like all the island men of the Moluccas, he was an experienced seaman.

He was adept in steering boats, reading the wind directions, currents, and waves of the seas. He also knew how to read the constellation of the stars to determine his course or when to begin sailing.

People called him Captain Tamela. Lucas knew he had a very good reputation among the seamen and secretly respected him deeply. Lucas knew almost nothing about sailing.

When Lucas heard they were ready to sail, a memory of his father transported him for a brief moment to the past.

He remembered his father taking him to lunch in a fancy restaurant in Amsterdam where the aristocrats and men of high society used to gather. He had just finished school and felt uncomfortable being in the midst of aristocracy.

His father told him that Holland was on its way to becoming a maritime kingdom, by conquering new territories, especially on the islands where spices came from and asked, "Lucas, do you notice anything different in this soup?"

"Yes, Father, it smells good and it's making me hungry."

"You've a good sense of smell, Son. You're able to recognize an exotic aroma."

Lucas had noticed his father's ravenous appetite. The way he gorged on his food almost came across as greedy. The thought had sickened him for a brief moment. He decided to let it go; after all, it was his grandmother's business to have raised his father. He had wondered if he would become rich if he grew into a tall, stocky, and gluttonous man.

They had brown, fragrant cakes for dessert. The pastry was spiced with cinnamon, cloves, and nutmeg.

"What d'you think of this cake, Lucas? Isn't it delicious?"

"This cake has a wonderful aroma as well, although different, Father."

"You're a bright and meticulous young man, just like your teachers said. I'm proud to have a son like you. My father refused to let me marry your mother. Well, the past is in the past. We can't change the course of history, can we? Let us look toward the future," his father said. He proceeded to tell Lucas about the spices and the distant lands where they were harvested and the long and arduous struggle to obtain them.

"You're an excellent painter, Son. That's a wonderful gift. Not many people are that lucky. Be grateful and make good use of your talent. The company that imports these spices to Holland is in need of painters; spirited young painters, who are willing to work hard. I've invested in this company."

While eating his cake, Lucas had tried to figure out the connection between his father's spice story and his talent to paint. From time to time, the aristocrat paused and waited for Lucas' reaction. Lucas had only smiled and looked at his father. He started to have the courage to call the man "father," like the man had asked.

"Our company is offering you work in the faraway Spice Islands. You'll be an archivist, and responsible for painting the environments and the natives of the islands for the company's archives. The company will study and analyze your paintings and later, perhaps use them as guidelines in formulating its policies. Will you accept the job?"

Lucas was surprised. He had always pictured himself back at the Wijnens after he graduated. Perhaps he would start a career as a painter, as an aside to helping Mrs. Wijnen with the cows. Never in his wildest dream had he pictured himself sailing to distant lands. He stopped eating his cake and was silent for a long time. He needed some time to let the unexpected news sink in.

"I know this isn't what you had in mind in terms of a career. You want to be a painter, don't you?"

"That's right, Father."

"No one forbids you to become a painter. I admire you. Perhaps, someday, you'll become famous. Is being an archivist in the east not the same thing as being a painter? Furthermore, you'll secure a stable position, and experience. This job will give you a good foundation for your work as a painter. Your paintings will be so much different from other painters who've never been abroad, who never worked hard. Think about it. I'm not forcing you to take this offer. I just want you to have some advantages over other young men who are desperately looking for employment."

Lucas had no idea where to inquire more about the offer, at least about the situation in the Far East. He wondered about the safety of the long voyage and what the natives would be like. His father had never gone there himself. Lucas was overwhelmed and nervous too. He thought the offer had come too suddenly to respond to now.

"Very well, Son. I will give you some time to think this over. I'll have my coach pick you up at the dorm three days from today. I'll see you then," his father said before they parted ways.

Three days later, Lucas accepted the job offer. He then prepared for the long journey to the east. The aristocrat's coach took him to the Wijnens' residence to say goodbye. He could only spend one night there, which was hardly enough time to satisfy his longing to see the Wijnens.

Sonya and Erick regretted his leaving. They missed their time together as a family, sharing everything. They shared food, beds, pillows, and blankets. They missed performing together with their cats and dogs on the sidewalk or at the front of the rich people's residences and afterward being rewarded with candies.

They missed the warm summer, the applause they received after the pet show, and the coins people gave them. Pillow fights, snowball fights, were hilarious and fun. It would be a long time, if ever, before they would experience that warmth again.

Lucas cheered them up by saying that he was not going for the adventure of his lifetime without them. It was just hard for him to turn down the aristocrat's offer, the man who had done a great deed for him. When he finished his residency, he would return to Holland and come to the Wijnens' house. He had always wanted to be a painter in his own country.

He had never imagined how perilous his long voyage to the east would be, nor did he have any idea about his life in the Spice Islands. Mr. Wijnen had again given him some pocket money. "Keep it, in case you need it," the old man said. He seemed to doubt that he would ever see Lucas again.

Now, Lucas looked at Tamela, and wondered if the valiant captain had told his wife and children that he was about to face danger and was unsure if he would see them again. Since he was incapable of vocalizing his question in the local dialect, Lucas kept the question to himself. Ever since he started his long voyage in Holland and sailed across the great open sea to the east, past West Africa to Banten, and then on to the Moluccas, death had always been near. They constantly faced danger and the mood on the ship was tense during the entire time.

Every single one of the VOC employees he met aboard the ship, his future colleagues, was greedy. All they talked about during the entire voyage was the quantity of the spice harvest and approximately how much they could "pinch" and divide amongst them. In addition, there were always hostile natives waiting at the new places where they had to stop to replenish their provisions. Many of the passengers and crewmembers died.

Lucas felt sorry for Tamela. He risked his life, yet he would not benefit from the profit of the spice trade. Lucas snapped back to reality and boarded his ship. The captain signaled the other ships to weigh their anchors. The fleet started to sail away from the fort of Saparua. The hoisted sails soon caught the tailwind.

The noise of the port slowly faded. Now the activities on board sprang to life. The rhythmic sound of the gongs from the natives' ships filled the air, and the oarsmen soon picked up the beat.

The captain of the main ship had ordered the fleet not to sail straight southward. They were to sail along the shores southeast of Seram. The maneuver was a show of force to remind the natives of the VOC's control over the seas and their preeminent presence. The maneuver was intended to deter the natives from revolting against the VOC.

Not long after they weighed their anchors, the resident was having a discussion with the captain when suddenly the crewmembers made a racket. They had spotted two men on the beach who might be looking for edible plants or firewood, but could also be spying on the fleet.

The captain and the resident did not see anyone in the small woods by the beach. At first, they argued angrily with the crewmembers. However, after given a detailed explanation they were willing to check on the story. The resident ordered the ship to halt. They had to detain the suspicious men.

"What if they're gone by now, Mister Resident? Or if it takes too long to pursue them?" a crewmember of the kora-kora asked.

"You've one hundred men aboard your ship. Overpower them and bring them here," Lucas yelled.

Their language barrier prevented further arguing. The only kora-kora in the fleet turned around and headed for the beach. The crewmembers jumped ashore as soon as they neared the beach and started to search for the two men they had spotted earlier.

It was easy to find the two men who were gathering firewood.

Aimuna and Makela were stunned by the ambush. They only had one machete and were unable to put up any fight. Makela wondered why the VOC was here when according to Makasuli they were supposed to be sailing north for a hongi expedition. She was certain their group had been traveling south. The sailors were upon them and she quickly whispered, "Pretend to be mute or crazy. Don't answer any question. Never tell them where Gamati and the others are."

The sailors started to beat them when they did not answer any of their questions. Makela worried the men would hurt Aimuna's belly. She prayed for the safety of the baby. Sobori's offspring would have to continue the legacy of Gamati's bloodline. Suddenly, a hand grazed against her head and her headscarf fell off.

The crewmembers were bewildered. The man they had captured turned out to be a woman. Someone then pulled off Aimuna's headscarf and yelled, "This one is also a woman." They immediately notified the resident and captain of the fleet.

The two leaders were tremendously relieved. Women were harmless. At least, they were not enemy spies. They did not want to take two women to Banda. Women never joined a hongi expedition. Still, there was no need to kill them.

Lucas said, "Take both of them to the Saparua Fort, use the kora-kora. Report to the commanding officer at the port, and tell him to send them to Mak Uti, my housekeeper. They can live with her and learn household chores until I come back."

One of the captains pointed out that the kora-kora most likely would be unable to regroup with the fleet on course to Banda. Besides, shouldn't they keep this military operation a secret?

Lucas responded that the kora-kora did not need to follow the fleet. They only needed to take the prisoners to the fort and deliver them directly to Mak Uti. They were relieved of their hongi duties until the next hongi, Captain Tamela included. He ended, "Have Captain Tamela report to me when I'm back in Saparua." Thus, the fleet of warships continued their voyage while the kora-kora sailed back to Saparua.

Makela paid close attention to everything on board the kora-kora, including the conversation between crewmembers. She understood some of their language. Apparently, their original mission had been to sail north, but then was changed and they went south instead. As Gamati's boat was headed for Banda, there was a possibility they would run into each other.

Makela realized Gamati and Makasuli had received incorrect information about the hongi. They were obviously unaware about the VOC's change of plans. She tried desperately to find a way out of the situation. Makela was a good long-distance swimmer and diver, and so was Aimuna. However, Aimuna was pregnant and in no condition to perform strenuous physical activities. If Makela were to escape by herself, the crewmembers might torture Aimuna to find out where they were hiding in the forest. Makela had decided not to appeal to the native crewmembers as they could easily betray her and Aimuna.

When the kora-kora entered the Saparua harbor, the villagers were surprised. The boat had barely left Saparua. They reported to the commanding officer at the fort, a tired-looking white man who could have been ill.

He did not understand the crewmembers and became angry. When the name of Mak Uti and the Saparua resident's house were mentioned, he ordered some of the soldiers to take the two prisoners to Mak Uti. The residence was still in the fort complex, although not in the military compound.

Makela noticed that the fort was empty and quiet. She had imagined the fort to be teeming with armed soldiers guarding the place. Her family, refugees from the hongi on Banda, always said that the VOC was merciless and had fierce armed forces. Apparently, most of the soldiers were on the hongi and extirpation mission southward. Tamela, captain of the kora-kora, brought the women to the quarters of the Saparua resident.

Mak Uti was surprised. Luckily, she understood Tamela. They had found the two women in the forest by the beach, dressed as men. Perhaps they lived in the forest of Seram and got lost.

"What should I do with them?" Mak Uti asked.

"The resident wants you to take care of them until he returns from the hongi. Teach them to help you with household chores." Tamela added, "We're excused from the hongi, because we had to bring these prisoners here. The rest of the fleet has sailed. We'd never be able to catch up with them."

After Tamela left, Mak Uti was silent for a while. She did not understand the order; it was unclear. *Who are these two women? They were dressed as men; are they able to fight and use weapons like men?* Mak Uti was a frail, old woman. *What if they threaten me while the resident is gone?* There were only a handful of soldiers at the fort. Mak Uti wondered how to approach the two women. She decided to start with asking their names and if this was their first time in a white man's house.

Even before Mak Uti could open her mouth, Aimuna started to sing and dance, hiking up the loose fisherman's pants she wore. She sang off key, sometimes in shrill high notes and sometimes in false notes that turned into an agonizing wail.

Makela told Mak Uti that Aimuna was insane and she looked after her. They were looking for her husband when they got lost in the forest. Aimuna had gone crazy after she lost her husband. The elders said that perhaps she would recover after she reunited with her husband.

Mak Uti just nodded. She empathized with the two women.

During their captivity Aimuna pretended to be unable to follow orders. She would not listen to anything Mak Uti said. She never bathed or combed her hair and smelled terrible. Her uncombed hair turned into a tangled mass. Makela told her in whispers not to refuse food. The baby in her womb needed it.

Mak Uti was confused. She was supposed to teach them household chores. However, the two women were not of sound mind. At least Makela swept the yard and carried water from the well. Mak Uti had assigned them to sleep next to the kitchen, in the room where they stored dry food supplies.

Language was a problem as well. Makela spoke only a few words of Malay. She often used her arms, legs, and facial expressions to explain herself to Mak Uti. Makela often gazed beyond the yard. She picked up the information that farther away from the fort was the first clove plantation planted by the VOC. And, even further up, the natives had their clove plantations.

A small river ran between the plantations. Its stream was swift and clear. Its estuary was at the southern side of Seram. That meant she and Aimuna were not far from where they hid in the forest last night, which was not far from Tuna kampong and Tuna was not very far from Saparua and Ambon. If only she could send a message to Makasuli or Sobori.

Aimuna and Makela knew their husbands would try hard to find and rescue them, but wondered how they would go about it. Their lepa-lepa was obviously too large to sail around to peddle their catch.

They tried to guess if Gamati, Makasuli, or Sobori would be steering the boat and who would look after the rest of the group of fugitives in the forest. The young men were inexperienced and did not know the seas around Seram.

One night, Makela whispered she wanted to run away in the dead of the night and swim across the ocean until she reached the shores of Seram. Then she would walk along the edge of the forests by the beach, until she reached the place where their group was camped. She was sure that she was still strong enough to make it.

Aimuna did not approve of Makela's plan. She was afraid that Makela would be lost, or run out of energy. The seawater was very cold at night. If Makela was lost at sea, she would be on her own. The VOC might kill her, since she was insane and not fit to be a slave.

Aimuna was convinced that Sobori would try to find them, wherever they might be. Maybe Sobori, Gamati, and Makasuli were trying to figure out how she and Makela had disappeared from the place where they were searching for firewood.

Aimuna speculated that Gamati and Makasuli would take the rest of the group on board the lepa-lepa to safety on the Banda Islands. Afterward, perhaps Sobori would borrow a boat suitable for a fisherman. Then, disguised as a fisherman, he would be able to look for information about them in many places.

Sobori had always feared that the pirates or the Papuans would kidnap her and Makela. The Papuan pirates sailed in a fleet with many crewmembers. They had no regard for human life and were not afraid to kill the people they pirated, or sell them at the slave market.

Makela canceled her plan to escape by swimming away at night. Aimuna thought that it would be best if Makela followed all of Mak Uti's orders. During its course she could pay attention to many details regarding places and things: the distance between the house and the river, pathways to the beach, the location of the villagers' huts, etc. The knowledge would come in handy later.

Aimuna continued to play her "role" as an unruly lunatic, too filthy to get close to. She was sure Mak Uti would pity her. She hoped that Sobori or Makasuli would find them before the white men returned.

Grandpa Gamati and Sobori had always told the group that if one of them was kidnapped, they would find them, as long as they were not killed or sold as a slave far away from Seram. Aimuna did not say that Grandpa Gamati owned gold that could be used to redeem her or Bori. She did not know if Makela knew about the gold; Bori had only told her about it recently, after swearing her to secrecy. If Makasuli had not told Makela, Aimuna would not reveal the information to her.

Muna also hoped they still would have some buried gold that belonged to her father and that Grandpa Gamati had left in the ruins of Tupawaroka kampong. Muna was a smart girl and knew many secrets. Grandpa Gamati raised her to be an independent free woman, in case Bori passed away before her.

Mak Uti was only a domestic worker with no salary. Her entire wardrobe consisted of only a few simple tops and sarongs. The resident of Saparua was a bachelor so she did not have any handed-down women's clothes. Still, the kindhearted old woman gave some of her clothes to the prisoners.

Aimuna and Makela continued to live their days in captivity according to their plan. Aimuna wandered around the compound acting as an unruly lunatic. Shrieking and dancing she strayed further and further away from the house. Aimuna figured that if she managed to dance through the fort's gates, she would be on the beach and hopefully be able to escape.

She did not worry about Makela, who was capable of swimming a fair distance and was a proficient diver.

Unfortunately, the armed guard at the gate yelled at her as soon as she approached the gate and ordered her to return to the house.

Mak Uti, the gardener, and another household helper were nervous around Aimuna. They wondered why she never took a bath. She reeked.

***

Gamati and his group of fugitives were highly anxious. Makela and Aimuna had gone to look for firewood and still not returned. There was a long drought and there should be plenty of it nearby.

Gamati ordered two of the young men to search the area. "Don't go far," Gamati said, "You might get lost."

The two men searched the area and soon found two stacks of dry branches and leaves. A machete was hidden among the branches in one of the stacks.

They hurried back to report their finding. Gamati, Sobori, and Makasuli immediately went with the young men to the place where they had found the stacks of firewood. It wasn't far from where they were camped. The women could not have gotten lost looking for water as the river was nearby. Gamati, Sobori, and Makasuli did not understand how the two women went missing. A multitude of questions tumbled through their minds.

Had they been killed? Who would have killed them? There was no Halefurus in the area. The tribe lived in the mountains, not along the shores.

Had they been attacked by pirates? It wasn't the time of the year for the Papua pirates to sail westward.

The Papuans usually attacked with cries and drums to create a racket that would intimidate the natives they were attacking.

Could it be Lissanei? If the arumbae was somewhere close to the place where Aimuna and Makela had vanished, Gamati was certain he and the others would have heard the noise of the ship's crew who took baths, cooked, or cleaned the ship. Besides, this shore was still near Tuna. Lissanei would definitely moor his ship in Tuna as his parents lived there.

Sobori felt his hair stand on end. It was as if his curly hair straightened and poked into the sky. He shivered at the memory of his parents' murders. Then rage took over. His blood boiled; his heart beat fast, he saw red. Grandpa Gamati used to say a traitor had led the VOC to their isolated kampongs and secret plantations. Their plan to relocate to the northern islands was a deep secret they had only whispered about. How did someone find out their plans? "If I ever find out who the traitor is, I'll kill him, Grandpa. You always told me not to commit murder so it wouldn't happen to our family as well, but look what happened. Both my parents were killed. Damn traitor, I swear I'll kill you." Sobori growled and clenched his jaw.

Gamati did not answer. He squatted to pick up the machete that was left behind and wondered if the machete belonged to Aimuna or Makela.

No one suspected the VOC. They trusted the information that the VOC was headed north to the islands the cloves originated from.

The entire group was devastated and hoped the two beloved women were still alive, somewhere. They were going to search for them in any way they could.

"We have to find them." Sobori tried to suppress his anger.

For some time they all squatted around the stacks of dry branches and leaves. Makasuli looked like a wounded bird. He was sad and felt powerless. His children wiped their eyes and stifled their crying. They were afraid to be heard. Young Sobori looked like a soldier ready for battle. Only Gamati looked calm and composed. He was used to facing danger and trouble. He was a rational leader.

After some time, Gamati said, "Let's get ready. Let's eat and then continue to sail to the Banda Islands. When we get there, Makasuli will arrange for everything. There are many Banda refugees who are survivors of hongi raids." He added, "They'll give us lodgings until we find our two beloved women. Then we will ask for or perhaps buy a boat or two, to sail north. We'll start our new lives there."

"Very well, Bapa. We'll prepare the food now." A young man rose and started toward their lepa-lepa. The other rowers followed.

Gamati, Sobori, and Makasuli remained to discuss their next plan.

Makasuli suspected a VOC ship had kidnapped Makela and Aimuna when it sailed by the shore. Perhaps their being here was related to the recent clove harvest. He said, "During an intense drought, it doesn't take long for the clove buds to dry. Maybe natives who lived near Tuna already sent their harvest to the Saparua Fort. Maybe, Pani-pani was patrolling the seas to prevent them trading with Tuban, Makassar, or Chinese traders and when they sailed by this beach saw Aimuna and Makela."

Sobori added, "That's possible, Grandpa Makasuli. Later, after we take the rest of the group to safety on Ai, we'll try to get information from the surrounding islands."

"How do we do that?" Makasuli asked.

"Like usual. We'll use a small boat, like a kole-kole. We catch some fish, and peddle it in the kampongs around here, or go to Ambon. We'll make small talk until someone tells us about the capture of two native women."

Gamati asked, "Didn't the Pani-pani hongi fleet sail north? How could they have seen Muna and Makela? We're south of Ambon."

"I meant the regular Pani-pani patrol ship, not the hongi warship. It's possible that it sailed by this shore."

They were silent for quite some time. The waves gurgled and swished as they rolled on the beach. It would be high tide soon. All three men were occupied with their thoughts. The cool sea breeze whistled in their ears.

Makasuli finally broke the silence. He proposed they leave soon.

Sobori jumped up and ran to their camping spot. He asked the rest of the group to load their cooking utensils and sleeping mats in the lepa-lepa. "Get ready to sail," he said. They checked the sail, ropes, fishing hooks, the oars, and the cabin. Everything was in good condition.

They decided to take turns rowing and keep sailing day and night without stopping. They were all highly motivated. It was as if something had possessed them. The boat moved fast, although they had not hoisted their sail. A lepa-lepa only had one mast.

The men felt a great urge to arrive quickly at Ai, where they at least would be safe among the islanders. At sea, another vessel could easily spot them.

Makasuli, who was still under the understanding that the VOC was sailing north, steered the boat further away from the shores of Seram. He took a shorter route through the open sea, in the direction of the islands southeast. The narrow straits between the islands were shallow at low tides. The large and tall VOC ships were unable to maneuver through these waters. Moreover, dense, dark green vegetation covered the small islands, making them into an ideal hiding place.

Everyone took turns rowing. Sobori and Makasuli were the most eager. Ages and Dopa, two young men of Banda descent, were able to row continuously with only a few hours of sleep. The currents were in their favor.

It took them three full days to reach Ai, where Makasuli's relatives lived. They received a warm welcome. They slept in the yard of the kampong's community hut. The next day the young men of the group went to the forest to cut some trees, and searched for the leaves of sago palm trees so they could build their own hut.

The villagers called their settlement Ketapang Patta kampong. The story behind this name went back to the time refugees from the Banda Islands first came to this island. They were the first settlers on Ai Island. A very tall and lush Ketapang tree grew on the beach where one could moor a boat. A big storm had compromised the tree's trunk, but the tree was alive and still growing.

The elders made the big and crooked Ketapang tree the hallmark of their new settlement and even named their new kampong after that particular ketapang tree.

Since then, many of the villagers had come from other areas such as Makassar, Tidore, even Tuban. Each had their own language, traditions, and beliefs. However, they never emphasized their differences in social settings. They all spoke the unifying colloquial Malay language, which was understood and spoken by natives as well as those of Portuguese, Dutch, and Chinese descent who lived along the coastal areas.

Gamati ordered everyone in his group to learn to speak the Banda dialect immediately. They went right away to ask the kampong chief for permission to stay there. Since he originally came from the Banda Islands, Makasuli led the group in socializing with the kampong's inhabitants.

It took them ten days to settle and recover from their journey. Makasuli, Gamati, Sobori, Ages, and Dopa searched for a small fishing boat to sail to the nearby kampongs on the islands. They also wanted to peddle big fish on Saparua and Ambon. There were VOC forts and some native-owned clove plantations that sold their harvests to the VOC on the two islands. There was even an occasional slave market.

Lontor, a fisherman who owned a small rurehe that only needed three to twelve rowers and came equipped with a roofed cabin, was willing to let Gamati's group use his rurehe in exchange for the use of their lepa-lepa. The exchange was only temporary; they agreed they were not trading the boats permanently.

All the men in the group were glad. A rurehe was much safer and balanced, although it lacked in speed. Makasuli was relieved that Lontor had not asked for gold or large porcelain plates.

Sobori asked Lontor if they could buy all of his catch, so they would not have to fish before they could sail to the other islands.

Lontor remembered his wife and children needed some clothing. He asked Bori if he had some dark-colored cotton cloth like the ones the Malaccan traders used to bring.

Sobori shook his head. They were all refugees; they sailed light; they only brought essentials. Lontor had no other needs; he had to go to his hut and ask his wife.

While they waited for Lontor's return, Gamati said that they could not agree if Lontor asked for gold, since then everyone would know that they were in possession of some gold. Besides, they did not know how long and how far it would take them to find Aimuna and Makela. They had already traded six gold necklaces; he hoped they would not need to trade more gold.

Several honorable elders passed in front of their newly built hut. Makasuli bowed and invited them in. Lontor returned at the same time.

One of the elders who guarded the beach told them important news. "I bet you haven't heard this. A rurehe from Run Island moored here. The skipper ran away with a half bahar of good-quality nutmeg and mace from Banda Besar, right next to Banda Neira," he said, excited, and continued, "A Javanese *nutmeg coolie* had long hidden this stash of nutmeg; he wanted to trade it with the white men in Run at nighttime, when all of a sudden, in clear daylight, Pani-pani's hongi fleet from Ambon ambushed the island. The coolie is one of us here in Ketapang Patta; he is used to trafficking illegal nutmeg. He immediately left Banda Besar and came straight home, skipping his stop at Run where he was to trade with other white men. He was afraid of getting caught; Pani-pani would surely confiscate his cargo of nutmeg and kill him and his men."

Sobori, Makasuli, and Gamati were shocked. The VOC had raided Banda Besar, near Banda Neira, while they were supposed to be headed north. They tried to figure out how the VOC could suddenly appear in this southern region.

Lontor was also surprised. He was supposed to help the man transport the secret nutmeg to Run in small packages at safer times, usually at the time of a new moon. That was why he wanted to borrow the lepa-lepa from Makasuli. The news was rather unnerving to everyone.

Makasuli asked the elder respectfully if they could soon meet the trader. They wanted to hear about his encounter with the VOC warships.

The elder agreed and left for a short moment. He returned with a well-built young man who spoke fluent Malay.

Timur came from Banda Besar. His skin was as dark as a mangosteen, and his hair was curly. He made his living by collecting wild honey in the forest; sometimes he fished. He sailed between Seram and the Banda Islands. If he caught large fish, he traded them on Ambon. The people around the Ambon fort really fancied fresh large fish.

Timur did not know the objectives of the VOC troops that came aboard the three warships. The plantation slaves said that the troops were going to war with the powerful white men on Run Island. The white men on this island always traded nutmeg with the natives even though the VOC prohibited such trade.

"Now, Pani-pani is furious. They want to execute the offenders." Timur had only seen three large VOC ships with hoisted sails and flags. At a glance he saw many white men go ashore. There could also have been several natives' boats, but he did not look closely. He was lucky to have been able to escape, because he knew about their coming early on. If he had been one or two hours late, they might have seized his boat.

Timur had no other information. He had left the island in haste, sailing for his life. He had no time to ask questions, let alone to watch troops come ashore.

Gamati and Makasuli thanked Timur many times; his information was of great use to them. They concluded that they had received false information. The hongi expedition did not sail to the islands of cloves, but to the islands of nutmeg and mace. This meant that it was very dangerous to sail in the outer seas of the Banda Islands. If the VOC happened to patrol the surrounding seas, they risked a chance meeting. The VOC would seize their boat. At the very least, they would have to answer many questions and have their boat searched. It seemed they were heading toward the enemy, instead of sailing in the opposite direction to avoid them.

There were no decisions they were able to make without thinking things through first. Ages, Dopa, and Beilang were tasked to cook papeda with the fish Timur gave them, and also some pumpkin stew.

Sobori and Makasuli, who had lost their wives, sat in silence in the front yard of their hut till the young men called them for lunch.

Toward dusk, Gamati went to the beach, alone. He wanted to have some quiet time to ease his mind and heavy heart. The cool waves tickled his feet and he wished they could wash his anxiety away.

He gazed at the broken trunk of the Ketapang tree. Its leaves were changing color. Despite its broken trunk the tree had not died and did not look withered. Gamati figured the tree must possess a very strong root system that gripped the earth underneath it. *We, the people of the Moluccas, should be like this tree*, he thought.

Meanwhile, the giant ball of fire in the sky turned into a fiery red. It resembled a glowing ember. All of nature seemed to bathe in an orange-golden light that illuminated the sky.

Gamati gazed across the tranquil water surface. The water that covered the white sand ocean floor was crystal clear and he saw schools of colorful fish. Some distance away from the beach, a pod of dolphins jumped and dove merrily. Sadly, he thought of Aimuna, who loved to watch the dolphins. All the animals he saw as the giant red ball slowly sank into the western horizon appeared to be happy.

"How beautiful this beach is," Gamati whispered to himself.

For a moment, he contemplated the sea. *Is this where happiness resides?* he wondered. During his sailing days he had noticed that all creatures of the sea always moved happily, gracefully and seemingly carefree. They had no enemies, except for the humans who liked to catch them, and bloodthirsty sharks. Perhaps he should pray to his ancestors and gods to turn him into a fish or a sea turtle. He would swim here with his wife, Arande, and take their children and grandchildren to play among the beautiful coral reef. They would dance to the rhythm of the currents.

At sea there were no fearsome VOC, sultans, rich people, and kampong chiefs to whom he had to pay his way. He very much missed the warmth of being with his family. He missed his freedom, his happiness. He also longed for peace.

Ah, the freedom, the peace.

It had been dark for quite some time and the stars had come out when Sobori approached Gamati and gently took his grandfather back to their hut.

***

The governor of the Banda Islands was a native of Holland. He was blond and blue-eyed, tall, and well built. In his youth, he had joined the military for a short time. He stood upright at the dock, surrounded by high officials and administration officers of the islands. The Banda Islands were considered the largest producer of one of the most sought-after spices at that time: nutmeg and mace, the dried aril that covers nutmeg seeds. They were waiting for the arrival of the military expedition from Ambon. Behind the governor's entourage several perkeniers gathered.

The large cloud formations in the blue sky looked like a flock of white sheep. When the wind moved them, patches of blue sky became visible. The intense midday sun brought perspiration to the men's heads.

The main ship's captain and resident of Saparua took stock of the hills ahead. The many dried-up, withered trees were a harrowing sight. The landscape was very different from the forests of Seram he enjoyed looking at from the Saparua fort.

Lucas had not expected the severity of the great drought. He had heard that the supply of nutmeg in Europe was on the decline. People worried that if the great drought persisted, there would be no nutmeg available at all. This would definitely threaten Holland's monopoly on spices. And, even more importantly, food harvested during the summer could not be preserved for winter consumption. This had to be prevented.

Lucas remembered, back before the Europeans found the sea routes to the eastern hemisphere and the origins of clove and nutmeg, they depended heavily on traders from the Middle East and China. The Chinese traders transported the spices along with silk and porcelain items produced in their land using camel caravans to Baghdad or Damascus. During the yearlong treacherous journey the caravan had to cross vast stretches of desert and snowfields as well as navigate uninhabited ravines and gorges. They were also subjected to attacks by bandits and wild animals. Consequently, the goods they carried were priced exorbitantly. This was the reason why Holland had felt pressured to explore the previously unknown sea routes to the origins of the spices, at the cost of many lives and enormous expense.

After they found the sea routes to the Spice Islands, greed soon transpired. Holland was not satisfied with the old-fashioned ways of trading of the earlier traders who preceded them for hundreds of years. They craved to control the entire market. They deployed soldiers to serve that purpose and searched for slaves as enforcements. Now only Holland had the capacity to control the prices of the spices on the international market.

These thoughts about the history of the clove trading occupied the mind of the resident of Saparua until seconds before he arrived on shore. The governor of the Banda Islands and his staff greeted Lucas de Vries and his crew after they docked at the port of Banda Neira. They went immediately to the governor's office for a meeting.

The governor said that the biggest problem was to immobilize the English at Run, west of Banda Neira. The English had built a sturdy fort there. They possessed small and slim boats that were highly portable at sea. It was rumored that most of the soldiers at the fort were natives.

"Where do these natives come from? I thought that all the natives on the Banda Islands perished when Jan Pieterzoon Coen raided the islands in 1621," Lucas said.

"I was unsuccessful in gathering information about them. Perhaps they came from Seram, Saparua, and Ambon. Maybe they were the survivors from the Banda raid. They're the ones who're helping the English there." The governor shook his head. He was overheated and apologized as he took off the jacket he had worn as part of his uniform since morning. Everyone else at the meeting immediately followed suit and now only wore white cotton shirts as their tops.

The men spread a large, patched-up map of the Banda Islands on the table. Banda Besar was the largest in the cluster of eleven islands. Nearby there was Banda Neira, the rather small island of Ai, and an even smaller Run. All islands had their *perken.*

The governor pointed at the perken. The owners were pure or half-Dutch. They had obtained ownership through credit the VOC had provided. Their payment installments were determined by the amount of perken they managed. The installment payments and interests on the loans were of course paid to the VOC's treasury. None of the perkeniers were Banda natives. They came from Java or Ambon.

At first, the perkeniers lived lavishly. The price of nutmeg in Europe was high at that time and even though they were only allowed to sell their harvest to the VOC at a very low price, they still made a significant profit. After all, the plantation workers were all slaves. They did all the work for three meager meals a day, lived in dilapidated huts, and worked for unlimited hours.

With the great drought, the supply of nutmeg was declining. Things would take a turn for the worse when the perkeniers would not be able to pay their debts to the VOC. The governors of Ambon and the Banda Islands were deeply concerned about provoking the Assembly of the Lords Seventeen. Their concern did not involve the lot of the natives or their land.

Run was a tiny island. Steep, solid rock walls barricaded the island. The cove where boats usually moored was located behind the rock wall. If they dared to moor their boats in the cove, the English would instantly know of their landing.

The chief captain of the Saparua fleet measured the distance between the islands. He asked, "How loyal are the natives here? I mean the nutmeg coolies and the fishermen on the island, are they loyal to the VOC?"

The governor only shook his head. He had never employed any informants. All the information he knew came from the natives or fishermen they had taken prisoners. They had told him that there was a fort on top of a steep cliff on Run. The tiny island was impenetrable; steep cliffs surrounded half of the island.

The armed forces from Banda were not great in number either. Despite the well-built fort they had, they were incapable of launching an attack on Run. Neither could they survive an attack. They would have to find a way to carry out surveillance on that island.

The governor from Banda hoped it would be possible to launch a major attack on Run with the military reinforcement from Saparua.

It was hard to plan an attack without any information about the enemy, let alone to devise a complete military plan. The resident of Saparua thought it was strange that the governor of Banda had not obtained any information regarding the enemy who prowled in his own backyard. He was, after all, the highest authority on Banda and had military training.

"Who can we assign as informants?" Lucas asked.

"It must be the natives," the fleet chief captain answered curtly. "We don't speak their language. They would never welcome us even if we pretend to be lost because a typhoon hit us." He repeatedly pounded his fist on the table as he spoke. He continued, "While we're waiting for information, we must formulate our plan of attack on Run. Lucas and Bertie, you could visit several perken and see what you can find out while documenting the situation."

Now alone with the governor of Banda, the captain asked, "What, aside from the drought, kills the nutmeg trees?"

The governor of Banda thought for a moment then said, "A half-day sail away with a big boat is Gunung Api, a large island volcano. The mountain just pops out of the ocean and has no land around it. It often spits fire and smoke. When the wind blows the hot ashes to the surrounding islands and it settles there, the vegetation dies."

"When was the last time it happened? How often does it happen?" the captain asked.

"The mountain is unpredictable," the governor said and continued, "It always rumbles. According to the natives, the last big eruption happened several decades ago."

"What happened?"

"They say the mountain shot a large torch of fire into the sky while the earth shook. When the fire died down, it turned pitch-dark and the air was filled with dust and smoke while a strange sizzling red liquid flowed down the slopes straight into the ocean." The governor paused to wipe perspiration off his forehead, then ended solemnly, "Eruptions always cause casualties. People die, cattle die, vegetation, including nutmeg trees and java almond trees, dies." The governor began folding the map and the captain took his leave.

While waiting for the chief captain's orders, Lucas sketched the port viewed from the governor's residence on the slope of a little hill. Against the backdrop of the afternoon sky, rows of sailing ships and boats were bathed in vibrant colors as the sea birds flew back to their nests; it was a marvelous sight. When he returned to Holland, he would transfer these sketches to paintings of tropical islands and offer them for sale to private collectors. He was confident the paintings would sell.

In the evening, the governor held a modest dinner reception in honor of the newly arrived hongi fleet. He invited the rich perkeniers and their families, providing the wife was Dutch, rather than of Chinese, Portuguese, or Arabian descent.

The governor introduced his wife, a lovely, slightly plump, brunette. Her beautiful large brown eyes matched her hair. A pair of dimples rose to her cheeks every time she laughed.

She was his second wife. His first wife had died in Holland and left him with three children. The oldest one, the dark-blue-eyed Yakob, who went by the name Yap, was nineteen years old. The second child, Petronelli, Nelli for short, was as beautiful as her late mother. She was seventeen years old. The third child, blonde, blue-eyed Heidi, looked like her father. The tall sixteen-year-old seemed to be more mature than her older brother and sister. Unlike most people who lived in isolated places and were usually shy, she was an assertive and extroverted girl. Without further ado, she asked her father and Lucas' permission to sit next to the resident.

There were several other girls who were brought to the reception by their parents, but Heidi was first to claim the seat next to the resident. The governor's wife seated Elsye, the daughter of a perkenier from a neighboring island, at the other side of the resident. Therefore, Lucas sat between two desirable young women.

The talkative Bertie sat between Nelli and a daughter of the governor's office treasurer who was not very pretty but was a good conversationalist.

Yap sat between the chief captain and his mother.

Actually, the governor had thought of throwing a party with dancing and singing. Unfortunately it was hard to assemble a band. He would have had to send for musicians from other islands. In the end, he decided to invite a band for the victory party after they attacked Run. He was certain they would emerge victorious.

It was hard for white people who lived on isolated islands, especially youth, to meet a suitable mate. Therefore, it was important to approach Caucasian visitors, especially if they were still single.

The chief captain was already married, but the resident of Saparua and the botanist were still bachelors and the young women competed for their attention in hopes they would take a fancy to one of them.

Heidi, who had seen several sketches of the nutmeg plantations and the Banda Neira harbor from the resident's archives, asked Lucas to paint her. "Tomorrow, if possible," she said and ignored her stepmother's comment that the resident would have better things to do than bother himself with a schoolgirl like her. She kept insisting and overwhelmed Lucas with her sweet talk.

The shy and inexperienced resident became flustered and quickly succumbed to her advances. He asked the chief captain if he could still work on his sketches of the nutmeg perken tomorrow.

The captain said, "We certainly won't launch the operation tomorrow."

All of a sudden, the quiet Nelli asked Bertie if she could come along to the nutmeg tree nursery. Bertie wanted to investigate why the Banda nutmegs were of much better quality than those from Seram. The nutmegs from Seram were a subject of ridicule in Holland.

Bertie said to the governor's wife, "There are many nutmeg trees on Seram. The seeds are large, but the VOC doesn't want to buy them. The Dutch say that they're of poor quality; they're less fragrant. I wonder if the volcano has an effect on the quality and aroma of the nutmeg."

The woman smiled and shook her head. She knew nothing about it.

"Are there still any of you young ladies who want to join me?" Bertie asked eagerly, and added, "There'll be no helpers. We'll have to walk home."

Nelly quickly answered, "I'm coming. I'm strong enough to walk. I've been to the nursery with my father. I'm used to walking around the perken."

The governor said, "Yes, Nelli usually joins me when I visit the perken. She's quite capable of moving agilely around the plantation carried in a palanquin, along with plenty of water and a large basket of cakes."

Everyone laughed.

"Well, Nelli, what do you say? I won't bring any helpers. You could go with the resident, if you'd rather," Bertie said.

Even though Nellie was not sure she could endure the hard trip, she preferred to go with Bertie. Her parents did not offer her a palanquin since this was her own idea.

Nelli was envious of her younger sister, Heidi, who, judging by her trip with the resident, seemed to have found a partner. This had motivated her to join Bertie, who was a bachelor. She might have a hard time walking around every patch of nutmeg saplings at the nursery and planned to ask Bertie to hold her hand. A gentleman was supposed to help women. Besides, she was a beautiful girl.

The next day, while everyone went on their separate ways, as planned, the chief captain and governor discussed the attack on Run. They were sure that the English did not have a strong military force there.

Governor General Jan Pieterzoon Coen had killed all the natives of Banda and the surrounding islands in 1621. If there were natives on the island, they must be from another island, and only a small group of them. Most likely, they had not brought their wives and children to Run; the smallest of the Banda Islands was nothing but a large limestone rock.

The two commanding officers inspected the warships and their weaponry. The warships were equipped with various sizes of cannons. All the rifles and their ammunition, swords, and bows were in good condition.

They also inspected the native troops, with the assistance of an interpreter. Everyone claimed to be ready. The chief captain checked on the availability of extra rowers and provisions just in case they would run into strong resistance.

He hoped there would be a large supply of nutmeg and mace in the warehouse for the VOC to confiscate after they defeated the English. The governor planned to send the confiscated goods to Holland, since they would have time to fix the perken that had dried out during the long drought. Hopefully it would rain in the meantime.

None of the VOC authorities, including the governor who had a military background, worked on a backup plan in the event their plan failed. No one worried about or made provisions for leadership, shelter, or prevention of capture by the enemy.

Resident Lucas, Heidi, and a group of helpers who carried his painting equipment left town early in the morning. They went to the largest plantation, which was located on a hill. It had a lookout tower hidden in the lush trees. While the tower was invisible from the sea, it provided an excellent vantage point of the harbor and the surrounding islands.

Lucas went up there to paint and to have a lookout. The natural scenery was breathtakingly beautiful. Tiny dark green islands dotted a wide-open blue sea that was dark and enigmatic. Perhaps because the tower was far from the beach, Lucas could not detect any waves on the glassy surface.

Aside from the ocean and island's scenery, he also drew a medium-height nutmeg tree, the java almond trees, birds, and a few insects that flew around the withered trees.

Banda Neira was a small island. Its inhabitants had been annihilated. The remaining animals were only a small number of boars and deer. The governor had told Lucas that there were no human enemies here.

Nevertheless, Lucas felt anxious. He always felt that way when he was alone on any of the islands. He always worried someone lurked and waited for the perfect moment to kill him. He never forgot the dreadful incident when the mad slave attempted to kill him. The thought that he had no guards and had a young girl with him briefly crossed his mind.

Heidi watched Lucas work. She was pleased to be alone with him in the outdoors. She took a seat near Lucas' feet, took in the changing expressions on his face and followed his moves, fascinated. She found the courage to ask why he had not married and inquired about his type of ideal woman, and whether Lucas wanted to live in faraway places like the Spice Islands through his old age or, like her father, had to return to Holland someday.

When it was lunchtime, Heidi said, "Pardon me, Mister Resident, despite the breeze, it's always hot on the island at midday." She took off the jacket she had put on when they left early morning when it was still cold and now wore only a thin sleeveless top. She had forgotten her hat. She uncovered the various foods they had brought, and tried to draw Lucas' attention by looking at the recently finished sketches. "Are you sure you're done with these?" she teased and added, "They looked unfinished." She was testing him to see how he responded to flirting, and if Lucas had not started eating quickly, she probably would have fed him.

Lucas was in fact disturbed instead of pleased with being waited on by a young girl. Heidi was different from Rosamunda, who was gentle, kind, and tried not to interfere with his work as a resident. He was used to being independent and working in silence. Heidi kept on blabbering. She even told him she disliked her stepmother. She thought that her father and stepmother were too critical of her.

Heidi wanted to leave the island. It was too isolated and had no prospects. She wanted to travel to exciting places and enjoy her life to the fullest. Would Lucas take her off the island and take her somewhere else, preferably Holland, where she had many relatives?

Heidi went on saying that guests who came to the island said living conditions in Holland were now far more exciting than when she and her family left the country. It used to be a very boring place. Now there were shops and schools. Life over there was very different from what it was on Banda. Especially since the great drought, her stepmother said they had to live frugally. They had to eat simple meals. She had to mend her clothes instead of discard them. Even more annoying was her parents' constant reminder to go to church every Sunday morning and read the bible every day instead of storing it on the bookshelf.

Lucas' answer was not accommodating. "You should be grateful, Heidi. You have a father and mother who love and nurture you. I didn't have parents to raise me. My father abandoned us. My mother died when I was still a young boy. My teachers raised me. I think your parents are right, the bible is much more useful if you read it every day, instead of just displaying it on the bookshelf."

"Oh, Mister Resident, are you siding with my parents? How strange. You're a young bachelor, why don't you have a little fun? There are lots of pretty girls here. Why do you like to read the boring bible?"

"The bible guides me in life. It keeps me from turning into a madman in these strange lands. It prevents me from turning into a greedy man who idolizes fine porcelains, art objects, silks, and spices. And, it stops me from smuggling luxurious items out of foreign lands."

"I think everyone wants to be rich. People will do anything, however contemptible, to be rich when they return to Holland. Is that wrong?"

"To me, it is very wrong. If we read the bible every day, we will surely know that God despises, even forbids, such acts."

"Take me with you when you return to Holland. You would, wouldn't you?"

"Under what pretense am I going to take you? You're a girl, and I'm not your husband. It's impossible for us to travel together aboard a ship for months. Your father would surely kill me," Lucas snapped.

Heidi was stunned. She had expected Lucas to wholeheartedly agree with her.

The two of them remained silent until Lucas rose to start their descent downhill. He wanted to paint the female slaves who harvested the remaining nutmeg. They used a gae-gae. The long bamboo pole cut into thin blades at the upper edge and with the blades woven into a small basket had caught Lucas' attention. It was similar to the harvesting poles used during the pata cengkei on Seram. The female slaves wore saloi baskets slung over their shoulders, where they put the nutmeg fruit they prodded with the gae-gae. They took the full salois to the smoker.

Heidi was bewildered; she did not know how to sweet-talk Lucas. The male guests who came to Banda usually sweet-talked and joked with the girls and gave gifts. Many girls were promiscuous and slept with the male guests in the perken. There was no law against it, so there was no need to be shy about it. *Why was the resident different?* Heidi was still too young to know that sometimes one's background, one's childhood bereft of parents' love, and living under a constant murder threat could shape and alter one's character.

Heidi was less talkative on their walk home. She was afraid Lucas would snap at her again if she said something that did not suit him. She had gained a new experience that day; not all attractive bachelors liked the aggressive approach of a pretty girl. Lucas had not even so much as looked at her face once, let alone complimented her on her beauty. Heidi concluded that Lucas de Vries, the resident of Saparua, was indeed no ordinary guest.

During the trip downhill, they passed dried, leafless, and withered trees. The governor had explained that those trees were no good anymore; they had to be felled and replaced with new saplings. Meanwhile, they were unable to begin the seeding process, since there was no chance of a rainfall soon. The farmers and the local VOC administration had a difficult time to sustain under the circumstances. However, it was even more difficult to explain the gravity of the situation to the Assembly of the Lords Seventeen in Holland, and make them ease their demands.

Just before the exit of the perken, at the housing complex for the nutmeg pickers, they came upon a tiny structure. The clean yard had a small pond at its side and several shading trees. Heidi asked a man in the yard about the structure in broken Banda dialect.

"It's a mosque," he said.

"What is it used for?" Heidi asked.

The man answered, "You, Miss, go to church every Sunday. We, the natives of Banda, have our faith too; it's Islam. We visit this mosque every Friday."

Heidi interpreted the man's words to Lucas. Lucas said, "There's a mosque like this with a pond next to it in Ambon. People said that it was the natives' place of worship. And on Saparua, there's also a very small mosque outside the fort."

When they returned to the governor's residence, Heidi pretended to be cheerful. She hid her disappointment very well. She felt intimidated by the man she had wanted to seduce earlier and did not dare to remind him that she wanted him to paint her amidst the withered plantation. She hoped he would have time to paint her the next day.

They had dinner along with several other guests, such as the fleet's chief captain, the botanist, the bookkeeper, the storage head, and a few perkeniers who were close to the governor.

The large dining area was lit with oil lamps. The illumination was neither bright nor dark. No one seemed anxious about the pending military actions.

The governor's wife had prepared a lovely table in the dining area. She had set the table with her best cream-colored Chinese porcelain plates. She had also arranged a display of young, brownish-green nutmegs, and ripe, orange nutmegs. She had cut some of the nutmegs in half so the seeds were visible. Some of the dark brown nutmeg seeds still had the aril, the bright red lacy covering, of which mace was made. The aril was stunning and fragrant. Also on display were some java almonds with their dark casings. The governor said that the natives used the hard shell of the java almond in place of firewood in their kitchens. They processed the white and fatty nuts as frying oil.

Not all of the perkeniers knew this. Some of them expressed their surprise and admiration. They now knew the java almond trees had other uses besides protecting the nutmeg trees from the harsh sunlight and the fierce ocean wind. Lucas had sketched the nutmegs and java almonds, and their harvests.

The governor's wife recalled that the clove harvest was a sacred ritual on Banda. No natives had ever seen baskets of clove buds ready for shipment, especially those who did not work for the VOC. She had also put out a large plate of clove flowers in full bloom. Then there were also some fresh clove buds, reddish-green in color. In addition, there were, of course, the dried cloves buds; a tiny, burnt, dark brown nail-like spice. It was hard to believe that people would cross oceans, stake their lives, and forsake their morality for this tiny thing.

The wine was served. The dinner's main course consisted of every imaginable edible aquatic creature caught in the seas around Banda: shrimp, crab, sea cucumber, and large fish like tuna, snapper, parrotfish, and many others. They were talking about the sense of taste and the art of cooking in the East when there was suddenly a strange tremble on the ground; they first felt it through their feet. The alcohol could not have kicked in already. They had barely started to dine, and not begun to drink.

The guests exchanged glances when suddenly the earth shook and swung. In a matter of seconds, the large crystal chandelier came crashing to the floor. The room turned dark instantly and there was an earsplitting sound of shattering plates and glasses. The tables, chairs, and people sitting on them tumbled to the shaking floor. Next, loud booming accompanied the collapsing roof. The air filled with frightful cries, wailing, screams of agony, and curses. It happened to be a dark moon.

A surge of high tide, apparently triggered by the earthquake, flooded the island. The gushing water swept several warships and the native boats onto the island, or took them further to sea. It was ironic that the powerful hongi fleet prepared to launch a full military attack on Run was destroyed by natural disasters: an earthquake and tsunami.

The wide-open sea, thought of as a great roadway to faraway islands, the source of such fine delicacies like fish and sea cucumber, and where people looked for pearls and scarlet rock beads, had turned into a source of uncontrollable disaster.

The next day, Heidi and several household helpers were found dead in her bedroom. They had been crushed by the collapsed roof. The governor's wife suffered from a severe head injury. There were many casualties among the nutmeg plantation coolies as well. Nearly half of the crewmembers of the warships were missing. The sea most likely had swallowed them. Two boats that had drifted away were later found on the shoreline of Ai. Luckily, the boats had not drifted to Run.

For weeks, the able-bodied survivors worked hard to bury the dead while trying their best to care for the wounded victims, build temporary huts, and tend to many more tasks. Bertie and Yap, the governor's son, worked extra hard burying the dead. The nutmeg island was shrouded in grief and a somber mood.

The resident of Saparua could not use his left leg for a long time. Lucas de Vries suffered from a serious wound and had to be moved on a stretcher. When his wound healed and he was no longer in pain, he discovered he walked with a limp. He had to use a cane when he wanted to take a bath.

Two large ships came from Ambon to investigate why the hongi fleet that sailed many weeks ago had not returned. The crew was appalled by what they witnessed on Banda Neira. One of the ships sailed back immediately to report the tragic incident to the governor of Ambon.

Lucas' leg wound prevented him from attending Heidi's funeral. He remembered the girl's request to be painted, and her wish to leave the island. She did leave for good. The Banda Islands were prone to earthquakes, even when Gunung Api rested. Neither the nutmeg, Java almond, nor coconut trees would bear fruit for several seasons after an earthquake.

Chapter 9

Aimuna tried to stay calm. Bori and Grandpa Gamati always told her to stay calm during an emergency. Staying calm was pretty difficult knowing there was a likelihood she would be separated from the only two remaining family members she had after the VOC raids. Grandpa Gamati and Bori had also said that her first thought would be to fight back with all she had in her and she had often contemplated that option during her confinement.

Aimuna had never seen stone houses before. Unlike the natives' huts, which were built on stilts, the VOC houses had no room under them. They all looked the same and were built in neat rows. A tall fence surrounded their compound. An armed guard watched the only gate.

The fort faced the sea. A small road connected it to the beach. Aimuna assumed that the sea acted as a barricade for the fort. There were no settlements near the fort. Anyone who wanted to attack the fort had to come from the front, the sea.

This was the first time Aimuna and Makela saw white people. They looked at the Caucasians with great apprehension. They had never seen people with yellow hair and blue eyes. Aimuna and Makela figured that they must be the VOC people everyone cursed. Like anyone who feared the new and unknown, Aimuna was terrified.

Makela did not speak the local dialect. She only spoke the Banda dialect. Mak Uti only spoke Malay, which was often used along the coastal areas.

Muna was confident that Sobori would look for her, even if he had to comb all the slave markets in the Moluccas. She would simply wait for him to get her. Makela had to let her continue to act like a madwoman and not bathe. When she stank and looked disgusting, no man would be interested in her. She would also circumvent questions that could expose her kinship to Kurubela. She would act as if she were insane, and Makela had to pretend to be her caregiver. Aimuna was convinced Sobori and Makasuli would find them soon. She whispered, "They'll know how to trick these people."

Aimuna continued to act like a raving lunatic. She would not speak to anyone and refused to do any chores. All she did was dance. Pretending to sing, she shrieked and hiked up the sarong Mak Uti had given her as she spun.

Makela tried to please Mak Uti. She worried about what would happen to them once Mak Uti's white employer came home. The white man might separate her from Muna. What would happen if he sent her to the slave market? The person who purchased her would take her to a faraway place and it would be impossible for Makasuli to find her. Hence, she thought it would be best not to make Mak Uti angry.

As time passed, Aimuna allowed herself to be coached into sweeping the falling leaves in the front yard. The truth was that it enabled her to observe the areas outside the fort. When ships were loaded or unloaded, the guards left the gate open and Aimuna was able to make mental notes about the layout of the harbor and the way the gate operated. No one dared to approach her because of her offensive body odor.

Sometimes a few trusted native officers of the fort asked Mak Uti why the resident kept a madwoman in his residence. Mak Uti did not know. She was getting older and soon, the day would come when she could no longer do all the household chores by herself. Perhaps the resident planned to replace her.

The days passed relatively quietly. Makela struck up some conversation with a few men around the fort. A middle-aged native delivered rice and butter to the residence. Another delivered freshly caught big fish usually used for the resident's consumption.

Mak Uti gradually taught Makela to cook her employer's favorite dishes. Makela thought the way the VOC people ate was strange. When she was introduced to cheese, she was amazed that there was food other than salt that was as salty.

Meanwhile, Aimuna wandered around the compound dancing while babbling what seemed to be incomprehensible words but in fact were cries for help in the Manipa dialect. She hoped someone would understand her. After a while she had to assume there was no one from Manipa around.

In the still of the nights, Aimuna often told the baby inside her to be patient. She gently moved her hand across her growing belly and whispered, "Your father and grandfather will surely come to pick us up, my dearest. They love you, and they love me, who carries your tiny developing body. Please be patient, my little one, be peaceful. I'm protecting you."

While Makela did not fully understand Aimuna, she knew Muna soothed her baby. When Muna cried or whimpered, Makela worried she might have started birthing cramps.

The two women had lost count of Aimuna's due date. Muna was in her early pregnancy at the time they left Tuna. Then came the time they lived in the forest and the start of their journey to Banda before they were caught. They now had spent a few weeks in the fort. Makela hoped that Muna would not deliver her baby here. She feared the white men would consider the baby their property. She prayed their rescuers would come soon. It would be more difficult to escape with a newborn, especially if the VOC claimed the baby as theirs. She wondered who would come to rescue them. It made no difference whether it was Sobori, Gamati, or Makasuli or if they all came. Makela just wanted someone to come soon.

Mak Uti started to be nervous after the resident had been gone for about four weeks. She often asked the gatekeeper when the resident and his fleet were expected to return. Lucas had told her he would only be gone for two weeks to twenty days. He had to be back in time to supervise the delivery of dried cloves to the VOC storage in the fort. The farmers of Saparua had just finished their harvest and according to an old tradition, they would present their harvest to the highest VOC official in a region. Later, the cloves would be transported to the fort in Ambon. Some kampongs in Tuna and its surroundings had also just finished their harvest.

Mak Uti also worried about the decreasing food supply for the domestic help at the fort. The long drought had prevented them from growing vegetables in the yard, like they had done in the past.

They used to be able to grow chili peppers, cucumbers, pumpkin, sweet potatoes, white pumpkins, turmeric, yams, and golden lime as well as a few banana trees in the backyard. Almost all the plants had withered and died now.

Lucas had not told her how to replenish their food supply. Usually the officers in the fort took care of everything.

To make the situation worse, Mak Uti now had two more people to feed aside from the gardener, the water-drawer who also cleaned the house, an errand boy for outside-the-fort tasks, and two guards for the armory. So far she simply prepared the food for everyone while others provided her with the supplies. She had no idea how to obtain those.

One day, Aimuna wandered around the house, singing and wailing. The rest of the household help was cleaning the yard. Mak Uti was sweeping the warehouse outside the main building. It was a rather small room with a stone floor and a thatched roof. Small windows up near the roof kept the room ventilated and lit.

Muna was surprised to find Mak Uti there, sweeping the floor. Woven rattan baskets filled with cloves filled the room. Aimuna inhaled the fragrance wafting from the baskets.

The scent transported her to Tuna, where she had participated in the harvest. Her longing for Gamati and Sobori sent a sharp pain through her heart and she automatically placed her hands on her belly.

Mak Uti tried to be nice to Muna. Since they were alone, she was afraid Muna would attack her. No one knew what the crazy girl was up to. "Hi there, *Nona,* who are you looking for?"

"Hi Nona, who are you looking for?" Muna imitated Mak Uti.

"Do you want something to eat? Some papeda and fish, perhaps?" Mak Uti asked.

"Do you want something to eat? Some papeda and fish, perhaps?" Muna repeated.

Mak Uti was terrified. She didn't understand why Aimuna imitated her like a mynah bird. Aimuna had been around for a while and should have picked up some understanding of the local language. Afraid to make Muna angry if she sent her away, Mak Uti decided to leave the warehouse instead.

Aimuna paid attention to her surroundings and made mental notes of the warehouse's location and its size. The idea of setting the warehouse on fire with her in it began to develop. She preferred to die over having to succumb to a man other than Sobori or be forced to work as a slave and be whipped.

Aimuna sauntered behind Mak Uti, singing and hiking up her sarong along the way. When Mak Uti turned toward the house, Muna walked straight to the open gate and suddenly found herself at the Saparua harbor.

She quickly looked around but did not see a small boat with Sobori or Makasuli on it. She started to sing again, hoping someone who understood her cry for help would hear her.

Aimuna noticed an estuary of a small river in the distance. She wondered if the river provided a waterway to the interior of the island. If that were the case, it could also be used to reach the open sea around Saparua other than via the harbor, which was part of the fort. Aimuna wished someone could tell Sobori.

During the next few days, Mak Uti was preoccupied with the pending food shortage at the fort. She busied herself with cleaning the house, in hopes that the resident would come home soon.

Mak Uti's inattentiveness to her whereabouts gave Aimuna a chance to wander around the fort's gate. Dancing and singing, she followed the small river to the headwater from where she caught a glimpse of groves of clove trees. She wondered whom the trees belonged to.

Aimuna had become a familiar figure in the fort's compound. The soldiers at the fort and the workers of the VOC clove plantation regarded her as the crazy, stinking woman the resident had caught at sea. No one cared to approach her. She not only stank, she hardly spoke the local dialect. However, they did feel sorry for her. She reminded them of their own fate as displaced persons who had been separated from their families and sold as slaves.

A few native soldiers sometimes gave Aimuna bananas or boiled sweet potatoes, dried sago cakes, or garden fruits. She happily accepted since food rations had become insufficient at the resident's house. Two full moons had passed and the resident of Saparua had still not returned to the fort.

The food ration changed from rice to sago. Unless someone from outside the fort brought Mak Uti fish, she rarely served it. Sometimes they ate fresh vegetables or fruits from the garden near the residence. They ate it simply with chilies and salt. They even had to cut down the use of salt. No one on the island made salt anymore. They had to wait for deliveries from another island.

Makela and Aimuna restlessly waited for their rescuers and the arrival of the resident they had never seen in person, while guessing Muna's due date.

Aimuna looked filthier than ever. Mak Uti, who was a slave herself and did not have much, had to give her one of her own sarongs so she could change, but she still smelled awful.

Mak Uti gradually developed a dislike of Aimuna and Makela. The two women were nothing but trouble to her. While she had to feed them from their diminishing food supply, they were hardly of any help with the household chores and Aimuna, the crazy one, was a handful. Mak Uti, who was used to only receiving orders, had no idea of what to do with them. The resident's only order had been to let them stay at his residence.

Worried that the two crazy women would do something to the neatly packaged and ready-to-ship baskets of cloves, Mak Uti visited the warehouse twice a day. She could only imagine what punishment the resident would sentence them to if the baskets of cloves were damaged.

Aimuna loved to be near the warehouse. The aroma of the dried clove buds was pleasant to the point of being intoxicating. Her foul body odor bothered her, but served her as a weapon. Muna knew that Mak Uti was terrified when she came to the warehouse.

At night, it was hard for Mak Uti to fall asleep immediately. Not only was she responsible for the safety of their two female "guests," she was also responsible for the safekeeping of the baskets of cloves in the warehouse. She worried why the resident still had not come back.

Aimuna and Makela also had a hard time sleeping. They startled at the slightest noise. *Was it Sobori? Makasuli? Maybe it was Gamati, who finally came to rescue them?* But it turned out to be only a bat or owl looking for prey.

The fragrant clove buds brought neither happiness nor prosperity to the natives of its origin in the Moluccas.

***

Gamati and Makasuli refrained from borrowing a boat. They were going to use their lepa-lepa. Their crew of fourteen would be sufficient to work as rowers and fishermen. Aside from Gamati and Makasuli, two excellent captains, Sobori, a skillful captain to-be, was also aboard the lepa-lepa.

Makasuli proposed that they check out the situation around Saparua first, pretending to be fishermen. He vaguely remembered a small estuary somewhat far from the fort in the island.

There was a clove plantation on Saparua that belonged to the VOC. It was an experimental plantation. If it succeeded, the VOC would have no need to trade cloves with the natives whose harvests were getting smaller and smaller. Consequently, the price of cloves went up.

"That's what they hoped to achieve from the extirpation of clove trees up north and nutmeg trees on the Banda Islands," Makasuli said and continued, "How can one destroy trees created by the Almighty Upulanite? Can man withstand the heavenly force? It was a lunatic's notion." Makasuli and Gamati shook their heads in disbelief.

"That is what we think. However, Pani-pani has great weapons. They also have big ships and many soldiers. They're a bunch of warmongers. We won't succeed fighting them."

Makasuli said that since the VOC fleet was reported to be seen on Banda, and assuming they proceeded with their plan to conduct a hongi raid and extirpation up north, it meant the VOC was combating two fronts simultaneously.

"I believe that the troops sent to Banda came from the fort on Saparua. That young man Timur saw with his own eyes that they were raiding Run."

"There are English people on Run. They live inside a very solid fort. The natives certainly favor them, as the English people trade cloves with fine-quality goods," Makasuli continued.

"What about the fort?" Gamati asked.

"They have more soldiers on Ambon," Makasuli answered and continued, "So, that leaves the fort on Saparua empty. That's why I proposed to offer fish to Saparua first. We'll try to see the natives on the clove plantation and make a good impression on the fort's guards. If the guards happen to be natives, I'm sure they'll like some gold or large ritual plates from China."

Everyone agreed with Makasuli.

The group soon set sail for Sapura. They fished while on their way and caught two baskets full of medium-sized fish and a few large tuna. The large fish would buy their way into Saparua. They wanted to see if the fort was poorly guarded. Sobori prayed to his ancestors for the safety of Aimuna and Makela. He prayed to be shown the path leading to them and their search would not be in vain. No one could replace Aimuna and their child, thus he wailed in his prayer.

"What if no one has heard about them on Saparua?" Driven by his suppressed longing for Aimuna, Sobori pulled hard on the oars.

"Then we'll sail to Ambon. The harbor there is just outside the fort and livelier, but a seawater pool barricades the fort. It will be much harder to look for information, but we'll try our best. We'll sail to Ternate and Halmahera if we have to," Makasuli answered.

The sun had passed the tops of their heads but was not yet leaning west when they reached Saparua. They did not approach the fort or port right away, but circled the beach outside the fort.

They found the small estuary, its river winding inland. Makasuli, who had sailed it previously, said the clove trees neatly planted along the river in the island's interior were the VOC's experimental clove plantation and rumored to be a success. They had harvested it once. Who knows what had become of the trees during this long drought.

"I hope all the trees withered and died," one of the crewmembers whispered.

After some deliberation, the group appointed Makasuli, who seemed to be well informed about Saparua, to ask around.

Then they steered the lepa-lepa to the port, which indeed was quiet. There were no large ships with fluttering sails. There were no ships from faraway lands. There was only a medium-sized ship from Ternate. The crewmembers were unloading its cargo: salt. Another boat was from Ambon. The boat was supposed to load the clove harvest. However, without permission from the absent resident, the storekeeper did not dare to hand over the harvest.

The only other vessel in the port was their lepa-lepa from Banda. Makasuli offered their catch, and in the process engaged in a friendly chat with the harbor guard, who told him that the resident was off the island, and no one could dispense the recently harvested cloves from the warehouse.

Another native guard from the fort joined them on the beach. Makasuli repeated their offer of the fish they just caught. He added, "It will soon be dark. We need to get rid of our fish or else it will spoil."

At first the guards said they didn't have any need for freshly caught fish. However, Makasuli continued to push and asked for permission to enter the settlement of the clove plantation workers through the estuary north of the fort. There were surely many farm workers who'd like to cook fish. He wanted to offer them their catch.

The guards hesitated. By rule, no vessels could come close to the area around the fort and its port without a special permit from the VOC.

Makasuli noticed the absence of white guards. He took the two largest fish from the pile and handed them to the guards. "Consider this a gift; you don't need to trade it with anything. Please, take these." His cordial manner persuaded the guards. They took the fish and thanked Makasuli, smiling.

The harbor guard said, "All right, go to the estuary, but return before sundown. Don't talk too much to the plantation workers. I don't want them to know about our little agreement. Hurry."

As he steered the lepa-lepa to the estuary, Makasuli chuckled. During a long drought and when food was scarce, no one would be able to refuse large, fresh fish. He asked the rowers to pull hard. He wanted to reach the settlement as fast as they could.

When they arrived at the plantation, the workers had just finished their day's work and were getting ready to return to their huts. They were stunned when they heard Makasuli hawking the fish.

The workers had been living poorly, eating whatever they could find. The offer of freshly caught fish was very tempting. They wondered what trade items the fishermen expected from them. They were after all only poor plantation slaves.

Makasuli moored the lepa-lepa by the riverbank. Some of the slaves asked what they wanted to trade the fish for. Makasuli answered he would accept anything.

"We're poor people, we've nothing," one of the workers said.

Gamati and Makasuli started to lure the workers by showing their freshly caught fish.

Makasuli told the workers they could take the fish now and give their trading item in a few days when they had it. Then, he casually mentioned he was actually looking for two female family members who were kidnapped from the beach on the south side of Seram a few weeks ago.

"Have any of you seen them? Perhaps they were ordered to work on this plantation?" Makasuli asked.

Everyone shook his or her heads. Someone said there had been no new slaves added for the past couple of weeks. Makasuli gave away some of the fish. The group did not intend to trade with the slaves.

Suddenly, a man in the crowd said, "There's a crazy woman at the Saparua resident's house over at the fort. Her hair's long and tangled, and she smells very bad. She acts like a madwoman, always singing and dancing while hiking up her sarong. She looks pregnant. But I only saw her from afar."

"Does she often come to this plantation?"

"I don't know. We work all the time. We only knew she was here when we heard her wailing. Perhaps she was crying over her husband or the baby she's carrying."

Makasuli and Gamati felt a sudden rush of excitement when they heard the slave's words. Sobori's heart pounded with an irregular rhythm. It seemed that they were getting closer to their objective.

"Can we see her tomorrow? Please arrange for her to meet us here," Makasuli pleaded.

"I can't help you. She's inside the fort, while we're outside the fort, on the plantation. We're forbidden to talk to each other," the man answered.

"Who's ordered to guard the crazy woman? Another woman?" Makasuli asked casually.

"We don't know, ask the soldier at the fort's gate," another slave answered.

Makasuli handed out four more fish. "Just take it. It'll spoil if we have to take it home," he said and added they might return to bring them more fish.

"Don't bother to come again, we've nothing to trade for your fish," a worker said.

"That's fine. We'll go to other places first. We'll bring anything left over here." Makasuli turned the lepa-lepa. He had to report to the harbor guard that they had left the plantation.

The guard played his part in the charade. He stood erect, and nodded at the now-empty fish baskets.

Makasuli thought it was rather unusual that the native soldier guarded the gate alone without a white soldier with him. The gift of fresh fish during a time of great drought had won him over. Makasuli headed the lepa-lepa to the open sea and sped away from the island. The wind and current were in their favor.

They reached Ketapang Patta kampong on Ai in no time. The younger lepa-lepa crewmembers promptly cooked and spread a mat to sit on while they ate. Afterward, they cleaned and prepared the boat for the next day's sail.

They held a meeting just before they turned in for the night and talked about ways to gain the trust of the gate guard. Makasuli wanted to convince him to bring the crazy woman to the beach, so that Sobori and Gamati could take a good look at her to make sure she was indeed Aimuna. They also needed to convince him to bring Makela along. Makasuli had to make sure she was his wife.

They had to move fast since the resident was not on the island. He might come back soon, or a white official might be given the authority to be in charge of the fort. Makasuli said they had to study the guard's habits and likings. They had to make sure that he guarded the gate every day. They also had to be prepared if he suddenly was replaced by a white soldier. Makasuli wondered if it would be possible for a Dutch guard to replace a native guard. It would be strange to offer a Dutch guard gold. Makasuli tried to figure out what to do if that happened.

Sobori almost lost his patience. Longing, anger, and restlessness struck him, all at the same time. He became a loner; he often went to the beach by himself to reflect.

At dawn, the next day, they were again ready to sail. Suddenly, a long and slim *lesung* loaded with fish approached them. The crew wanted to return to their kampong and offered their catch. Makasuli gave them two new sarongs in trade.

The traded fish saved them some time. They would be able to reach Saparua earlier than yesterday. They did not go straight to the fort's gate at the port. They searched for a new entrance point by the estuary they used yesterday. Makasuli and Gamati thought that there was bound to be a kampong outside the fort and the VOC's plantation.

A lesung coming from the sea approached, and Makasuli drew their boat close. The men aboard the lesung were looking for fish. Their baskets were only half full. They said they lived in the interior of Saparua.

Makasuli immediately offered the fish he had. His tact and friendly approach proved to be very effective. The men aboard the lesung happily received their gift. Lambetta, the owner of the lesung, invited Makasuli and his friends to come to their hut on the island.

Makasuli accepted the invitation immediately.

There were many rivers, estuaries, valleys, and waterfalls on the islands in that area of the Spice Islands. The lepa-lepa followed the lesung to a different estuary from where they traveled upstream to Lambetta's hut.

It turned out that Lambetta was a respected elder in his kampong.

Makasuli frankly told him that he was a descendant of the refugees from the Banda Islands, who had perished over a dispute with the VOC about the nutmeg trees. Lambetta showed his empathy by inviting them to stay at his hut should they sail the seas near Saparua. He knew Ronasundu when he still sailed the seas back when he was younger. He had also heard of Kurubela and Tarambessi as the VOC's enemies. Strangely, he never heard of Gamati.

Lambetta served the customary betel leaves and a simple meal to welcome Gamati's group. He also told them that the VOC forbade the residents of Saparua to befriend outsiders, above all those who came from Banda and hated the VOC so much.

Makasuli, who was skilled in associating with other tribes, promised to leave soon. He would only like to ask for a small favor, and only if it was safe for Lambetta and his kampong.

After Lambetta gave him permission to speak about the favor, Makasuli told him that they had lost two female family members who had gone looking for firewood in the forest. They assumed someone had kidnapped them. Recently, they had heard that two strange women had been brought to the Saparua fort. One woman was crazy, and the other one acted as her caregiver. They supposedly lived at the Saparua resident's dwelling. Makasuli and his group would like to take a good look at those two women. If they turned out to be their missing family members, they would kidnap them back and take them home.

Makasuli recounted their encounter with the two guards yesterday and ended, "Since they're living inside the fort, we can't afford to make any mistakes."

Lambetta was silent. After a while he said, "It's very difficult if it involves the fort, my brother."

"Perhaps you, as a respected resident here, can find out if the resident's housekeeper can be asked to assist us. We're willing to give the reward she asks for in return for her help," Makasuli said.

"What kind of reward?" Lambetta asked.

"For instance, we can offer the gate guard something that will interest him. Later, he might ask for something more for his superior, and the superior certainly has a higher superior. Then, another, higher superior, possibly all the way up to the resident himself. Usually ships from Tuban or Makassar that are caught by the VOC make this sort of payment."

"That's a trade payoff. We need to make this payoff at the port. Tradesmen do that, but we're not trading here, are we?"

"We don't really care what you call it. Yesterday the guard was very happy with our gift. He was very friendly after we gave him two large fish. However, we were afraid they changed the guard today, and didn't go near the fort."

"I see, so you went to the fort yesterday. Which route did you take?"

"We took a stream near the fort's gate, then went to the clove plantation. The workers there told us about a crazy woman with long tangled hair and horrible body odor living in the fort."

Lambetta, who still looked fit for his age, nodded. He stared at Sobori, who looked restless and irate.

"Well, let me put it this way, my brother. I don't want to make promises for fear they might turn into a lie. Give me ten days. I'll try to find someone I know at the resident's house; maybe I can ask him a favor. I'll also approach the gate guard. Usually, for that kind of favor, people ask for gold in return. His employer could kill him if he was found out helping outsiders."

"I understand, my brother Lambetta. I sailed many seas when I was younger, and I've prepared several payoffs. We heard that the resident has not yet returned from Banda. We have to act fast, before he returns."

Makasuli was a bit surprised that Lambetta was not suspicious of the group, and almost immediately agreed to help them. It looked like he did not want a payoff for himself. Perhaps he was a rare example of the sincerity of the natives who were not yet marred by crime brought by outsiders.

Lambetta did not tell his guests that he hated the VOC who had conquered his native island and killed many of his family members.

After some chitchat, the group said their good-byes.

Lambetta solemnly asked them to return in ten days. He hoped to have news for them then.

Makasuli, Gamati, and Sobori felt relieved. They were seventy-five percent sure that the crazy and stinking women were Aimuna and Makela.

Sobori had told Aimuna to make herself unattractive if she was ever forced to be intimate with other men. He had told her never to bathe, let alone dress up, refuse to talk, and pretend to be a lunatic.

Makasuli wondered if the fort people would also bring Aimuna's companion to the beach. He hoped she would be Makela. It would break his heart if only Aimuna returned and not Makela.

During the following ten days, Sobori practiced sailing and rowing around the Banda Islands. He also busied himself with fishing and deep diving. He figured it might come in handy when they rescued Aimuna.

The other young men in the group also fished, swam, or rowed around Ai.

Before the ten days had passed, a small boat moored at the beach of Ketapang Patta. Apparently, it had just escaped from a disaster on Banda Neira. The owner told them about a horrible earthquake that had taken place a few days ago.

"It was terrifying," he said and continued, "The roof of the governor's residence collapsed. The governor's wounded, and his guest, the resident of Saparua, broke his leg and can't walk. He's being carried around on a palanquin. Many of the natives' boats are lost, swallowed by the waves. The governor's daughter was killed, along with many plantation workers."

"Why did you run away?"

"Pani-pani wanted me to work hard to take care of the dead. I didn't like it there. So I ran."

"Let's just hope that they won't come here to look for you. We'll all be doomed."

Thus, bits of information about the catastrophe on Banda Neira arrived. And, finally, Makasuli, Gamati, and his group heard about the misfortune that befell Banda's inhabitants. What really worried the three leaders of the group was the payoff. They wondered how much gold the guard would ask for and worried if they still had enough. If they didn't they would have to go back to the ruins of Tupawaroka and Tupamarangi. Gamati had already taken all the gold buried in Tupawalili before they left Tuna. It would be a long and difficult trip to get back there.

Moreover, they had to move fast, now that they were sure the resident of Saparua and his troops were on Banda Neira, and that he was wounded, and got around on a palanquin.

Gamati's one request was that they should not harm anyone, including the enemy, during their mission to rescue Aimuna and Makela. It was said by their ancestors, that to insure the safety of the baby's delivery, a husband of a pregnant wife can never shed the blood of others.

That night, Sobori went to the beach. It was a moonless night and very dark. The rushing waves licked his feet. He tried to picture his life without Aimuna. He wondered how dark it would be, if it would be just like tonight. His thoughts continued to wander and he asked himself, *Why would I need to relocate up north if Muna and our baby are lost? Will I still have the energy to go on living without them?*

Sobori gazed at the night sky. He wondered if the night would be as dark if Aimuna sat next to him.

***

After all the slaves owned by the VOC as well as the perkeniers had removed the debris the earthquake had scattered across Banda Neira, the beach at the port looked considerably cleaner. All around the island, most of the fallen trees, the broken perken fences, and collapsed bridges had been removed. They had also cleared the road to the port, especially the stretch between the governor's residence on top of a hill and the harbor.

A number of the Saparua resident's ships had sailed; even the VOC's warship had returned to Ambon. The only warship left was to transport the resident and the remaining members of his troops from Banda Neira.

Lucas sat on a stretcher. He did not wear a uniform. Instead, he wore a white cotton shirt without a lace collar and a pair of dark blue pants. He looked as if he had suddenly aged a few years and appeared moody.

The governor of Banda, who had lost a child in the earthquake and whose wife was still recuperating from an injury caused by the collapsed roof, was the only one who saw him off at the port. They nodded at each other and Lucas extended his hand from the stretcher before he was carried aboard the ship. Behind him, workers carried his art supplies, also the sketches he had made during his stay on the nutmeg island. Those sketches would undoubtedly be extremely valuable to the VOC.

Lucas looked around him for the last time. He thought of Bertie. The VOC had asked him to stay to take care of the nutmeg plantation.

Bertie was nowhere to be seen at the harbor. Lucas figured he had to be in the hills tending the nutmeg trees.

Lucas, Bertie, and Karel liked the beaches of the Spice Islands, especially those with lush green sago orchards or rows of coconut trees. Lucas always thought that shady spots at the blinding bright beaches were especially spectacular. The three of them used to relax on the beach after a day of work. Songbirds usually inhabited all the beaches.

Six java almond trees grew at the edge of the harbor. Lucas fastened his eyes on the spot and thought, *This'll be my last sight of this island.* He no longer wished to remain on the Spice Islands, or, for that matter, on any island of this archipelago. He wondered how long it would take for his leg to heal. *I'm a painter; how am I supposed to move around if I remain crippled?*

Lucas needed plenty of rest. While he had to write reports about the operation and the earthquake, he had more than enough time to reflect on his condition. He missed the gentle Rosamunda. Fate would keep them separated. Even if they met again in Ambon, things would be hard on them. The VOC rule was definite. Lucas believed that Rosamunda could add color to his barren and lonely life. He wondered if there would be a way to leave Ambon together.

He had made up his mind; he would resign from the VOC and return to Holland. He was sure his father would give him his salary once he arrived. He never received a salary during his residency in the East. The VOC met all his living needs. He had lived a frugal life.

He had a clean record. He always remembered his father's words, "Don't damage my good reputation in the company." Surely, there would be an award for his efforts, he thought.

After he resigned from the VOC, he would propose to Rosamunda. He would tell her that he was twenty-five percent Portuguese. Perhaps Rosamunda's father would find a way to marry his daughter. If necessary, he would not return to Holland. He could go to Portugal or other Portuguese territories in Asia for Rosa.

Lucas ordered the captain not to stop at Saparua but to sail straight to Ambon. The wind and the current were steady and they sailed smoothly with great speed.

The port of Ambon bustled with activities. Many large ships had unfurled their sails; perhaps they would soon raise their anchors. The clear blue, cloudless sky signaled that the dry season still prevailed.

Lucas was relieved when he noticed the governor's ship and other large VOC ships moored at the harbor. He wanted to give the governor a report about his journey.

Lucas' unexpected arrival caused quite a turmoil in the governor's office. The governor and his entire staff sprang into motion to receive the resident of Saparua and his entourage. Several high-ranking VOC officials hurried to the harbor. The governor quickly changed into his official uniform.

After Lucas arrived at the governor's house, he proceeded to give a short verbal report to the governor. He would write an official report later that evening, or perhaps the next day.

Then, it was the governor's turn to tell the resident about the hongi mission he had conducted to the small islands up north, from where the clove trees originated. His extirpation mission had sailed with warships, and only one kora-kora and two rurehes for his escort.

De Bruijn began his story, "Even though we displaced and killed some of them and in general made their life miserable, it turns out that the natives there are still resistant. They shot arrows at us from the forest. Some of our soldiers died, others were gravely injured. Right when we sent soldiers to cut down the remaining clove trees, a fire suddenly broke out from many directions."

Lucas only nodded. He was sick of hearing another story about hongi. There was no reason for the VOC to keep conducting hongi missions. The VOC had destroyed the origins of cloves and nutmeg trees, and enforced a monopoly on the trades. The VOC had also given the king a hefty allowance. The king and his family would not have to live destitute lives. There was no need to go to war and conduct hongi and extirpation expeditions.

Lucas did not openly voice his disagreement. He simply refused to comment on the governor's words. He was accustomed to living in poverty and dependent on others. He thought it would be best to keep silent rather than argue when there was a chance that he might lose the argument. He was, after all, speaking with the highest official in the Moluccas.

The governor continued his story. Some foreign ships still frequented the small islands where cloves originated. Apparently, the natives still traded with merchants from Java, India, China, and occasionally Europe. "Their ships were low and slim. With many rowers the ships sailed so fast they were able to escape." The governor sighed. "I'm sure they hid on the islands outside our territory. They couldn't go too far. They've no room to store food and water, let alone cabins for their crewmembers."

Lucas wanted to cover his ears and shout at the governor to shut his mouth. He already knew that the governor would end his lament with a proposal to execute another hongi. Lucas could already hear the order to send ships up north to destroy kampongs again.

The governor suggested that Lucas stay in Ambon for the next two to three days. He could rest up and meanwhile write his report, which had to be sent to VOC's main office. Due to the tragic deaths during both missions, the governor did not give a welcome reception.

The governor's wife hurriedly ordered some specialty cakes from the de Freytas cake shop. Rosamunda delivered the cakes herself; she came accompanied by a slave. However, Lucas did not see her since he was taking a nap. He regretted the fact no one had awakened him when Rosamunda came to deliver the cakes. Deep in his heart, he missed her very much.

The governor's wife tried to soothe him. "Who would dare to knock on your bedroom door knowing you are resting, Mister Resident? You did not instruct us to wake you. She would surely come again soon to deliver cakes. Why do we not order more cakes?"

Lucas simply nodded.

After spending three days in his bedroom writing his report, Lucas handed the papers to the governor. He had attached his letter of resignation addressed to the governor to the report.

The governor was stunned upon reading Lucas' resignation letter. He could not understand why the resident wanted to resign from his post. "You're still young, Mister Resident. A glorious career lies ahead of you. Our company has just started and already we're raking in high profits. Our kingdom defeated the kingdom of Portugal everywhere. You'll soon be a wealthy man."

Lucas was silent for a moment; he did not know where to begin. He finally said, "With all respect, Mister Governor, to be honest, I've been disheartened for a long time. I accepted the offer to work in this great company to return the favor from the person who financed my education. He wanted me to get more experience working abroad, so I could reach maturity physically and spiritually. In my humble opinion, I've put in enough years. I've never taken any home leave."

"I can grant you leave anytime you want. However, don't resign. It's hard to find a job back home. Yet, here you are, resigning from your job. Please, reconsider," the governor pleaded.

The governor knew Lucas was a well-respected official in the VOC. He was young and agile. He had performed very well. He was a renowned "clean" official who never took part in the illegal pinching of clove baskets. He did not drink; he was not ashamed of his unfortunate background as a poor orphan.

The governor's wife had particularly noticed that Lucas never yelled at his subordinates. Nor had anyone ever heard him shout at the natives who interacted with him. The latter was especially considered strange.

The governor knew that Lucas had been quoted as saying, "We're killing the natives. It's only natural they fight back. Don't we resist the Spaniards in Holland?" The governor had once told his wife that Lucas had learned to be soft-spoken and gentle in the elite schools he had attended and that life in the Spice Islands might not agree with him.

However, the governor now found out that despite his calm and courteous nature, the resident was unyielding. It was impossible to change his mind. At first, the governor was dumbfounded. Most Dutch officials were reluctant to return to their homeland. They thought it was far easier to live abroad.

After contemplating the fact, the governor reasoned that most of the Dutch who worked for the VOC, from the captains to the cabin crew, came from the bottom of Dutch society. In Holland, they were mostly unemployed, ex-criminals, ex-foreign legionnaires, drunkards, and such. Their education, and moreover their manners, left a lot to be desired. While the top officials were better educated, their conscience never prevented them from mistreating the natives if it meant they would gain higher profits. To them, the end justified the means.

The governor and his wife unsuccessfully tried to persuade the resident during dinner conversations. Lucas used his injured leg as an excuse for not yielding. He said, "Hopefully my leg will recover faster in Holland."

Lucas de Vries did not have any possessions in Saparua or Ambon. He did not have gold savings, porcelains, or a beautiful young woman of questionable moral. He could easily pack up his suitcase and his paintings, and leave in an instant.

However, Lucas had fallen for the gentle Rosamunda. Unfortunately, a VOC rule prohibited him from marrying her. VOC officials were only allowed to bring home wives who were pure Dutch. He thought the rule was absurd and it only strengthened his decision to resign.

Even though he was in love, Lucas was not the type of man who allowed himself to become irrational. He wanted to sort out his life in Holland. After he reported to his father and asked for his salary, he would deal with his personal life. He wanted to avoid his father's scolding.

Perhaps his plan would take too long and Rosa might fall in love with another man. Or, perhaps another man would ask for her hand in marriage. He still wanted to contemplate these possibilities.

The governor only shrugged, knowing that he was unsuccessful in changing Lucas' mind. VOC officials in Ambon or Batavia were not authorized to terminate an employee hired in Holland, nor could they approve their resignation. The governor only wrote a letter of recommendation for the Saparua resident, which stated that the resident was a dedicated official, and had performed his duties very well. He also noted that Lucas was a trustworthy man and his archives of paintings were admirable. He considered it a great advantage for the VOC should Lucas de Vries be willing to return to the Indies.

On the fourth night of Lucas' stay on Ambon, the sea was calm under an almost full moon as he visited the governor and his wife to show them the paintings he made on Banda Neira. The cluster of little islands had amazed him. They looked like flower petals scattered to welcome a bridal couple.

The governor had never set foot on the Banda Islands.

Lucas had sketched the small hills, with slopes of nutmeg plantations. Towering Javanese almond trees provided shade under their luscious green canopies that served like giant umbrellas.

Looking at a sketch of the nutmeg slave workers, the governor commented that they did not look like the natives of Ambon.

The resident explained, "They're Javanese slaves purchased on Java. Almost all of the Banda natives were killed by Jan Pieterzoon Coen in 1621. The few survivors from the Banda massacre were the ones who assisted the English in their defense of Run. Initially, the governor of Banda wanted to attack their fort on that island."

"Why did they postpone the attack?"

"They didn't have sufficient information regarding the English troops and weaponry. They had zero data and had to send a surveillance team before we could even begin to plan an attack. Unfortunately, the earthquake struck while we were planning our strategy. Next thing we knew, we were busy helping the wounded and burying the dead. Perhaps the earthquake also struck Run; we don't know."

The governor of Ambon and his wife scrutinized the sketches of the plantations. There were also drawings of the young and then ripe nutmegs, the cut-open fruit showing its bright scarlet covering that looked like lace and was called the aril. The Dutch used nutmeg as a preservative, especially for preserving cooked food. The natives said that mace, made from the aril, was used as an aromatic. Its subtle fragrance whetted the appetite.

"Mister Governor, this is another example of our kingdom's cruelty. The dried nutmegs had to be washed with an acidic liquid, either lime or vinegar, before being packed for shipping. This is done to damage the nutmegs. The treatment causes it to lose its capacity as a seed. It can't grow anywhere."

"Did the governor of Banda tell you this?"

"No, the perken coolies did," Lucas answered.

"Hahaha...so the dialect lesson finally came in handy, eh?" the governor's wife, who was known to have no interest in learning the local dialect, exclaimed.

"Let's think about it. Was it really necessary? None of the other foreign traders have done that," the resident said bitterly. "Monopoly has become our life philosophy."

The governor did not answer. He actually did not know any of this.

Lucas showed sketches of Heidi, the Banda governor's teenage daughter who yearned to leave the island out of boredom. He said, "She left the island the night of the earthquake," and added, "She left us for good."

The governor and his wife were saddened by Lucas' story. When they saw the sketches of Gunung Api they asked if the governor of Banda intended to plant nutmeg and Javanese almond trees on the mountain slope.

Lucas chuckled and answered, "Perhaps this is nature's answer to our greed; the mountain has no flat land. Steep slopes rise from the ocean. There's no safe place to moor. We could only jump onto the slopes. Some parts of the land are covered with vegetation, but the slopes that are frequently covered with lava are barren. It would be impossible to plant nutmeg trees there. The people on Banda Neira said that the mountain is an active volcano and erupts frequently."

The governor's wife said, "Who knows, in the future, a smart scientist might invent a tool to flatten the terrain and we can make more perken there."

"That's possible. In this world, the impossible is possible," Lucas said quietly. Documentation through his sketches of the Spice Islands and of the lands passed on the way to reach these islands was the fruit of his years of working in the Far East. He felt he had proven himself a dutiful son as well as having amply served the kingdom of Holland. He had even donated a perfectly functioning leg to the cause. Now, he just wanted to quit.

Lucas extended his stay at Ambon to find a trading ship that would sail westward. It had to be a large ship, capable of bracing the big and dangerous waves of the Pacific Ocean and with an appropriate storage place for his archives of sketches. He hoped the fact that he was the ex-resident of Saparua would give him a nice cabin. As an archivist, he was a rather important official of the VOC and the safety of his sketches was important. Even the governor helped Lucas with finding a decent ship.

While he waited for passage, Lucas often visited the beach, away from the harbor. There was a spot with three mature ketapang trees from where he could see a few uninhabited small islands that had very dense vegetation. When Karel and Bertie were still in Ambon, the three of them would go there and listen to the colorful songbirds. It was soothing to watch the birds return to their nests at dusk.

One afternoon Lucas was absorbed in watching some albatross hunt for fish, when he suddenly heard Rosa's voice. "Good afternoon, Mister Resident. I didn't expect you here." Rosamunda carried two large baskets.

"Ah, Rosa. I'm just watching these gorgeous beach birds. They're one of the charms of the tropics. Listen; their afternoon song is beautiful, isn't it? I really love the view from here."

Rosa nodded respectfully and said, "Very well, Mister Resident, enjoy your time here. I must get home before dark."

"I can take you home if you would just sit here with me for a while, Rosa. Do you have some cakes with you?"

"No. I am sorry, Mister Resident. I just finished delivering them and it will be dark soon." Rosa knew her place. It would not be proper to sit on the beach alone with the resident. She was aware that Portugal was an enemy of the Dutch kingdom that had conquered the island. It was a privilege that they allowed her family to stay here and keep her family's bakery in business. Rosa imagined how some Dutch women here would smirk when they found out.

The Dutch women on the islands were always looking for an opportunity to get close to the resident because he was a bachelor and, of course, his high position. There was no reason why she, a girl of Portuguese descent, would have that chance.

Lucas rose and limped toward Rosa. He took her hand and motioned her to sit next to him.

Rosa was surprised to see Lucas limp. She wondered if she should express her feelings or just be quiet about it. After a while, she said, "Please don't be offended, but I have to go home."

Lucas took her in his arms and kissed her on the lips. Neither noticed the baskets she dropped. He seated Rosa on the wooden bench and wrapped an arm around her waist. "I've been thinking about you for a long time, Rosa. Is that a reckless thing to do?" he whispered.

Rosa shook her head and moved away.

Lucas grabbed both of her hands. His grip was so tight, Rosa was afraid he would crack her fingers.

"Rosa, I've resigned from my job with the VOC. I'm a free man now. Hopefully, this decision will free me from their ridiculous rule that prohibits an official from bringing home a native wife."

"Does this mean you're in love, Mister Resident? Do you have your eye on someone?" Rosa played dumb.

"Yes, I do. She's a beautiful and remarkable girl. It's unfortunate I only had the chance to tell her today."

"Oh, what kept you?"

"I was utterly baffled by the rule. I didn't want any scandal. The girl's father is a respectable man on this island. I have to uphold his reputation. Hopefully, the young lady has not given her heart away." Lucas sincerely hoped that Rosa was still available.

Rosa did not reply at first. For the first time, she could muster the courage to look at the face of the Saparua resident. It was the face many girls on Ambon dreamed of. *He's so handsome*, she mused, *he almost looks Portuguese and is not as tall as most Dutchmen here.*

"Am I worthy of accompanying you, Rosa? I'm neither tall nor handsome and now I'm a cripple to boot." Lucas nervously interrupted Rosa's thoughts.

Rosa chuckled softly.

Lucas could not resist his feelings; he pulled Rosa back into his arms and kissed her again.

This time Rosa allowed herself to reciprocate and relaxed in his embrace.

"Do you love me, Rosa? I want to deal quickly with matters at hand."

"I don't know. My parents want me to look for a Portuguese husband, or at least half-Portuguese; as long as the other half is not Dutch."

"What's wrong with being Dutch?"

"They are the enemy of the Portuguese people. They despise us."

"Oh, Rosa, I am a quarter Portuguese. My grandfather on my mother's side was a Portuguese seaman."

"Are you sure? You're not just sweet-talking me, are you? My family and I have waited a long time for the arrival of a young and handsome Portuguese bachelor," Rosa flirted.

Lucas held Rosa close against his chest. For a fleeting moment, his father entered into his mind and he heard him say, "Don't get involved with a woman of Portuguese descent, lest you end up like your grandmother."

Lucas and Rosa stood for a while lost in each other's arms. Both wanted the moment to last. It was the first time for both of them to be intimate with the opposite sex. Social interaction between opposite sexes was highly limited at that time; women rarely went out by themselves. They were always chaperoned. It was unacceptable for Rosa to be out of the house by herself at that time of day.

Lucas took Rosa home, as promised. Despite his limp, he guided Rosa with ease through the small footpaths around the darkened beach, while she worried that he would trip in the dark.

"Is your father home?" Lucas asked.

"He was at home when I left earlier today. I'm not sure if he still is."

"Can I pay him a visit? I know I didn't make an appointment, but we just now met accidentally at the beach. It would surely speed up matters."

"Sure. In Ambon it's considered impolite to turn away a visitor. This is especially true for Asians and natives. My mother is a native."

Lucas was greatly relieved after he confessed his feelings to Rosa. Although he was crippled, it seemed his step was lighter. While Rosa had not answered his question about another possible suitor, he felt it was safe to assume that his feelings were reciprocated. He was truthful about his feelings for her and wanted closure.

The strict local custom that dictated girls had to be home before dark forced Lucas and Rosa to leave the beach.

Lucas hoped that Domingo de Freytas would agree to receive him. He had decided to ask for Rosa's hand in marriage that very night. He prayed Rosa's father would find a way for them to marry in an appropriate manner.

Chapter 10

Ten days had passed since Gamati and his group last saw Lambetta. According to Lambetta's instructions, they came to retrieve the information Lambetta had promised. They had left Ai at the break of dawn. Everyone's hope was as high as the Gunung Api and it boosted the rowers' morale. They hoped to find Aimuna and Makela in Saparua.

Sobori and Gamati had brought all of their gold. Makasuli had also brought his gold savings, which represented many years of hard work. He did not want to be empty-handed if he had to pay the VOC for Makela's freedom.

They tied the pouches filled with gold to their bodies with sturdy strings made of animal skin. Everyone wore loose, knee-length black pants with thin black tops and batik or cotton cloth headbands, folded in such a way the wind could not blow it away. These headscarves and sometimes woven bamboo hats protected their heads from the heat and rain. Fishermen of the islands around Ambon and Seram were usually dressed like that.

They arrived on Saparua a little past noon. It was an average distance from Banda. The blind hope had given them extra strength. The men seemed almost possessed. They sailed directly to Lambetta's kampong through the estuary they came through previously.

Lambetta had been waiting for them, and greeted them warmly. He invited the group to climb up to his hut. Gamati ordered two rowers to watch the boat and the load of fish.

Lambetta told the group immediately that the crazy woman and her companion were VOC prisoners.

"Who told you?" Gamati asked, tersely.

"Tamela. He's a captain who was in charge of one of the kora-koras in the resident's fleet. They were on their way to conduct a hongi mission when some of the sailors spotted two people in the forest by the beach. The resident ordered them to capture whoever was there. The kora-kora moored and when the soldiers captured the two men in the forest, they turned out to be women looking for firewood."

"Where did they take the women after that?" Gamati asked.

"To the fort. The resident said they were to be taken to Mak Uti."

"Who's Mak Uti?" Gamati continued to probe.

"She's an old woman from Ternate; she's the resident's housekeeper. She cooks, and cleans the house and the warehouse."

"I met Tamela, at the fort. He was very grateful that he did not have to sail to Banda. As of now, he is already returning to Seram. I have also met the soldier who was on duty on that day."

"The guard's name is Henri, a white man's name. I persuaded him to take me to the resident's house, where we saw Mak Uti. She said the crazy woman refused to bathe and stank real bad. Mak Uti also said the crazy woman cried when she didn't sing and dance in circles, while hiking up her sarong. Mak Uti is scared of her. She said the crazy woman never told her name."

"Are there one or two women at the fort, Lambetta?" Makasuli asked nervously.

"Two. The other one isn't crazy, but she rarely speaks. However, she did tell Mak Uti she took care of the crazy girl. She's afraid that the resident would relocate them once he returned to Saparua. They want to stay together."

For a moment, everyone was quiet. Gamati and his group tried to digest the rush of information they had just been given.

Lambetta continued his story. He did not speak to the crazy girl, since he did not want to raise the guard's suspicion. He was afraid that the guard would ask about his relationship to the two women. Only several days later he told Henri that the crazy woman had a husband. They had been recently married, and the husband had nearly lost his mind thinking about his missing wife. He also told Henri that the couple was on their way to relocate to another island and if Henri wanted to help, the distraught husband would amply reward him.

Henri argued that if he lost the two prisoners, he would get in trouble when the resident returned to Saparua. The resident might even kill him. The same applied to Mak Uti. She would be scared for the kind of trouble she would get into if the two prisoners went missing.

Lambetta knew Henri and Mak Uti had a hard time making a living and would appreciate things that eased their burdens. Things like nice silk cloths, gold jewelry, large porcelain urns or plates for traditional ceremonies, or farming tools would be tempting. He said, "I told Henri there were people who wanted to see the two women and all he had to do was to order the women to take a walk on the beach. If they were someone's wives, they would want to take them home."

It took Lambetta several days and many promises of rewards in gold before he was able to persuade Henri. Lambetta told Gamati how he went about it.

"I said to Henri, 'If the women turn out to be the missing wives, we'll tell them that they have to take off some of their clothes and leave them by the water's edge before swimming to their husbands' boat. You can then tell Mak Uti that the women went to wash themselves at the beach. Tell her the waves crashed into them and they drowned. Give her their wet clothes as proof. By that time, the women would be safely on board their husbands' boat.'"

Henri's response was that if they wanted to buy silence, there were many people who needed to be paid. There was the fort's overseer, Mak Uti, the gardener, storekeeper, the clerk, and also the weighmaster and the harbormaster.

Lambetta said, "We can't afford to forget to pay anyone, lest they would reveal everything to the resident. Gamati, Makasuli, are you ready to pay the rewards? If you are, I'll go to the fort now and ask Henri if he can arrange for the two women to be at the beach today."

Gamati said, "Let's figure out how many people we have to pay. I only brought some gold jewelry, two sarongs, some batik cloths and a few small jars from China."

"Very well," Lambetta answered, "then I'll head to the fort to see Henri. I hope he'll accept our offer. Let's hope that Mak Uti can convince the two women to take a walk on the beach."

Lambetta asked his wife to serve lunch to everyone in Gamati's group. He spread a mat on his front porch for those who wanted to rest and said he hoped to return before evening.

Sobori, Makasuli, and Gamati were anxious. They feared something might go wrong. They would have to continue their search to other islands if the two women were not Aimuna and Makela. They did not want Aimuna to deliver her baby in slavery.

The crewmembers took turns eating their lunch. Lambetta's hut stood alone. There were no neighbors; they had either died in a hongi mission, or relocated to another island to avoid the hongi. They used to trade nutmeg from the Banda Islands.

Makasuli, Gamati, and Sobori sat at a separate place on the porch.

Lambetta walked briskly to the fort, accompanied by one of his teenage sons. They returned before dark. Henri had finally agreed to help them, as long as all his superiors, except for the resident and his deputy, Verhoven, would also be awarded with gold.

Henri had asked for gold jewelry and porcelain items from China such as large plates or urns. He liked Chinese vases. Henri also asked that the crazy woman's husband would send some object that his wife would recognize. If she did, he could rest assured that the man was indeed the crazy woman's husband.

However, Lambetta thought this could potentially present problems since it required another visit to the fort. It would cost them time, while they were trying hard to finish the rescue of the two women before the resident of Saparua returned.

After dinner, the older men gathered for a discussion. Makasuli consented to Henri's entire request. He said, "It'll only waste precious time if we try to negotiate or argue with him."

"What about the gifts? Do you have them with you now or do you need to retrieve them from Banda?" Lambetta asked.

"We brought some gold with us, a few small porcelain urns and one very large porcelain plate. Can we have a safe place to take inventory of the gold we brought? We won't have to go back to Banda if we have enough." Makasuli was beginning to tense. He and his children missed Makela terribly.

Lambetta invited them to come inside his hut.

"How many people does Henri think we should pay?" Makasuli asked Lambetta.

"Henri said seven. That includes the harbormaster and the weighmaster. It is quiet in the fort since almost all of the soldiers went to the Banda Islands. The best gift must go the fort guard. He is a native from Sapura like me, but he likes gold and drinking."

"Why do they let a drunkard guard the fort?" Gamati asked.

"He's the only drunkard in the fort. He's just a substitute. All of the other soldiers are on the hongi mission."

"How do we present them with the rewards?" Gamati asked.

"I think we should prepare them individually. Decide which item to give to the fort overseer; it should be the best gift. A porcelain plate or an urn for the harbormaster; he likes items from China," Lambetta answered.

When they entered an empty family room, the hut's wooden floor creaked under their weight.

Makasuli told Lambetta to take all the fish on board his lepa-lepa and the latter ordered one of his sons to go to the river to deliver Makasuli's message.

Lambetta then left the room. He disliked dealing with issues and wanted to stay out of their business.

After Gamati and Makasuli finished proportioning the rewards, they wrapped each in pieces of sarong the size of a handkerchief, and asked Lambetta to come back into the room.

Sobori asked Lambetta what would happen if the two women were not Aimuna and Makela. Would they still have to pay the bribes even though there would be no need for anyone to lie to the resident?

Lambetta regretted the fact that he had forgotten to ask about that possibility. His recklessness resulted from the fact that Makasuli, Gamati, and Sobori had looked so convinced that the two women were indeed whom they were searching for.

Sobori thought that if the two women turned out to be strangers, they only needed to pay Henri and Mak Uti. They had to save the gold to bribe officials on other islands.

Lambetta nodded and then asked for the object to hand to the women.

Sobori confessed that when they were newlyweds, he had instructed Aimuna to pretend to be crazy and never take baths should she get captured. At that time, they were scared of Lissanei, who had boasted that he would kill Sobori and take Aimuna with him. They were also afraid of the deputies of the sultan of Ternate, who were searching for palace entertainers. "I really hope she's Aimuna, waiting for us to come to her rescue," he said sadly.

"What object would Aimuna instantly recognize?" Gamati asked.

Sobori suggested, "A salted fish from the kitchen will do, I think. We can say that it's a fish from Manipa. If she's not Muna, she won't understand what Manipa means. Makela also knows that we came from Manipa. Done."

Gamati and Makasuli were silent for a while, then nodded in agreement.

Working continuously for two days made Gamati realize that he was no longer young. He was exhausted. He quickly agreed to anything Sobori or Makasuli proposed.

***

Makasuli opened the door and motioned Lambetta to come in. After he told Lambetta their decision he handed him a small package wrapped in a piece of sarong. It contained a small gold necklace and pendant. He said, "Please accept this as a token of our gratitude for all your help and kindness. We shall always remember it, even if the two women are not the ones we're looking for. If that's the way things turn out, we'll continue our search to other islands."

"Lambetta, let's be brothers in good or bad times," Gamati added.

Lambetta was clearly astonished. He had never expected to be awarded, especially in gold, by a group of ill-fated, miserable people. The people of Saparua also had been victimized by hongi. He truly understood what it was like to lose family members. "With all due respect," he said softly, "I'm saddened by your separation and loss. I don't expect any reward. I'm only trying to help, that is all."

"It's alright, my brother. Please accept it. Gold is imperishable; just like our bond. You can leave it to your children and grandchildren. If an emergency arises, you can use it the way we're doing now. It's a token of our gratitude."

Lambetta was perplexed. If he insisted on refusing the gift, he feared that he might offend his guests. On the other hand, he felt taking gold from unfortunate people showed greediness on his part. They silently looked at each other for a long time.

Makasuli finally broke the silence. He said, "Lambetta, please accept this. If the two women are our family members, we'll sail northward straightaway. We might not see each other again. Pani-pani is conducting many hongis and extirpation missions. People can disappear in an instant." Makasuli looked at Lambetta, pleading.

Finally, Lambetta accepted the small pouch with a heavy heart. In the dim light of the oil lamp, his cheeks glistened. He had a hard time not bursting into sobs.

"Please accept my deep gratitude, dear brothers from Banda. I pray you'll have safe sailing tomorrow. I hope we'll meet again someday. Who knows, I too might need to move up north." Lambetta's voice shook.

The meeting finally ended. Gamati, Sobori, Makasuli, and several crewmembers slept on the front porch. The rest of the crew slept on the lepa-lepa.

They all rose early the next morning. Some of the young men went to fish using a net. They caught a sizeable amount of medium-sized and small fishes. The fish would be useful for their disguise as fishermen later. Next, they took some salted fish from Lambetta's kitchen to offer near the fort.

Lambetta's wife and children boiled many bananas and cassavas for their breakfast and provisions. After everything was ready, the lepa-lepa sailed to the fort.

Earlier, Lambetta and his son had walked to the fort to look for Henri. As soon as they met, Lambetta asked, "How's everything? Where shall they meet?"

Henri nodded knowingly.

Lambetta continued, "Henri, they'll come through the river. Tell Mak Uti that she needs to speed things up. If the two women are the ones they're looking for, both of them have to take off their clothes and swim to the boat. The men will pull them aboard. They have prepared some clothes for the women to wear."

Henri quickly agreed. He already pictured a warm welcome from his wife later that day when he would bring her gold jewelry.

Lambetta asked Henri to memorize his orders.

"Don't make a mistake, lest the resident punish you. Say that the crazy woman got hysterical. Dancing and running around, she suddenly ripped off her clothes and ran into the sea. The older one did not follow her at first, but when the crazy woman did not return, she also took off her clothes and went into the sea. She also disappeared in the tall waves. Mak Uti has to confess she didn't see the women leave the property."

"I understand, Bapa Lambetta."

"Let's hope the two women are really the ones the group is looking for. If they're not, only you and Mak Uti will get a reward. Keep this a tightly sealed secret, so the resident won't punish you. Now, don't let anyone go near the beach by the fort. Get rid of them. You're in charge."

"What's the object that we'll show the crazy woman?"

"Salted fish from Manipa Island."

Henri nodded and asked, "Where will they moor the boat?"

"At the estuary at the fort's left. You have to empty the beach there. Just say the resident will return today."

Henri hurriedly walked to the fort's gate. He combed the beach around the port. It was impossible to empty the area. There were always activities around the harbor.

He walked along the left beach to the small estuary that was a waterway fishermen used. Located close to the fort, the area was restricted for the natives who could not justify being there. It was also the place where he first met Gamati's group.

Henri hurriedly returned to see Lambetta and his son. "Tell them to come through the left side of the fort, the place they used the first time they came. I'm off to see Mak Uti to ask the two women to come. Tell the group to wait if they get to the estuary before I come back. Do you have the salted fish?"

"Yes. Don't make a mistake when you relay the message: 'Here is a salted fish from Manipa.' If they don't understand what you're talking about, they're not the ones we're looking for. If they look happy, tell them to come along quickly." Lambetta handed Henri three salted fish wrapped in dried banana leaves.

Henri ran to the resident's house and shouted Mak Uti's name. The resident still had not returned. As a native soldier, Henri had no reason to visit the residence. He usually just served as an errand boy for the resident or the fort's overseer.

Mak Uti hurried to the front yard when she heard Henri. He handed her the fish and taught her the message for the two women, 'Here is salted fish from Manipa.' After Mak Uti repeated the words correctly, she ran into the house to look for her charges. She found the women by the well. Mak Uti handed the parcel to Makela and said, "Here's salted fish from Manipa."

When they heard the word *Manipa,* Aimuna and Makela immediately knew there was someone nearby to free them. Muna danced and hiked up her sarong. Her movements filled the air with a bad odor.

Mak Uti led Aimuna and Makela to the fort's gate. Aimuna danced and sang all the way. Mak Uti was afraid to go farther. As the resident's housekeeper she had no business beyond the gate.

Henri took over and showed them to the small estuary off the beach left of the fort.

Once outside the fort, Aimuna relaxed. She did not want to attract anyone's attention. She wanted to avoid trouble for her guide and Mak Uti. Muna knew that the gold saved by Grandpa Gamati and her and Sobori's fathers would be used to pay for her and Makela's rescue.

Lambetta observed the women from a distance. The crazy woman was pretty. She had a sharp nose and pointed chin. Nevertheless, her hair was a formless, tangled mass.

It didn't take long before a lepa-lepa emerged at the estuary. Aimuna wanted to swim to the lepa-lepa immediately, but remembered she still had to play along. She started to dance and sang with a shrill voice.

The boat approached the river's edge. Sobori stood at the bow, his head covered with a special scarf.

Aimuna could hardly control herself. Yet she had to think of the safety of the native guard and Mak Uti.

Sobori also knew that he must not show himself as part of the rescue team. He acted like a fisherman who hawked his ware, "Salted fish. Salted fish from Manipa."

Aimuna and Makela understood the code perfectly. Intermingled with the sound of the sea breeze and the rushing stream in the river, they heard Sobori call out a pantoum,

> *The glaring beach of Manipa*
> *dazzling white the color of its sand*
> *Is it really you, my darling Aimuna?*
> *I'm asking, because I'm worried.*

Aimuna continued to sing in a shrill voice, spinning wildly she replied:

> *The sky is blue, here on Manipa*
> *Filled with parrots and eagles*
> *Bori, don't hesitate,*
> *I'm truly Aimuna.*

Makasuli had already spotted Makela from afar and could hardly contain his joy. He had not dared to hope they would find her so near. He took a deep breath.

Sobori continued,

> *The beach on Manipa is smooth.*
> *Come ashore to pick rattan,*
> *My dear Muna, please forgive me*
> *for leaving you alone in the forest.*

Aimuna pretended to fall into another crazy spell and sang,

> *Manipa is far away*
> *surrounded by coral reef*
> *Bori, we're waiting for orders*
> *what should we do, right now?*

Bori shouted to make his voice louder than the wind,

> *Manipa, beautiful beyond compare*
> *where Papua boats moor*
> *Dear Makela and Muna,*
> *We're coming for you.*

Aimuna's heartbeat quickened; she felt as if she soared into the sky. She recalled the private conversation she had with Sobori about things she needed to do should they become separated.

Sobori had instructed her not to allow any man to touch her, to refuse to bathe and to act crazy. Sobori had promised to rescue her, even if it would take years. He said that if he died prior to that, he would let her know through her dreams.

Aimuna promised that should she die in the process of self-defense, she would come to Sobori in a dream. This secret conversation had been triggered by the threats of Lissanei, the hongi draft, and the recruiters for palace entertainers.

Muna knew that she had to get into the sea. Continuing her crazy act, she took off all her clothes and dove into the sea. Gamati had trained her to hold her breath for a long time under water. This was the perfect time to exercise this skill.

Then it was Makela's turn to act out her part. She shouted, pointed at the sea, and wept for the missing Muna. Next, she took off her clothes and plunged into the sea with a big splash.

Following Lambetta's orders, Henri retrieved both women's clothes. He had rehearsed his story. Later, he would say, "I noticed the two women wildly dancing on the beach outside the fort. They were uncontrollable. When they took off their clothes and ran into the sea, I thought they could swim, and were just washing themselves. It turned out that they could not swim. Neither resurfaced after a wave washed over them." Their clothes would serve as proof that the two prisoners had intentionally dived into the sea. Henri hoped the resident would believe him and no one would tell on him. He was not worried about Mak Uti. She was also involved, and would receive a reward for telling the exact same story.

Muna swam in the direction of the lepa-lepa. Someone pushed an oar into the water, and Aimuna grabbed it. It was hard to hoist herself on board with her large belly. The men respectfully turned their heads to not see Bori's wife naked.

Several minutes later, Makela followed. She was also given an oar to help her climb on board and again the men aboard respectfully turned their heads.

Sobori fought his urge to take Aimuna into his arms right then. He had missed her tremendously for a long time. Instead, he only handed her a pair of loose black pants and a shirt, the customary fisherman's outfit.

Aimuna and Makela had to disguise themselves as crewmembers and covered their heads with the common fisherman's straw hat. After she dressed, Makela kneeled at Makasuli's feet and wept as she thanked him, stammering.

Makasuli caressed his wife's shoulder and said, "It's all right, Makela. Please don't cry, everyone's looking at us. We're all together, we're safe, that's enough."

Sobori checked his pants' pockets for the pouches with the rewards and made sure they were secure before he dove into the sea.

Bori reached Henri in a short time. He held on to large tree roots along the edge of the estuary, and handed Henri all the pouches.

"This is for you; a necklace and a bracelet. This one is for your boss. This is for the storekeeper, and this is for the woman who takes care of the house. This is for the clerk, and weighmaster, and this is for the harbormaster. That is all. For your own safety, please keep all of this a secret."

Sobori quickly swam back to the lepa-lepa. As soon as he climbed on board, Gamati ordered the crewmembers to row hard; they had to leave immediately.

Makasuli acted as the lepa-lepa's captain. They headed for a small river's estuary at a beach on Seram. They would follow the river into the interior, where they would rest for a day or two to recharge their energy and collect provisions in the nearby forest.

After that, they would sail nonstop from dusk until dawn, around the north side of Seram to the northern islands where they planned to start their new lives.

Luckily, there were enough young men who had decided to join the initial group members, which included the two women. Aimuna was not allowed to row since she was pregnant.

***

Domingo de Freytas paced his front porch. It was getting dark and Rosamunda had not returned. She had gone out by herself. He rubbed his eyes. *Where is she?* When he peered down the street again, he spotted Rosa walking toward the house. A man walked beside her. He looked like the governor's young guest, the resident of Saparua. Domingo squinted, not trusting his sight. It was impossible that such a high-level official would visit his house. When the governor's wife needed cakes, she sent a soldier.

Rosa called out a greeting and said that the resident of Saparua had something to say to him.

De Freytas was a courtly man. He politely invited the resident to have a seat in the modest family room. He had already closed the bakery at the front of the house.

While a housekeeper lit several oil lamps, Rosa excused herself.

De Freytas anxiously wondered about the reason for his honored guest's unexpected visit.

Lucas did not make the usual preliminary small talk about the objects in the room or delicious cakes. Instead, he cut to the chase and said, "Mister de Freytas, forgive me for this unexpected visit. I hope you can give me some of your time."

"Certainly, Mister Resident. I'm done with my work. It's an honor to have you visit our humble home."

Lucas cleared his throat a few times and tried to compose himself while de Freytas waited and wondered whether or not to invite his wife to join them.

Lucas said, "Mister de Freytas, again, I apologize for barging in. I wanted to tell you that I'm in love with your daughter, Rosamunda, and I intend to marry her as soon as possible. However, a VOC rule dictates that the wives of VOC officials must be born in Holland, not in Ambon. If you would accept me in your family, I'd appreciate your help with finding a solution to this problem. I don't want to cause a scandal."

De Freytas brought a hand to his face and rubbed his knuckles against his thick sideburns. He was clearly taken by surprise. "Mister Resident, where and how did you learn to know my daughter so well that you fell in love with her? You have to forgive me, I'm totally baffled."

"With your permission, I often sketched Rosamunda to depict a woman of mixed native Moluccan and European blood. I also sketched the delicious cakes from your bakery. I have been attracted to Rosamunda for a long time. However, my position as resident forced me to keep my distance. I was not at liberty to approach her. My job with the VOC requires I maintain a certain decorum."

De Freytas simply nodded. He offered Lucas a glass of wine but Lucas declined. He did not consume alcohol.

Lucas returned to their conversation. He asked de Freytas if he accepted his marriage proposal on behalf of his daughter. Lucas added that he was a quarter Portuguese by blood.

De Freytas confessed that he and his family had often talked about Lucas' Latino looks, and wondered how he came to have his Dutch surname. He asked Lucas to tell him more about his life starting with his childhood.

Lucas then told de Freytas everything about his father the aristocrat who had financed his education and given him the job as an archivist of the VOC.

De Freytas said, "I'm sure you know that the kingdom of Holland and Portugal are not on good terms. Would this impact the family?"

"I won't continue to live here. I'm returning to Holland, to work as a professional painter," Lucas answered.

"When are you sailing back? Much later, I suppose?"

"I've given my resignation to the governor. He could not accept it. It's something the head office in Holland needs to do. It suits me well since I can return directly to Holland and see the directors there myself. I have an immense collection of sketches. The governor is getting me a good cabin aboard a ship returning to Holland."

"Have you told the governor you plan to marry Rosa?"

"No, I haven't. I wasn't sure that you would accept me. I am Dutch, and Rosa is half Portuguese. I didn't know if she was already spoken for. Besides, I was held back by the ridiculous VOC rule. That's why I kept my feelings to myself."

Lucas continued, "This afternoon, I had the opportunity to meet Rosa in private. I was alone, bird watching on the beach, when Rosa passed and greeted me. I immediately took the opportunity to convey my feelings to her. Rosa did not object and I thought it was best to immediately discuss this with her parents, so we could find a solution to this matter."

It was de Freytas' turn to clear his throat. After a moment of silence, he said, "Mister Resident, I'm honored to have you, a high official, ask for my counsel. Prior to your visit, Antonio, my eldest son, and I had been discussing our plan to sail to Europe. I wanted to teach him more about our Portuguese heritage and take him to our motherland, Portugal. There he can study Portuguese and learn everything he needs to know in the event, one day, he can go to Brazil. I don't want my children to live their entire lives here in the Moluccas."

"That is a good plan, Mister de Freytas. Rosa once told me about your plan to take the entire family to Portugal. She said it had not happened yet as it was very expensive to take everyone."

"That is true, Mister Resident."

"Please don't call me Mister Resident, just call me Lucas. My name is Lucas de Vries."

"As you wish, Lucas. If we need to take Rosa out of Ambon to marry you, I will take her to Europe with Antonio and me. We could stop in Holland and go to Portugal from there. Can you arrange to come to Portugal after you finish all your dealings in Holland? We will wait for you; meanwhile Antonio could enroll in a school or take courses. We could also board a ship to Holland and we could meet there. You two can then get married. As her father, I can give Rosa away."

Lucas was stunned. He wondered if the solution for his problems with marrying Rosa could indeed be that simple. De Freytas was truly an experienced man, Lucas thought in appreciation. He was silent for a moment, pondering why he had never thought of that earlier. Surely, Rosa could never travel to Europe without Antonio and her father accompanying her. No young, unmarried girls traveled without a family chaperone.

Lucas added, "There is one more thing. I am not a wealthy man. I never received a salary during my post here. However, I expect to receive some money in Holland upon my return. To provide for my family, I will paint, professionally, in Amsterdam. Or perhaps I will move to Paris."

"I'm surprised. How is it possible that you didn't get paid here? All Pani-pani officials are busy acquiring wealth in any way possible. Those who live here own property, like a plantation. They return to Holland every so many years. Their pantries are stocked with wine, cakes, and meat."

"I tried very hard to stay away from the illegal business of clove pinching and trading the stolen cloves with porcelain or gold. I do not wish to be a slave of stolen wealth. I sincerely hope that the de Freytas family will judge my character and morals, not my material wealth. I'm a good and honest man, if I may say so. My love for Rosa is straightforward. I wish for nothing else but true happiness in simplicity."

"Certainly we all want to live happy and dignified lives. If Rosa returns your love to her, here and now, I, her father, accept your proposal. I'm glad that you are of Portuguese descent. Do we practice the same religion as well?"

"Yes, we do."

"Then there are no problems. We can discuss other things as the situation develops. Please come to this humble abode if you want to discuss anything. Antonio and I will start to arrange our trip."

Lucas understood that with those words, de Freytas had subtly signaled that the meeting was over and it was time for him to leave.

De Freytas called Rosa with a booming voice. Rosa entered the family room, smiling happily. Lucas shook hands with de Freytas and said good night. He then took Rosa's hand and joked, "Do I need to start learning Portuguese as soon as tomorrow?"

"Yes, yes, you can. Rosa is an excellent language tutor," de Freytas laughed.

Lucas left. Although he used a cane, he climbed the stairs at the fort easily. Perhaps it was because his mind was unburdened since de Freytas had accepted his proposal to Rosa. His path was clear now; he would return to Holland and resign from the VOC. It was a very good reason to be happy.

Lucas entered his bedroom and for the first time noticed that it was a very well-decorated room compared to other rooms in the governor's residence. He was definitely in a relaxed and good mood.

In the morning, he had breakfast with the governor and his wife. The governor brought up Saparua. He said, "Mister Resident, you haven't visited Saparua since you returned from Banda. I think it's a good idea to go there after you're done writing the reports. There was a clove harvest before you went to Banda. The baskets of cloves are stored. Shipment requires your presence."

"I do plan to visit Saparua as soon as possible. I need to take care of the administration, check on the armory, and inspect the pilot plantations. Since we don't know how long Bertie will have to stay in Banda to help revive the nutmeg plantations, do you think we could send Karel to supervise the plantation on Saparua? The trees might flower if watered properly."

"We'll make those special arrangements later. We first have to appoint a new resident. Although it's small, Saparua has strategic value; it's perfectly located to control the sea traffic around Seram."

"Precisely. I also left many of my sketches there. I have to take all my sketches to Holland. People in Amsterdam will want to learn more about the situation in the Spice Islands."

The governor ordered the preparation of a boat with a deck. Lucas left before lunch and planned to stay in Saparua for several nights. When boarding the boat, he tried to appear fit despite his limp and cane.

Lucas was sure that during his absence, his assistant Verhoven had written reports about what had been going on at the fort. When he proposed they promote Verhoven to be the new resident of Saparua, the governor said that while Verhoven was qualified, the fact his wife was half Ambonese and Makassaran presented a problem. Lucas thought Verhoven's wife was a beautiful and smart woman and he hated the VOC's ruling. Nevertheless, he did not pursue the matter further.

Before the boat set sail, the governor said he planned to throw a farewell reception for Lucas. He planned to invite families with young girls and lads. The reception would offer music, dancing, and singing. They would serve freshly caught fish and delicious cakes from the de Freytas' bakery. The governor ended, "The de Freytases also love music and own some musical instruments."

The governor's wife hoped that during his final days on Ambon, Lucas would fall in love with one of the Dutch girls. Lucas only chuckled when she whispered her hopes to him. He knew her hopes were empty, since the de Freytases had accepted his proposal to Rosa.

Many people stared at Lucas when he limped and used a cane as he boarded the boat to Saparua. The same thing happened when he arrived there.

It had been a while since the people of Saparua had seen the resident. The last time they saw him was when he sailed to lead the hongi mission on the Banda Islands. The crowd wondered what had happened to his leg.

One of the boat's crewmembers ran to the resident's house. Mak Uti was sweeping when she heard someone shout, "Mak Uti! Mak Uti, the resident has returned. Quickly, get to the door to greet him." Mak Uti threw the broom into the front yard and ran outside where she was met by a noisy crowd.

It was the first time the people of Saparua saw the resident since he left with his fleet almost three months ago. When Mak Uti greeted him at the yard entrance, the old woman could not hide her sadness when she saw the crippled resident. She burst into tears and lamented, "Ah, poor Tuang Resideng. What happened?" The resident had always treated her very kindly and she had no reason to hate him.

"Mak Uti. Please don't cry, Mak Uti. There was a big earthquake on Banda Neira. *Tana goyang, Mak Uti.*" Lucas struggled to speak the local dialect. He soothed, "I'm fine; I didn't die, right?"

Mak Uti asked amidst her tears, "Tana goyang, Tuang? What do you mean by the ground shook? How bad was it? How can the ground shake?"

"Yes, it's like when we are aboard a boat and the wave hits hard. Instead, the ground shakes, not the water. A house collapsed, and the falling stones hit my leg. It was very painful; I could not stand at all for some time. Now I need to use this *tongka* when I walk."

Lucas' explanation calmed Mak Uti. She first thought that the enemy on Banda had wounded her employer with a weapon, perhaps a sword or spear. She regretted the resident had not sent a messenger to notify her of his arrival on Saparua. Now she had no food other than some rice and smoked beef from Holland.

When Lucas heard there was hardly any food at the house, he ordered to bring whatever food they had from the fort. There were some VOC officials and crewmembers of the boat in the harbor and they needed to eat too.

Lucas asked Mak Uti whether it had rained on Saparua and she told him that it had never rained during his absence. Lucas worried about the extremely long drought. If this situation continued for a long time, many plants would wither and die. Starvation could be next. They did have an abundance of sago trees and innumerable fish in the sea and rivers. However, humans could not survive on sago and fish alone.

That night, Lucas told Mak Uti that he had come to check on the VOC's experimental plantation outside the fort. He also had to check on the warehouse at the back of his house where they stored the clove harvest from the natives. Mister Verhoven would accompany him. Lucas ended with telling her that when he was done, he would return to Ambon and wait for the ship that sailed to Holland.

Mak Uti was devastated. The news of the resident's imminent departure came totally unexpectedly. She had happily served him for several years in that house. Since Lucas was a bachelor, she did not have to deal with a nagging wife who ordered her around. Before working as a housekeeper for the Saparua resident, she had worked for a Portuguese family on Ternate. Sometimes she improvised her cooking and combined Portuguese and Ambonese ways of preparing food. She always used fresh and fragrant ingredients, such as nutmeg and cloves, and *pandan* leaves. The fish and fruit she served were always fresh. She had been able to please Lucas with the meals she prepared for him.

Mak Uti had neither home nor family. Abducted from an unknown island, she had been a slave in a colonialist's household ever since she was a child. She had worked all her life and was old now. Mak Uti wondered where she would go after the resident left the island for good. Her position as the resident's live-in housekeeper had isolated her from the social life with other natives on Saparua. The issue tugged at her and questions like, *Where will I live when I can no longer work? Who will take care of me then? And who will take care of my body when I die?* filled her mind.

One evening, when Lucas sat reading after dinner, Mak Uti steeled herself to approach him. She dropped on her knees near Lucas' feet.

"What is going on, Mak Uti?" Lucas was surprised. She had never done this before. Watching Mak Uti, he remembered his mother who had worked as a housemaid. The memory saddened Lucas.

All of a sudden, Mak Uti started to sob inconsolably.

"Mak Uti, please, please, tell me; what can I do for you?" Lucas asked quietly. As he tried to soothe the old woman, a memory flashed through his mind. The aristocrat's wife and her children beat him and his mother with a stick as they threw them out of the house where his mother had worked for a long time and where he had lived all his life. They didn't mind the aristocrat who tried to stop them. He was too young to defend his mother and himself. The incident scarred him permanently.

"Tuang Resideng, what will happen to me when you return to your country? I have no home, no kampong to return to. I have no child. And I'm old; I can't work anymore." Mak Uti broke into his thoughts.

Lucas was stunned. He fixed his eyes on Mak Uti and noticed she was indeed very old and frail. At some point she must have had a home and family. Perhaps the VOC had destroyed them. Lucas wondered whom he could leave this kind old woman with. He wanted to leave her in good care. Listening to her laments made him compare their lots. He too had no one after his mother died.

After they were silent for a while, Lucas coaxed, "You could still stay here, Mak Uti. There will be a new resident, I'm sure he will treat you well." The thought of leaving Mak Uti in the care of the island's priest crossed his mind. He needed to ask the priest and would be lucky if the priest had a spare room. Also, Mak Uti needed to agree to the arrangement. He realized that he did not know her religion. It had never occurred to him to ask for that information. He said, "Let me think of a solution, Mak Uti. Just be patient. I have to check things out first."

Lucas suddenly remembered the two women caught at the beach on Seram during his sail to Banda. He had completely forgotten about them. He asked, "Mak Uti, where are the two women who were caught in the forest?"

Mak Uti began to wail again.

"They're dead, Tuang. The crazy one never wanted to take a shower. She stank terribly. And she was pregnant. All she did was cry, sing, and dance while she hiked up her sarong. I was so scared of her, Tuang."

"What about the other one? There were two of them."

"The other one followed the crazy one everywhere. One day they walked to the beach just outside the fort. The crazy one took off her clothes and dove into the ocean. The other one also took off her clothes and dove into the ocean. They never resurfaced. The fort's guard told me that they drowned."

"Is that true, Mak Uti? I find it hard to believe that two women drowned together. Could it be that the guard pushed them into the ocean?"

Mak Uti said, "I don't know, Tuang. The guard said so; you can ask him directly."

"Mak Uti, I sent those women here so you could take good care of them. I wanted to put them to work at the clove plantation. How come you didn't know they left the house?"

"I was busy cleaning the house, and checking the warehouse. Forgive me, Tuang. The crazy one did not like me; she always got mad around me. I was scared of her."

Lucas remembered how a recently purchased slave had flown into a rage and nearly killed him when he had just arrived on Saparua. Perhaps the woman was also angry because they had separated her from her family. She might have known that there was no way out from the devilish fort. Such tragic incidents could happen anywhere, he thought.

He solemnly recalled the many lives lost, when the earthquake struck and even when he left Banda. The angel of death was rather busy in this foreign country. The urge to return to his homeland surged.

For the next several days, Lucas was busy. He inspected the VOC's clove plantation. Many saplings had withered. The soil of a number of plots was cracked. The lack of irrigation had left the trees in dire straits. The situation was inevitable, as several wells on the plantation had dried up.

No one knew when it would rain. Every day, the skies were a clear blue without a hint of clouds. By midday, a forceful, blistering wind blew from the sea and cooled the nights. Yet, not a single drop of water fell from the sky.

The VOC had stationed Bertie on the Banda Islands to rebuild the nutmeg plantations owned by the perkeniers. There was much more capital at stake there. Besides, there were no native nutmeg plantations to fall back on if the experimental plantation did not succeed.

"That's what they get for being too greedy and destroying nature. Now, nature is getting back at them." Lucas cursed the VOC under his breath. As for cloves, the company still relied on the native-owned trees. They traded the harvests at a ridiculously low price. The high officials in Ambon thought that this arrangement was better than having no nutmeg and mace at all.

Lucas was saddened to see the fruit of his labor nearly ruined. He wondered why the Assembly of the Lords Seventeen was still adamant about continuing the monopoly, although they were fully aware that it had cost countless lives and immeasurable damage. He could not understand why they could not trade fairly with the natives and listen to them.

Lucas used a palanquin for transport this time. He spent many hours inspecting the plots of the VOC plantation and took notes for his final report that was some kind of farewell for him. He even visited a white-sand cove with shallow water, where he used to swim with Karel and Bertie after a hard day's work. He also visited the three majestic ketapang trees that he admired so much. He did not get into the water because of his injured leg, but Verhoven went for a short swim.

Lucas noticed that the banyan trees were still green; their foliage still had a lustrous sheen. Apparently, the long drought had not affected them. His admiration for the tree species deepened. The sago palms that marked the plantation's boundary showed the same resilience. Green and thriving, the trees provided relief from the glare of the sun on the water surface.

Lucas also inspected the warehouse where they kept the natives' cloves, harvested prior to his visit to Banda.

He ordered the officers to feed the plantation workers even though they were unpaid slaves. He pointed out that if they were to die, the VOC would suffer a great loss.

Lucas instructed Verhoven to gather the officers and told them to collect as much sago as they could, and also some rice. He said that if needed, the officers could trade with ships from Tuban.

Unlike other VOC officials, Lucas cared, and thought that all workers, whether they were Dutch or natives, needed to be fed. It was common for the white VOC officials to take care of their personal affairs in the absence of their superiors. Lucas knew that all too well. Their excuse was that they were underpaid and thus had to find other means to support themselves.

Next, he had to make sure his sketches were properly packed and protected from seawater, in case the ship met turbulent waves.

Lucas still did not know what to do with Mak Uti. He thought of the de Freytas family. They probably could have used Mak Uti to help in the bakery had she not been so old. She might not be able to place the cakes in the charcoal oven or beat the eggs for the batter.

Since the VOC provided for all of his everyday needs and he did not receive a salary, Lucas had no means to build a modest hut for Mak Uti. He finally decided to leave Mak Uti in the care of the kampong chief just outside the fort and the VOC plantation.

A Dutch family he had helped during the earthquake disaster on Banda had given him a beautiful Chinese porcelain plate. He knew that the natives prized large porcelain plates, which they used in their traditional rituals.

On his last day on Saparua he visited Watari, the kampong chief. His kampong was under the control of the VOC. The inhabitants only traded their cloves with the VOC. Watari was well respected by the natives as well as the VOC officials. Lucas knew him closely because of his involvement in the administration of the VOC's pilot plantations on the island.

The villagers agreed with Lucas. Mak Uti was very old, and it was unlikely she would cause a problem. Besides, the kampong could use a beautiful porcelain plate.

Lucas explained in his limited local dialect that his own mother had been faced with a similar fate as Mak Uti. He told Watari about his miserable childhood and ended stating that he now wanted to return the favor of the Wijnen family, the kind neighbor, by making sure Mak Uti would be cared for.

Watari felt sorry for Tuang Resident's tragic life.

Lucas asked Watari to pick up Mak Uti at the fort. He hoped it would make her understand that he was leaving her with a family who would care for her for the rest of her life.

Watari patiently explained to Mak Uti why she needed to move to his family's hut. He told the old woman the resident had given him a beautiful porcelain plate and in return, he and his family would take care of her as long as she lived. He said, "Mak Uti, I made a promise to Tuang Resideng. We must always uphold a promise; we are not allowed to tell a lie. The porcelain plate is proof of my words. Don't be afraid to live with me and my family."

Mak Uti was stunned; she did not know what to think. Everything was happening so fast. Overwhelmed, she nodded and dropped herself to the floor. After she stammered her gratitude to Lucas, Mak Uti packed her belongings in a small bundle. She had given most of her clothes to Aimuna and Makela. Her only prized possession was the gold necklace she had received for looking the other way when Aimuna and Makela went to the beach to escape.

Lucas told Mak Uti to take a good look at the large porcelain plate he gave to Watari. It was what bound the family to her.

The VOC prohibited natives from entering the fort, let alone visiting the resident's house. They needed to leave fast.

That night, Lucas spent a long time alone in the dining room. He felt tremendously relieved that Mak Uti was taken care of. Before she left, she had prepared a large grilled fish seasoned with nutmeg and mace for him, but he lost his appetite as he recalled the years he had spent in the Spice Islands. All the devastating confrontations he had witnessed during his travels in the Indies flashed through his mind. He remembered the severe punishments of the crewmembers and their suicides during the long voyage to the East. The speared bodies at the West Africa beach; the attack with a machete by a crazed slave the day he arrived on Saparua. He vividly recalled the captured people who later were sold as slaves, and then the earthquake on Banda. He thought of Heidi and other VOC women who had tried to seduce him.

Lucas closed his eyes and prayed to God for a safe trip home. "Father, I have seen enough greed on these islands. Please use me for a nobler mission to reflect Your grace," he ended.

The sea was calm and the sky a brilliant blue when Lucas sailed from Saparua the next morning. No one saw him off. Lucas had not told anyone he was leaving Saparua for good. It saddened him to leave Saparua. Mak Uti held a special place in his heart and it was on Saparua he first learned to be a leader.

As if pulled by a large magnet, he turned around to look at Saparua one last time. He gazed at the fort and imagined Mak Uti standing on the beach, waving good-bye. Yet Mak Uti had already taken her place as a member of the Watari family. The old woman's kindness, as well as her loneliness, had reminded him of his own childhood. Lucas hoped the Wataris would give her the same good care he had received from the Wijnens.

***

The lepa-lepa quickly left the beach near the Saparua fort. The group did not want to take the risk of the guard Henri suddenly changing his mind and reporting them while they were still visible from the beach. Or, worse, for the resident's fleet to suddenly appear on the horizon as it returned from the hongi mission. In either event, they had to sail away as fast as possible.

With Makasuli acting as the lepa-lepa's captain, they sailed along the beach line of Seram. They stayed close to the coast. In the event they had to escape a chase, they could easily enter one of the many estuaries of Seram or alternatively hide in one of the lush coves or passages.

The rowers took turns eating lunch. Aimuna and Makela sat on the roofed deck. The crewmembers asked Gamati to rest, so he would not get sick.

Aimuna grimaced in pain, and held her large belly. From time to time she caressed her belly and muttered to the baby to be calm inside her womb.

Makela knew the signs and she was on the alert. Apparently, Muna would soon go into labor.

Aimuna had forgotten how long she had been pregnant. She had been tense when they left Tuna, and their capture by the VOC had been nerve-racking. During the time of her imprisonment, she had poured all her thought and energy into playing the part of a crazy woman while she waited for the rescue that seemed never to arrive.

Sobori suggested to Aimuna to have her hair shaved. It was regrettable because her hair used to be beautiful, but it now had turned into such a tangled mass, no comb could be run through it. And the odor. Actually, the crewmembers were tormented by the horrible smell, yet, out of decency, they did not pinch their noses.

Aimuna did not object. All she wanted was to rest. She did everything Sobori told her. Makela cut her hair. Then she shaved Muna's scalp. Gamati forbade Makela to throw the hair into the ocean. "We will bury it decently as soon as we reach land," he said.

When the sun leaned into the west, Makela asked whether there were sarongs or mats on board. If Muna suddenly went into labor while they were still at sea, they would need the mats to lay the baby on and sarongs to cover Aimuna and the baby, so they would not get cold.

Alas, many of the group left many of their belongings, including some sarongs, tops, and headscarves, at the Ketapang Patta kampong. At the time of their departure, they had been too preoccupied with the rescue plan, the gold, and the baskets they had to fill with fish. They forgot to bring along objects they would need in their relocation, let alone things needed to assist a birth.

The sun started sinking into the horizon. It's fiery red seemed to radiate anger. Everything was bathed in an orange glow. There was not a single cloud in the sky. Sobori suddenly recalled the ill-fated night at his old kampong near the forest, the night when everything was lit by a large orange torch. Even though it was supposed to be dark in the middle of the night, everything was ablaze. For a moment he felt the hair on the back of his neck rise. That night wrapped his parents in an orange blaze and separated them from him forever.

As the last rays of sunlight dissolved in the dark, the lepa-lepa entered a small river's estuary. They were on the south coast of Seram, facing the vast Banda Sea.

Protected by the darkness of a dense virgin forest, they moored the lepa-lepa. Gamati ordered everyone to be quiet.

The small river emptied into a cove that forked deep into the interior of the land. Although they were in a virgin forest, there was always a possibility that there were some Halefurus hunting. Or perhaps a VOC ally was out spying on Makassar or Tuban traders who refused to pay for the VOC's license badge.

Half of the crewmembers went to sleep by the river; the other half slept on the lepa-lepa. Gamati warned to stay aware so they could flee immediately in the event of an attack.

They still had some of the boiled bananas and cassavas Lambetta's family had given them. It was too risky trying to find a water source in the dark, so they did not drink that night. They did not intend to spend more time than was necessary there. They worried about trouble that might be lurking.

As soon as a glimmer of light was visible in the east, the lepa-lepa set sail again. They still followed the coastline for an easy escape. Displaced people had enemies whether they were on land or at sea.

Makela and Aimuna had already washed themselves earlier at the riverside. It was hard for Muna to climb down from the boat into the freshwater. Gamati helped her. Makela washed Aimuna's stinking body. She scrubbed Aimuna's entire body numerous times. Muna needed to be clean. After she delivered her baby, she would not be able to climb out of the boat just to bathe.

It was the third night on their way northward. Everyone aboard the lepa-lepa felt sorry for Sobori and Aimuna. They were still newlyweds and supposed to spend their time together and eat fine meals. However, unfortunately, the VOC with their hongi mission and extirpation plans had turned them into fugitives on their own land.

The group's meals consisted mostly of an abundance of freshly caught fish. They fished using hooks and nets. Sometimes they caught so many fish, they threw the smaller ones back into the ocean. Their ancestors had taught them not to be greedy. They roasted the bananas, cassavas, and also some wild taros after making sure they were not poisonous.

On their fourth day of sailing, Makasuli speared a fawn. Gamati was a bit upset as he had specifically asked everyone not to spill any blood before Bori's child was born. On the other hand, Makasuli was concerned about their provisions. They still had far to go and needed more food in case they were faced with hard times, and no safe hiding place. Makasuli reasoned, "We need as much food as we can get."

Gamati did not pursue the matter any further.

The group worked hard to skin and cut up the meat. Since they had no cooking utensils, they seasoned the meat with salt and roasted it on a fire made by dry twigs from the forest floor. They put the rest of the meat on the deck roof for later consumption.

Aimuna became bored just sitting around all day. She was not allowed to row or cut meat. Sobori went with her if she wanted to walk on land. She had to always be near the boat. Some of the crewmembers had made small bamboo flutes to blow as a signal if they were lost in the forest or encountered danger.

Bori observed Muna silently; she was clean now. She behaved respectfully; she greeted all the young men who were relocating with them. The long sail in the narrow boat was dull and tiring. Especially during the daylight, the long drought struck them at its worst. It was very distressing. However, their common goal and desire to find a safer place to live was stronger than the temporary inconveniences.

The two women refrained from grumbling. They never made comments or demands. Everyone's spirits still soared; they were still in the seas around Seram, but were now in the northern waters.

Gamati and Makasuli knew that inside the lush forests they saw from the distance were secret clove kampongs. Gamati used to live in one, and Sobori was born in one.

Muna prayed that she would not deliver her baby on board the boat while they were sailing the vast ocean. The lepa-lepa was very cramped.

Everyone on board the boat did not mind his or her hardships during the voyage. After all, they were used to sailing the vast Moluccan seas as they often sailed from one island to another. Besides, swimming and diving were as natural to them as walking on land.

Makela had experienced childbirth and would be of great help should Muna deliver her baby on board the lepa-lepa, Sobori thought. He hoped that they would have arrived in Misool, part of a cluster of islands up north, when the time came for Muna to deliver their baby.

The islands in that cluster were small and close together. The strait was shallow and curvy, tracing the coastline of the islands. These natural features caused the islands to be impenetrable to the VOC. Some of the islands were uninhabited. Only fishermen or pirates or seamen who looked for temporary shelter from raging storms sailed its waters.

They rested for a while on a deserted beach. Makasuli briefed the crewmembers on the distance they still needed to sail to get to a relatively large and inhabited island. Then, they would have only covered half of the distance they had to cover to reach the islands up north. After they rested, the crewmembers cleaned the lepa-lepa and replenished their food and drink supply.

"I hope Aimuna's birthing can wait until we get to Misool. There's a kampong there, and the cries of a baby won't attract the attention of the boats sailing near the beach," Makasuli said and continued, "If Muna went into labor in the middle of the ocean, there's a possibility the wind will carry the sound, and it could be heard by other ships' crewmembers. A baby crying in the middle of a vast ocean is definitely a strange thing. It probably would make them curious and decide to look for its source."

Everyone agreed with him.

Sobori had been aching for Aimuna. He wanted to embrace and kiss her, caress her bald head and round belly. Unfortunately, the lepa-lepa was always crowded with the crewmembers and the young newlyweds could only exchange glances.

Aimuna usually just sat or lay down on the small raised deck with Makela. She tried hard to remain calm, even though she was tormented by her deep longing for Bori. She wanted to be in Bori's arms and cry on his shoulder. She wanted to tell him how lively their baby was inside her womb. Sometimes her stomach felt stuffed; it was very uncomfortable, but she restrained herself from talking about it. She did not want to trouble all the crewmembers and silently endured the repeated stomach cramps.

After a half day of sailing, they rested in a concealed and cool cove. Gamati took this opportunity to tell the other crewmembers that their destination for relocation was actually Halmahera, way up north. It was a very large island, perhaps even larger than Seram. Only a small part of Halmahera was inhabited. The kampong chiefs were mostly noblemen from Tidore, a kingdom on a nearby island.

Gamati stated that he knew there were terrains with good soil in the hills that stretched across the island from the north to the south. The land was free of ownership claim. Gamati was sure that the group could live there. First, they could clear a small patch of forest to grow their food and later clear enough land to start a clove plantation.

Their plantation was going to be a secret plantation, just like the ones they used to have on Manipa and Seram. It would take several years for the clove trees to mature and bloom. They could trade their first pata cengkei harvest on the islands east of Halmahera, Misool, Kofiau, Gag, Gebe and other islands.

There were already settlements of refugees in the interior of eastern Halmahera. They were located far apart. There were kampongs of people from Makassar, Malacca, and also from India. There were even settlements of people from Portugal, India, and China. The Portuguese were enemies of the VOC, he said.

The people from the various faraway lands had native wives and children. When they acquired bahars of cloves, they returned to their homeland to sell the cloves. They would come back after a year or two.

They did not build forts or houses, to avoid attracting the VOC's attention. These large foreign ships sailed far out of the VOC's range, deep in the vast ocean. The VOC might not even be aware of those seas. The traders used small and lean boats to pick up the cloves.

The small boats moored in designated beaches and loaded the neatly packed baskets of cloves. All the traders had to do was to count how many bahars or catties of cloves there were and then trade it with their trading items. Their native wives also protected these foreign traders. When it was not sailing season, they hid in their huts among the natives, deep in the interior.

Makasuli agreed with Gamati. Sobori and other young rowers listened attentively. From Gamati's description, all the young men realized that once they had safely arrived at Halmahera, they had to be able to be self-sufficient.

The next evening Aimuna sat on the deck and stared into the distance across the ocean. They had stopped to rest. Gamati was bathing in the sea. Makela and Makasuli were preparing their meal. The younger men were checking and cleaning the boat, or helping Makela with the meal preparation. It was almost time for dinner.

Sobori slipped away to the deck. For a moment he just stood, watching his wife.

Muna was oblivious of his presence. She stroked her round belly, thinking that the time to deliver the baby was near. Her contractions were becoming more frequent, with regular spacing in time. She tenderly whispered to the baby inside her to be calm since she was in pain.

Bori edged closer to Muna's side and whispered, "Muna, when will our baby be born? We'll be very happy having a child; someone to fulfill my parents' wish."

For a moment Muna startled, but she quickly calmed herself. She turned around to face Sobori. The ocean wind stroked the headscarf she wore to cover her shaven head.

She looked at Sobori with radiant eyes; she had not had a chance to look at her husband closely since she had returned from the fort on Saparua. A surge of warmth and happiness coursed through her body, made her tingle from her head to her toes. She had never experienced the sensation before; it was warm and invigorating.

Suddenly Bori pulled her into his arms and held her tight. He whispered close to her ear, "Muna, pray to Upulanite for the safety of our baby. If the baby is born at sea, then he or she will be a hero of the ocean, one who will possess great knowledge about our seas, down to the bottom of this ocean."

Muna did not know what to say. She was consumed by a yearning she had suppressed all this time. A thundering desire accompanied by deep gratitude rushed through her, coursed through her veins. "Bori, thank you. I hope nothing will separate us again, ever. Until the day we die." Unable to fight her tears any longer, she sobbed on Sobori's shoulder.

Sobori could barely contain himself. His wife's words moved him and his eyes moistened. The idea of losing his wife forever was devastating. His tears were also tears of joy now that he had Aimuna in his arms again.

He first stroked Muna's shoulder, then her head. He whispered tenderly, "My dear Muna, I hope we will have a peaceful life in our new kampong. We will be far enough from Pani-pani. We can plant some clove trees, save some gold. Then one day we will build an arumbae and sail to faraway places like Tuban and Makassar."

Muna nodded. There were only Sobori, Grandpa Gamati, and also Grandpa and Grandma Ronasundu in her life. Makela was a new entity. She would rather die than live without them. She quietly cried in Bori's arms, while Bori continued to caress her head and back.

They broke apart when someone called out that dinner was ready. They had boiled venison, some cassavas, and yams. Aimuna did not have an appetite, but Bori pleaded with her to eat for the sake of her baby and her own health. Muna could not resist Bori's pleading and ate her portion of the meal. After dinner Muna started to have another series of contractions.

Makela went up to the deck. She knew Muna was going into labor and sat down by her. Bori refused to leave Muna, making the small deck even more cramped.

Makela had prepared all the things she needed for Muna's delivery. She had torn some sarongs to make a makeshift cloth, mat, and blanket for the baby. She also had a pair of clean clothes for Muna, and some seawater, taken far from the beach, to wash the baby and Muna. They had no fresh water, and the torn sarongs actually belonged to other crewmembers; they were their spare clothes.

Muna continued to moan. Gamati sat down on the floor of the boat and chanted a mantra. The other young men, including Makela's sons, climbed down the lepa-lepa and swam ashore. The older adults knew that delivering a baby was dangerous and could be a matter of life and death.

Sobori could not stand to hear Aimuna's painful moaning. He told her to lie down and lay her head on his lap. It was unusual for a man to be with his wife during labor; however, this was an unusual situation. Bori needed to stand by his wife's side during this crucial time. He remembered how Grandpa Gamati used to coach Aimuna when they were little and said, "Muna, darling, please be strong. You have to push hard. You're a strong woman, I know you can do it."

Makela murmured a mantra for Muna and the baby's safekeeping.

Aimuna's screams were getting louder; it was obvious that she was in great pain. Then, suddenly, Aimuna's wailing was interrupted by the shrill cry of a newborn. No one dared to cheer as they were, after all, in a hiding place. They whispered their gratitude and joy. Little Kurubela had come into the world. The VOC had to face another opponent.

Makela was relieved that the delivery had gone relatively well. She washed the baby and wrapped him with the sarong she had prepared. The baby boy kept screaming in a loud and penetrating voice. He looked strong and healthy; his body was well proportioned, his hands and feet nimble. He had thick curly hair. Makela wrapped him tightly; they were in the open air and the wind was fierce.

Makela also washed Aimuna. She rubbed Muna's body with an aromatic oil she had prepared with a mixture of mace, cloves, and other spices. The treatment would keep her warm and fragrant.

Muna stayed awake long enough to hear her baby's loud cries, but then drifted into sleep. She was exhausted.

Sobori, happy and beaming, was surprised to see his wife silently lying with her eyes closed. He anxiously wondered why she did not move or show any sign of happiness. He suddenly panicked and blurted, "Muna! Dear Muna, why don't you say something?"

"Shush, be quiet, Bori, Muna's fine. She's just exhausted. Let her sleep," Makela calmed him.

Bori put his palm on his wife's chest. He felt Muna's heartbeat and whispered, "Ah, right. She only fell asleep, right?"

Relieved, Bori remained seated. Holding Muna's head on his lap, he almost did not move. He was very touched by what his wife had gone through. After Muna awakened he washed everything that was soiled during his wife's delivery.

Gamati said they should not throw the afterbirth in the sea, but bury it in the ground instead. He feared that the blood would attract sharks. Aimuna had delivered a healthy baby boy and everyone was relieved. Since they were not on land, it was their duty to protect mother and son from dangers and perils.

Makasuli shook his head as he looked at the baby who was born at sea, under the wide open sky. "What a brave boy you are, Son, choosing the sea instead of a clove plantation for your birthplace. I bet you want to be a captain just like your Grandpa Gamati," he cooed and smiled when the baby puckered his mouth and waved his arms and feet in the air.

Muna, healthy and young, quickly recovered from giving birth. She had ample breast milk and the baby boy had more than enough to eat.

During the next several days, everyone on board of the lepa-lepa tried to come up with a name for the baby. Because it was a boy, they called him temporarily, *"Nyoong,"* which meant "boy" in the islanders' dialect. And since he was still a baby, they called him Nyoong Kacil, Little Boy.

Their next stop was on Misool, which was a very scenic island when viewed from the sea. The natives were much like the natives of Ambon and Seram. They had curly hair, dark skin, and were of medium built. It was the first land they encountered after several nights sailing. They could meet people on the island since Misool was an inhabited island. The islands where they had previously stopped were uninhabited.

The lepa-lepa did not receive a warm welcome. The natives were not fluent in the colloquial Malay, a common everyday language in the Spice Islands, although they lived by the seaside. Makasuli and Gamati went ashore to see the kampong chief and tried to communicate using body language.

Makasuli was an outgoing and sociable man. He asked the chief to allow them to stay for one night to have a good rest and to collect food supplies from the forest. In almost all forests of the Moluccas, there was always an abundance of seasonal fruit, like banana, mangosteen, cotton fruit, sweet rose apples, and durian.

Tubers were mainly cultivated; caladiums, yams, and cassavas, also types of pumpkins. Several young crewmembers picked some yellow pumpkin, which they could keep fresh on the lepa-lepa for a long time. Fruit trees and plants located close to the kampong were usually owned by the natives, while the ones in the forest belonged to everyone.

From their limited conversation using gestures, they learned that pirates frequently attacked the island. It was understandable; the island was rather close to Seram, and it was fairly easy to moor in its cove. The kampongs were also close to the beach and were an easy target for the pirates.

The natives fought back by setting traps around the beach, similar to the ones they used to catch boar and deer. They just dug deeper holes and used sturdier, sharper stakes that had been previously soaked in a deadly poisonous liquid derived from a toxic plant. People who fell in the trap would die in a matter of minutes.

Makasuli and the young crewmembers who were present felt a chill. "How terrifying," they whispered to each other.

"That will definitely teach the pirates a lesson," Makasuli said. His curiosity piqued, he asked the chief to show him the toxic plant. If they came across the same plant up north, he would tell the others to stay away from it. And surely they could use the plant to "welcome" the pirates or intruders who wanted to enter their kampong and plantation.

The Misool chief laughed; he understood Makasuli's body language. The people of Misool did not plant clove or nutmeg trees. Their soil was not suitable for those crops. They fished and dried their catch and traded it around the many kampongs around Seram. And, the sago they made in large quantities was relatively popular in kampongs even as far as Ambon.

When Makasuli asked whether the VOC or its accomplices ever visited their kampong to collect tax payment, the chief shook his head. The natives there were poor, and they rarely interacted with outsiders.

The chief asked who they were and where they were going.

Makasuli signaled that they were fishermen sailing to the north.

They stayed for two nights in Misool. It was the pirates they worried about now. However, the drought might keep the pirates from patrolling the seas north of Seram. They knew that the natives of the seasides often evacuated to the forests to look for food during long droughts.

Gamati's group said good-bye and thanked the people of Misool. During their stay there, Aimuna and Little Nyoong never left the lepa-lepa.

It still had not rained yet. During the day the sky was still brilliantly blue and turned orange at dusk and dawn. Gamati had discussed the lack of rain with other crewmembers. They would soon start sowing many plants for their food source in their new settlement. They would not need to plant sago, since it was very easy to find. However, fruit trees, seasoning herbs for the sago porridge, rice, and tubers definitely needed some rain. Clove tree saplings also needed regular watering.

They needed water. It would be one of their biggest challenges in the new settlement.

The group hoped that the long drought did not extend to the north, which was located very far from Seram. They found solace in the thought that should the dry season stop and it start to rain while they were still at sea, the rain would give them nothing but trouble. Fierce wind and typhoons would render their tiny deck useless in protecting Little Nyoong and the two women in their care.

"Let the drought continue until we reach our destination, the east coast of Halmahera," Gamati said pensively.

One evening, after they finished dinner, Gamati explained to the group how they would start their new lives. First, they would loosen the soil with hoes and dig the forest floor for some compost. Then, they had to dig a new well and visit friendly neighboring kampongs to search for seeds and saplings. Last, they needed to build a dugout canoe for their daily transport.

"What about our custom and traditions?" a young man from the nearly vanished Banda people asked.

"What do you mean?" Gamati asked.

The young man explained, "The people in our group come from many different islands, like Manipa, Banda, and Seram. Maybe, later, other people from other islands will join us. Which custom do we use when we need to have ceremonies, like for instance at a wedding proposal, a new ship's first sail, a first harvest, et cetera?"

"Ah, I see. Let's not complicate things; we can still use our own rituals and traditions. Those from Manipa can still use their traditions. However, living as refugees made us forget so many of them. The same thing applies to those coming from Ambon; feel free to practice your own traditions. We, the people of the Moluccas, are all brothers. Our traditions are very similar. There were the alliances of uli siwa, uli lima, and many more alliances, which are now destroyed. Pani-pani is the one to blame. They forced the people from the mountains to relocate on the beach; they drove people out of their kampongs to live with other people from other kampongs. They severed our strong bond with each other and our heritage. We used to sing our kapata, but now we can't even remember the tunes. Now we all speak Malay just like the people on Ambon. Let me ask all of you, is there anyone here who can still speak the Banda or Manipa dialects? Or sing our sacred kapatas?"

Makasuli added, "For now, let's just concentrate on getting there safely. We can think about customs and traditions later, particularly our beliefs. We now practice many different beliefs. Some of us practice a new belief and call ourselves Muslims. I used to have Muslim relatives on Banda; however, they are all dead now, killed by Pani-pani. Some of us are Christians. I know some of Ronasundu's family on Ambon are now Christians."

"I think we just have to respect others; their customs, their beliefs, so we can live together peacefully in our new kampong later. I still want to pray to my ancestors, Upulanite. There is nothing wrong with that, is there?" Gamati inquired.

"No, there isn't," the young men answered almost in unison.

"Gamati, my brother," Makasuli spoke, "let me say something. I no longer pray to the ancestors. My family and I are Muslims. It's different from going to the baileo. When we arrive at our destination, can we practice our new belief?"

"I see. Certainly, you and your family can practice your new belief, as long as you don't cause trouble for others. We will continue to pray in the baileo. I think we can live together peacefully, caring for and respecting each other. Our lives are difficult already. We sailed far from our islands and faced danger throughout our escape. Why make it harder, and fight among ourselves in our kampong?" Gamati answered.

Makasuli added that his ancestors on Banda were Muslims, long before they perished.

"Why don't you pray to your ancestors? Where do you go to pray? Do you have your own baileo?" Gamati asked.

"We have to make a prayer hut. It has to be clean. There can't be a mess on the floor. It has to be equipped with a small pond to clean our bodies. We don't eat boar."

"When it comes to food, no one can force someone's taste. Some people don't like papeda. Some hate yams. Some hate salted dried fish and others dislike steamed fish. Don't overthink it."

"We also need a tutor to teach us to read our holy book. It has been a long time since the last time we heard a recital of our holy verses, and celebrated our holiday."

"Who was the person who taught you?" Gamati asked.

"Our clergy usually came from Tuban, or Makassar. Sometimes from India or Malacca," Makasuli answered.

"Where are these people now?"

"Pani-pani forbids them to enter our seas. They have not bought that thing...what's it called, the permit badge?"

Gamati was quiet for some time. Then he spoke, "India, Gresik, Tuban? They're Pani-pani's enemies, so they are our allies. They will be welcome in our new kampong. I'll be glad if they join us, Makasuli."

"Yes, Gamati; we did not own a holy book, have a tutor, or anyone to share our feelings with when we lived on Seram."

"How very unfortunate; I didn't know you went through such a trying time. No worries, my brother, we will live as free men later, in our own kampong."

Everyone was silent for a moment. They were taking in all they had just talked about.

"Gamati, you would be the elder in our new kampong. Are there people among us who pray to something other than the ancestors and are not Muslims?" Makasuli asked.

"I don't know. Is there anyone here who is Christian?" Gamati asked the group members.

No one answered.

Makasuli spoke. "I know that there are natives on Saparua and Ambon who are Christians. They wore the same pants and clothes like the white men. They also sing a lot and they no longer pray to their ancestors. They have a house where they get together and pray."

Gamati nodded and said, "That's fine, my brother. We escaped this far because we want to be free men, just like our ancestors. We want to be free to trade our cloves and nutmeg on our beach for farming tools, salt, sugar, clothes, and also porcelain plates, and urns from China. We won't allow anyone to force their belief on us. That's all for now, my brothers."

Everyone nodded in agreement. The group started to move around. Some of the younger members of the group started to yawn. They did not have hot drinks or something to snack on, like fried banana. Little Nyoong cried for a short while then was quiet again once his mother breastfed him. It was time to get a good night's rest. Most of the men went to sleep on the shore. The older men slept aboard the lepa-lepa, with their machetes by their sides. Makela, Aimuna, and Little Nyoong slept on the raised deck.

Between his waking and sleeping, Gamati imagined he saw Arande, his beautiful late wife, appear on the ocean's surface. A wave carried her to him. She wore a Timor woven sarong like the one she wore on their wedding day and smiled ever so sweetly at him.

After she reached him, she said slowly, "Gamati, my love, Ranila's grandson has to be named Kolosia. It means 'waiting.' We have long awaited his birth, haven't we? He not only will become a great captain, he'll even become a *tamaela,* a captain of an entire fleet. Sobori and Aimuna will live until they are old and grey. Congratulations, my dear Gamati. I love you." She smiled her sweet smile as she moved away from him.

Gamati wondered why she kept moving. Perhaps the wave she rode kept rolling. Then the wave flattened and Arande disappeared all together from his vision.

Gamati jolted awake. Everything was very still. High in the sky, the moon lit the rolling waves with a silvery glow. He was the only one awake. Gamati rose. The waves rocked the lepa-lepa gently. He gazed into the distance across the sea and peered at the distant waves looking for Arande, his lovely wife. A hongi raid had separated them.

Gamati lay down again. His heart ached with longing. *Ah, I was only dreaming,* he thought and muttered, "A very pleasant dream indeed." He reached for his machete before drifting off into a deep sleep.

Chapter 1

Salawaku: A wooden shield designed to guard against the slash of machete or sword in combat.

Kampong: Local village or community; settlement.

Pani-pani: The natives' nickname for the VOC.

VOC: In Dutch, the "Vereenigde Oostindische Compagnie," or the United East India Company, known in English as the Dutch East India Company, a chartered company established in 1602, when the States General of the Netherlands granted it a 21-year monopoly to carry out colonial activities in Asia. Also known to locals as "Kompani."

Hongi: Short for "hongi tochten," sailing expeditions by VOC warships designed to destroy clove and nutmeg trees in order to control the spices' supply and thereby protect the Dutch monopoly of the trade.

Arumbae: A traditional Moluccan ship, a large, long-distance vessel with more than one hundred crewmembers and room for cargo.

Bapa: A polite form of address to an older native man.

Pikul: A unit of weight measurement used during the 17th century equal to approximately 30 kilograms, or the load one man could carry on his back, usually using a big rattan basket with a sling.

Saloi: A traditional basket, conical shaped and made from woven rattan. It is slung across the shoulder like a backpack.

Halefurus: Natives of the islands' wild interiors much feared for their alleged headhunting traditions.

Tabea: An expression of greeting in the Moluccas.

Papeda: A staple food of the Moluccas, it is a jelly-like porridge made from sago flour or pulp, to be eaten along with various fish dishes.

Kolak pisang: Traditional caramelized banana compote with coconut milk.

Masohi: A tradition native to the Moluccan Islands, it signifies the spirit of mutual cooperation, of working together arm in arm through thick and thin among villagers or kin.

Gotong royong: The Javanese tradition equivalent to masohi.

Tuak: Alcoholic drink made from the sap of the coconut palm flower.

Kole-kole: A traditional small dugout canoe.

Lepa-lepa: A single-mast sailboat that can carry between ten and twenty passengers.

Tuang: A polite form of address to a foreign male; sir.

Mardijker: A community of freed slaves whose ancestors, originally from South India or Mozambique, were brought over by the Portuguese as domestic help for their forts and households. The term derives from the Indonesian word "merdeka," which means "free" or "independent."

Ikang garang: Salted dried fish.

Chapter 2

Selampuri: Painted chintz from South India used for scarves and veils.

Extirpation: A VOC policy designed to control the clove supply on the European international market by cutting down, uprooting, and burning listed clove trees, especially trees that had been harvested once.

Sultan: A Muslim ruler.

Mak: A form of polite address to an older native woman in the local dialect.

Kora-kora: A large rowing boat, sometimes with hundreds of crewmembers. Very slim and long in shape, it had high mobility and was often used in wartime.

Rurehe: A catamaran-like fishing boat with ten or so rowers mainly used for inter-island travel.

Uli Lima: Living compounds organized according to traditional customs of the Moluccan natives; its inhabitants are descendants of five patrilineal kinships.

Uli Siwa: The same as uli lima, but based on nine patrilineal kinships rather than five.

Pela: A traditional custom of alliance through kinship or an agreement under oath.

Kapata: Traditional singing in the tribe's respective dialects; it usually glorifies the heroic deeds of a chief and recounts the sagas of the tribes.

Takarao: Now widely known as "sepak takraw" or kick volleyball, it is a popular sport native to Southeast Asia and is played with a ball made of rattan twigs.

Enggo lari: A sprinting race.

Gici-gici: Hopscotch.

Chapter 3

Sasi: A Moluccan tradition designed to mark and protect property ownership. The tradition forbids touching or taking someone else's belongings and also honors the rejuvenation process of nature. For example, the ban on the harvest of sea life imposed to give the fish, sea cucumber, seaweed, and other life forms a chance to recuperate. To violate a sasi-marked entity will cause the violator to suffer serious consequences.

Mauweng: A shaman and caretaker of plantations and forests, able to communicate with the spirits.

Henas: Small settlements governed by traditional values before the arrival of foreign colonialists.

Arbabu: Stringed fiddle with coconut shell body, originally from Ternate Island.

Lenso: A large handkerchief or scarf. A lenso dance (The Handkerchief Dance) is a social dance for young men and women, usually taking place during folk celebrations and festivities such as wedding balls, clove harvests, New Year celebrations, etc.

Raja: A term for a monarch or princely ruler in Southeast Asia.

Chapter 4

Kadeira usung: A type of palanquin used to transport passengers.

Langsat: A fruit that resembles small potatoes and grows in clusters similar to grapes. The flesh tastes sweet and sour, somewhat like a grape.

Pata cengkei: Roughly translated as "picking cloves," refers to the harvesting of clove buds, which are handpicked just before the heads open. The harvested buds are separated from the clusters and then sun-dried.

Catties: A catty is a unit of weight measure used during the 17th century in East Asia and Southeast Asia equivalent to approximately 6.25 ounces.

Borgo: The term for Dutchmen who were not VOC employees but who worked in private sectors such as partnerships, etc. Some natives were also called "borgo" after they performed great service to the VOC.

Chapter 5

Moyang-moyang: The souls of ancestors who were believed to still be present in the form of spirits and were still worshipped, as in animism.

Baileo: A traditional home that served as a community center, a repository for sacred objects, and a place where traditional ceremonies were held.

Gambier: The extract from the leaves of the uncaria climbing shrub native to tropical Southeast Asia, originally used as a sedative. It is often chewed with the betel nut.

Bapa-bapa: A traditional term to reference an older, native man.

Bahar: A unit of weight measurement; one bahar equals 400 kilograms.

Perkeniers: Owners of large plantations who were white men the VOC had lured to Banda with empty promises of high rewards.

Chapter 7

Juanga: An elaborately decorated sailboat that is part of the sultan's flotilla.

Chapter 8

Nutmeg coolie: Pejorative term used to describe an unskilled native worker tasked with   harvesting nutmeg.

Perken: The plural of "perk," Dutch for a garden bed or parcel of land.

Chapter 9

Nona: Common Moluccan form of address to a young, unmarried woman.

Lesung: A long dugout canoe holding between five and twenty rowers, made out of one tree trunk and used for short distance inter-island travel and fishing.

Chapter 10

Tana goyang: Earthquake. Literally "the ground shook," in the local dialect.

Tongka: Walking cane.

Pandan: The leaves of the pandanus amaryllifolius are widely used in Southeast Asian cooking as an aromatic flavoring while the leaves of the pandanus tectorius are used to make baskets, mats, and sails.

Tamaela: The captain of an entire fleet.

About the Author

Indonesian author Hanna Rambe started her writing career as a journalist at the *Indonesian Observer*, a Jakarta newspaper, in the late sixties. She has subsequently worked as a reporter and an English-to-Indonesian translator for *Indonesia Raya*, another Jakarta newspaper, and was a contributor to the popular *Intisari* and *Mutiara* magazines.

Rambe's work as a journalist provided her the opportunity to travel, and her journeys provided inspiration for her biographies and works of fiction. *Terhempas Prahara ke Pasifik, Mencari Makna Hidupku* (Sinar Harapan, 1992) is a biography of Suyatin Kartowijono, a pioneer in the struggle for women's rights in the 1920s, while *Pelayaran Cadik Nusantara* (Sinar Harapan, 1992) is the true story of a youth who traveled by himself from Jakarta to Brunei in a fishing boat.

In her works of fiction, Hanna Rambe explores Indonesian history and draws attention to the fate of the indigenous people. Two of her most noteworthy novels are *Pertarungan* (Indonesiatera, 2002) and *Mirah dari Banda* (originally published by Universitas Indonesia Press in 1983 and reissued by Yayasan Pustaka Obor Indonesia in 2010), which has been translated into English under the title *Mirah of Banda* (Lontar, 2010).

Today Hanna Rambe is retired from journalism and spends her time teaching English and writing. She is currently at work on a three-volume historical novel set in seventeenth-century Eastern Indonesia.

About the Translator

Miagina Amal is a translator, writer, and editor. She was born in Ambon and raised in Manado and Bandung.

Shortly after acquiring a diploma in Food & Beverage Management from Sekolah Tinggi Pariwisata Bandung, a vocational institution for culinary arts and tourism, and then working as a bakery manager, she switched careers in 1994. Her love of language and literature was a strong motivation for her becoming a translator. She works primarily with works of art, literature, culture, and history.

Mia is a native Indonesian speaker with language pairs of Indonesian-English and English-Indonesian. Her debut translation into Indonesian was *Di Tepi Sungai Piedra Aku Duduk dan Tersedu,* a novel by Paulo Coelho published in English as *By the River Piedra I Sat Down and Wept.* (Harper Perennial; Tra edition, 2006)

Mia's translations of short stories from Ben Sohib, Triyanto Triwikromo, Arup Kumar Dutta, and Hao Yu-hsiang, and poetry from Joko Pinurbo, Sharanya Mannivanan, and Sean M. Whelan, among others, have appeared in anthologies of Utan Kayu and Salihara International Literary Biennale (2007, 2011 & 2013). She is currently working on a translation of *The Da Peci Code* by Ben Sohib. In addition, Mia volunteers at Intersastra (an Initiative for the Improvement and Promotion of Literary Translation in Indonesia) and is also the poetry editor of Intersastra's on-line magazine.

As an editor, Mia served as a member of the revision team for *Tesaurus Bahasa Indonesia* by Eko Endarmoko from 2010 to 2013 and has edited several works of fiction and non-fiction, including *Tobelo Tempo Doeloe,* a history book by M. Adnan Amal (Disparbud, Halmahera, 2013), and *Mirah Mini,* a children's picture book by Hanafi and Nukila Amal (Kemendikbud, 2012).

Mia also co-authored *Cerita Rakyat Halmahera* (Disparbud Maluku Utara, 2013), a collection of folklore of the island of Halmahera, with M. Adnan Amal.

She currently lives in Jakarta.

My Name is Mata Hari
Remy Sylado
Translated from the Indonesian by Dewi Anggraeni

My Name is Mata Hari tells the story of Margaretha Geertruida Zelle, a young Dutch woman married to an older military officer assigned to the Dutch East Indies. Claiming her mother's Javanese ancestry, she changed her name to Mata Hari, Malay for "eye of the day."

As Mata Hari, she danced on stages across Europe and the Middle East, and took many high-ranking military and government officials as her lovers. Convicted of espionage during World War I, she said at the end of her tumultuous life, "I am a genuine courtesan. And I am a dancer in the true sense."

Price: $17.95
Paperback: 334 pages
ISBN: 978-0-9836273-0-2

Potions and Paper Cranes
Lan Fang
Translated from the Indonesian by Elisabet Titik Murtisari

In Lan Fang's award-winning novel, Sulis is a young woman selling potions in Surabaya's harbor district. She meets Sujono, a day laborer with dreams of becoming a freedom fighter, and whose passion for Matsumi, a geisha called to Java by a Japanese general, is destined to ruin all of them. Each tells the story of their lives during the Japanese occupation of Java and Indonesia's transition from a Dutch colony to an independent republic.

Price: $17.95
Paperback: 252 pages
ISBN: 978-0-9836273-3-3

Kei
Erni Aladjai
Translated from the Indonesian by Nurhayat Indriyatno Mohamed

At the end of Suharto's New Order, the Kei people hold on to their traditions as they flee the violence that divides Muslim from Christian and destroys the villages. Namria, a Muslim girl, works as a volunteer in a refugee camp when she meets Sala, a young Protestant man. Grounded in the islander's belief of "We drink from the same spring and eat from the same land, the land of Kei," the two fall in love amid the chaos that will soon separate them.

Price: $17.95
Paperback: 224 pages
ISBN: 978-0-9836273-6-4

Daughters of Papua
Anindita Siswanto Thayf
Translated from the Indonesian by Stefanny Irawan

Seven-year-old Leksi lives in modern-day Papua with her grandmother Mabel and her mother, Mace. Pum, an old dog of unknown ancestory, and Kwee, a pig, along with Leksi, look back at the past as they face an uncertain future. In *Daughters of Papua,* the present is marked by a contentious election, with the gold company that wants to rob Papuans of their heritage the only winner.

Price: $17.95
Paperback: 224 pages
ISBN: 978-0-9836273-9-5

The Red Bekisar
Ahmad Tohari
Translated from the Indonesian by Nurhayat Indriyatno Mohamed

The *bekisar* is a fine crossbreed between jungle fowl and domestic chicken that adorns the houses of the wealthy. Lasi, whose father was a Japanese soldier, fair skinned and beautiful, is such an acquisition for a rich man in Jakarta. She is born in a village where the main source of income is tapping coconut palms for their rich sap, or nira. Her life takes an unexpected turn when she is betrayed by her husband and flees to Jakarta. She meets Mrs. Lanting, procuress for men in high government and social circles, who sells her to the rich Handarbeni. Lasi enjoys the new splendor as a much-desired ornament, but is alarmed when she discovers the marriage is a sham. Kanjat, a childhood friend, is now grown into a man. Lasi and Kanjat rediscover their affection for each other. Their bond is the village, its people and traditions. They struggle to free Lasi from a net of power, corruption, and deceit.

Price: $17.95
Paperback: 294 pages
ISBN: 978-0-9836273-2-6

Love, Death and Revolution
Mochtar Lubis
Translated from the Indonesian by Miagina Amal

During the early days of their nation's revolution, Indonesians were driven by passion and built a future on dreams. In a world still reeling from World War II, Major Sadeli of the Indonesian Army Intelligence travels to Singapore tasked with establishing naval and air routes to Sumatra and Java as well as securing weapons and radio equipment vital to the revolution. His desire for Indonesia to be prosperously independent, independently prosperous, and no longer dependent on other nations' pity forces him to choose between personal happiness and commitment to a higher cause.

Price: $17.95
Paperback: 298 pages
ISBN: 978-0-9836273-5-7